DEATH GAME

VAMPIRE TOWERS

KELLY ST. CLARE

DEATH GAME

ABOUT THE AUTHOR

When Kelly is not reading or writing, she is lost in her latest reverie.
Books have always been magical and mysterious to her. One day she
decided to unravel this mystery and began writing.
Her works include *The Tainted Accords, Pirates of Felicity, and The
Darkest Drae.*
Kelly resides in New Zealand with her ginger-haired husband, a great
group of friends, and whatever animals she can add to her horde.

Join her newsletter tribe for sneak peeks, release news, and disjointed
musings at kellystclare.com/free-gifts/

This series is dedicated to my grandmother.

Frances Carolyn
13th August 1936 - 19th March 2019

~

I miss you.

1

He was awake.

For the last hour, I'd felt Kyros climb from the relative peace of slumber, but after a week at his Lyall Bay property, I knew he'd spend another hour pretending to be asleep.

All to avoid time in my company.

"We have zero tolerance for sexual harassment," I told Eric over the video call. He was one of my many CEOs. "Sack him without a payout, and if Rhiannon wishes to take legal action, give her our full legal and financial support."

Eric dipped his head. As cold as ice, the guy acted like I'd just told him to yank weeds out of the garden instead of fire a human being.

"I will send confirmation when it's done, Miss Le Spyre."

I withheld my wince as his firm tone cut through my tender ears.

"Good. Did we win the contract for Gyron-Easting Pharmaceuticals?" I scrolled through his latest update on my phone, leaving his face on my laptop screen. I was missing my office space big time.

"They met your additional terms. I expect the revised contracts today and will forward them to your legal team before they're presented for your signature and final approval."

Eric was one of my youngest CEOs, but also one of the best, and one of the few who hadn't tried to assert their dominance on the twenty-one-year-old heiress of the Le Spyre Estate. Advice from those with more experience, I'd happily take—though Grandmother ensured I was capable of managing and increasing the family fortune. A few of my employees had learned the hard way that I wasn't a normal twenty-one-year-old.

I'd grown up in the shark tank before learning humans were really the fish. Business interactions seemed insignificant now. A lot of things did.

Disconnecting the call, I leaned back, stretching my arms overhead. *Carefully.* The bruises on my abdomen had faded to yellows and greens, and the jagged scar on the right side of my neck from Theodore's brutal bite had formed a hard red scar with the help of Kyros's saliva and surgery, but I was still sore.

My jaw cracked as I yawned.

Blood loss was a bitch. Dr Olivia said it would take between four and eight weeks for my blood cells to be replaced, and that I could feel dizziness and fatigue in the meantime.

I glanced at my phone. *2:00 p.m.*

Nap time. At least I was down to one nap a day. I wasn't sure what Kyros would do once I got rid of them altogether. He only left his room to leave for work once I left the open-plan kitchen and lounge area around this time.

Familiar anger gripped me, and his own anger flared in response. Even in pretend sleep, Kyros was mad at me.

Guilty. Sad. Uncertain.

I woke one week ago after a brush with death and had patiently waited for him to snap out of this *mood ever since.* He just wouldn't. The distance was swelling and freezing, and I had no idea what to do about it.

He couldn't be distant. It wasn't just that I needed to complete two more blood exchanges with him. Whether because his emotions were infiltrating my own or otherwise, his sorrow was breaking my fucking heart.

His uncertainty occupied my every thought, accompanied by frustration and yearning in turn.

I felt terrible, and yet regretting what I did to save Tommy was ludicrous.

A one-hundred-and-fifty-year-old vampire creeping around his own home was equally ludicrous...

Maybe he just needed more space.

Now I was mostly healed, returning to the estate may be best.

I slowly got to my feet. My head spun, but I forged through it, walking to my room just down the hall from Kyros's. The damage to my ears and general blood loss had set me back in adapting to the changes in my senses after the fourth exchange.

I stared into the shadows of the sprawling house. The house wasn't a mansion by any description. The spaces were minimalist and efficient with ingenious custom additions that gave the home a unique edge. The décor was modern, but the natural textures and earthy palette with occasional splashes of colour lent the space ample warmth. The property perched on the cliff tops overlooking Lyall Bay. The birthday gift was kind of perfect for the crown prince of the Sundulus clan.

Through the shadows of the hall and the heavy wooden door at the end, I could feel Kyros focusing on me.

I was focusing on him focusing on me.

This was ridiculous.

Scrolling through to Fred's number, saved under *Butler Badass,* I hesitated.

I'd hurt Kyros a lot. Even if I couldn't regret the action. Even if I'd do it all over again to save Tommy... when I decided to enter Fyrlia territory alone, to actively *prevent* him from following me there, I'd cut the cord between us.

He was adrift.

Be the bigger person.

I whispered, knowing full-well he could hear. "I'm sorry that you feel so shitty after what happened with Clan Fyrlia. I think you need space, so I'm calling Fred to come get me and take me back to the es—"

The door to his room slammed open against the wall. *Into* the wall.

Kyros stalked out, stopping halfway down the hall. He crossed his arms, and I swallowed hard as my eyes roamed over his bare chest. Sweatpants on this vampire should be illegal. The ridges of his abs disappeared under the dark waistband, and I dragged my gaze back to his arms and the expanse of his pecs.

The current I hadn't felt since the fourth thrall ended began to vibrate again.

Oh yeah. The blood bond definitely wanted our pelvises on speaking terms.

Having been there once with Kyros, I was in *no way* adverse to a repeat performance. Especially because it would close the emotional gap between us to some degree. Or was it unwise to use sex for that reason?

"You will *not* leave this house." His deep voice rumbled down the hall.

We just needed pistols to make this a stand-off.

"Yes, I am. It's for the best," I said calmly.

Kyros stepped forward, meadow-green eyes blazing. "*Try it.*"

Rolling my eyes, I steadied myself on the wall to turn on my heel.

Reaching my room, I ripped out the bag Fred dropped off last week, throwing my few belongings into it.

The bag was torn from my hands.

I blinked as it crashed against the far wall. Heat flooded my cheeks. "Kyros, you have some fucking nerve trying to stop me when you haven't uttered a single word in a *week*."

His short laugh twisted with bitterness. "The problem in this is *me*?"

Stay calm.

Kyros was precariously close to losing control. Not only was that bad for the human in close proximity, but he'd feel worse afterward.

"I'll always do whatever is needed to save Tommy, just as you'd do for your family." I tipped my head back to meet his gaze. "I'm not sorry for meeting Theodore, I'm not sorry for calling your siblings to stop you coming after me, but I am sorry for how it made you feel. As I've said." *Multiple times.*

Inwardly and outwardly, I watched him struggle for control over his alpha power. His body shook with the effort. Closing my eyes, I sent him calm, soothing thoughts. We'd managed to send each other cautionary vibes a few times, and his emotions gave me strength two weeks ago. I wasn't sure if calm thoughts would be any help right now, but it was worth a try.

When I peeked again, his shaking had stopped.

Good. "It's best if I go—"

His roar shook a painting off the wall.

Not good!

My heart erupted into a flurry, and my legs folded. I sank onto the bed behind me, wide eyes locked on the furious Vissimo.

He took one look at me, cutting off the roar, and his anguish swept through me, leaving a heartsick ache in its path that belonged to *both* of us.

Why was this so damn hard? Why couldn't he understand that I didn't blame him for not saving me? I'd saved myself. He was furious that I'd made him powerless in the equation. I got it.

If the tables were turned, he'd have zero qualms locking me in a room to go save his family.

Kyros strode to the door, gripping the framing. It cracked under his hand, and his shoulders heaved as he said, "Do not leave this house."

He wanted me here but didn't want anything to do with me?

Kyros felt inadequate. Welcome to the fucking club. *No one* but Kyros could make himself feel worthy again, certainly not me. This was his battle.

And yet I hated witnessing such uncertainty in someone who'd walked this earth for so long. This bottomless, falling feeling was horrible. It was like he'd given up the right to our blood bond.

I sighed. "I'll stay if you sit down and talk to me tomorrow

5

morning instead of waiting until I fall asleep to leave for work. You're one hundred and fifty years old, not thirty."

Apparently the thirties were a hard time for Vissimo.

He didn't turn. "You want to negotiate? Here's a negotiation for you, Basilia. Stay in the house, and I won't kill the Indebted who failed to protect you on the estate."

I stopped moving. Stopped *breathing*. "You wouldn't do that."

Evie would be the first in the firing line. When I misled her, it was in the knowledge Kyros would never cross that line and hurt her because of my actions.

The vampire glanced over his shoulder, fangs lengthening. "Test me."

I stood, staggering slightly with dizziness. "So, what? You're trapping me here?"

"You can't be trusted not to put yourself in danger. You'll remain in my personal territory until that trust is earned again. Look at it however you want."

He was there one moment and gone the next.

The door to his room slammed.

Sitting heavily, I stared at my hands. What the actual fuck?

I couldn't be trusted to put my safety first? I only had *one person* whose needs I put above my own. Kyros had eight of them.

Yet guilt rose hard and fast.

You can't be trusted.

Little did Kyros know just how true those words were. When I got back to the estate, I wouldn't just be picking up where I left off with my grandmother's legacy of winning *Ingenium*.

Nope.

Two weeks ago, I pretty much handed Clan Fyrlia everything they needed to win the game. Unless I put Clan Sundulus back in the game somehow, not only was my grandmother's work and death for nothing, but most of Kyros's family would be murdered. I couldn't let either of those things happen. Equilibrium had to be restored.

So Kyros was right—yes—I couldn't be trusted.

Just not for the reasons he thought.

2

I inched forward, peering over the cliff edge at the ocean crashing below. In the distance, to the left, the golden shores of Lyall Bay called.

My head spun and I closed my eyes, inching away. My ears were mostly healed according to Dr Olivia. Tests had confirmed permanent damage to the canal. I couldn't hear a whisper at farther than fifty metres away. Considering human norms were a few metres, I wasn't shattered over the disability, but the news devastated Kyros; one more punch to the stomach. I'd genuinely feared for Olivia's life when she presented the results. Poor woman.

A safe distance from the drop, I opened my eyes again and settled into my senses practice. I worked to stretch each individually and then mute them one by one. I worked on operating two at once. Looking as far out to sea as possible, I did my best to block out the crashing noise of waves. Once I achieved that, I dialled each sense in the opposite direction, pulling in my vision to the grass by my feet while flaring my hearing to maximum despite the tender twinge of protest.

After repeating this for paired combinations of each sense, I returned to sight and sound, adding touch to the mix. Holding the sensation of wind on my skin at a *medium*, I proceeded to juggle the three around, dialling them up and down in turn.

I was a shit juggler.

Blowing out a breath, I walked to the house, aka my prison. The cabin fever was real. Kyros had cooled off from our talk three days ago though, so when he woke, I'd open the estate talk again.

I had to.

I'd ignored Tommy's calls for the last week, texting her that I was with Kyros and couldn't talk. She'd read between the lines, but I needed to see her with every fibre of my being. And I had so many freakin' apologies to make—to the Indebted—that I didn't know where to start.

I shat on a lot of friendships to save my most important one.

"Kyros! Wake up. We brought pizza."

I wrenched to a halt, my eyes lifting to the house. His siblings were here. At least one. And generally they—

"Why are you still asleep?" another asked.

—moved in a pack.

Shit. Just what I needed.

Their brother wasn't asleep, but maybe our talk could wait until tomorrow. It was my turn to avoid *him*—and his family who would soon be dead unless I could undo the damage I'd caused, and *fast.*

How long until they figured out the truth?

Maybe Fyrlia would tell them before that happened. King Mikael couldn't wait to turn Kyros against me.

I managed a single step toward the hidden garden I found two days ago.

"Basil!"

A wincing glance confirmed Lalitta was waving at me from where she stood in the bay windows of the open kitchen-dining area.

Fuck my life.

"Oh, hey," I said weakly, wobbling as I pivoted back to my initial route.

Neelan appeared next to his sister. Then Gerome and Dierdre.

I picked up Safina's dry voice and Francesca's higher whine.

"*Darling*," Rory purred as soon as I walked through the patio door.

I grunted in reply, throwing myself on the couch next to Lionel—by far my top pick for most empathetic sibling. Lalitta was the sweetest person I'd ever met, but she didn't pick up on low moods and her chatter always remained at high.

Lionel wrapped an arm around my shoulders. "What's happening, babe?"

Shrugging, I mumbled, "Nothing much."

"I don't buy that for a second." His voice was low though everyone could hear.

Maybe I shouldn't have chosen Lionel to sit next to. He'd make me cry.

I cleared my throat, blinking rapidly. "Your brother hates me. But also won't let me leave this house. I nearly died seventeen days ago while killing the man my best friend loves."

Silence reigned.

Gerome whistled low.

"Yep." I let my head thump back.

"Kyros won't let you leave?" Safina asked, rounding the charcoal sofa.

The devil himself strode into the kitchen at that moment, wearing nothing but his sweatpants again. I forced back the surge of lust that told me jumping him was probably the best way to live my life for the end of time.

Damned loins.

Kyros threw back the lid of a pizza box. "He won't, no." The vampire even managed to sound cool and collected about it. Kyros didn't look my way. He didn't make any comment about Lionel's arm around my shoulders.

The siblings exchanged long looks.

Neelan opened his mouth, and Kyros's menacing rumble filled the room. I couldn't blame Neelan for shutting his gob.

"*She* will be leaving once he stops sulking," I replied in the same even tone.

His fury nearly left me gasping, but I was sick of this.

I'd tiptoed around his bullshit when I should have pushed him to breaking point from the get-go. At least when he was furious, he actually spoke to me. I wasn't leaving because I was bored out of my mind or because his behaviour was tearing at my insides. Not really. There were things that I couldn't do outside of my grandmother's office. I hadn't contacted my Churchill team for a fortnight. I needed to see Tommy with my own eyes.

"You know the repercussions," he replied. Not even his siblings were fooled by his breezy tone.

"More death?" I shot back. "Because there hasn't been nearly enough of that."

He lowered the slice of pizza in his hand. "No, there hasn't." His green eyes blazed.

"Kyros," Dierdre said, her gaze lowered. "Father has ordered that Trenit and Tynan are off limits. You know what the consequences for killing them would be."

She darted her eyes to me.

Wait, wait, wait. I'd die? *Fuck me.* Sure, why not? That made total sense.

"Father and Mother are here," Francesca announced, zooming to lay a kiss on Kyros's cheek. "I love you, brother."

"I love you, too, Frannie." His gaze softened though his jaw didn't unclench. Kind of like his ass cheeks.

The king and queen were coming for the pizza party. That was my cue.

I scrambled to my feet. "Time for my daily nap. Kyros is such a chatterbox today. I'm worn out."

His eyes narrowed.

"One thing," Gerome called.

Ugh, nearly made it to the hall.

"It can wait," I replied, high-tailing it out of there.

He zipped in front of me and threw me over his shoulder, carting me back to the lounge. Unfortunately heightened senses didn't mean heightened reaction time or strength. It just meant I could see and hear it was coming.

The world had a great sense of humour.

His shoulder pressed on my stomach bruises, but I gritted my teeth until he set me down between Rory and Neelan on the window seat.

"I'm calling in the favour you owe me," he stated.

I stared. "What in the ever-loving hell are you talking about?"

He grinned. "I gave you the name of the nightclub owner so you could buy the lease. You promised me a proportional favour with no nudity involved."

Groaning, I rubbed my face. "I remember. What is it?"

"I'm giving the favour to Francesca."

"Nope. It's non-transferrable."

He glared. "*Fine*. In return for my boon, you'll participate in Frannie's fashion parade next week."

It took a few moments to click. "The launch of the boutique stores in Green?"

The vampire nodded.

Dammit. I'd known this would come back to... well, *bite me*. "Participate how?"

Francesca smirked. "Catwalk."

I fixed her with a flat look. "This is your turn, isn't it?" Her *sibling* turn to fuck with me and piss Kyros off.

Because he wasn't *nearly* pissed off enough.

"Whatever," I said, pushing at Neelan's thigh until he budged over.

"Have you considered asking politely?" he snapped.

Honestly? No.

Growing up a billionaire heiress could do that to a person.

I tensed as the front door opened, and blood pounded in my ears, surging as Neelan sniggered over my automatic reaction to the king's arrival. He was one powerful fucker, and I hadn't seen him since waking.

The queen wasn't happy that I'd put her entire family at risk by entering Fyrlia territory.

It occurred to me her husband may not have taken it well either.

"Children," the queen said happily, sliding into the kitchen ahead of her husband. Her nipples were covered today. The world should mourn the deprivation. They were art.

"Hey, Mom," the siblings murmured back.

The king scanned the room when he entered, not speaking, his gaze settling on his eldest son.

My phone buzzed.

Thank fuck.

Drawing it out, I read the message from Rory.

Who dis?

I rolled my eyes.

Beside me, his thumbs blurred, and another three messages buzzed through a second later.

What's happening between you and gyros?
Oops. *Kyros
#autocorrect LOL

Was he serious? Texting while beside me? Sometimes, it took a lot of effort to remember how old these vampires were.

He nudged me until I typed a reply.

He thinks he failed your family and me. He's pissed.

<3 <3

Rory showed the message to Lalitta on his other side, then typed again.

I read his reply.

Can you un-angry him?
He's being a pain at work and we need him on the ball.

They did? Were Fyrlia already moving on the information I gave them?

I sent my text.

Why? What's happened?

Rory cast a look at his father, who prowled about the room looking about as out of place as a wolf at a roller disco. My tension inched upward as he passed close by, flicking his ancient blue eyes to the wound on my neck.

Please keep moving, please keep moving.

My shoulders didn't relax one bit as he stalked past the window before returning to his queen's side.

I opened Rory's message.

Things have stalled with the recent distractions

Things like the Mr Ringly bluff? *Fuck.* It *was* starting. The Sundulus clan, unknown to most of their minions, were doing their best to sabotage a subdividing project that would trigger the end of the game.

Mr Ringly was a drug addict, and one month ago, Kyros was certain of the win.

Until I opened my big mouth to save Tommy.

If Fyrlia was pushing back, I had to get out of here and figure out a solution without delay. Which meant, it really was in my best interest to *un-angry* Kyros.

I nodded at Rory and Lalitta, texting:

I'll try

How the hell I'd achieve that was the next question. Nothing came to mind.

My phone buzzed incessantly and I glared at Rory before seeing it was a call from Tommy. This had to be number fifty at least, despite my messages to her. I got her neediness. It was the same for me too. I just couldn't stand for her to be compelled after everything Theodore did to her.

"Do you intend to answer that?"

My chest seized at the king's silken voice though he was speaking quieter—like all of the Sundulus royals—because of my ears.

I darted a glance at him. "No, I—"

His eyes narrowed to slits. "Answer it, human."

And when the fuck King Julius's questions were rhetorical was anyone's guess.

Shit. Tommy knew about Vissimo. What if she let something slip on the phone?

Swallowing, I obeyed, holding the phone away from my ear. "Tommy."

"Basi! Oh my fucking god. You better have a great reason for fobbing me off for two weeks. Where the hell are you?"

I winced as she erupted into a stream of cursing and wandered to face a bookshelf against one wall of the large lounge area.

She paused for breath, and I slipped in. "I'm with Kyros in the Bahamas, Tom. And we've been... busy."

Consider me non-plussed—because I could lie through my teeth to anyone else—but lying to Tommy wasn't in my skillset. I really, really wished it was.

"Sex?" she snarled. "Really? I've had to put up with texts because you're bouncing on the D?"

I bit back on a groan, my cheeks burning.

Francesca snorted.

Reaching up, I rested my hand against the spines of a few books. "I'm sorry I haven't called. I've been worried sick. Fred has sent me updates, but are you okay?"

"Not worried enough to come home?" she said quietly.

I squeezed my eyes shut, but I had faith in my friend's intelligence. She knew what *I'm with Kyros* meant even if the sadness and anger in her voice was real. "I love you, Tom."

Her gulping sob nearly tore an answering one from my lips. "I miss you, Basil. I really need you right now. Theo's gone missing. I woke up in hospital and no one has seen or heard from him. I don't know what to do."

It was like a sledgehammer slammed into the middle of my chest.

I covered my mouth with a trembling hand, robbed of speech. Kyros's anger cut through my shock, and I dug the heel of my palm against my ear until the pain shoved away the urge to cry.

"Theodore's missing?" I rasped, slightly too late. "Why didn't you tell me? You think the people who drugged you took him?"

Her voice shook. "I've called the restaurant to ask what they remember. They said we were there until after dinner and then disappeared. Their cruise boat doesn't have any cameras onboard. His phone is dead or something. He won't answer my calls. I filed a missing person's report with the police five days ago, but they haven't found anything."

I listened to her frantic babbling, wondering if I'd ever felt less human.

"Tom, slow down."

She choked. "I *love* him, Basi."

Tears thickened my voice, and my vision of the books blurred. "I know you do, girl."

"I can't sleep. I can't think. What if he's injured or worse? I need to know. Basil, I swore I'd never ask you to use your influence and money on my behalf," she whispered. "But I don't know what else to do. I need your help."

My face was slick with tears. "Of course. You have it."

This is what I'd hoped to avoid. Back at the estate and away from prying ears, I could have told Tommy the truth, especially now King Mikael had given me the key around the compulsion. The presence of Kyros and his family was backing me into a lie Tommy would never forgive me for, even if I came clean as soon as possible.

Theodore was dead and cold. *In pieces.* I hated giving her false hope. I wanted her to know what that bastard did. He didn't deserve her grief. Not one bit of it.

"The circumstances were dodgy with your drink being messed with," I said after wiping my face. "I have to play devil's advocate, Tom. Is it possible Theodore did that to you and ran after?"

Her silence was awful. Worse than her tears.

"Or," I added, "is it possible he got cold feet with your relationship and doesn't want to be found? Maybe when you were roofied, you guys had an argument? Anything could have happened."

"*No,*" she whispered. "Stop saying those things."

"I just... What if he's okay?"

"Then I need proof of that. One way or another. I can't move on without the truth."

My heart was made of glass, and her words shattered it. "Please tell Fred to grant you whatever help he can. When I'm back, we'll get through this together." *And I'll break your heart.*

"You'll be back soon?" she croaked.

I'd witnessed Tommy sounding pitiful once in my life. She was broken.

My voice firmed. "As soon as I can. I promise you."

Hanging up, I slipped the phone into the back pocket of my high-waisted shorts, feeling my holey crop-sweater ride up. Staring at the bookshelf, I didn't turn until my face was dry and I had rein on my emotions again.

Thank you, Agatha Le Spyre.

The quiet was leaden. Too heavy.

I needed pizza, ice cream, and Avril Lavigne's *Let Go* album.

Dierdre punched me on the shoulder as I passed.

Love that bitch. Screw Lionel. Next time, I'd sit next to her.

Throwing open the pizza box, my stomach unknotted somewhat as the royals began to converse again. All but one.

Green eyes trained on me, and I ignored him, stuffing as much of the margherita slice into my mouth as possible.

Actually...

Grabbing the box, I rounded the bend, walking to the hall.

An arm looped around my bare waist, stopping me.

Resigned, I peered up at Kyros. "What?"

He didn't say a word, so I listened to the war within him instead. *Sorrow, fear, guilt, uncertainty, frustration, anger.*

So much anger. And yet it was a tiny blip on what he'd feel toward me when Sundulus discovered the truth. If Fyrlia was starting their countermove, then I needed Kyros to hold the fort until I could figure out some way around what I'd done.

I sighed as Rory cleared his throat dramatically.

Jesus. I hadn't forgotten the damn messages!

"Driving lessons," I said, sighing.

Kyros's eyes dimmed.

"You promised to show me how to drive. I want a lesson." Striding back to the bench, I threw the pizza box down and faced off with him.

Kyros's face hardened though he turned to watch me. "No."

"You're going back on your word?" I challenged. "Knew it was too good to be true."

He began to vibrate.

"A simple lesson." I pressed. "We don't have to leave the property if that makes you feel better. Or are we so far gone that you can't be in the same car as me?"

He agreed with my words. Not out loud. But *fuck*, he couldn't stand being that close to me? That's how unworthy he felt?

Which was just so messed up, I wanted to throttle him.

Kyros reached behind, hooking a set of keys on his finger. "You want a driving lesson?"

"I do." I folded my arms, wary of the ugliness filling him.

He tossed the keys to the ground between us. "Then pick up the fucking keys and let's go."

Shock and hurt cannoned into me. Kyros had one rule—don't fuck with his family. Within those bounds, in possession of his control, he'd never done anything to disrespect me or make me feel less.

"That's how you made me feel," he said quietly.

My mouth dried as the vampire studied me. I could feel his pain and his triumph and his relief.

This wasn't a punishment for me—for what I'd done. He was punishing himself by shoving me away. And if I didn't have front row seats to his emotions, the ploy would have worked.

Not today. I had too much riding on this bullshit.

"You'll have to do worse than that." Stepping closer, I swooped for the keys.

A massive hand stopped me.

King Julius picked up the keys with his other hand, still holding my hand. We stood together, and he placed the keys into my hand, cold eyes on his son. His ire filled the space, and my knees knocked together. Pretty sure my heart was decaying and crumbling to dust from the proximity and contact.

"Your true mate has killed two of my enemy," he said, dark menace crawling with each word. "She walked to certain death out of loyalty to her family. She outsmarted fifty of your best Indebted to do so. She ensured that our family would not be in danger from your loss of control. You *dare* to disrespect her so?"

That one was rhetorical.

Kyros usually kept his gaze lowered around his father. Not this time. Green fire could leap from his eyes and I wouldn't be surprised.

King Julius's voice lashed out. "*Answer me.*"

Wrong again.

He didn't give Kyros time to respond. "Tell me, eldest son. How many of my enemy have *you* killed?"

I sucked in a breath. *Whoa. Fucking harsh.*

I swear that I only *blinked*, but in that split second, blood erupted from Kyros's mouth, his head snapping to the side. The king stood before him, fist clenched.

Savage growls ripped from Kyros's mouth of the like I'd only heard once. Black was overcoming him, but Julius didn't react or move back.

This was getting out of hand.

Moving, so Julius wasn't between me and Kyros, I closed my eyes and sent warm fuzzies to the vampire. Why the fuck I had to comfort him when he'd been a jackass was beyond me. Other than the knowledge that Kyros had never, not in *one hundred and fifty years*, felt so off-balance. I'd made him this way.

His growls died down.

When I opened my eyes, it was to find King Julius's shrewd gaze on me.

"You calmed him," the vampire king said under his breath.

Glad to know it worked both ways. Because only Kyros got the GPS location benefit from the second exchange and that was bullshit.

Nodding, I gripped the keys, my palms sweating.

My attempt to close the distance between me and Kyros did not turn out how I expected at all. Actually, I'd just expected Kyros to say no—not to treat me like crap and then cop humiliations and a smackdown from his dad.

I'd made him feel roughly three times worse by trying to make him feel better.

Go, Basi.

"Take your mate on the driving lessons you promised her," the king said in a tone that brooked no argument.

Not from me anyhow.

Kyros didn't seem inclined to acquiesce, and that would lead to round two with his father.

I set the keys on the bench and picked up the pizza box again. "That's okay. I don't much feel like a lesson anymore. I'm going to leave you guys to it." The wobble in my voice was fucking pathetic.

"Okay, dear," the queen called softly from the window seat. "Call if you need us."

It'd be a cold day in hell before that happened.

3

"We brought Thai food!"

No.

Double no.

They were here again? Like, the *afternoon* after they were last here?

"Touch the green curry, and I will rip your eyes out."

Francesca sounded bitchier than usual.

I was closer to the hidden garden this time. Grinning, I slipped between two low-hanging trees and crept to one of the swinging chairs positioned around the sunken fire pit area.

Gerome snarled. *"Don't touch my Khao Soi if you don't want me to touch your green curry then!"*

Dodged a bullet.

Victory!

Kyros's deep voice rumbled. *"What are you doing here? Again."* His resignation nearly drew a snort from my lips. I tempered by recalling his douchebaggery from yesterday.

"Brother," Safina said, *"do you really need to ask why?"*

What did that mean?

The king's voice stopped Gerome and Francesca's bickering. *"Heir."*

Everyone was here. Fucking great.

"Father."

"Why is your mate hiding in the garden?"

I bit back my groan.

The king's voice cut through the walls of the house toward me. *"You are yet to apologise to her."*

Simultaneously, I appreciated and did *not* appreciate the king championing me. He was one of the few Vissimo in existence who could exercise control over Kyros. I objected to his humiliating methods when his son already felt so worthless.

"I was about to if you hadn't all shown up," Kyros growled back.

Shit. He was playing with the fire that was his father too often of late. Though powerful, Kyros was considered a growing Vissimo. He'd just turned the vampire equivalent of twenty-one.

Which meant his six-hundred-year-old father could give him a literal smackdown that would make the punch from yesterday look like a game of Pictionary.

"I suggest you do it, heir."

Yep, I had front row seats to Kyros's emotions. He in *no* way intended to apologise for throwing the keys on the ground. I tensed as the front door opened, wondering if I should hide better.

Bit hard when I had a figurative homing beacon inside me.

"Basilia," Kyros called from the front door.

Maybe I'd just stay quiet and—

He growled and stalked from the house toward where I sat.

Today was not a day to push me around. I'd tossed and turned all night after the call with Tommy. Plus, a peaceful doze was impossible with Kyros beating himself up so freakin' much after acting like an asshole.

And I wanted Thai food.

I sent Kyros a flash of warning through our bond—a lion's roar of sorts.

"That's about as strong as a growling puppy," he spat, striding between the two trees and stopping at the edge of the sunken pit.

Turning my face away, I stared at the rolling expanse of his garden, spotting a few Indebted in the distance. My insides twisted.

"I have time for a driving lesson now," he said, folding his arms.

I hummed. "That's a shame. I'm busy for the next few months. I'll let you know if there's an opening."

Kyros dropped into the pit and approached me at a slow stroll. "You want to learn."

"Someone else can teach me at the estate."

"Basilia, just—"

I burst to my feet. "No, *you* just."

I gasped, swearing as he picked me up. Cradling me in his arm, he began striding back to the house.

When kicking proved futile, I thumped my fist on his chest. "Kyros Atagio, put me down *right* this minute."

"Has anyone ever told you that you're spoiled?" he murmured.

Who did he think he was fooling with his calm façade? Anger thrummed just beneath the surface of the massive vampire.

Sarcasm filled my voice. "Have you ever met a billionaire who wasn't?"

We entered the garage, and I was transferred to the driver's seat of his usual black car. I would have preferred the flashy orange number at the far end of the row of vehicles.

And he thought *I* was spoiled?

"Seat belt," he snapped, sliding into the car.

Glaring, I did as bid. "Are you going to be a dick the entire time?"

Waiting patiently as he struggled to grip the tatters of his control, I pushed the doodacky that started the car.

He took a deep breath. "Check your side and rear-view mirrors as you reverse out. Swing to the left when the front of the car is clear. We'll practice on the front grass."

"There's a reverse camera."

"That you can't always rely upon being there. Use the mirrors."

Whatever.

Touching the accelerator gently, I jolted as the car jerked back. I slammed on the brakes and whacked the wheel. "Why is every car different like that?"

Kyros hesitated before answering, "Your altered senses may have something to do with it."

True.

Focusing on my touch, I pulled the sense right in before easing on the accelerator.

The vehicle glided backward. *Ha!* I ripped the wheel down as we left the garage, spinning us to the left on the gravel.

"Woohoo," I crowed.

"Easy," he said between clenched teeth.

I quirked a brow. "Why? The result is the same."

"Because reckless driving is against the law."

Really? Who knew?

Not waiting for him to boss me around again, I directed the car onto the wide expanse of grass between the house and the ocean. "What next?"

"Drive around. Get used to the feel."

Yes, sir.

I planted my foot.

"*Basilia.*"

"This thing really flies."

"Do you have any self-preservation whatsoever?" he hissed as I eased up on the pedal.

We were going there then.

"As much as any human," I answered, easing the car in a wide arc to go back the way I came. "Why? You got a problem with that?"

A long beat went by.

"Yes. Though I have no right to. Yes," he said in a hollow voice.

It was the first time since I awoke that he'd pushed past anger.

What exactly did Kyros mean by the *no right* part though? Was it centred around his feeling of powerlessness? Or was this another Vissimo thing I didn't understand? I didn't dare hope that he'd gracefully accepted I didn't *need* help.

Scrap that. There were times when I needed help, but there was no way, *no way*, that I needed him or anyone for everything. I didn't even need Tommy for everything. Or Fred. I hadn't needed Grandmother for everything.

"The triplets were very clear about what would happen to Tommy if I didn't enter alone," I said.

Silence.

"I'm trying to understand why you hold me to different standards than you hold yourself." I continued. "You *blame* me for saving my friend?"

Fuck, he was so incredibly hard inside right now—an emotional barrier. I hated when he pulled that crap.

"No," Kyros said, glancing out the window to the sea. "I blame myself because you deemed me inadequate of your confidence."

That was just so... *messed up.*

Sorrow tinged my words. "I find it really hard to grasp Vissimo values. You know that I don't see us as a team, Kyros. I've known you for a handful of *months*, and most of that, you weren't my friend by any means."

"*Friend?*" he said incredulously.

I didn't take the bait, but my knuckles whitened where they throttled the wheel instead of his neck.

"I had minutes to come up with a plan, Kyros. *Minutes.* If I'd had longer, I likely would have thought of a way to involve you without risking Tommy's life. I *wanted* to involve you because I was so afraid. But in hindsight, I'm glad that never happened. I wouldn't be able to live with myself if harm came to your family. In my mind, that's how the matter lies."

"Your death would have been my end, Basilia," he said, defeat hanging heavy around him.

I shot him a frown, swinging us back around again. "Like, killed you?"

Shit, I hadn't known that.

Kyros shook his head. "Others. I would have lost control. Safina would have paid the debt of my crimes once my father managed to kill me. When a vampire goes berserk, there's no coming back. Ever. The death of a true mate is a sure way to trigger it."

... *Oh.*

I bit my lip. "I never knew that."

He closed his eyes. "Because I didn't wish you to carry the burden. When you entered *Gingers,* I nearly lost control. After I extracted your promise not to enter Fyrlia territory again, I thought it a non-issue."

That there was a massive problem. "So you deemed that as your burden to carry, your issue, and made the choice not to include me?"

Green eyes cut to me. "It is not the same thing as walking to your death to save your friend."

I disagreed. "Both proved life-threatening. You're used to working by yourself. I'm used to working by myself. Double standards, Kyros. And I can tell you're deflecting. Tell me what the real issue is."

Were we going to do anything other than loop in circles? Not that I was going to mention that now Kyros was talking.

"You—" He started. "You killed that Fyrlia scum. As a *human.* Through sheer intelligence and bravery and loyalty to your friend, you defeated him. I'm inadequate to call you mate."

There it is.

My heart squeezed tight as his emotions barraged my mind. "You're treating me like shit to push me away. *That* behaviour, nothing else, is what makes me doubt the blood bond. Why are you acting this way?"

There was something more.

I could feel it. And hey, I could flatten this grass all day while he put his anguish into words.

Kyros growled, avoiding my gaze. "You know why."

"I can't read your mind, so no, I don't know why."

Glass poured into the car as he smashed the passenger window. "I'm your fucking mate—your *true mate*—and you don't have faith in my strength or my power or my ability to keep you from harm. You don't want to be in my company, on my property, or in my territory. You don't *believe* in the blood bond or see us as a single entity. How the fuck am I meant to change your mind? How do I show you when killing more of my enemies means losing my family? What gives me the right to show you when you're just so *untouchable*?"

Understanding trickled to me slowly.

Really, *fundamentally*, Kyros's torment had the same roots as many of my childhood demons. He felt trapped and incapable of taking action.

I may not completely grasp his inherent Vissimo need to protect me as the male, but I could understand the emotion making him feel helpless. And I knew from clawing my way back to self-worth that I couldn't make him feel better.

He had to do that himself.

But maybe he needed a kick-starter.

Guiding the vehicle around again, I said, "You think I don't trust you to protect me? That's the issue?"

That was just so... moronic. Who else was better equipped to do so *and* had more motive to save my butt?

"I can feel your uncertainty around me," he answered after a beat.

I hit the steering wheel, pushing down on the accelerator. "I only feel that way because you're acting like a caveman who didn't spear a pig for dinner!"

"Slow down."

In reply, I wrenched down on the wheel to circle us around, gauging the distance between us and the cliff edge. "What if I could give you proof that I trust you with my life?"

Kyros whipped his head to me. "You can't."

My heart spluttered uselessly in my chest. I gripped the wheel, firming my resolve on the fucking craziness I was about to unleash.

"I can. In the boot. There's a bag."

He stared at me. "No there's not."

I groaned. "Because you look there all the freakin' time? Check the damned boot."

Massive vampire in an itty-bitty space? He lowered his seat back and wrangled his way onto the back seat.

As soon as he pulled the seat down and stretched into the trunk, I planted my foot, wrenching the wheel to the right. His startled snarl was lost to the roar of the engine as we hurtled toward the cliff ledge.

Closer.

"Basilia!"

Closer.

His hand closed around my seat belt.

The engine whined as the ground disappeared and I gasped as we glided straight in thin air.

The nose tipped, and a scream lodged in my throat as we plummeted down to the ocean.

Kyros ripped my seat belt off. Moving me too quickly for me to fathom up and down.

Metal screamed. Light poured in. My new senses were overloaded. *Shot.*

I couldn't take it anymore—though I'd created this.

Terror forced my scream. "Kyros!"

His arms were around me. Wind rushed past as we catapulted to who knew what, and yet still his soft words were audible in my ear.

"I have you."

He did.

So why was I afraid?

The calm spreading through me wasn't mine but worked all the same. My head cleared, and I was able to focus on the cobalt blue rushing up to meet us.

Kyros curled around me, covering my ears an instant before we crashed through the surface.

Water closed over us.

Forever passed as we forged a path through the depths. When our downward movement stopped, Kyros kicked upward with me in tow.

Just as my chest began to tighten, we broke the surface.

The vampire whirled me to face him.

"What the fuck were you thinking?" he hissed, water dripping from his toffee hair.

He hadn't touched me in weeks, and as his words floated away, we both gasped at the electrical contact.

The current underneath my skin exploded.

I panted for air, wiping water from my eyes to better see him. Call it adrenaline, call it the blood bond, or call it something else entirely —throwing myself at Kyros, I looped my arms around his neck and pressed my lips to his.

His moan was immediate.

Saltwater seasoned our kiss as our tongues moved together, our union working both of us to a frenzy. I burned with the need to draw him closer, to tie him to me by whatever means possible.

To never exist as separate from him again.

I bobbed under the surface without warning. Surfacing, I coughed for air.

Kyros joined me above water a second later, glancing around in confusion.

"Did you just forget we were in the ocean and you had to swim?" I asked, breathing hard as I treaded water.

His lips twitched as the dreamy haze left his eyes. "You have that effect on me, vixen."

Vixen.

My bottom lip must have trembled because as Kyros drew me against him once more, he stroked it with his thumb.

"I'm sorry, my beauty," he said over the crashing of the waves.

A handful of words made me realise just how much his distance had hurt. "I missed you. Are you back for good?"

His reply was dry as he turned around. "You proved your point. Destroying my favourite car in the process."

"That was collateral for your little move with the keys yesterday."

"Fair enough. Hold onto my neck."

As soon as I did, Kyros swam for the cliff face.

"But?" I asked him.

"*But* you are not Vissimo. And I am not human. I need to figure out how I fit as your mate, seeing as you won't accept me acting like a caveman who didn't spear a pig for dinner."

His amusement embraced me and if it was a tangible thing, I

would have hugged it and never let go. Kyros was happy, and I just felt so *right*. So centred and sure.

"No, I won't," I mumbled. "I promise to figure out the same. For y—" I grimaced as we reached the bottom of the cliffs.

"What?" He tried to glance back.

We were exchanging wedding vows. What the hell was wrong with me? I'd forgotten everything.

I shook my head. "Uhm, nothing. Just grossly unprepared for the emotional content of this conversation."

That didn't amuse him one bit.

"You drove a car off a cliff, and this conversation worries you?"

Make that a big fat yes with a side of fries. Not answering, I linked my legs around his waist and adjusted my grip.

Kyros started up the one-hundred-metre drop, and I didn't give it more than a passing thought. I really *did* trust him to protect me. As it turned out, knowing that and proving it to myself were different things.

Why did I have the feeling I'd just crossed a line that I couldn't erase?

"Kyros. Basilia. Your dinner is getting cold!"

I craned my head to see Queen Titania peering over the ledge. She waved, beaming.

How did this become my normal?

Because it did feel normal to me now. This absolute insanity where vampires were real and I drove cars off cliffs to prove a point.

I rested my head against Kyros's back. "I'm hungry. Let's go feed me."

A growl filled his chest as his powerful arms and legs worked to move us to the top. "Kyros spear pig."

Ugh.

I'd never hear the end of that.

4

It took another two days to return to the estate under the not-so-ideal negotiated conditions of my release.

I'd needed time after Kyros came around to decide my plan of attack for Tommy and the Indebted. Plus, things felt so right with him after the car thing, and I truly hadn't wanted to leave his company.

In the end, the danger of *that* spurred me home more than anything.

My duty to my grandmother's memory and her friends came first. Always. I'd known my feelings would get tangled as we continued to exchange blood, but I had to keep that from interfering with my strategy.

"Fuck," I muttered under my breath as Fred pulled into the estate.

This was going to be a shit of a day.

One I'd brought on myself.

Tommy was out the massive front doors of the main house before I'd opened my car door.

"Good luck, Miss Le Spyre," Fred said.

Fred.

Although he'd known the truth of what happened that night, I still felt like I owed him an apology too. Yet he'd take that as a mortal offense.

"Thank you so much, Fred," I whispered, reaching forward to squeeze his shoulder.

Tommy ripped open my door and nearly dragged me out.

"You're okay," she gasped.

I shook my head at her in warning before pulling her into my arms. "Of course I am."

"Everything has been so fucked up," she blurted. "I'm getting paranoid."

Good save.

"Tom, please tell me you're alright?"

I'd done everything I could to prepare for this moment, even reciting lines. But I couldn't have prepared for seeing her for the first time since she was lifeless on the cold, concrete floor.

The memory choked me. "Y-You nearly died."

My entire body shook as I clung to her.

I never expected to be able to hold her again—hear her voice or her laughter.

"I'm okay, Basil," she hushed, squeezing me just as tight. "I swear."

"I'll be the judge of that," I said, pulling her toward the house as I scanned her from head to toe. "What was the latest verdict from the doctor?"

Why I was rushing toward what had to happen next, I had no idea. My only reasoning was that if Tommy's heart had to be broken, it was up to me to do it and I should do it without delay.

"I'm right as rain now. Took ten days or so to feel human again. They said an hour or two more and I wouldn't be alive."

I closed my eyes as we entered the office.

"I'm so sorry that I wasn't here, Tom. Really." Shutting the door, I switched on the noise-cancelling.

She rushed me. "What the fuck did he do to you?"

"What?" *Theodore?*

"That fucker. He held you prisoner? Did you do another exchange?"

31

She meant Kyros.

I exhaled slowly. "Not a—" I gurgled with the effects of the restrictions on my mind. Crap, I hadn't had to worry about the compulsion while in Kyros's company.

I focused on the thought of a mouse in a trap.

"Not prisoner," I managed.

Taking her hand, I led Tommy to the chaise. "Sit, please."

She sat but bounced straight back up, face stricken. "It's Theo, isn't it? Your private investigators found something."

There weren't any private investigators. I'd asked Fred to string her along until I got back.

I'd considered my lines carefully before coming and really hoped to get through this without the compulsion cutting me off. Kyros would have already been alerted by my slip before.

This was it.

I had to believe our friendship could survive the coming moments. But unless I owned up to this now, I could kiss Tommy goodbye forever.

Pulling my hair back, I leaned so she could see the jagged red scars on my neck. It was a mess of a thing. Looked like I was cut with a broken bottle. I had no idea how Kyros was able to save me.

Her mouth rounded and her shocked eyes flew to mine. "You were hurt. That's why you couldn't come. I knew it. That bastard!"

"It wasn't Kyros," I told her.

She inspected the scar. "What do you mean *it wasn't Kyros*?"

I captured her chestnut gaze, wondering if I'd be physically sick. Unfortunately, saying names had never been an issue. "Not Kyros. It was Theodore."

Tommy stared at me, unmoving.

"Theodore," I repeated.

"I don't understand," she said, slowly standing.

A lie.

I could see her put everything together, and fuck, how I *wished* repeating the details of the triplets' plan to win the Le Spyre fortune was easy as blurting them out. Because maybe then she'd believe I'd had no choice. The explanation was going to take hours. I wasn't even sure if I had the creativity to force the direction of my intention for so long. It was fucking hard.

"He was a—" She clapped her hands over her mouth.

Hope stirred in my chest.

Not shifting, I waited for her to process that Theodore was a vampire, watching as her eyes darted and she gasped at intervals.

Eventually, she turned to me.

"He must have had reason to attack you."

I directed my thoughts to Bluff City Bank. "My money and power."

Ingenium was involved. I wracked my brain, then thought of Twister. "A game."

She shook her head, backing away. "That's not possible. I met him at my last job. Before you started at Live Right." Her chest rose and fell. "You're wrong."

My chest tightened as she crumbled. "I wouldn't ever make this up."

Tommy whirled, anger twisting her face. "*You're wrong!* Where is he? What the fuck did that psychotic fucker do to him?"

She rushed me, and I didn't glance away though my insides shrivelled to dust.

The word was bitter on my tongue. Because Theodore shouldn't carry this much power in death. Not when he was a twisted, cruel piece of shit. He didn't just drug my friend and use her body to get information on me; he made her fall in love.

He didn't intend her to leave the underground chamber. He broke her for fun.

To get to me.

Later, to get back at me.

I forced the lump in my throat down, thinking of my grandmother in her coffin.

"Dead," I said in a low voice.

She reeled back as if slapped. Pain suffused her anguished

expression and her usually warm gaze that filled most of my best memories.

Taking a shuddering inhale, thoughts on the toast I managed to make myself this morning, I broke what was left of my best friend. "I did it."

The sound coming from her chest was awful. Air wouldn't fill her lungs. Or it couldn't get out.

She backed away again, stumbling over the leg of the chaise.

Lost.

Betrayed.

Fixing my mind on the day I kicked Harriet Gregorian and my other rich friends out of my life for good, I said, "To save you."

Standing, I moved closer.

She stilled, anger coating her grief. "*To save me*? Are you fucking serious? You mean to save yourself! Or that animal you keep running to over and over again. Theod—" She blanched, clutching at her chest. "Theodore *loved* me. I *loved him*. We had a future together."

Tommy crossed the gap, and I made no effort to move. My head rocketed to the right as her palm met my cheek.

"What did you do to him?" she screamed in my face. "Where is he?"

I clutched my ears, tears of pain pricking the corners of my eyes.

"He's not gone," she said, gasping for air. "You're hiding him. You and that asshole. This is a game. Part of the game. He found out. And t-tried to get you free and..."

He never took photographs with her because I would have recognised him. I was willing to bet the estate that he manipulated Tommy to feel she shouldn't introduce us.

I stepped toward her. "Tom—"

"*Stay the fuck away from me*," she choked out. "You're just like them. How did I never see it? *You're* a fucking monster too. Everyone you touch ends up dead."

Pain struck me and my legs nearly buckled.

Her words were far more effective than her slap.

"That's right," she said. "I see you, Basilia Le Spyre. What a fucking wake-up call. I'm leaving. Don't send your fucking freak squad after me. My father and I are cutting ties with your family. Come after me, and I won't be responsible for what I do to you."

I watched her leave in the numb grip of disbelief.

My worst nightmare just came true.

"Laurel," I said when I could trust my voice.

The second I allowed myself to feel was the second I crumbled. There was another apology to get done first.

The Vissimo appeared less than ten seconds later. Her expression was cool, something I'd never seen on her face—not even when we first met.

Weariness piled thick on my shoulders. "I owe you an explanation," I told her. "But first, please send ten Indebted with Tommy."

Tommy's words rang in my ears, but the triplets were able to get close to her because I tried to uphold her sense of freedom. Our friendship was destroyed, but her life was still my responsibility. "Tell them to stay as close as needed to protect her, please."

Laurel nodded, raising her voice. "Patrick, Sheena, take your teams and protect Miss Tetley. No restrictions on range."

My ears picked up their distant replies of *Roger that.*

I stood aside. "Please come in."

She shut the door, and I reset the noise-cancelling.

The Indebted woman tilted her chin, watching me with cold blue eyes.

"Laurel, I—"

"If you *ever* put the lives of my Indebted at risk like that again, not only is our deal void but I will go to Kyros with every single thing I know."

Already numb, I absorbed her threat on autopilot. "Fair enough. But you should know that if Tommy is in danger, I'm capable of doing nearly anything to bring her back. That does *not* include putting the lives of any Vissimo here at risk."

"I told you what he'd do to us if you died," she snarled, crouching forward. "Evie would have been first to face execution, do you realise that? Barring the handful of seconds that decided you'd live instead of die, she'd be dead in the ground along with the rest of us."

I had. Sweet Evie.

Heaviness swept through me, and I nodded. "I should have listened. In my defence, I didn't know what happened to male Vissimo when their mates are killed. Laurel, I asked you to tell me everything you knew about the laws and intricacies of the mate bond. Why didn't you tell me that part?"

Her face smoothed.

It was confirmation she'd left it out on purpose. "I see. Whatever your reasons for omitting that were, I can't say if that would have changed my actions that night. What I can promise is that I will never leave you out of a plan again."

Not because of her threat.

Because we were partners and she had an equal risk in this venture.

Her blue gaze narrowed.

"I nearly died, Laurel. *Tommy* nearly died regardless of me trying to control the situation. I've learned my lesson, and I can only apologise sincerely for the risk my behaviour put you and the other Vissimo in from Kyros."

Her eyes trailed over my scarred neck and lingered on my face. She straightened and smoothed her expression. "I believe you have."

"You accept my apology?"

She quirked a brow. "I hear you."

Damn, throwing my own words in my face. Forgiven but not forgotten. I grimaced. "I deserve that."

The two-hundred-and-eighty-year-old vampire dipped her head. "Yes. But you've survived one beating. Don't be so eager to beat yourself up again. Worse mistakes have been made, and your goodwill toward the Indebted cannot be erased by one night."

That meant so much to me. I hadn't expected their forgiveness. I'd expected Tommy's.

"Okay," I said hoarsely. "I'll apologise to everyone soon, I swear."

"They'd appreciate that," she answered, then her gaze snapped to mine. "What's the state of the game after what happened with Fyrlia?"

"Shit hit the fan. That's what."

Her eyes searched mine. "Sundulus is going to lose."

"I need to restore balance in the game without delay," I said. "It's the only way." I had to catch up on a landslide of reports, not to mention filling Tommy's now-vacant position.

Laurel stood to attention. "What do you need me to do?"

There was a list a mile long.

But I'd considered filling Laurel in on my betrayal of Clan Sundulus before deciding nothing good would come from it. The iota of respect King Julius held for me would vanish the second he learned or guessed the truth. It was possible he'd interrogate the Indebted at that point. The less Laurel knew, the better.

My life would be forfeit, or at least my freedom. The bond with Kyros? He'd snuff it out quicker than I could recite his siblings' names. I'd have destroyed my grandmother's legacy of *decades* in mere weeks after swearing that I'd win—for her, for me, and for everyone Vissimo had ever used and abused.

Now, the battle wasn't winning. It was ensuring Fyrlia *didn't* win. And to do that, I needed help.

It was high time I paid my grandmother's closest friends a visit.

5

Sir Olythieu, owner of Bluff City Bank, and *human liaison* of Clan Sundulus spoke from across the round table. "We've anxiously awaited your call, Basilia."

I bet they had.

Weeks had passed since Grandmother's funeral. Then a few more while I got my head around Kyros's betrayal. Then a couple more while I recovered from death's door.

It settled something within me to be sitting in Sir Olythieu's massive office with my grandmother's nearest and dearest. I'd craved normalcy and familiarity for so long.

"Circumstances delayed me," I said. "Firstly, you should know that my mind is caged."

Sounds of dismay echoed around the room. I hadn't told them the reason for this meeting, but I was sure they'd guessed it had to do with Grandmother's work.

"All of us are controlled to varying degrees," Mr Hothen said. His eyes filled with an empathy that I hadn't thought him capable of. Being the owner of Bluff City's largest mall complexes and shopping streets required a certain pragmatic calculation he was renowned for.

"How long?" Mrs Syrre asked softly.

I regarded the genteel woman—by far the kindest elite in Bluff City. If my grandmother hadn't tucked the woman under her wing after the death of her husband, the Syrre fortune would be long gone. Their ship freighting company had been around for nearly as long as my family name. "Three months."

So little time for so much chaos and destruction.

Mr Dithis set a board on the table, and the oldies spread out all manner of cards over the square table.

Dame Burke jabbed her finger at two of the cards. "Which cunt did it?"

I couldn't point. Not without the right intention anyway. I *could* say a specific word out of context, usually, but that would be useless here because the context was fixed—and exactly what the compulsion worked against—me spilling Sundulus and Vissimo secrets.

Fury warped Lady Treena's face. "They got her good. Only Olythieu has trouble pointing. Must've been a strong beast."

"Think of something unrelated, Basilia," the regal man who always reminded me of Colonel Sanders said. "Hold that in your mind as you talk and move."

I nodded. "Yes, I know." I'd practiced more before coming here to keep my mind off Tommy.

Sir Olythieu's grey brows slammed together. "You know?"

I glanced around the table, which had stilled.

Mr Dithis rubbed his jaw. "Took us nine years to figure that out."

They shouldn't congratulate me. I'd been told by King Asshole himself.

"Even with that knowledge, I'm afraid we must often rely on the others guessing to get information across," Olythieu said quietly.

A reflection of my pain and frustration lurked in his dark-grey eyes. I'd previously thought that my intention had to be closely aligned with whatever I was trying to say. But if I focused hard enough, any random thought was effective. Thinking of lavender bushes, I placed my hand atop the table on the Sundulus side.

"Bastards," Dithis seethed. "Which one?"

"Kyros," I answered, feeling a twinge of guilt as his name passed my lips.

Hothen sighed. "He's one of the worst. The eldest son, as I'm sure you know by now. I am so sorry, Basi dear. The trapping was a permanent one?"

The trapping. Singular.

I held up four fingers.

"Four," Lady Treena said, frowning.

Syrre held a hand to her pale cheek. "Four times, Treena. Is that what you mean, Basilia? He did it four times?"

Hurrying around the table with a speed belying her age, Dame Burke placed yes and no cards before me. These cards were a really good idea. It would make the coming explanation so much easier.

Maybe if I'd had them with Tommy, she'd still be here.

I tapped a finger on *yes*. I could point to normal words.

A heavy tension filled the room at that revelation.

When it came to the people around this table, I'd had nothing from my grandmother to go on. Fred merely said that she met her friends every week. But if they were in the power of the clans, each of them had to report in some way—probably to the royals or their seconds. I needed to know who they were compelled by and how tightly. My grandmother may have been the ringleader because she wasn't controlled in any way, but I'd continue her work regardless of my compelled state. That meant I had to feel out how much I could tell the others.

"I need information on each of you," I told them.

"You're taking the third seat?" Sir Olythieu's gaze sharpened.

"Give me the information and I'll answer that question," I replied, settling back.

He smiled. "Very good. Burke, do we have the file from when we first started?"

Dame Burke pursed her lips. Her restraints had to be the loosest. She seemed to be the nominated spokesperson. "I'll dig it up and update it."

She cut me a look. "And none of us have orders to freely report.

We answer during interrogation, and only to their direct questions, which are always business based. In fact, most of us have minimal contact with the beasts now they've caged our underlings. Nothing more than a phone call every few months. Olythieu and Lady Treena have it the worst. They're pulled in for questioning once or twice every year."

That wasn't surprising. Neither of them was richer than me, but their assets were entirely located in Bluff City, whereas Grandmother had moved the vast majority of ours international. Their estates were far more valuable in *Ingenium* than mine. And when it came to power and influence, Lady Treena was mayor for over seventeen years before retiring. Her father was mayor in his time. And her grandfather. Five generations ago, the head of their family had married a woman of vast mining fortune.

"We need to meet twice weekly until I'm up to date," I announced. "This is around my hours for *Live Right Realty*."

Kyros never eliminated that term from my repertoire. Kind of hard to if he wanted me to secure properties.

"You're working there?" Treena said. "We thought you were trapped. That's why Rory Senrite was on such familiar terms with you at the NJB function."

Uhm, kind of.

"I don't just secure houses." *Hmm*, how best to tell them I worked on Level 66 with the royals?

Hothen stiffened. "What hours do you work?"

Dithis moved to place a clock before me. My grandmother had fondly referred to the man as *Pie* because he had his fingers in so many. There wasn't any Bluff City industry that Mr Dithis's wealth didn't touch.

I was able to answer that without help. "Midnight until 3:30 a.m. Weekdays."

"You're there for the..." He trailed off, eyes lighting up.

The roll? Yes.

My shoulders sagged. It was such a fucking relief to get some of this out, no matter how frustrating the process. Once they knew my situation, and I knew theirs, things would move faster. But to have their support—even their knowledge of what being compelled felt like—it meant *everything* to me right now.

"Wait. You're in *the place after it too*." Mrs Syrre gasped.

The six sets of eyes that unofficially ruled Bluff City alongside my family estate watched me.

"Yes," I answered, then thought of Queen Elizabeth. "Royals."

Dame Burke swore long and hard. "You're in on the strategy meetings with the royal siblings."

She exchanged a shocked look with Lady Treena.

Six identical smirks spread across their faces.

My lips curled too.

"There's a problem," I told them. "A big problem. One that could end the..." *Game.* "Battle. Not on my terms. Soon."

"One of the groups is going to win?" Mr Hothen asked, straightening. "They've been locked evenly for so long."

Yeah, I'd get to that part eventually. As much as I wanted to hide it, *these* were the people who could help me restore the clans to an even match. As soon as that happened, my guilt would be assuaged and I could continue playing *Ingenium* in relative peace.

The details would be tortuous to convey, but it was torture I longed for. Because then I wouldn't feel so damn alone anymore.

I dragged an alphabet board toward me and fixed the rake-thin woman on my left with a grim smile. "I'll need your help first, Lady Treena."

I had one idea to pursue at this point.

Mr Ringly had lodged a development application for rezoning agriculture land to residential. There had to be some way to stall the project until I could sort things out. I needed to comb his application with a fine-tooth comb.

My grandmother's best friend raised her champagne glass. Tipping the chute back, she didn't drink a single drop. "Naturally, Basi dear."

I woke more comfortable than I'd been in my life. A perfect warmth suffused me. Heaviness filled my limbs. A massive erection rested in my hand.

I froze.

What. The. Fuck!

Nearly giving myself whiplash, I twisted to discover Kyros behind me.

Kyros in my bed.

Kyros on the estate.

I blew out a breath as quietly as possible.

Shoot.

Okay, we'd agreed on him sleeping here. Well. I'd agreed so I could get off his territory.

When Fyrlia rolled, he would stay at the estate.

When Sundulus rolled, I'd sleep at the tower.

What he hadn't agreed to was my fingers around his junk. Dying inwardly, I eased my hand away, wincing as his hips jerked at my touch.

I tucked Kyros Jr safely beneath the waistband of his black sweats and eased back down.

I stole a peek at the vampire.

"You can leave it there if you want," he murmured, eyes closed.

"*You!* How long have you been awake for?" Slapping his chest, I climbed to my knees.

His lips curled.

Laughter choked in my throat as his amusement soared. I toppled back to the bed beside him, laughing my ass off.

"Oh my god. I'm so sorry," I choked out, staring up at the canopy as my body shook. "I was asleep."

Mortifying much?

He rolled to face me, eyes still closed. He draped an arm over my hip. "I arrived at 4:30 a.m., climbed into your bed, and fended you off twice before I fell asleep. You're persistent."

Heat flooded my cheeks. "Oops."

How long did I hold his penis for? That seemed the most pertinent question.

"Not a complaint. I kissed you when I arrived. We're even."

Were we though? They seemed to be on different levels.

I cleared my throat. "I really hope I don't do that again."

I'd spend *every* night with Kyros for the foreseeable future, and my body had a secret agenda. When I agreed to his terms after driving off the damn cliff, it didn't seem like such a big deal. That was before sleep Basi took matters into her own hands.

Literally.

"Time?" he muttered, toffee strands splayed over his cheek.

I needed an air conditioning unit installed in my uterus. Rolling over, I tapped my phone, squinting. "Eleven."

Knowing Kyros would be here every second day, I'd rearranged my schedule to work from midday until eight at night. Really, it made sense to sleep in one chunk instead of breaking it into two shifts so I could work normal hours.

My stomach gurgled. "Breakfast time for me."

He rubbed his face. "Us."

I shot him a look, dragging my eyes over his biceps. "You sleep until one. I can just—"

"You can *just* have breakfast with me," Kyros rasped, cracking open his eyes. Humming low, he drew me flush against his body.

His lips brushed against mine. "You look damn good in the morning, Basilia Le Spyre."

Was it weird to be freaking out because Kyros was in my space? I had a vampire in my room. A really hot one. Which was ridiculous because this was the most normal location we'd spent time together. The current between us steadily climbed and an answering languidness spread through me. Doing my best to force the will of the bond to one corner of my mind, I tilted my head back and regarded him.

Kyros rested his head against the pillow and regarded me right back.

He had the appearance of someone my age—in terms of the

smoothness of his skin. At a glance, a human would see a genetic royal flush. Now I knew him better, the surety in his eyes and the serious set of his mouth were two signs of his immortality. When he spoke or moved, it was the same. Old people didn't give a shit what people thought because they'd learned there was no point to it. Kyros had lived one-and-a-half-human lives so far. That quality, in contrast to his youthful appearance, told me he was *other* more than his fangs did.

The closer I dared to look, the more of Kyros I was forced to acknowledge.

His uncertainty about who his father was.

His guilt over a game he never asked for.

The burden of his siblings' lives on his shoulders.

The playfulness that may be a much larger part of him if he hadn't been drawn into *Ingenium* from birth.

His constant battle to remain in control. He could never relax entirely, and that would only get worse as his alpha power matured.

Kyros had lived through one hundred and fifty years of that already. Wanting to fight that battle took a dedication so deep, I couldn't fathom it.

Ambition, cunning, confidence.

There had to be an end to this man, but I hadn't found it.

"A million dollars for your thoughts," Kyros rumbled.

I blinked and met his green gaze. "Isn't it meant to be a penny?"

"I wasn't sure you knew what a penny was."

Pssh. "I was *thinking* that you have more than one level. That *maybe* I assumed a few things about you at first appearance."

"A few things?"

"That's all you're getting."

He captured my bottom lip with his teeth, eyes dancing. My eyes widened and my chest rose in surprise.

Releasing me, Kyros murmured smugly, "I'm the penthouse."

The penthouse? *Yep*, couldn't deny that.

I was far more worried he was all sixty-six levels.

Gah. A shudder overtook me.

This freakin' current was about to leave me in a quivering mess.

I rolled over to tug the bell.

He snorted. "You have bell pushes? Rich people used those in my childhood years. Or people who wanted to appear rich."

"A lot of the house and furniture are original, including the... bell pushes? I had no idea that's what they were called." I shot him a look. "You must have interesting stories. I can't imagine living one hundred and fifty years ago. No televisions. No rocket ships. Weird."

"I'm relieved it's only occurring to you that I could recount the invention of telephones and the women's rights movement," he said drily.

I grimaced. "Right. I didn't mean it that way. I forget how old you are because you don't look old. It's your hair."

He chuckled sleepily. "No, I really am relieved. Remaining current is easy for the first thirty years, then you develop paranoia about becoming outdated. We do our best to listen and observe and adapt, but it can feel like an act. We always wish to do things from our own era."

Huh. "That's eye-opening. What old things do you like to do?"

"My mother always instilled in us an interest in changing times. Those who don't change become isolated. But I've always worn suits. I wear other clothes if necessary—when sleeping or going to the beach. Otherwise, suits are most comfortable for me."

"Good. Because they're comfortable for my eyes."

He arched a brow.

"And?" I pressed, clearing my throat.

"Things weren't as noisy when electricity wasn't widely used. My childhood and most of my teens were blissfully free of the buzz. I prefer quiet spaces still. I don't understand why people feel unsettled in silence or like they constantly need to fill it."

I wasn't sure how to take that. "I find that time hard to imagine if I'm honest. I'm imagining dirt roads and Mr Darcy."

"Maybe we can look through pictures one day."

My stomach gurgled.

Hopefully it covered my discomfort. I didn't know whether

uncertainty or guilt was more rampant inside. When he spoke long term like this, I couldn't make head or tail of it. In fact, it was gravely important that I *didn't* think long term when it came to the blood bond. I had a job to do.

A knock sounded.

I straddled the vampire, grinning wickedly. "Come in!"

Rosie opened the door, and I screeched.

"I apologise, Miss Le Spyre," she said calmly. "Shall I return at a more convenient time?"

Damn, nothing could shake her.

I huffed. "Do you play poker, Rosie?"

She flicked a glance at Kyros, cheeks pinkening. "I dabble, miss."

Mmm-hmm. Sure she just dabbled.

"We'd like breakfast. Better make a lot," I said, studying the half-naked male between my thighs. His eyes were fixed on me.

"At once," she bobbed a curtsey.

"By the pool, please."

She curtsied again, shutting the door.

"Do you always mess with your staff like that?" Kyros rested his hands on my hips. He pulled me down hard and circled his hips.

A breathless moan slipped between my teeth as my legs shook. "Why does that feel so fucking *good*?"

He ground his erection into me again, and my head dropped forward until our gazes locked.

"Do you like that, my beauty?"

"I can't think when we touch," I said between pants.

Both of us trembled against the urge to drink blood and fuck for three days.

"You're not the only one. To my memory, I recently forgot we were in the ocean and I should swim to keep us afloat."

My husky laughter trailed off as I dragged my fingernails through the middle line of his torso.

His sharp inhale was music to my ears.

"We should discuss the fifth exchange," Kyros said in a ragged voice.

I stilled, returning my hands to my lap. "Uh, that's..." *Sudden. Fear. Resolve.*

"Kyros?" I pushed backward so I was crouched between his legs. "Is everything okay? Why do you feel that way?"

He followed me up, capturing one of my hands. "There's nothing to fear."

"Is that so?" I scowled at him. "How about this then? I'm going to have a shower, to which you are not invited, and you can have another think about your plan of attack because the *nothing to fear* line didn't work."

Kyros's lips twitched, and I jumped off the massive bed and snatched up my kimono on the way to the bathroom. Part of me was just proud I managed the move without face planting.

When I exited ten minutes later, feeling unusually bubbly about the day, Kyros was looking through my stuff.

"Having a good snoop?" I asked, entering my closet.

He followed close after me, inhaling deeply. "Just returning the favour. You have a lot of clothes and shoes. I like how they're organised."

That actually hit me in the feels. "Thanks."

His anticipation curled around me like a litter of puppies.

"You're excited to be here." I grabbed jeans and a T-shirt seeing as he was just in sweatpants and a black Tee.

"To see the home of my *true mate*, yes. I'm excited. You continue to keep me at a distance. I've wished to know you better for some time."

"Your penis entered my vagina, Kyros. Your face has been between my legs. Not sure what distance you're talking about." Grabbing underwear, I dropped my kimono and dressed in the black panty and bra set.

His storming lust left me breathless. "You're purposefully being obtuse. I refer to emotional distance, not physical. And what we shared was much more than me pleasuring you, vixen. Don't make it sound empty."

I glared at him. Why wasn't he letting me get away with shit this morning? I didn't do deep emotions before midday. Or after midday. Not with him.

"I'm unsure how to respond to that." I tugged my jeans on and slipped the see-through T-shirt over my head.

Kyros's eyes tracked me like a hawk. "You're beginning to relent. Soon you'll be mine."

Reluctant laughter fell from my lips. "Can you stop? What woman wants a man saying that to her?" I picked up a sandal and hurled it at his head.

He caught the shoe. "You see me as a man?"

I wrinkled my nose. "Stop being weird."

Relief.

"Weren't we discussing the fifth exchange?" I huffed, snatching the sandal from him and locating the other.

Kyros whirled me around, pressing me against the wall. "Were we?"

Good try. "You wanted the fourth exchange because it would prevent others from compelling me, but why the fifth? Why, *really*?"

"Things are reaching a head in *Ingenium*, Basilia. I wish you to have every possible advantage in case things don't go as planned. Our blood will further merge in the fifth exchange. You will heal at an accelerated rate and become faster and stronger."

Unease stirred within me. "I thought you said I wouldn't become a Vissimo."

He cocked his head. "Not through the exchanges alone, and you must be invited by the clan alpha. Am I to take it you don't wish to join my kind?"

We'd never talked about it. But no, I didn't.

I was human—lifespan, wrinkles, and all.

Kyros caught my frown and tilted my chin up. "The fifth exchange is all we're discussing."

I tried to free my face, glowering at him. Like he never downplayed anything that may freak me out.

"I'm just not sure why I'd do the fifth exchange," I said, abandoning my attempt to shake his hold. "I'll be better able to protect myself, yes, but each exchange makes it harder to think of anything but you. If we exchange again and you're taken away, it will be harder to live without you."

A hardness settled over his emotions—something I'd noticed Kyros did when he wanted to guard me from something.

"Can you say you're immune to the drive to continue the mating exchanges?" he eventually asked. "That your entire being isn't desperate to intertwine with mine?"

The urge to blame the urge on the blood bond stalled on my lips. Because that excuse wasn't true anymore. Even if I hated that lines were blurring, feelings *were* becoming tangled.

He crowded me against the wall, threaded his hand through my hair and tugged until my head was tipped back to see his face. "When will you admit how you feel for me, my beauty?"

My breath hitched.

"You drove off a cliff for me," he whispered, trailing his nose from jaw to temple.

My hands shook. His were in the same state.

"I..."

His growl slipped between us. "The thought of claiming you as my mate keeps me up at night. I want to bite and fuck you through the three remaining exchanges back to back." He leaned in for a kiss that I could tell would leave me legless.

I placed a hand on his chest, mind scrambling. "Is losing *Ingenium* a possibility? You said winning was a certainty a few weeks ago. Why the rush to jump into the fifth exchange?"

"There are no certainties in life," the vampire purred, slipping his leg between mine.

"Kyros, I can literally feel when you're downplaying shit," I said angrily.

I needed this to happen and didn't expect Kyros to come out with it so soon. Yet I was putting up more barriers than security at a Justin Bieber concert.

In response, the vampire tapped my ear gently, his eyes sliding to the left.

Oh, right.

"Time is always slipping away. If the opportunity is now, who am I to fight my instincts?" Kyros trailed kisses between my pushed-up breasts, pulling up my thin T-shirt to continue down.

I clamped my thighs together.

He undid the front of my jeans, dragging down the zipper.

My insides clenched and I clutched for his shoulder as everything disappeared; sound and smell and sight, gone.

"Can I touch you, Basilia?" He sounded almost furious.

He wasn't.

We were as desperate as each other.

I needed him to touch me. Just another fucking line blurred that I couldn't bring myself to care about.

Looping an arm around my waist, Kyros held me upright, hovering his mouth just over mine. "Tell me."

In answer, I grabbed his hand and slid it down my stomach and beneath my panties. "It won't take long."

Like, one touch. Seriously.

His eyes flared and his fingers unfurled under my panties, making me jerk.

I slapped my hands back on the wall. "*Please hurry.*"

Kyros hummed, watching me as he supported my weight entirely. "No."

One thick finger entered me, pressing in with agonising slowness. I cried low as my body tightened from my toes to my fingertips, my insides drawing in to the tip of his finger.

"*Fuck,*" Kyros whispered, his rapt focus on my flushed face.

His thumb circled my clit *once*. And the tightening catapulted to the peak with unfathomable speed.

Twice.

White obliterated my senses as Kyros's hand moved rapidly.

Kyros's thumb was circling.

His finger moving. So fast.

I couldn't make sense of anything but the weightless bliss being wrung from my body.

His forehead was against my shoulder as he milked my orgasm for all it was worth.

Pleasure turned to pain as he continued.

His name lodged in my throat and I wiggled to dislodge his thumb from my sensitive flesh. It was so much. "Ky—"

He growled, unrelenting. The pain morphed to a slow heat that built, spreading through me again.

My shocked gaze flew to the ceiling. I was...? The pleasure jumped up and up again, bowling through my shaking frame.

Oh my god, *I was*.

This time I heard the scream that tore from my lips as my body tried to implode around his hand. He didn't let me collapse and curl into a ball, keeping up a steady pressure until the hazy grips of my second orgasm left me.

After one last pulse, he slid his hand free.

"I need to set you down." His voice was strained, and I shivered. Blurring me to the futon in the middle of the wardrobe, Kyros raced from the room.

Pure possessiveness rolled through him. His mind shook with the need to claim me again.

And I was in no position to help matters.

Sprawled on the futon, I reached blindly to do up my jeans. *Fuck me.* I couldn't believe what just happened. Twice. Really?

I wanted to stretch like a cat in front of the fire. I wanted to return the favour. I wanted nine days of mind-boggling sex from back-to-back thralls.

The shower turned on, and I flashed a smile.

What's the bet it was cold?

6

Almost weirder than anything that had happened during Kyros's sleepover was driving to work with him. Earlier than my shift demanded I needed to go.

He'd woken, delivered multiple orgasms, and left. I spent all day with him between my appointments. If he kept this up, I'd have to schedule Churchill meetings on Sundulus roll days.

Then there was my constant fear Mrs Gaughton would want to introduce herself and tell him about how she'd come to move in. Kyros thought of Bluff City residents as addresses; there was no way he'd recognise her, but still. His curiosity about my life may lead him to question her.

"I'll drop you at the tower," Kyros said as I waved goodbye to Fred.

Yep, my butler knew Kyros was a vampire and his face gave away nothing.

And *yep*, pretty sure the whole house heard what went down this morning, including Fred.

Damn. "Drop me there? You're going somewhere else?"

He hesitated.

I narrowed my gaze. "Tell me."

Kyros tilted his head. "You'll find out anyway."

That was his only incentive to tell the truth?

"After the Tonyi triplets took you into Fyrlia territory, the clans made a deal to avoid involving an impartial clan."

I knew that much. "What was the deal?"

"Part of the deal is that I spend two and a half hours with King Mikael every Friday night from 10:30 p.m. until 1:00 a.m."

Wow.

For starters, that would mess up Kyros's ability to lead his team for that day's roll. *More* importantly. "This has been going on for a few weeks?"

Kyros nodded, directing the car through Black.

There was no way he was okay with this. "I'm willing to bet that Mikael spends the entire time filling your head with twisted shit about you being his son."

Resignation.

I gritted my teeth. "That's so messed up. Why would your father agree to that?" I just couldn't understand what made Julius tick. He loved his children. Humiliated his son. He'd displayed the occasional good quality but was an all-round cruel fucker.

"I made the offer," Kyros said.

What?

"Why would you ever do that?"

Reluctance filled him.

"You don't doubt who your real parents are, do you?" I pressed.

He pursed his lips. "No. Not really. But you'll get angry."

"And angrier if you don't spit it out."

We pulled to a stop at a red light. "If I hadn't, the impartial party would have interrogated Tommy. If what I suspect about how much your friend knows about my kind is correct, she'd now be dead. At the best, she'd currently be compelled. I didn't tell you because you don't like me interfering in her life."

I nearly choked on the irony of that. *Interference* didn't include him saving her life.

"How did you know?" I asked him softly.

"You're happier when she's in your life. You were lonely and very suddenly happy. I then discovered she'd re-entered your life. Friendships like the one you share don't tolerate lies. Therefore, you'd figured out some way around my fucking excellent compulsion."

Eek.

I couldn't take the credit for that. Angelica gave me Tommy back. My hands twisted on my lap.

"Don't ask what you're about to ask," he said quietly. "I told you I wouldn't harm your friend and I meant it."

My exhale shook, and I felt his frustration swell at my mistrust.

It was *Tommy* though.

Kyros slid me a look. "Will you tell me how you were able to get around the compulsion?"

"Hmm, what?"

The vampire rolled his eyes. "I'll figure it out."

The light turned green and he guided the car—an identical vehicle to the one I'd driven over the cliff from what I could tell—through Blue.

"You told Tommy the truth about Theodore and she didn't take it well," he murmured as the tidy apartments and community gardens whizzed by. "I felt your pain yesterday morning. She left?"

"She loved him and couldn't accept he was dead, that I did it, or that he was Vissimo. Any of it. She won't be back."

I hadn't dared to let myself feel anything but numbness about that yet.

"She'll return."

"No," I replied, hugging myself. "Last time, there was a spark of friendship remaining. I watched it die yesterday. I know her. That was it for good. I sent ten Vissimo with her, but that's the extent of things."

Kyros was silent for a long time. "Then she has lost a great treasure."

"Pretty sure it's the other way around," I said in a hollow voice.

He didn't speak for the rest of the ride, dropping me in the garage and waiting until I was in the elevator to leave again. What a fucking joke. I wished I could wrap my hands around King Mikael's neck. Kyros wanted to pretend this didn't affect him, fine. I knew otherwise.

The current dissipated to bearable levels as the lift shot up. Thank Zeus. A day in his company had me aching in the worst possible way. I took a steadying breath, recalling the way I came undone in my wardrobe.

There was another hour until the dice were rolled. I'd spend the time catching up on the last few weeks with Conrad, Ilion, and Danielle—three of Kyros's seconds. They'd be eating their lunch on Level 50.

"Miss Le Spyre." Ilion greeted me when I entered the cafeteria. He was my favourite of the seconds—reminded me of Fred with his watchful ways.

I shrugged out of my jacket and swung it over the back of the chair. I tended to sit at the front of the room closest to the elevators to avoid Vissimo overload, but the seconds sat right in the middle of the hundreds of round tables and being around bulk vampires bothered me less and less.

"Hey, Ilion. Thanks for meeting with me. Probably best I catch up before tonight."

"Danielle and Conrad will be along presently," he replied. "Can I extend my sincerest relief that you are recovered from your ordeal?"

He made it sound like I'd bounced back from a sprained ankle. "Thank you. I appreciate that." I opened a notepad. "Okay, what properties has Fyrlia acquired in the last week?"

Ilion tapped on his tablet. "It isn't good."

My face fell. "How bad are we talking?"

He glanced around the level and lifted his tablet, reciting the list. The list went on and on. In comparison, Sundulus's acquisitions were pitiful. He moved through changes in each of the industries. Though the results weren't as drastic as in the realty sector, Fyrlia had increased across the board.

"The thing is their purchase prices," he muttered. "They're throwing money at these properties. Everywhere, really."

I knew why. "That doesn't make any sense."

"It does if they feel they're about to win," he said quietly. "Our efforts to stall the Ringly development are proving ineffective. If our forecasters are right, we have a matter of weeks to turn this around."

Shock found me. Then anger. Kyros had grossly underplayed how dire things were. He'd slipped in a *worst-case scenario* comment off the cuff and then used the listening Indebted as an excuse.

I mean, of course I'd known Fyrlia would swing the game as soon as possible with the information I'd imparted. "So what's the game plan?"

Ilion sighed. "Kyros is investigating the legitimacy of the council documents surrounding approval of Mr Ringly's DA. We already ran through the documents, but the royal family is certain something there is amiss. Other than that, Prince Rory has approved a doubled budget across the board."

Ilion and the other seconds had no idea about the bluff. I wasn't sure if I should be bothered that Kyros and I had the same thought to investigate the DA.

Danielle and Conrad joined us, and we settled into a more in-depth discussion of how the game board was stacked. By the time the Vissimo around me filtered upstairs in preparation of the roll, I was exhausted and my real shift hadn't begun.

"Thank you," I told them wearily. "That helps a lot."

Conrad rested a hand on my shoulder. "We'll figure it out, Miss Le Spyre."

Considering he wasn't a big fan of mine, I appreciated the reassurance.

We entered the lift, a group of minions scrambling out when Ilion growled.

Just as the doors began to close, Angelica slipped in.

She smiled at me.

Fuck. "Whatever shit news you're delivering, get it over with," I told her flatly.

Her smile widened, and she held out the dark-green envelope in her hand. There was a gold wax seal on it.

FA.

Fuck All. Or Francesca Atagio.

Maybe both.

"Do I want to open this?" I muttered.

"Probably not."

Snorting, I slipped my finger under the seal and pried it apart, sliding out the thick paper.

It contained the details of the fashion show. Next Sunday, nine days away.

Ugh.

Danielle took the invitation when I held it out.

"Kyros's siblings are going to kill me one day," I told them.

"If they didn't accept you, they wouldn't bother," Danielle replied, her lips twitching.

Francesca would dress me in the ugliest creation in existence. The papers would have a field day that Basilia Le Spyre was dressed in rags.

Had to respect her effort though.

"Francesca's may be the best one," I admitted.

"I liked Lionel's," Conrad said. "Even if Kyros painted the billboards over two hours later."

Yeah. In terms of enjoyment, Lionel's was my favourite. Or Lalitta's.

"Safina still hasn't shown her hand," Ilion said. "She will deliver."

I took the fashion show invitation back, tucking it in my purse. "Why do I get the feeling you guys are enjoying this?"

Angelica patted my hand. "Because we are."

By the time we got to the glass tube, the rolling chamber where the kings and their queens gathered each night was already up.

The monarchs glided into the room, but they weren't alone.

I inhaled as Kyros strode into the room in the wake of King Mikael.

Angelica slid a look at me. "You didn't know."

"I did." *That downplaying bastard.* "Seeing it is just a shock."

The monarchs faced each other and Kyros bowed low to his

father and mother. King Mikael's face didn't change, but he had to be *totally* pissed.

I wasn't sure that I'd felt protective over Kyros before, at least not to this degree, but I felt capable of violence on his behalf in that moment.

A foreign soothing wound around me, and I narrowed my eyes as Kyros tried to calm me down from the ringside of Fyrlia's roll.

Whipping out my phone, I typed:

Great seats. How much did they set you back?

Send.

The kings were facing each other when Kyros's phone buzzed. His expression didn't change, but I felt his jolt of surprise.

Shit. Why wasn't his phone on silent!

All four of the monarchs paused to look at him.

Meeting their gazes, he slid the phone free.

Kyros read the message, and a wide grin spread across his face. His gratitude swept through me, and then my phone chimed.

Like we'd orchestrated it, the Vissimo on Level 66 pivoted my way.

"What are you doing?" Angelica asked.

"Fucking with Mikael. He's a dick."

A few gasps rang out.

Was that a no-no? My bad.

I read Kyros's message.

Freebie. Couldn't turn it down

King Mikael was picking up the dice now.

Pursing my lips, I readied my text.

The fifth exchange is a yes from me.

As Mikael crouched forward in preparation to fling his arms wide, I sent the text.

The buzz made him twitch as the dice left his fingertips.

I laughed, and Angelica looked at me like I'd lost my mind.

Pretty sure I lost that about the time I drove a car off a cliff to prove a point.

The kings zoomed back to their seats as Kyros read my message. He lifted his head, and *holy shit*, I swore he looked straight at me through the camera.

"What did you just say?" Conrad whispered.

My cheeks warmed. "Just discussing the weather."

He snorted.

The dice catapulted over the chamber, but as they slowed, everyone quieted. We couldn't afford Fyrlia to land on Agriculture again. It was the only industry where neither clan had a large foothold yet. With Mr Ringly's ongoing development, if Fyrlia gained traction there first, we were *really* screwed.

The dice by Queen Titania's foot was a five.

The other was a four.

A nine. Which put them firmly on Agriculture.

"Fucker." I booted the glass tube.

Ilion gripped my arm as excited murmurs erupted at my back. "*No*, one of the dice is touching Queen Bethany's shoe."

Cool. I hoped they could sell it on eBay for a good price.

"If either dice touches someone, they have to roll again," Danielle said.

Oh. "That's great!"

Inwardly, Kyros was roaring with laughter though not a speck of it showed physically.

"Distraction from the same side isn't considered interference," Conrad said, gripping my shoulder tight.

Peering back to the live streaming, I studied King Mikael. The only sign of his fury was the white skin where his lips pressed together.

The kings stepped forward again. I had no idea how to gauge Julius's reaction, but I felt he'd be all for the humiliation of his enemy.

Kyros was typing back.

What has changed in the last two hours?

I waited until after Mikael's roll to respond this time. He'd be braced for the distraction and messing with him twice felt like tempting fate.

Hmm, what had changed in the last two hours? I'd learned Kyros sacrificed his time and happiness so my friend kept her freedom and life.

But really?

Sighing, I messaged back.

Nothing

Not only did I need the fifth exchange with Kyros. I fucking wanted it. *Bad.*

Desperately.

He was the whole damned tower, and I was so far gone that denial was futile.

Every speck of hope and anticipation I felt turned to fear and guilt... and resolve. Backing down wasn't an option. It hadn't been since I entered *Kyros Sky,* and so really, nothing had changed except what I was willing to admit to myself.

One way or another, I'd lose him anyway. If not because of my betrayal, then because I was working against him.

This was all so fucked up.

"Four," someone exclaimed.

Ilion grinned. "Orange. *Well done*, Miss Le Spyre."

Conrad clapped me on the back and nearly sent me sprawling.

Well done?

They wouldn't be saying that before the end.

"Thank you for gathering today," I said to the crowd of fifty Indebted, my voice pitched low.

I stood atop a pool-side table, ready for my afternoon shift visiting trouble properties for *Live Right*. I'd work through the weekend to get my game plan and various teams back on track.

I could always rely on work to distract me from feeling too much. From thinking about Tommy and the long list of shit I'd gotten myself into.

The Indebted were stone-faced. The smiles they always shot my way were just a memory. *Yep*, sneaking out without telling them was a dog act. I'd known it at the time—if not the threat Kyros's berserk rage presented to them—but I'd acted in the knowledge it would place them in some difficulty.

"I'm sorry for putting each of you at risk by sneaking off the estate," I told them. "There's no excuse for it, other than Tommy's life was on the line and I did not understand how badly Kyros would take it."

Some of them softened, but would I just forgive some human for putting my life in danger when I was helpless to protect myself in any way?

Nope.

I chewed on my lip. "I didn't intend to put any of you in a position where you felt helpless and threatened. I also understand that if someone did that to me, I'd have a really hard time forgiving them. I've already promised Laurel that I'll never put the Vissimo on this estate in such a position again and know that I don't make that promise lightly. You've seen what I will do for a person I care about. By making that promise, I've agreed to trust all of you with the people I love too. That's something I've never done in my life."

Scanning them, my stomach twisted anew with guilt. "With that said, I'd planned a surprise for you guys before I acted like a massive butthole, but I'm no longer sure the gift is welcome."

Laurel had stood to one side throughout the conversation, her face as hard as the others. I was on my own for this and hadn't expected any less.

She frowned at my comment.

If they rejected the gift, I'd deserve it. "I bought a nightclub a month ago. Tonight is the opening night. I'd like to invite any of your Vissimo brethren not on duty tonight and those on estate duty to come party. If you don't show, it will be a seriously lame opening, but I respect that attendance is your choice. I'll give the details to Laurel for those who are interested. And you can expect cameras to be there."

I exhaled and nodded to them before leaping down from the table.

It felt like fifty sets of eyes bored into my back on the walk into the house, but I was glad to have the guilt off my chest at least. Though I felt so much guilt, I wasn't sure I'd made a dent.

"Miss Le Spyre," Fred said, bowing slightly as I passed through the music room to my office.

"Hey Fred, can I help you with something?"

"Just a few housekeeping points I wished to discuss."

"Sure, come in."

He followed me into the office and as soon as the door was shut, he reached for the noise-cancelling button.

I blinked as his face dropped into serious lines.

"Are you okay? The man in your suite two nights ago. We heard you screaming."

... Oh my god.

The butler was stricken. "He hurt you, but I wasn't sure if it was part of your strategy. I didn't want to act without confirmation one way or another."

"You were right to wait, Fred," I said firmly, rounding the back of the desk. The computer was already on. Stacks of papers lined up. "If a similar thing happens in the future, don't intervene."

The butler stared at me. "He didn't hurt you?"

Uhm. He hurt me in ways I didn't know I *wanted* to be hurt.

I cleared my throat. "Right as rain, Fred. Thank you for the concern. And I mean that."

"That vampire is an important one," Fred said as his impersonal butler mask fell back into place.

An important one? In the game, absolutely. To the kings, yes. To me?

I inclined my head.

Fred's face twisted. "I know it's not my place to be saying this, but the thought of such a monster in your personal space makes me sick inside. I'm certain your grandmother never intended you to take the game so far."

His words were a punch in the gut. Despite his initial bluff, he knew exactly what those screams were about.

The words *fucking awkward* came to mind.

I opened the first email, an update from my stockbroking team. "You're right. It isn't your place. Is there anything more I can help you with?"

When I glanced back at him, red had flushed across his cheeks. Not the angry sort. The butler appeared absolutely mortified.

The truth was, I felt disgusted at the thought of what my grandmother would say if she knew what I was doing. My words came out harsher than intended, but I couldn't back down now.

"I apologise for overstepping, miss," he said, bowing. "There's nothing else to discuss. I will leave you to your correspondence."

And the guilt is back.

"One more thing," I called when he was at the door. "Is Mr Tetley gone?"

He turned, mouth pulling down. "Yes, Miss Le Spyre. I'm in the process of finding a replacement."

Tommy kept her promise then. I wasn't surprised her father would follow his only daughter. She was the moon, stars, and sun in his life.

"Hey, Freddy boy, is Basilia in there?"

Mrs Gaughton sidled into the office without waiting for his reply. "Hey, Basi."

I smiled at Fred over her head. "That will be all, Fred. Thank you."

Sorry.

"Mrs Hannah," I said when the door was closed. Reaching under the table, I started the frequency generator. It wouldn't stop the Indebted who really wanted to listen in, but they'd have to be close to overhear, and I knew my main crew of seven stuck closest to the house.

She eyed my clothing. "Heading out on *Live Right* business today?"

"Sure am. Have to catch up after the three weeks off."

"I like you, Basi, but I've got to say that I think Live Right is seriously dodgy. If you ever want to work for a business who have the best interests of Bluff City residents at heart, you come to me."

Was Mrs Gaughton vetting me for my own company? She had no idea I was the owner.

I loved her.

"You're enjoying the new job with Tommy then?" I asked her. Tommy's name left a sour taste in my mouth.

She winked. "I'm not supposed to talk about it. But yes. Tommy is actually on leave, so I've stepped into her HR position for a little bit. I've been doing some hiring."

I made a mental note to read the latest report from Churchill without delay. "Anyone I know?"

"Well, get this. There's such a thing as *trouble properties* in Bluff City. We're having a hard time acquiring them. So I thought... why not *hire* some of them?"

Considering I did the same thing to her, I'd say that was great reasoning. "We have the same trouble list at *Live Right*, I'd say. I probably know the names of your new employees."

"Mr Triffz was my first one."

My jaw dropped. "Mr Triffz? You're kidding me! That's the bastard who threw compost at me."

"All he needed was a battle to fight." She eyed me. "He wants to take down *Live Right* and *Foremost*. He thinks they're secret agents who put old people in homes."

And now he was working for me.

65

"When I sold his home to a lovely family from Spain, I helped him find a smaller rental. One thing led to another."

I absorbed that as best I could. "Anyone else?"

"Mr Trenington. And a Mrs Franger."

Both off the trouble list. I'd only met the suspicious Mr Trenington. Mrs Franger put on her sprinklers each time I reached her letterbox. "You acquired all their houses too?"

She cackled. "Not so hard, really. Just got to talk to them like they're people."

I bit back on my smile. "Sounds like you're a HR natural."

"Yeah, but it's only until Tommy is back." The older woman sounded moderately miffed. "You know when she's back?"

Hesitating for a beat, I decided to impart some of the truth. "Tommy and I aren't in a good place at the minute. I was the reason behind the breakup with her boyfriend. I told Theodore what I thought of him and he took off without telling her where. She's really angry at me."

The older woman studied me. "I've never known you to be unnecessarily mean. He was hurting her?"

I nodded. "Badly. Without her knowing."

"Then he's a fucker. If Tommy has any sense, which I know she does, she'll come around in time. Never easy to deal with a broken heart, especially if it's her first one."

They were words I so desperately wanted to believe in.

"And the pure hunk of god I saw walk in here the other day looked familiar. Strutted as if he owned the place, too, I might add."

"Who?" I asked her innocently.

She waved a hand in the air. "None of that now. We all heard the screams."

Ugh. I choked on laughter. "Stubbed my toe."

Her gaze darkened. "I'd like to stub my toe like that a few times."

I grinned. "Can't say I'd mind a repeat."

She scowled. "You went back there with the guy who wanted you for your money? I mean, not that I blame you. He's a tall drink of something."

"He told me he's not after any of that," I replied, grimacing. "I'm not so sure. So I'm testing him. Could you do me a favour?"

"Sure."

"If he asks you anything about how you came to be here or about the work you and Tommy do, could you lie through your teeth and let me know? He'll assume that you work for me or are a family member, so if he's here for the wrong reasons, I believe he'll speak to you first. Make sure to bullshit him."

The glint in her eye was 110 percent evil. "It would be my pleasure." Her gaze turned shrewd. "So we can expect him around here often?"

I arched a brow. "Yes. Why's that?"

"Just wondering if you'll have soul-destroying sex all the time."

Leaping up from the table, I shooed her out of the room, husky laughter bursting from my lips. "Time for Mrs Hannah to leave so Basilia can get her work done."

"Tell me!" the woman blurted just before I got the office door closed.

7

"I got hold of all the papers relevant to Mr Ringly's development approval," Lady Treena said. "And everything in his file. Thought we should be thorough. There may be a past transgression we can use to stall things."

Pretty sure Sundulus already tried that.

I sat with my grandmother's friends around the round table.

After a few agonising hours at the last meeting, they knew most of the details of my exchanges with Kyros—everything except for one tiny thing.

They had no idea Kyros was anything other than an evil tyrant who controlled my mind. I just couldn't bear to tell them I was considered his true mate or to see the horror and disappointment on their faces.

Whatever I saw on their faces would be what I would've seen on Grandmother's face.

Dame Burke placed a stack of papers in front of me, next to the file I'd brought along for reference. It contained details of their compulsions.

Lalitta compelled Dame Burke thirty-five years ago. Not tightly—which was such a Lalitta thing to do.

I flicked my eyes over the first page.

"This is all the correspondence and rejections for his development approval request for the last ten years. You'll notice the main issue was the concern of necessary agricultural land being re-zoned and lost to residential land. He spent an arm and a leg trying to win approval. Idiotic if you ask me."

Which is why I believed the answer rested here. Fyrlia wasn't new to this game and neither was Sundulus. But neither of them were human. It was a desperate hope, but all I had to bank on right now.

I skimmed through the pile and passed it to Mr Dithis on my left. He was controlled by Gina, but he was able to converse about anything Vissimo-related in metaphor. How he'd even figured that out was anyone's guess.

"Did you spot anything amiss, Lady Treena?" I asked, consulting my other file.

Lady Treena was controlled by King Mikael himself. Her compulsion was nearly as bad as mine except she could nod and shake her head in answer to direct questions. He usually contacted her for information on council affairs via his minions, and contact had dwindled considerably after her retirement. She'd been compelled for as long as Sir Olythieu.

"No," she replied. "And I went through it thoroughly."

Mr Dithis passed the stack to Mr Hothen.

Mr Hothen belonged to Francesca and discovered Vissimo and *Ingenium* fifteen years ago. He could say pretty much anything if he was vague enough, something I attributed to Francesca's youth.

"Sandra Hoyt was the town planner in charge of this deal?" he asked.

"Why?" Sir Olythieu asked drily. "You know her?"

He belonged to King Julius, and his compulsion was as tight as mine. Like father, like son, I supposed.

Mr Hothen smirked. "For a while."

Which surprised no one. He had the silver fox look down to a T and knew it. The ladies flocked, and his only rule was twenty-five plus and highly educated.

Mrs Syrre made a small sound in the back of her throat. It was strange to think that Neelan drank the genteel woman's blood while compelling her.

"Let me guess," she said. "You dumped her via letter."

Was that the original dumping via text move?

"Actually, no," Mr Hothen said, frowning. "She moved to Frankton Gorge and ended things."

I stilled.

Sir Olythieu beat me to asking, "How *long* ago did she move to Frankton Gorge?"

Lady Treena snatched the stack away, pacing the room as she scanned the pages.

"I should cut you out of shares in my new plaza for that," Mr Hothen said to her, leaning back.

She eyed him briefly. "Empty threats are for the lower class."

I snorted with the others.

"It's possible I missed something," she announced, setting two papers before me.

Dame Burke whispered under her breath, *"Never thought I'd hear the day."*

"It seems that Sandra Hoyt managed this case until three months ago when there was a change to Julia Dinh."

That name rang a bell. But I was certain Julia Dinh was under Sundulus control.

"She *might* have just moved away," I said slowly, my gut already telling me that wasn't so.

Mrs Syrre countered. "She *might* have run for her life. Or been forced to relocate."

Exactly.

"I'll track down her current address," Dame Burke said, jotting a note in a diary.

I smiled tightly. "Let's hope this is a lead. If I can take proof of a shady deal to them, they'll be locked in battle again." An impartial clan would rule the development deal as void—at the minimum— according to Kyros's seconds.

Mr Hothen leaned back. "Sometimes I wonder if it would be better to let someone win."

I located the F on the table. "Not these ones," I said, holding it up and thinking of the kiss Kyros gave me that morning. "They're worse."

"They're as bad as each other," Sir Olythieu spat.

Shaking my head, I swept back my heavy braid to show them the red scar. Then I stood to show them the nearly gone bruises on my stomach.

Murder was etched on each of their faces when I resumed my seat.

I held up F again. "Believe me. I know."

Maybe I thought the same for a while, but having met both royal families, having been questioned by both, I could say with certainty there was a difference.

Fyrlia wasn't wholly bad, but the bad parts were evil to the core.

"What can you tell us about the clans, dear?" Dame Burke asked.

I focused on sunflowers. "S is scared."

Man, focusing so hard made me sweat.

"They would be. From what I understand, only one flock of eagles can fly the skies," Mr Dithis said.

The royal family of the enemy survived. Yes. "Two from S survive. Kyros and Titania."

Mr Hothen's expression darkened. "It's a shame the lot of them won't die. Good riddance."

I withheld a retort, my guilt soaring. If they knew I was sleeping in the same bed as a vampire each night, they'd never look at me the same.

I should tell them. Maybe I could convince them it didn't mean anything. They'd have ideas on how to turn the development to our advantage.

But maybe that's why I hadn't told them.

If they knew, they'd expect me to use Kyros. If I *didn't do that*, they'd know my dirty secret.

That I didn't want to hurt Kyros anymore.

Yet disappointing my grandmother's memory and her friends? I couldn't do that either.

I'd landed myself firmly in the middle of a battle I could never win.

8

Only Jessica Alba could wear black leather. In *Dark Angel*, specifically.

I'd broken my rule twice.

White leather didn't count. Right? Why did I get the feeling my standards were crumbling? How long until I wore black leather and felt no remorse?

It was a slippery slope.

"Will you require me to pick you up later, Miss Le Spyre?" Fred asked from the front seat.

My new club wasn't far from *Kyros Sky*. "No, thanks. I'll be back at the estate by 4:00 a.m. or so."

"As you say, miss." He glanced out the window. "I better help you into the club."

I eyed the stack of camera fuckers either side of the red carpet. They could get brusque. And nothing cried rich woman like a bodyguard. "I'd appreciate that."

Of course, if no one had shown up—or showed up later—the headlines tonight and tomorrow would ruin the club. I'd made the Indebted feel vulnerable, and now it was my turn.

Glancing down to make sure my bits were inside the white

leather leotard, I waited for Fred to open the door. When he did, I extended one long leg out of the limousine and paused.

Because great shot.

White leotard, silver feather shoulder pads, dark eyes, and messy curls that tickled my lower back? Nude stilettos gave my legs the endless illusion. I looked untouchable. *Forbidden.*

I straightened and waited for Fred to close the door before moving down the red carpet behind him. Indebted had to be all around me—there was no way they wouldn't be protecting me right now—but I couldn't see a single one through the throng of reporters.

"Miss Le Spyre, can you tell us why you renamed the club to *Forbidden*?" one shouted.

Uh, because Ricky Pikar fucking named it after me. In numbers.

Turning my smile on full wattage, I twisted to glance over my shoulder at him. "Figure it out yourself. It's a secret."

I held a finger to my lips.

If Tommy could see me right now, she'd bust a gut, but I'd had to attend sessions with the estate publicist during my business training. The media gobbled this cheesy shit right up.

My stomach flipped.

"Basilia! Bottom right! International business success, why a nightclub?"

I located the journalist, cocking a hip and flicking my hair back as the cameras flashed. I hated stuff like this. I wasn't a natural mover. MET Gala clips on YouTube were a fucking godsend. "You don't enjoy doing things you know you shouldn't?" I asked her, tilting my head. That would reinforce the nightclub brand.

"Is this a sign of what's to come from the Le Spyre empire?" she called in reply. "A left-turn from your grandmother's plaid vision?"

And *this* is part of why I hated events. In a bid not to show my reaction, I turned my gaze to a camera, dropping my chin to deliver what I *hoped* was a saucy smoulder. Part of me was glad I'd done the photo shoot with Lionel.

"My grandmother hated plaid," I said mildly.

They had enough shots to do what I'd invited them for. As long as the Indebted hadn't stood me up, whether the media painted the club in a good or bad light, this place would be filled to the brim for months to come. A promise of mixing with the rich and famous— with a healthy dose of exclusivity—very few could resist such an allure. Probably just Mrs Gaughton, Mr Triffz, and the rest of my realty trouble list.

"Middle left! Who can we expect to come tonight?" a man in a greasy T-shirt boomed.

Who indeed.

I scanned him up and down. "No one you'd know."

The other journalists laughed.

Old money bitchery. I was kind of great at faking it. At least, I hoped it was mostly fake...

I'd settle for 50 percent fake.

Fred directed me through the alleyway to a small square sign halfway down. Ricky's flashing neon 2274 sign was replaced immediately. If a person didn't know where *Forbidden* was, they'd never find it.

Exclusive.

To my surprise, the doors were pulled inward as I approached.

My heart leapt at the sight of Marcus and Kirsten in their black leather outfits. I grinned at them as I entered. Cameras flashed from behind to get a glimpse. All they'd see were two beautiful creatures and a black curtain.

I faced the two Vissimo when the doors closed. "Glad you could show up."

Two were here at least, and the squeeze in my heart at the sight of them was borderline painful.

Sweeping back the black curtain, I stared at the vampires filling the club. More than my fifty were here. Way more. Several hundred at least.

I located as many of my estate crew as possible in the crowd. "Thank you for coming," I said to the gathered group.

My voice only wobbled a *little*.

Laurel dipped her head. The tension in my shoulders drained

away at the smiles on those filling the dance floor. We were on the bottom floor of the building. The club extended for several levels, becoming *more exclusive* the higher you went. Or darker and more boring, in other words.

"Whatever clan you've come from tonight, welcome! Between you and me, my ears still can't handle loud music. So tonight, for what may be the first clubbing night ever for some of you, I declare a silent disco."

I gestured to the carts of headphones around the room. "Grab headphones and dance to your heart's content. Take whatever you want from behind the bar. Drinks are on me tonight! And rest easy, there are no human staff in the building."

I'd asked my club manager to purchase a pre-recorded set from a local DJ. For legal reasons, my three home chefs—each with a bartending license—were registered as working. The regular staff would begin next Thursday, and the club manager would usually be in residence instead of me. Though I'd pop in once a month or so.

We were a three-days-a-week nightclub. Quality not quantity.

Vissimo blurred to the headphones as I strolled to the bar, watching as they figured out just what silent disco meant. I grinned as they began to dance, blurring and twisting. The reporters outside would have no fucking idea why the club was so quiet.

I slid onto a stool, and Laurel, Josie, and Kelsea approached. They alone wore something other than black leather. They'd come in the dresses I gifted them when trying to catch the spy in the tower.

"Thank you for coming," I repeated, unsure if we were cool.

"You were shitting yourself before you came in, admit it," Kelsea said, nudging me.

I glanced behind. "Sure was. A white leotard was a terrible choice."

Josie laughed, reaching for the tequila. "We're even Stevens now. We could hear your heartbeat."

I bet.

"We're good then?" I fixed my eyes on Laurel.

She nodded. "Water under the bridge."

Leaning forward, I hugged her tight. "Love you, Loz."

The vampire froze in my embrace.

I released her and slithered over the bar like a whale mermaid—because the bar was fucking mine. I stared at the wall of alcohol. Where to start?

"Shots," I murmured. "Not that they'll work on you heavyweight fuckers."

And the Indebted wouldn't take anything unless I forced it into their hands.

Loading up trays, I waved over Jillian and Evie. "Hand these out, would ya?"

I passed the tray to Jillian, and snagged Evie's hand, looking her directly in the eyes.

"I'm sorry, Evie. Really, I am. I consider you a friend, and that was a shitty thing to do to you."

She shrugged a shoulder. "It was. And I'd do the same for any of my family if they were still alive. You're forgiven."

Pulling her into my arms, I kissed her cheek. "Thank you. I'm not sure I deserve you being so understanding, but I'll never forget it."

The pixie-faced blonde relaxed in my arms and squeezed me back. "I'll go help Jillian pass out those shots."

I handed trays to Kelsea and Josie, too, then lined liquor bottles along the bar in an attempt to make the vampires more comfortable taking them.

Grabbing the last tray, I set to work plying my guests with high-percentage alcohol they'd burn off quicker than I could disperse it. The sound of their dancing feet and laughter filled the space. Headphones on, their conversations were shouted, and I sniggered to myself.

I went back and forth with trays, squeezing between leather-clad bodies.

On my fourth return journey, the bar was emptied of the bottles I set out. Ha! That was more satisfying than Santa eating the fig and olive tapenade I used to put out on Christmas Eve.

Setting another twenty bottles on the bar, I glanced at Laurel as she approached the bar next to a dude double her size. *Dude* wasn't the best term for him. He'd look more at home in a galley with a broad sword in his hands.

Hot damn. Was he in Laurel's harem? She tended to go for the Viking type.

"Miss Le Spyre," she said. *Formal.* "I'd like to introduce you to Vladymir. He holds my position amongst the Fyrlia Indebted."

Their leader in other words.

Viking Vladymir extended his hand, and I felt a twinge of warmth. *Huh.* Consider me surprised my lady parts could twitch for anyone but Kyros. I couldn't help it. This guy exuded promises of wild sex.

I cast a look at Laurel, who arched a brow.

She was totally into him.

"Nice to meet you, Vladymir. The Vissimo attending from Clan Fyrlia are welcome here."

His grey-blue eyes gleamed. "So it's true you don't call us Indebted."

I shrugged a shoulder. "You're *in* debt. That's not all you are. For most of you, it's not even your debt. I hate when people treat me like a token rich brat. Whoever decided people should be stereotyped by our most insignificant quality was a fool."

"I heard of your battle with Theodore Tonyi," he said.

Stilling, I peered up at the massive fucker. "Not my favourite memory."

"But an honourable one. You're not without bravery, young one."

I didn't feel honourable. I didn't feel brave.

Swallowing, I muttered, "Thanks. I'm just sorry you have to work for that psycho, Mikael. I wouldn't wish that on anyone."

He exchanged a look with Laurel. She arched a brow, and his lips twitched.

And what that was about, I had no clue.

"You're not drinking?" I held up a shot to Laurel.

She shook her head. "None of your estate crew are. We need to uphold your safety."

I grimaced. "Right. Yeah. I guess indulging in hard liquor wouldn't go down well with Kyros."

She gestured. "You're not drinking?"

Things were too shit to drink right now. Which was ironic because that was usually my go-to when manure hit the fan. "Nah, I've got to work at the tower later. Is Vladymir in your harem?"

Oops.

That wasn't the smooth conversation change I'd envisioned.

The Vissimo perused each other the same way I scanned abstract art—like they were trying to figure what the splashes meant and if it was art at all.

"We did discuss the possibility once," the Viking eventually answered. "The issue being that we both like to be dominated."

These conversations were miles above my pay grade.

I cleared my throat politely. "How lovely."

Laurel threw me a grin. "We decided it wouldn't work."

"Yeah, but wouldn't it be like a fight? Like a reverse fight? You'd both be goading each other to take control until one snapped."

Blinking, I leaned back.

Jesus. When was the fifth exchange? I needed to get some.

The two vampires scanned each other anew.

Now *that. That's* how I looked at strawberry mojitos.

"The children from our union would be strong," he said in a low voice.

Laurel hummed. "The thought of goading you to dominate me appeals."

He lowered his head. "It is not I who will lose control, *skjaldmær.* Your womb is mine."

Fucking hell.

My phone buzzed. I read the message from Kyros.

Where are you and what are you doing?

Uhm, replying that I had front row seat to a Viking porno may not go down well.

I sent back a puppy GIF.

On second thought, that drink sounded really great.

I teetered around the bar on my stilettos. "Maybe I'll just have one drink. I'm rich enough to drink strawberry mojitos again after all." I stared at the Bacardi. "Shit, what other stuff goes in a mojito?"

Josie appeared to my left. "I used to bartend at clan functions. Got strawberries?" She didn't wait for me to answer, opening the cupboards and drawers in a blur. "No strawberries, but I found passionfruit. Passionfruit mojito?"

I sighed dramatically. "Fine. But I'm texting the manager to get some damn strawberries for next week."

Some people have no idea.

Vladymir and his testosterone were gone when I returned to my seat, passionfruit mojito in hand. "I'm surprised that guy doesn't impregnate women and men just by standing within a five-metre radius. Can't believe you haven't tapped that. Let him pillage you, for god's sake."

Laurel's lips trembled. "He heard you."

I regretted nothing.

My phone buzzed again.

Tell me. You're turned on

Blood heated my cheeks. *Ugh*, awkward much? I couldn't help it. Waking up next to Kyros each day was hell on my libido. With our laughable control around each other, we had to be so careful of toeing the line.

If I was a rabbit, the world was dangling a carrot just out of reach. Except that carrot was the best sex of my life.

Thinking about naked you...

Send.

Probably shouldn't have done that.

"I have dabbled with the idea for a few decades, but sexual compatibility is the most important factor in our relationships," Laurel was saying.

"Try before you buy," I told her sagely.

She shook her head, smiling. "Is that off *Truth Ranges*?"

"What? No. That's advice my grandmother gave me on my eighteenth birthday."

Laurel threw back her head and laughed.

I slurped on my drink and my eyes widened. "What in the name of the mighty cocktail gods is *this*?" Where was Josie? Probably didn't matter. "Josie, this is amazing!"

A thumbs up appeared from the midst of the writhing bodies.

"I may be a convert," I said in awe.

My phone buzzed, and I choked on my next sip, staring at the GIF from Kyros. A fucking carrot dangling in front of a rabbit.

That was... disturbing on a whole new level. He couldn't read my mind, so it was just a freaky coincidence.

A really freaky coincidence.

"Thank you for giving this to them," Laurel said, twisting on her stool.

Shaking off his message, I did the same, watching as Kelsea grabbed the waistband of a vampire who would have looked at home playing the drums for Queen.

If things went to plan, the Indebted could expect more experiences like this. Cruises, private island parties, gambling nights, musicals, and outside cinemas. My life was falling to pieces around me, but their lives had been chaos for decades and centuries. I'd give them as many first experiences—or happy memories—as I could.

"Despite what this turned into," I said quietly, "you know I intended this night just for their happiness only. There are already more activities in the works."

She glanced at me. "More?"

"Oh, yeah." I grinned into my passionfruit elixir.

The vampire sighed, crossing her long legs. "You aren't entirely to blame for how events unfolded. You were right with one of the observations made in your office."

The part about Kyros going berserk if I died? "You did gloss over the consequences."

"You don't know who I was, do you?" she asked. "Before I was Indebted."

I pulled a face. "Does it matter?"

She studied me for a long time. "Not usually. Not for a long time. In this instance, it explains the glossing. My mother and father were mates. Not true mates, but when they met, mating was still the mode, so they completed all seven exchanges, and even received two mating gifts."

"I've never heard of anyone else being mated," I told her.

"Mostly only the very old or the poor do so now." The vampire swallowed.

"Your mother was killed and your father went berserk?"

She cast me a surprised look. "Correct. He was a king—alpha—and old, so very powerful. His control couldn't hold after her murder. It took three other kings to kill him. And I inherited his debt. The rest you know."

Laurel was a princess. Or had been.

Her life was changed forever because her father lost control. Then I'd walked into Fyrlia territory and nearly triggered the same mindless rage in Kyros.

I rubbed my forehead. "Whenever I think I've grasped the depth of Kyros's struggle to control his power, the reality hits me all over again."

Maybe I really should apologise for putting Kyros in that position. And Safina. And his whole damn family.

"I need to apologise again for placing you guys in that situation," I told her, lifting my gaze to hers. "It must have opened old wounds."

The vampire nodded, her black hair slithering forward. "Yes. It also highlighted my weakness in letting painful memories dictate me in small ways after so long. I should have told you."

I doubted a person could ever get over such a tragic end to their family. "Do you miss your parents, Loz?"

She shot me a look. "I do. They loved each other. Their people loved them."

Tilting my head to the dancing Indebted, I said, "Much like your people love you."

Blood welled in her eyes and she blinked rapidly.

"I hope the sick fuck who killed your mother got their reckoning," I added.

"King Julius let me kill them."

He had a heart in there somewhere, I knew it. He showed it half as regularly as Christmas, but it was in there.

Still didn't like him.

Laurel leaned in as I slurped back some more tart, sweet, alcohol goodness.

"You understand Kyros's power better now. Maybe you understand why some didn't wish for your union though your combined blood sings. Kyros already rivals some kings for power *now* with another seventy years until he is fully matured. His power was even evident in the womb, I've been told."

I set down my drink, reading her glimmering expression.

That's why Mikael was fighting for him? Not because he'd wanted the son of his union with Queen Titania, but because Kyros's power could be felt before he was born?

Cold, cold bastard.

He wanted to use Kyros.

"He's going to be really powerful one day, isn't he?" I asked after an explosion of laughter from the dance floor.

In seventy years, he'd reach maturity. I'd be ninety-two. Surviving that long was something I hoped for while knowing I'd be dead at seventy-five like a good little statistic. The only way to be with Kyros when he matured was to become a Vissimo. If I died, he'd go berserk and be killed too. Yet seeing as my various sources of guilt wouldn't let me consider our relationship as anything long term, turning into a vampire was still something I refused to contemplate.

Laurel regarded me through hard blue eyes. "One day, he'll rule all Vissimo, *Basi*."

I jerked, frowning at her. Was she serious?

She continued, "He'll rule us. Or he'll destroy us. And which path he takes is entirely up to you."

9

"You're kidding. Eight percent?" I stared at the screen which currently showed my Churchill team on the other side of the video call.

A woman in the middle flipped through a file. She stood, addressing me. "Yes, ma'am. Last week saw an increase of 8 percent in house acquisition. A 2 percent rise in rentals and leases."

Well, shit.

"I take it the new employees are doing well." My trouble property employees were behind this change. Led by Mrs Hannah.

The CEO cleared his throat. "Correct, Miss Le Spyre. Interestingly, our four newest employees were previously owners of properties from the trouble list. The houses sold last week were all from the trouble list too."

I smiled despite my fatigue. "Good."

In coming weeks, I'd hire more of them. But I needed to see how Sundulus reacted to the surge first.

Disconnecting the call, I climbed the stairs to my regular office, and pulled out my phone.

Staring at Tommy's number, I chewed on my lip, typing.

Please message so I know you're okay

I hovered my thumb over Send. She was physically okay. Laurel gave me a report every day on Tommy's status. But was she *okay* in her heart, in her mind, and in her soul?

Hitting Send, I scrolled through my contacts until I reached the name *Get Strawberries*. I held the phone to my ear.

"Miss Le Spyre."

Two rings. Not bad.

"Jordan," I greeted. "Give me an update."

I heard frantic rustling. Jordan was young, and managing a nightclub was a massive step up for her. During the three-month trial, she'd sink or swim. I had a feeling she'd swim—and well.

"Publicity after the opening night is insane. Exactly what we were going for. Nobody could hear a peep. They have no idea what was going on inside. I had Quin put up one post across our social media detailing opening hours next Thursday."

Opening my Instagram that I'd never posted with, but always stalked *Truth Ranges* celebrities on, I pulled up the post. Black background. A handful of words in the middle.

Forbidden.

"Perfect. What else?"

I listened as she detailed various themes and edges she had planned. I'd already used my influence to pull in renowned DJs from outside Bluff City.

When she finished, I said, "Discuss your ideas with the marketing team and research which will be better received. I'd like a schedule by the end of the week. In addition, approach the four most popular bars in Black. Invite them to participate in a club crawl—with a better name, obviously. The crawl will end at our club at midnight."

"I'll get onto that immediately," Jordan said.

My phone chimed as I ended the call. 1:00 p.m., and so many calls to make and emails to answer. I was mostly caught up, but a queue of CEOs waited for my approval on proposals. The sleepless nights were getting to me.

I glanced at the message.

[MESSAGE NOT SENT. This number is disconnected or no longer in service.]

My mouth dried. Tommy changed her number.

Of course she did.

Rubbing my chest, I opened a message from Dame Burke.

I stared at the address in Frankton Gorge.

There wasn't a name attached to the message, but I knew who it belonged to.

Sandra Hoyt. The last case manager for Mr Ringly's DA.

Hope and fear warred for first place. If she'd moved due to pressure or threats from Fyrlia, then I could stop the end cascade by bringing it to King Julius.

Which meant I couldn't delay. If I left now, I'd be back before my tower shift.

The problem being my personal GPS tracker. Tapping a finger on the table, I frowned at the Tom Hanks autobiography on the shelf.

Picking up the landline, I dialled for Fred.

"Miss Le Spyre. How can I be of assistance?"

"Fred, please send Mrs Hannah in." It was Sunday, so she shouldn't be working.

Oh fuck.

"Scrap that, Fred. She'll be at her extended lunch."

Hmm, I needed a reason to go to Frankton Gorge. Screwing my face up, I dismissed half a dozen excuses.

Kyros understood family and business.

I picked up the landline again. "Fred, get the car ready. We're going to Frankton Gorge."

"As you say, miss."

Laurel would have heard that too.

Kyros left mine an hour ago, which made this look more suspicious. Since the first night, he tended to stick around the estate until midday, then we went our separate ways until midnight. There hadn't been any repeats of what happened in the wardrobe, even after my text last night. Part of me was grateful despite the aching of my body. It was just a rabbit GIF, but I'd literally thought the same thing minutes before he sent it through. That our connection was changing and deepening was undeniable. With physical intimacy as intense as ours that trend would continue. I had to be careful. Losing myself over and over like that could break me. Not that I had to fend him off each night or anything. In Kyros, I detected fear each time we touched. He was afraid of losing control and starting the fifth exchange before the agreed time.

Next Sunday after the fashion show, we'd take the next step.

I'd wanted to do it tonight, but Dr Olivia recommended we wait four weeks from the attack in the hope my body would have replaced a fair amount of lost blood cells.

I sent Kyros a llama GIF.

His amusement trickled through a second later, and I hit Dial.

"Basilia." His voice slid over me, through me, and bumps erupted on my skin.

"Kyros."

His lust surged, and mine answered, pushing his higher. We were like a positive feedback system; with each rebound, the heat catapulted higher.

"I'm heading out to Frankton Gorge for the afternoon, and I wanted to tell you. Because you'd know."

A growl slipped down the line. "That's the only reason you're telling me?"

Well... "Yes."

He sighed. "Of course it is. Why are you going to Frankton Gorge?"

"Don't mistake this for asking your permission, Kyros. This is a courtesy call only. I'll take two cars of Vissimo."

"Take four." He cut me off.

Ugh. "I'd prefer the residents of Frankton Gorge not to mistake me for the Madame President."

Contemplation wound through the vampire. My ears picked up the squeak of leather as he leaned back in an office chair. "Then I'll come."

That was a big fat no. "You're so frustrating."

"Believe me, I'm nothing on you," he said, anger splicing between us. "Twenty Vissimo. No less. Or I'll follow, and you won't like the consequences."

"Chill out, *Dad*," I said, hanging up.

Consequences, my butthole.

I paced the office, hands curled into fists. Kyros wasn't allowed to dictate how and when I went places! Who the fuck did he think he was talking to?

Plus, Sundulus placed tails on Trenit and Tynan Tonyi after I killed their brother. Kyros knew where they were at all times.

He was just being a possessive control freak.

I blew out a breath.

Except, maybe he wasn't.

He'll rule us. Or he'll destroy us.

"Stupid male," I informed the room.

Striding to the door, I beelined for the patio doors that Laurel tended to guard.

She didn't turn. "Frankton Gorge?"

"Yes, could you get a team ready, please?"

"How many?"

I ground my teeth, increasing the number he gave me. "Twenty-five."

Her expression smoothed, and I pivoted on my heel, striding for the lobby. If taking that many would shut Kyros up, then whatever. No skin off my back. There were more important things to focus on—like climbing out of the six-foot grave I'd dug myself.

I'd take twenty-five Vissimo with me, and hopefully by the end of the day, I'd be in a position to confess everything to the Sundulus royals.

There was still time.

Sandra Hoyt, I'm coming for you.

The two-hour drive here wasn't totally wasted. My estate work was up to date—for now. The frenzy would continue until my CEOs believed I wouldn't disappear again. Unfortunately, there were no assurances of that. Each day could be my last if I didn't find a solution to restore equilibrium in *Ingenium* soon.

I'd made the Indebted wait at the ends of the street. My crew surrounded Miss Hoyt's house, out of sight.

I knocked on the door of the narrow townhouse. Frankton Gorge was wine country. The houses lining the main street were charming Victorian-style apartments. I'd come up here a couple of times with Tommy. We got all dressed up and consumed far too many bottles of sacrificial grapes.

Light footsteps echoed through the house before the door swung open. A towering woman with red hair regarded me warily, her eyes darting to the black car where Fred sat in the driver's seat.

This was Sandra Hoyt. I'd googled her.

"Miss Hoyt, I'm a family friend of Mr Hothen. My name is Basilia Le Spyre."

Her eyes widened. "*Le Spyre*. What are you doing here?"

Smiling, I said, "The subject I wish to discuss is of a sensitive nature. Do you mind if I come in?"

The thing about a last name like mine was people knew better than to say no—especially if those people worked for the council.

Yet she hesitated.

"I haven't come to harm you," I told her, dropping my smile. I could spot her brand of fear from a mile away. Maybe literally with my sharpened vision. She didn't leave Bluff City for her career. She'd been scared by Vissimo.

Badly.

She took another look at the car. "It's just you?"

And twenty-five vampires. "Just me. I'm not here to cause problems."

Sighing, Sandra gave up and opened the door wider. "Come in. I don't have long though. I have a meeting in an hour."

Sure she did.

I followed her into an elegant lounge room that matched the architecture of the house. Miss Hoyt was tasteful—and if Mr Hothen's interest was piqued by her, the woman had smarts.

Smart enough to get out of danger when things heated up.

"How is Walter?" she asked.

I thought of the silver fox. "Fine last time I saw him. You know him. Doesn't sit still for too long."

Her expression turned wry. "He doesn't. Are you dating him then?"

Ew. "Mr Hothen is more like a grandfather to me."

A small smile played on her lips. "Indeed. Then how may I assist one of the richest people in the world?"

I leaned back, watching her. "For several years, you were the town planner on a rezoning application. Last year, you moved to Frankton Gorge. Six months later, the development proposal was approved."

Her mouth tightened. "I don't know which—"

"Mr Ringly's DA for the 70 hectares known as Lot 42, previously agricultural land."

She blinked. "I can't discuss cases as I am sure you know."

I did. But she would.

Focusing my thoughts elsewhere, I said, "They scared you, didn't they? Was it just one of them or more?"

Sandra Hoyt froze.

"They threatened you... your life or career. They wanted you to approve the DA and you wouldn't."

"H-How do you know about them? Are you human?"

I waved a hand. "As human as they come." *With some alterations.* "However, Bluff City is not in a good state. I'm hoping to stop it falling into... unsavoury hands for good. To do that, I need proof that something was amiss in the Lot 42 DA."

She wet her lips.

I lowered my voice. "To do that, I need your help."

"They'll kill me."

"They won't," I told her. "No one's aware that I came here. Your statement won't be put forward to the correct parties until I am positive my people can use that proof to overthrow our enemies."

Sandra stood abruptly. "I can't help you."

"You're not safe here, Sandra. You think they don't know where you are? Do you think leaving Bluff City was protection enough? If you had the sense to get out of that situation, then you're smart enough to realise there's nowhere in the world they can't find you—should they choose to."

Tears pooled in her periwinkle-blue eyes.

I steeled myself, focusing on the texture of her wallpaper. "I can protect you. I say that with complete knowledge of their capabilities. But to protect you, and the city, I need to know how they tried to force your hand."

Julia Dinh took over after Sandra, but approaching her wouldn't go unnoticed by either clan. I'd looked up her name and confirmed she was a Sundulus human liaison. Yet she'd pushed through the DA for Fyrlia.

Which meant she was working both sides. Or Fyrlia had a larger hold over her.

Sundulus hadn't detected any wrongdoing in the Mr Ringly case. No bribes, compulsion, or apparent blackmail. Seeing as the rules prevented compulsion of anyone who signed contracts, Sundulus couldn't compel Julia for the truth. It would nullify future deals made with her as the signatory.

Had she figured that out?

That's why the clans compelled the very powerful—people who delegated tasks to others. Mr Olythieu was in their power and couldn't sign over anything himself; however, he could introduce them to a range of financial CEOs and advisors who could do the work they wished, as well as his direct underlings.

Sandra sat again, and I scanned her striking features, wondering if the stress of being a pawn in *Ingenium* caused the fine lines around her eyes. She couldn't be older than her mid-thirties.

We were all victims in this. But if we acted like victims, they'd win.

"You're living in fear," I whispered. "I know the feeling, Sandra. That's why I took my chance to live a life free of it. And the chance is good, or I wouldn't be here."

The woman plucked a tissue from a box on the table and wiped her face. "How can I be free? I've seen them. Seen what they can do. I just made it out of there with my life. As full of fear as life now is, why would I risk drawing their attention my way again?"

"For the others you may have in your life." I held her gaze. "You cut ties with Mr Hothen, so you know what I'm talking about. Will you live alone forever? What if you have children one day? What about your parents and siblings and their children? That's what you must protect. The information you have could be the thing that will protect them. Not only will I protect you during the proceedings, but afterward, if you still wish to hide, I'll help you do it properly. You and whatever loved ones you wish to take with you. You don't have to believe this, but you can see the same fear in me. I know what you've been through and what you feel. Believe that I'll do right by you and everyone else who has suffered."

Sandra closed her eyes, and I listened to the rush of breath in her throat and focused on the bead of sweat trickling down her neck.

The silence swelled and the ticking of the clock a few rooms away boomed in my ears.

Her lips trembled and she opened her eyes. "You'll help my family?"

I nodded. "I will."

She exhaled and her shoulders sagged. "I need time to—"

"There is no time. Unless you want the enemy to win, it has to be now."

Her hands shook. She opened her mouth twice before speaking. "I'd been working on the Ringly case right before I finished work that day. I usually left him until last because he tended to erupt on the phone each time I knocked his DA back. That happened a lot over the three years I worked with him. That particular day, I left work and found a list of my family's home addresses in my letterbox. I didn't know who the list was from at first. As time went on, each time

I had an interaction with Mr Ringly, a new copy of the letter would appear. First, just in my letterbox. Then at my workplace. I'd get off the phone with him and a letter would be sitting there on my desk. Toward the end, I found them in my bedroom. Sometimes while I'd been sound asleep."

Fuck. Even without knowledge of Vissimo that was terrifying.

"I told my superior and hoped that would be an end of the trouble. Instead, he asked me to stay on the case so Mr Ringly wasn't alerted to the police investigations. It took a while to realise he hadn't told the police about the harassment at all. I contacted the police myself and tried to go directly to the mayor. After that, the police stopped returning my calls. The mayor blocked me at every turn. I started to believe he must have some kind of stake in Mr Ringly's plans. It was the only thing that made sense."

She cut off and took a deep inhale. "That was about the time I began to spot the same man everywhere. I'd see him at the supermarket, and then pass the same man in the parking lot three seconds later. I'd stop beside the same man *again* at the traffic lights. I'd pass him twice on the same escalator and see him again on the next level walking out of a store. Meanwhile, each day at work was hell. Everyone thought I was creating trouble—I don't know what they were being told, but my colleagues turned against me overnight. No one would help or listen. Whoever was threatening me was extremely powerful, and I still had no idea who they were or how they were doing these things to me."

"What did you do?" I whispered.

"I sent my family away, out of Bluff City. I told them the truth and told them they had to leave. For how long, I didn't know. The man was following me at that point, and I was going crazy. Because how could he be in so many places at once? He was everywhere."

There was a very good reason for that. "Hazel eyes and brown curls? Tall? Cold eyes?"

Her gaze flew to mine. "Yes."

The triplets. I'd wondered how Fyrlia got away with this kind of shit. They hadn't directly approached her or compelled her. They'd broken her. Or tried to. Focusing on something unrelated, I said, "There's more than one of them."

"That did occur to me at first. But then they came closer, and I began to see stranger things. Things that couldn't be possible. Their teeth were long—*fangs*. Once, the man blurred across the road a-and ripped the head off the neighbour's cat. I woke up and the cat's head was sitting on top of my letterbox. My neighbours reported me to the police. I saw the man break a street post in half with a twitch of his hand. I tried moving house after that. I moved three times, changed banks, but they found me over and over again."

And she still held strong against approving Mr Ringly's deal. "What you did took some serious fucking guts."

She shook her head. "Not bravery. If I did what they wanted, they'd either kill me or I'd be in their pocket for the rest of my life. I had a plan. After my family was safe, I applied for a transfer despite knowing I should cut all ties and get another job. I'd worked too hard to get where I was. I'd leave my reputation behind, and that was bad enough. I'd hoped to use that reputation to become a private town planner. Giving up everything was too much."

I reached for her hand, squeezing it tight. Her pain was real and so very familiar. Just like my grandmother's friends, like Rhys, like me, Sandra Hoyt was an innocent pawn in *Ingenium*. I came here to save Sundulus so I could continue my own game, but I'd help this woman with everything I had. She'd gone through that alone. As much as I hadn't wanted Kyros's protection at the start, things could have been so much worse if the triplets got to me first.

"There was one problem. No one would take me," she breathed. "The CEO was blocking me, or my colleagues were spreading the news of my behaviour at work. Council staff gossip like nowhere else I've ever worked. Regardless, after two months of submissions and rejections, the council here offered me a position."

Fyrlia let her leave because she wouldn't approve the plans.

"It was too close for my liking, but I leapt at the opportunity. Two hours from Bluff City was better than being *in* Bluff City."

They wouldn't have followed her. Not in the same way. They

would have compelled her or killed her once her use had expired. She spoke far too openly to have been compelled. "They've never showed here?"

"No. And my team here didn't act strangely. They were welcoming. The man—or men—never showed their faces again. The letters stopped. I have a bag packed in case they do, even now, just in case I needed to cut ties and run. But Bluff City never followed me here until today."

I released Sandra, thinking over her words. This was surely proof of coercion. They'd forced her out of the city to make way for someone more pliable to their harassment. They must have done something similar to Julia. Even if they hadn't, what they did to Sandra had to be enough to break the deal. Except I wasn't sure. I couldn't make my move until I was certain. I owed her and her family my full diligence in the matter.

"They're vampires, aren't they?" she said dully.

Thinking of my body lotion, I managed a nod and gave her a minute to absorb that confirmation.

"Do you know what happened in council after you left?" I asked.

She shook her head. "I didn't care. I just wanted out. I was so angry at the people I worked with. I just didn't want to know."

Julia Dinh was going through the same hell, most likely—and yet I couldn't blame Sandra one bit.

"Here's what I need you to do," I said, holding up my phone. "You need to repeat everything you just told me so I have proof. After that, you need to take the packed bag you mentioned and the cash I give you and leave Frankton Gorge."

She opened her mouth. "Where?"

"That's something you must never speak aloud." I tapped my ear. "Don't take your phone. Don't take your computer. Not your car. Nothing. And don't go to your family. Do you understand?"

"Can't I come with you?" she asked.

"I need to make sure my move is solid before I make it," I told her. "If I play it wrong, you suffer. Not only that, I almost definitely have eyes on my estate." If Sundulus got hold of Sandra, and I didn't have a leg to stand on, they'd take a walk through her mind, and then she'd be tied to them for life. There were worse things in life—like being tied to Fyrlia—but I'd avoid her compulsion if possible.

When Sandra nodded, I took out a card. "This is my personal email. Find a new phone. Message me if there's any hint of trouble or if you need more money. I'll see that it gets to you. And after, when things are safe, I'll see that you find a council position equivalent to what you now hold. Better if I can wrangle it." Lady Treena shouldn't have any trouble with that.

"I just..." The woman blinked. "It's so fast. No one has ever helped me. I've been afraid for so long. I don't know what to think or do."

I pressed my lips together. "What is your body telling you to do, Sandra?"

"T-To run. To not look back."

"Stop ignoring your instincts. They're there for a reason. I have you now."

Tears tracked down her cheeks. "I want to believe you. That you'll help me."

"That's enough for now," I said, holding out another tissue. "Dry your face and let's get to work. These fuckers are going down. You might have been their victim until now, but you'll stand beside me when we have the last laugh."

Hatred glinted in her eyes. "I want that."

Revenge was a strong motivator. It had fuelled my grandmother for decades. It fuelled me for a while too. I missed the mindlessness of revenge after all Kyros's lies. When I hated him, my decisions were blissfully black and white.

"Then take it," I replied, lifting my phone up. "Tell everyone what happened to you."

Sandra squared her shoulders.

"I'm ready," she said.

10

My body had begged for rest, and sleeping on the drive back was tempting to the extreme, but I had shit to sort through. This development was huge, and I had to play it exactly right. The lives of Kyros's family depended on this. Kyros's forgiveness hinged on this too.

"Fred, please pull over when you can."

I fired off a text to Laurel, and in short duration, she slipped into the car.

"Laurel," I greeted.

I pressed a button on the console next to me and the soundproof screen between us and Fred slid up. Soundproof for human ears anyway.

She took the seat opposite me. "Basi."

"You heard?"

The vampire inclined her head. "I worry about leaving her unprotected."

"Same here. But I can't leave you guys to protect her without questions being raised by Kyros and Sundulus. I'm not prepared to answer their questions yet."

Sandra got this far without being compelled. I'd do everything possible to keep her out of chains.

Twenty-five Vissimo came with me to Frankton Gorge. I had to assume twenty-five heard Sandra's story. All of them knew the confidentiality rules when with me on the estate, but I couldn't depend on Laurel keeping them in check when they had so much motive to pay off their debts.

The sooner I hammered out the finer details, the better I'd feel.

"What do you know about the rules surrounding the presentation of this kind of evidence?" I asked.

Laurel's eyes darkened. "Nothing. The rules of Vissimo are well known to me. The intricate rules of *Ingenium* are not."

Fuck.

I couldn't move in the dark.

"You need the rule book," she said. "The manuals are readily available. Children in both clans are taught the rules during their schooling."

I lifted my head. "You're shitting me?"

She shrugged a shoulder. "How else would the clans keep track of everything? The rule book is a direct copy of the original contract between the two kings with any new rules inserted with passing decades."

This was... "I needed this, like, yesterday."

"Might I recommend consulting Deana on this point?"

Deana was the woman who introduced me to vampires when she sank her teeth into her boyfriend.

"She's not here today." Laurel continued. "I keep the newest of our kind in the tower and away from the estate. Their loyalty must be proven first. However, you're part of the inner circle on Level 66 now. You can use that as a cover. With some caution, she'll be one of the best to quiz on the complexities of the game. She's the only one of us to have worked in *Ingenium*."

Talking to her would be a risk, but nothing on the risks I'd taken to get here. "I need a copy of that book regardless." I hesitated before adding, "Are there books on the rules of Vissimo and mating?"

"Publications are held in high esteem in our world," the vampire replied, blue eyes scanning passing cars. "You know every clan is dedicated to a cause. They tend to write these things down and disperse the copies to various clans to show what they've achieved. But I warn you, they're generally long-winded and complex. That's why I didn't bring them up. Incorrect interpretation is dangerous." Her eyes glimmered.

Maybe. I was sick of relying on what others told me or didn't tell me. "I'll take them all the same. I'll double-check details before acting."

The tension left her shoulders. "Then I'll see that copies find you."

"Thank you," I said, blowing out a breath. "The fifth exchange is set for next Sunday."

She met my gaze. "I see. How does that tie in with the current state of *Ingenium*?"

Not good. No point having completed six exchanges to buy myself an army if the game was fucking over. "I'm another step toward keeping a promise," I answered, letting my head thump back against the headrest.

Laurel leaned back, surveying me. "What happens to you?"

"Nothing like a bit of uncertainty in life." I cracked a smile.

My phone rang. I checked in on Kyros mentally before checking the name. He was focusing.

I checked the name. *Yep.*

"Kyros."

"Basilia. Are you on your way back?"

He knew I was. "Missed me, did you?"

"Today wasn't an easy day. You're an hour away—"

"Does my GPS signal give you an ETA and take traffic conditions into account?" I frowned as a flutter of exasperation tickled my senses. "Did you just roll your eyes?"

"Yes."

Ha. "I felt it. Who knew eye-rolling had an emotion? Hey! You did it again."

His amusement was a trophy I wanted to keep winning.

"If you listen for three seconds strung together…"

I kept quiet and then deliberately rolled my eyes.

The vampire growled. "Woman."

"*Man*." I grinned. "Spit it out."

"Dinner," he said. "At my Lyall Bay property. Maybe one of us can cook."

I burst out laughing. "Kyros, really? Do you know how to cook?"

He was silent for a beat. "No. Do you?"

"I'll let you think about that one."

He snorted. "I'll pick up something. See you there in an hour."

"*Hold on*, I never—"

The line cut off, and my phone beeped.

I opened the waving kitten GIF. "Bastard."

Laurel cleared her throat, and I jumped.

"You forgot I was here." She quirked a brow.

I spluttered. "No."

The vampire leaned forward and plucked my phone from my grip. She stared at the kitten GIF and tossed the phone back on my lap.

Explanations died on my tongue. There was no good way to explain a kitten GIF from an alpha vampire prince. In my limited experience of them. I lowered the car screen. "Fred, take me to Lyall Bay, please." I rattled off the address.

He glanced at me in the rear-view mirror. "Yes, miss."

"How's that going?" Laurel asked when I raised the screen again.

That? "What do you mean?" I mumbled.

"Don't be obtuse. The blood bond with Kyros."

I glared at her, but she didn't back down. With what she stood to lose, I couldn't blame her.

"Balancing is difficult. I will still do right by my grandmother. As promised," I said carefully. The Vissimo with me were aware I was doing things I shouldn't be, but they didn't know everything. Neither did Laurel. Neither did my oldies or any of my teams. Only I knew all the various parts.

She scanned me. Was she judging whether Kyros had rendered me to a pile of goo?

"I'd let you know if that ever changed," I said as Fred drove us over the crest of the gorge. Bluff City glittered below.

"*Will* it change?"

Would I spit on my grandmother's memory, her friends, and people like Rhys and Sandra? "It will not."

Laurel blinked, and I was finally released from her attention.

"Anything good happen at the club after I left?" I asked in the lull after.

Her brows shot up. "Music and alcohol mixed with a race inclined to have as much sex as they can? No. Nothing."

I laughed and settled in as she rehashed the night. Vampires were worse than horny teenagers. Except they actually wanted babies out of the union and couldn't get STDs.

Laurel trailed off as we drew closer to Kyros's place. I took a steadying breath. Why did coming back here feel so normal? The tower and lair never felt that way, but this house did. I was happy to be here. What I felt was above and beyond the usual relief to be within touching distance of Kyros.

Fred stopped in front of the house. Kyros was waiting outside.

My heart thumped at the sight of him standing there waiting for me.

"Laters," I said to Laurel.

"See you later, Miss Le Spyre," she said.

I pulled a face, and her lips twitched.

Play it cool, Basi.

Fred was watching. And Laurel.

My butler opened the door, and I slid out, smoothing my black jeans and knit sweater combo.

I'd control my steps toward Kyros.

I would.

Kyros ran toward me at human speed. The air whooshed from my lungs as he spun me in a circle. I laughed and looped my arms around his neck, lifting my legs to wrap them around his torso like the koala I was in a past life.

He walked toward the house, kissing my cheek. "I'm glad you're here, true mate."

And I was glad to be here.

I opened my mouth to tell him so, but snapped it shut, resting my head on his shoulder instead.

"Nothing to say?" Kyros asked as we entered the house.

"Nope," I mumbled against his neck.

We tensed at the contact, but he relaxed after a breath. Maybe that wasn't the smartest place to put my mouth.

He shifted me higher. "I can feel how content you are."

It was true and I couldn't deny it. Just as I wouldn't confirm it, but I was so content that the current wasn't as uncomfortable as usual.

"What did you get for dinner?" I asked.

A tiny sadness stirred within him. He grabbed a bag off the bench and then he was lugging me back out of the house, one hand under my ass.

"Thai food. I didn't know what else you liked."

"I'll eat anything but olives and anchovies," I answered, locking my legs tighter around him. The guy could toss cars around, but the one-arm hold was disturbing my human sensibilities.

Fred was gone when we reached the front door again. Exiting the house, Kyros left the door wide open and walked us off between the trees lining the driveway.

Throwing off the remaining awkwardness, I said, "Do you want to know a fun fact about human women?"

He glanced at me warily. "No."

I tapped his nose. "We have legs that we can walk with."

Kyros caught my finger in his teeth. Ouch, those fuckers were sharp! I sucked on it when he let go.

"You want to be in my arms, so why don't you let yourself be in my arms?" he replied.

He dropped down into the outdoor area that I'd sat in while

avoiding his family. The fire there was roaring. A bottle of wine sat on a low table between the swinging seat and the fire pit.

I tried to lower my legs, but he carried me to the swinging seat and set me on it.

Breathing thinly, I surveyed the setup, something akin to panic rising within me.

"My beauty," Kyros murmured. "What did you think dinner with me meant?"

We'd had meals together before.

We slept in the same bed.

Stayed in the same house for more than a week.

This was a *date*, our first date if I excluded the beach—which I did because Kyros had coerced me into going. When I agreed, dinner was just casual. Sharing takeaway food at his kitchen bench before work didn't hold the same terror as this romantic gesture that I didn't want.

That I didn't deserve.

I curled my legs under me, glad I wore ankle boots today. The days were getting chillier now. A woollen blanket rested beside me, and although heat poured off the fire, I draped the throw over my legs. Blood loss would do that to a gal.

Kyros didn't push the issue as he dished the food onto plates and poured the wine.

My hands were shaking when I took the glass from him.

His green eyes settled on me.

I turned my face away, sipping on the white wine. Crisp fruitiness exploded on my tongue. I hummed in approval. "Yum."

That satisfied him enough to sit on the seat beside me. I eyed the seat springs, wondering if this thing could hold him.

"What do you want?" he asked, picking up a plate.

Peeking at him, I set my glass down on the small table and reached for the plate. "I'll get it."

He grabbed my hand.

Blinking, I glanced across at him. "What?"

We locked gazes.

Sighing, he let me go and passed over the plate.

Frowning, I loaded it with papaya salad and grabbed a fork.

He poured Tom Kha Gai into one of the two small bowls and I breathed in the rich coconut scent of the soup.

I was ruining the dinner he'd organised because I couldn't get a handle on my guilt. Swallowing my bite of the spicy and sweet salad, I asked, "How was your day?"

"Hectic," he answered.

Every Sundulus roll was hectic these days. Their clan was working overtime, all of them believing the deaths of their royal family was a near certainty. "Is everything going downhill then?"

He knew I was speaking about the bluff.

"If you don't mind, Basilia, I'd like to leave work for later."

My brows shot up. Kyros didn't want to talk about *Ingenium*? I didn't know the concept existed. Not that he couldn't talk about other things, but he enjoyed the game—even if he hated the potential outcome. He loved the challenge of conquering and understanding the complexities of economy.

I took another bite.

We ate in silence, and I set my plate down after, staring at the dancing flames.

This area was beautiful, and imagining endless nights like this, just me and Kyros, was a hell all of its own.

"So young and so serious," he murmured, stroking the top of my cheekbone.

He'd set down his bowl.

I frowned at the boxes of food. "You haven't eaten enough."

"Neither have you, my beauty. You never eat enough."

"I'm not an oversized vampire. I've seen what you can put away."

Kyros smiled. "How about a deal then?"

"I'm listening." I folded my arms, shivering slightly.

Grabbing a deep-fried money bag, he held it against my lips. "I'll eat if you do."

I inhaled, eyes wide on his. Opening my lips, I took a bite of the minced pork parcel. He ate the rest, grabbing another.

"Stop trying to hand feed me," I complained.

Kyros held another to my lips.

When I sighed and opened my mouth, he snatched it away, shoving the whole thing in his mouth.

"Very funny." I whacked him, leaning forward for some of the coconut soup. I shivered again as the hot sweetness trickled down my throat.

He draped an arm across my shoulders. "You're still cold."

"Hmm? Yeah. The blood loss, I think. I get it for a bit after each exchange too."

His brows furrowed at that.

"I didn't say that to make you feel bad. It's just fact."

Kyros tightened his hold, his warmth seeping into my body. I shuffled closer, trying not to spill my soup.

"Why is it that the more time we spend together, the more uncomfortable you feel?" Kyros asked, staring at the fire.

I tensed, swallowing hard. Fear surged within me. He couldn't discover the truth yet. I hadn't figured everything out.

"Fear," he stated. "Guilt."

Closing my eyes, I rested the bowl on my lap.

"Longing," he whispered. "I can't understand it. You fear the bond between us. You feel guilty about it. Yet you want me. Sometimes, your behaviour and actions suggest you feel as strongly as I do. Other times, you're impossible to reach as though you're locking yourself away."

He drew my face toward his. "Why do you deny yourself? Why do you deny *me*? I'm trying to understand. To be patient. But the distance between us in those times, like now, drives me mad."

Opening my eyes, I met his intent green gaze.

"I—"

"*No lies*," he said harshly.

I pressed my lips together and tried to break free of his grip. He let me go, watching as I established fresh distance between us.

"Answer me one thing then," Kyros said.

"Depends what it is."

Anger flashed in his eyes. Or hurt. Both?

He tucked the anger away before asking. "Why do you want the fifth exchange if you don't always want me? Or if something about me, my situation, or my family makes you doubt the future we could have?"

I set the bowl on the table, appetite gone. "You've heard what I think about *Ingenium*."

"I can't promise there won't be games if Fyrlia wins."

My breath hitched. "It's happening then?"

Jaw clenching, Kyros glanced away. "Yes. We believe our human liaison at the council, Julia Dinh, is not as fully in our control as we previously thought."

They thought Fyrlia was evading their efforts to tear down Mr Ringly because of Julia Dinh?

I took his hand in mine. "Kyros, is there anything I can do to help?"

He regarded me for a long time. "I won't drag you into this further. To see how knowing me has changed you. You were always this young, but you weren't always this serious. Not before me. Thinner. Scarred. Wary. Hurt. Too aware of danger."

I struggled to understand what he was saying. "You find those things unattractive?"

"No, my beauty. They're nothing more than regrets spoken in a regretful moment."

"Those things are nothing more than a moment in time," I told him. "And not all of those things you listed are bad. I had lessons to learn. Would you rather lock me in your tower?"

"Yes."

Fell into that one. "You've changed, too, since we first met."

"But I don't run from you because of them."

"Kyros, you've run from me twice. Once after your siblings found out our bond was far stronger than you'd let on. And again after the third thrall. Not only that, you *still* keep me at arm's length whenever you fear I can't handle something. Like the other day when you tried to brush aside what happens beyond the fifth exchange."

"What else should I do when you feel panic and fear at every turn? What lies between us overwhelms you with its intensity, but our bond will only grow stronger. That's why you run."

I rubbed my temples. "That's... No. I'm not running."

"Move into the tower then, or this house. With me. Permanently."

"Kyros, that doesn't prove anything. That's asking me to leave my home. Why don't *you* leave your home?"

His eyes gleamed. "Why don't you ask and find out?" My chest rose and fell, and his expression smoothed. "I didn't think so."

"I've only known you for three months," I choked. "What's the hurry?"

"When two people are true mates, time is meaningless."

The urge to get up and leave was nearly unbearable. Not for any of the reasons he thought he'd correctly deduced. My reasons had everything to do with everything *else*. Grandmother. Tommy. The triplets. King Mikael. Grandmother's friends. Sandra. Rhys. The game.

For the first time, I truly wished everything else would disappear. If it were just me and him, things could be so different.

Kyros closed his eyes. "If you want to leave, then leave, Basilia."

"If I have a tendency to run," I withered, "then you have a tendency to push me away."

He growled, facing me. "Pushing you away? Everything I do is to keep you by my side, including the lies. Without that, you'd be long gone."

"Maybe in the beginning," I acknowledged. "I'm here now when I don't have to be."

"And if I told you all, vixen, would you stay?"

I shifted, hugging myself. "I don't know what you're talking about."

Kyros gripped my hips and slid me toward him until we were nose to nose. "How long will it be before telling you that I've never cherished another as I cherish you doesn't fill you with dread?" He searched my gaze.

My heart leapt at the words. Then twisted, plummeting to splatter on the ground.

"You know, my beauty. Don't you?"

I held a finger over his lips. "Don't."

Please don't tell me you love me.

His gaze darkened.

"Please don't," I whispered against the pain filling me, not all of it mine. "You're older than me. And I—" Taking a steadying breath, I tried again. "I'm not ready for that."

"Why did you drive off the cliff?"

"Because I trust you to always keep me safe."

He opened his mouth, and I covered it. "I don't want this to happen now."

A lump rose up my throat. *God*, I felt so fucking trapped. Like my feelings for Kyros were one wall, and my grandmother was another, and they were slowly pressing in. There was no way out.

His beautiful green eyes fixed on me. Right now, all I wanted was him. I wanted to run *with* him.

"My beauty," Kyros said softly. "I didn't intend to upset you. I won't say more on the subject tonight. Come here."

I resisted his attempt to tuck me against his body. Before he could voice his frustration, I climbed onto his lap and kissed the base of his neck before craning to kiss the corner of his mouth.

"What were those gifts for?" he said, a shadow crossing his face.

My vampire was never darker than in my presence. Dark for me. Light for me.

"Thank you... mate," I replied, meeting his gaze for as long as I could.

Working myself as close to his warmth as possible, I rested my head against his chest.

His shock battered at me for a long time before his arms came around me.

A perfect fit.

I stared at the fire, doing my best to pretend the world away.

Doing my best to pretend that only this dark creature and I existed in the here and now.

11

When Laurel first handed me the *Ingenium* rule book, I'd celebrated the Jane Austen thickness of it. Until learning the font size was suitable for a flea.

I had vampire eyesight and still had to hold the book in front of my face.

Beside me was a notebook filled with what sense I could make of the three chapters in the rule book dedicated to *Vissimo-Human Relations*. The edition I held was from last year, so everything from media to technology was covered. These weren't Monopoly instructions. Like Laurel said, this was a contract—filled with all the lawyer jargon that came with it.

I re-read the section on coercion of signatories.

From what I could tell, I was right. Humans surrounding the signatory could be coerced and compelled, but the actual signatory had to sign of their own free will without influence.

Sandra had detailed what the Tonyi triplets did to her. That was coercion and extortion by *human* standards.

That's what worried me.

There was the section under Clause 14.3. *Whereby the signatory is believed by either party to be victim to the transgressions listed in Clause*

10 to Clause 12.8, proof must be obtained and presented to an impartial clan.

The impartial clan would make the judgment and, if deemed guilty of a transgression, the offending party's deal would be nullified.

But what constituted as proof?

I didn't want Sandra dragged before an impartial party. She'd be compelled for sure.

I jotted the word *proof* down and circled it.

Rubbing my temples, I closed the rule book. I'd read it from cover to cover as many times as it took to know everything about the game. Sliding it aside, I picked up the much thinner volume beneath.

Mating Rituals & Blood Bonds
A Complete Collection

Ugh, I called Kyros mate last night. He'd been so lost and completely off base about why I felt so much guilt and fear.

The word slipped out. Far too easily.

During my pretending act around the fire, it even felt right to say aloud.

I woke alone in the house, in his bed, at 10:00 a.m. I couldn't remember falling asleep but thank fuck he wasn't there this morning. It gave me time for an appropriate freak-out session.

Kyros pretty much told me he loved me. I called him mate.

Cringe.

I mean, that's technically what we were to each other, but I'd crossed a massive line in our relationship. One I shouldn't have crossed while betraying him and his entire family.

Messed up didn't touch what I'd done.

With the walls crashing down around me, I felt like Kyros needed to hear the truth from my lips and soon. If this lead with Sandra didn't eventuate to anything, I had to come clean. At the very least so Sundulus could redirect their offensive strategy.

Kyros spent every Friday night with King Mikael, and after my latest stunt texting during the roll, it was a very real possibility the

Fyrlia royals would tell Kyros what I'd done to drive a wedge between us.

A wedge should be what I wanted.

I shouldn't care what Kyros thought.

I should be as ruthless in achieving my game as Agatha Le Spyre.

There were so many things I should be.

Opening the cover of the thin book, I flicked to the first chapter, which detailed the difference between mates and true mates. After that, it summarised the history of mating rituals through the ages, and the current fashion of forming harems over the mating ritual.

Harem trend. How did that even become a thing? Imagine if humans did that?

Snorting, I skimmed over the next chapters, which detailed the first four exchanges. I stopped at the chapter titled, *The Fifth Exchange.*

In following with the pattern thus far, the fifth exchange between true mates heightens the libido of both participants while furthering the exchange of power. The strength, speed, and healing capabilities of each party will improve, and the ability to be apart will decrease.

The paragraph went on to detail how the exchange usually affected normal mates.

I blew out a breath. One week left as I was. With the setbacks to my ears, I'd only started feeling comfortable with my new senses. The dizziness when I suddenly turned was gone. With each passing day, the overwhelming feeling from clashing stimuli decreased.

Yet Kyros was right. The clock *was* ticking.

If Fyrlia won, Mikael wouldn't allow Kyros to continue the exchanges with me. In fact, I was certain that if I stayed in a Bluff City ruled by their clan, my life would effectively be over until I died.

I had to leave before that happened, and make sure everyone I cared about left too.

Kyros wouldn't lead Fyrlia to my hiding spot, but I'd live separate from those I loved just in case. I didn't spend much time amongst the working class, but I was confident that with better preparation, I could cover my real identity and live as economically as needed to stay off the radar.

When it came to the exchanges and my game strategy, I was determined to uphold my deal with the Indebted. Even with the very real possibility of Fyrlia triggering the end cascade, I had to push on with the mating ritual. I had to continue on as though winning was an option.

Because in no way, shape, or form did I intend to lose.

There was an answer to all this. I'd already found a potential solution with Sandra, really. Now, I had to make sure that it was bulletproof for her sake. And for Kyros.

I read the chapter on the fifth exchange and squinted at the sixth before deciding to quit while I was ahead.

Picking up the third book, *The Law & Etiquette of Vissimo*, I scanned the index, finding the section titled *Human-Vissimo Mating Bonds*. The subject was covered by two sections, one for expected etiquette and the other for all legalities.

"*Any mated human must walk in front of his or her mate at all times, head bowed, and hands clasped at the waist,*" I read aloud, my jaw dropping. Laughter burst from my lips. "They can go fuck themselves."

Kyros preferred me to walk in front, but the head bowed part could climb a tree and sing a beanstalk into existence for all I cared.

Shaking my head, I read through the rest of the section—which was as ridiculous as the first sentence.

I flicked to the legal half of the book. "When was this shit even published?"

I checked the date. *1907.*

That explained a few things. Was this the most recent edition Laurel could find? The other two books were at least revised during this century. The law section was much larger, and my heart sank at the third clause.

Unless the transition ritual is invoked at the seventh exchange, the human or elevated-human mate will not speak in formal gatherings unless permitted by their Vissimo counterpart.

I'd broken that about a million times.

Trailing my finger through the legal clauses, I flicked through the pages until finding the topic I was specifically interested in.

After the sixth exchange, a human mate is considered an elevated human.

"Elevated human, my butthole," I muttered. But Laurel was right. Clause 7.6 stated—in much clearer terms than the *Ingenium* rule book stated anything—that I could own and direct Indebted, who were considered lesser than an elevated human.

Asswipes, ranking people like that. Not that *humans* didn't do that to themselves and everything around them. But still. Immortality clearly didn't correlate with increased wisdom.

My phone buzzed on the office desk.

Safina.

"Go away," I grumbled, clicking on the green button despite myself. "What?"

"Basilia. We have something to discuss."

We did?

"I've been meaning to apologise about going into Fyrlia territory and putting you at risk. I didn't understand it completely at the time, but I gather now that if I died and Kyros lost the plot, you would have paid the price. And Kearra."

"Life is too short to apologise for things that never happened. Your intent was not malicious. You warned us. Everything worked out."

No, it didn't.

"Okay, I'm still sorry though."

"My time is precious, Miss Le Spyre. You're wasting it."

Total badass. I'd said it once, I'd say it a million times. "Spit it out then, Safina."

"Most of my siblings have spent quality time with you—"

I spun in my chair. "That's what you guys are calling it? *Quality time*?"

She was walking around a room. I listened to the rustling of papers, imagining her in the penthouse of her own tower. Aside from *Kyros Sky*, I'd only been to Lionel's tower—to look at his model of the vertical farming developments.

"Call it what you will," Safina said breezily. "Because my time is short these days—"

"—You're not going to do anything to me?"

"Quaint. No. But I will make things easier if you're cooperative."

I groaned. "That's where Lionel learned it."

"What?"

"He used that exact line on me during his turn."

Safina hummed. "We must teach our younger siblings all we can to survive."

They could have stopped at *don't touch the hot oven, Lionel.*

"Tell me straight then. What crap have you got planned?"

She purred down the line. "A week's worth of outfits, shoes, and jewellery are about to arrive at your estate. They are labelled Monday to Saturday. You are to wear them each night with your hair styled in my usual bun. Make-up is to be kept simple. I will send you a picture to mimic. This week, you'll sit next to me when we're in the same room. You'll mimic my actions. Bonus points if you copy some of my other mannerisms and speech patterns."

I absorbed that. "You want me to be a mini-me?"

"Yes."

My lips trembled. "Safina. That's seriously messed up."

"The only thing worse than not fucking your true mate is for her to look like your sister while you obsess over it."

Brilliant.

Husky chuckles tumbled from my lips. "I really like you. I'm totally behind your *Game of Thrones* mindfuckery."

"Thought you might be."

This would create the barrier I needed to erect between us again.

And Safina didn't even know I'd called Kyros mate last night either.

The seconds' furious debate bounced overhead as Kyros stared at me in consternation. He'd been frowning at me since I arrived on Level 66, but until Safina got here, I doubted the vampire would put it together.

"Enough," Kyros said.

Fangs retreated, and everyone sat.

I studied my hashtags.

There was only one.

#amscrewed

Angelica strode into the room per her usual cue. Everyone tapped on their tablets. I did the same, opening the House Acquisition file. Usually, the first page contained the properties in whichever suburb the roll had landed on.

"Today, a slight detour from the norm," the Vissimo began. "For the last three decades, rates of privately sold properties have held steady. Last year, the rate doubled as tourism spiked and vacation homes became a trend. Or so we assumed. While that theory was supported by the purchase of houses in waterfront locations and townhouse purchases in Black and Blue, there has been a recent and dramatic shift."

Uh-oh.

"The rate of privately-purchased properties has doubled again in the last two months."

I arched my brows. "So much?"

Angelica dipped her head. "I had my team do some digging. It appears that over 9000 homes in Bluff City were purchased by offshore owners."

Ilion jerked. "Nine *thousand*? That's 15 percent of the residential market."

Think of Tommy leaving. Think of Tommy leaving.

"Private transactions usually operate at a word of mouth and local level, but the scale of this is suspicious to the extreme. Someone is brokering these deals, and yet our staff have never come across other realtors, beside *Foremost* workers. Not only that, the private owners we consider problematic are increasingly selling to overseas buyers."

I'd known this moment would come as I accelerated acquisition. I needed to focus on the conversation as much as possible.

Angelica bowed. "I leave the seconds to discuss the possible reasons behind the surge; however, you can find a list of proposed theories at the bottom of the second page. If *Foremost* isn't behind these purchases, this could be a potential market to hit with everything we have."

Scrolling down, I skimmed through the theories of her team while doing my best to focus on what I had for breakfast that morning.

"Have you had contact with any of the owners or buyers?" Kyros asked, glancing up at her.

"I was awaiting your decision, sir." Angelica straightened.

"You'll have one by the end of the night."

She bowed again, then launched into an abbreviated version of her usual spiel. Sundulus landed on Purple tonight. After her report, the stream of other team leaders delivered their reports. The door had barely closed on the Forecasting Head of Team before Conrad erupted.

"*Foremost* is behind the private sales," he said, bursting to his feet. "It's a safety net. They broker a deal and keep the details of the sale under wraps. They can then purchase the properties back when they wish. It would be perfectly within the rules."

Danielle tapped her pen on the table. "No. If they had over nine thousand properties, then they could have won the game by now. Why would they broker private sales to overseas buyers instead of keeping the homes for themselves?"

Kyros was watching me.

I had to say something. "Because the trouble properties are demonstrating resistance to *Live Right* and *Foremost*. They likely prefer to sell privately than deal with either company. When the property is sold, Foremost can then approach the overseas buyers, who don't have any resistance to their offer. Holiday homes are often an investment. Convincing overseas clientele to sell due to plummeting house values would be child's play."

Ilion scrolled through his tablet. "But some of these properties were purchased nearly thirty years ago. The rate has greatly accelerated in the last month, but prior to that, the rate was steady—between 300 and 350 properties were privately purchased each year."

Go, Agatha.

"Just a theory."

Kyros peered at me over steepled hands. "There's more."

Dammit.

My palms grew slick with sweat, and I reasoned away my thumping heart. All the seconds were looking at me. At least part of my reaction was masked by the natural instincts of my body around them. "Having visited a lot of these trouble properties, I can tell you that public favour for this company and *Foremost* isn't good. I don't think you should discount the possibility that the residents of Bluff City talk to each other. You know word of mouth is the strongest marketing tool there is. The information we've spread about plummeting house prices would have only skyrocketed that word of mouth. I also don't think you should dismiss that someone might have seen an opportunity to make money. You may have forced other realtors out of work, but if someone is brokering overseas deals, they're filling a niche where there is no competition. Of course they'd thrive."

Satisfaction thrummed through Kyros, and I held onto the very real passion I'd felt during my outburst so relief didn't edge in.

I tuned in as the seconds launched into their usual debate. The fury level was at a record high. Everyone felt the stress of what was looking more and more like an imminent loss to Fyrlia. The forecasters reported that the end cascade would be triggered within three weeks unless Sundulus did something huge.

Beforehand, that *something huge* was the bluff with Mr Ringly that hardly anyone knew about. That was gone now, though Kyros's family was still hoping it would turn around.

Three weeks to make everything right.

So little time. And yet I'd decided to sit on my information from Sandra Hoyt. When I brought that information forward, I'd tell Sundulus absolutely everything about what I said to Mikael. Kyros would be pissed. Mega pissed. Possibly *never-talk-to-me-again* pissed.

So I couldn't risk him cancelling the fifth exchange over it.

If the book on mating rituals was correct, we'd be almost inseparable at that point. The opportunity to trigger the sixth exchange with Kyros's tenuous lack of control would be easier. He may even be more inclined to forgive me.

Which only served to show me how desperate I felt.

And what a coward I was.

Shaking that off, I settled into listening, tapping out hashtags when a comment caught my fancy and slipping in my opinion when something unvoiced occurred to me.

When the seconds zoomed out per their usual exit, Kyros switched off his tablet and stalked slowly toward me. "What do you type down during every meeting? I thought it was notes at first, but you're always amused."

That's because I was within the sad percentage of the population who found their own jokes funny.

I opened the notes app and tilted the screen toward him.

He tore his gaze from my pantsuit and pearl necklace to the device, reading, "Hashtag am screwed more."

Dang. Maybe it wasn't funny to other people.

"It's how I keep track of the conversation when the Vissimo power turns up a notch or ten."

Kyros read the others, his lips twitching at #juliadoublecrossingdinh.

Not a complete loser. Go, me.

"Hashtag Fyrlia crumb trail," he said, pointing at the last hashtag. "What does that mean?"

"I think Ilion's right. There should be a team dedicated to fishing out corrupt deals that Fyrlia has made. The team could target the larger deals from, say, one to two years ago. I feel like they would have taken care in recent months as they drew ahead, but before that, I feel like there's a chance Fyrlia won't have bothered to cover their tracks as diligently."

"Very good, mate. Let's put it to my brothers and sisters." Placing a hand on my lower back, he directed me out of the room ahead of him.

Mate.

He had to go and say it.

"Do you regret saying it then?" he murmured at my back.

I shivered, already tense from having him behind me. Did I regret calling him mate? "No."

Biting back my smile at his answering growl, I scampered into the next meeting room, beelining for Safina. She turned as I approached.

"Ah, Basilia."

"Ah, Safina." I copied her slightly bored tone. Was that how this worked?

Gerome's mouth dropped open and he whacked Francesca. She hissed, fangs lengthening, then glanced at me and Safina. Her fangs disappeared.

She whipped out her phone, and in unison, the other siblings drew out theirs.

Kyros scanned Rory and Neelan as they snickered. "What's—?" He froze as his gaze landed on Safina and me.

"Brother?" she said, tilting her head.

"Kyros?" I said, tilting mine.

Horror filled him, and I nearly lost it on the spot. His gaze snapped to mine, and I worked to keep my face smooth even though he could feel me hooting inside.

"Oh my gosh," Lalitta hushed.

Dierdre was crying with silent laughter. *Go figure.*

Kyros's throat worked, and he shuddered visibly *and* internally. "Please be seated. We have much to discuss before the call to King Julius."

Safina leaned back, crossing her legs. I did the same a beat later.

Lust and revulsion warred for first place within the massive vampire.

Oh, yeah.

This was going to be a fun week.

12

The video recording of Sandra Hoyt came to an end. I surveyed the shocked faces around the table.

"*Fucking monsters*," Mr Hothen spat. "Why didn't she come to me for help?"

The desperate weren't known for 20/20 vision.

I placed my phone on the table. "I consulted a rule book. Proof must be examined by an impartial, uh, group. I fear that presenting it to... S... will result in Sandra being caged." I hadn't just consulted the rule book, I'd also clarified the point in vague terms with Deana.

Sandra would be dragged in for questioning and compelled to silence afterward. That was the absolute verdict.

"I want to find another angle. I won't involve her unless there's a way to do it safely," I told them.

She'd been through so much already.

Lady Treena set her champagne flute down. "Julia Dinh."

"Possibly. S is aware that she's playing both sides. Or at least is being controlled by F somehow. They're pouring resources into an investigation in that area. It's likely we'd be noticed trying to do the same. The same with Mr R. He'll be under close surveillance by both sides."

I was getting pretty good at talking around the compulsion while calm like this, but it was still a frustrating process.

Sir Olythieu hummed, stroking his short white beard.

"I could put through a request for a site inspection via one of the council workers," Lady Treena said. "If there's a planning breach, then development will be delayed while a retrospective application is put through. Or ideally, there'll be something there to warrant an enforcement notice."

I shook my head. "S has done that stuff already. I'm more worried that Sandra is our only bet to restore order."

Mr Hothen placed both hands on the table. "Then we're best to set our sights on how to achieve that without her being hurt. Human lives will not be sacrificed for this endeavour."

"Agreed," I murmured with the others.

"I wish I could kill every one of them," Mr Dithis cursed, standing and whirling away to pace the room.

Dame Burke leaned back. "I used to dream of dropping bombs on their homes."

Mrs Syrre. "Animals, the lot of them."

My stomach twisted at the hatred etched on the six faces around me. I hesitated, wondering if I should say something. It wouldn't do any good though. They'd hated *Vissimo* for decades—longer than I'd been alive. Not all vampires were cruel, but I only knew that because of my unusual position. If I wasn't Kyros's mate, I'd hate their kind just as much. My position as his true mate granted me a lot of leeway with his minions and even the sane members of the other clan.

I picked up my buzzing phone and studied the name.

"Be very quiet," I announced, cutting off Mr Hothen.

Fixing them with a warning look that they immediately understood, I answered the phone.

"Kyros. I'm in a meeting."

"What meeting?"

Standing, I turned away from the table. "A boring one, but a necessary one. What do you need?"

"The agricultural lot you secured for us," he said. "That was from a family friend, correct?"

I paced, setting my mind on my grumbling stomach. "My grandmother's friend. I didn't ever meet him. Barnaby Dwelt."

"I was mulling over Angelica's report last night. *Live Right* staff are trying to locate the previous owners of offshore-owned properties this week, but you've had contact with one already."

Fuck balls. Think of lunch. Think of lunch.

"Well, yes. Except I had his contact information already."

He inhaled. "That's what I wanted to ask you. Lot 91 was purchased fourteen years ago, so it may be irrelevant to the recent surge, but it's all we currently have. Could you get in contact with Mr Dwelt and ask how the private deal was brokered?"

I pursed my lips. "I can do that, yes."

His relief poured through me, and I squeezed my eyes shut.

"Is there a chance you may have connections to any of the other privately sold properties?"

Uh, just a few of them.

"What's funny?" he asked, a smile in his voice.

"There are over nine thousand properties, Kyros. I have no idea. Ask Angelica to send a list of the addresses and names through. I'll look."

He spoke rapidly over his shoulder. "Done. One more thing. Barnaby Dwelt. I couldn't find any information on him through our systems."

Because he doesn't exist. "The very rich have that privilege. Search my name. I'd gather it's the same."

I listened to him typing.

He swore. "When did you wear that?"

"What?" I glanced at the oldies, who were as still as wrinkled statues.

"White leotard. Looks like leather." Kyros swore again.

I choked on a laugh. "The opening of *Forbidden*. I changed before the tower." Neither of us could handle the heat that would have erupted if I'd shown up in that.

"Do you still have it?"

"You realise there are a bunch of people waiting for me right now?"

His lust didn't dim. "I've had to watch you parade around looking like my sister all week, Basilia. Cut me some slack."

"I knew Safina's would be the best."

"Gerome won't stop sending me Jamie Lannister memes. I had to look up the reference. He's a character who sleeps with his sister in some show."

Laughter burst from my lips. "Originally a book series. And he would do that. I'm just surprised you know what memes are. I mean, you have a handle on GIFs, but this is getting ridiculous. Next thing I know, you'll stop wearing suits."

He laughed low. "I'm watching *Truth Ranges* here and there. They talk about memes and GIFs, so I looked them up a while back."

I clapped a hand over my mouth. He'd kept that fucking quiet! "You're kidding me. What episode are you up to?"

"Nine."

"Trissa is hanging between two buildings by her cardigan and it's starting to tear!"

"Episode nine. Season *two*."

Oh. My. God. "Doctor Khang is forced to complete emergency brain surgery in a basement with one hand tied behind his back."

My mouth dried. If Kyros was here right now, I'd jump him. It was that simple.

Leather squeaked as he shifted. "I set up a romantic dinner equipped with fire and wine at the start of the week and it made you want to sprint in the other direction, but you're turned on by me watching a show?"

I didn't make the rules. "Don't hurt yourself trying to understand me, Kyros."

"I'll just be happy when you stop wearing pantsuits. Please tell me it's over at the end of the week? I can handle two more days. Not an entire month."

"You'll have to wait and see."

Kyros growled.

I placed a hand on my hip. "Don't get growly with me. I'm not messing with Safina for anything. All your siblings will gang up on me, and I still have Francesca's fashion show to get through on Sunday."

And the fifth exchange after it.

"I'm looking forward to Sunday night," he said.

I shifted, suddenly remembering the six gazes boring into my back. "It'll be a... real party."

He groaned. "Gerome just sent me another meme. I'll let you get back to your meeting."

Snorting, I said, "Okay, see you tonight."

Disconnecting the call, I avoided the gazes settled on my face as I sat again. Glancing up, I rose my brows. "Something wrong?"

Their faces were smooth. I saw those expressions on their faces all the time. Just not usually directed at me.

Dame Burke was the first to break the tension. "That was Kyros—crown prince of Clan Sundulus?"

I nodded. "Correct."

Sir Olythieu met my gaze. "How close are you with Sundulus?"

My own gaze cooled. "Close enough to be invited to their innermost meetings. What are you implying?"

The six oldies exchanged looks.

Lady Treena watched me from beneath hooded eyes. It was the look she gave me before trumping me in Scrabble. Her vocabulary was legit. "Basilia, the way you just spoke to him..."

"And I'm still not certain what your question is," I answered mildly. "Stop beating around the bush."

Mr Dithis broke first. "Is what we just heard an act or is it real? You were discussing a television show? You scolded him like a child."

I did?

"Don't get growly with me," Dame Burke quoted.

Shit. I did say that.

In my defence, it was really hard to remember others were in the room with the state Kyros and I were in.

Maybe I should just tell them about the mating thing.

One look at their hard faces decided it for me.

"Some of it was an act," I said. "Not all. Your experiences with them have led you to believe they're all monsters. That's not the case."

It was like I'd slapped them. Mrs Syrre reeled back.

"Led us to *believe*," Mr Hothen said.

I straightened. "Yes, led you to believe. And you can't be blamed for that. That's what they wanted you to think. So you'd obey without question."

These weren't narrow-minded people I was talking to. They used emotion as data, but emotion didn't dictate their decisions. Yet how could a person not hate creatures who'd forced them to live in fear for decades on end?

"I've spent a lot of time with them in the last three months," I continued. "Whether you wish to accept my words or not, their... kind is as varied as our own. Very few are wholly evil. Very few are wholly good. Humans think differently, I grant you. I often struggle with some of their ways. But for the most part, what motivates our race also motivates theirs."

Sir Olythieu slammed his cane on the table. "Listen to the words coming out of your mouth, child. Are you their servant now? Is that what this is? Have you lured us in to betray us and your own grandmother?"

"*Bartley*," Lady Treena gasped.

I held up a hand. "It's okay, Lady Treena. I am aware of how this looks. That's why I tend to listen to talk of killing them all or dropping bombs without comment."

Tilting my chin, I stared across the table at my grandmother's most trusted friend.

"I will uphold my grandmother's legacy because I loved her. I believe in what she started. Bluff City is not a game board. The humans within it are not pawns. I say that with absolute conviction."

The older man relaxed.

I raised my voice. "With that said, don't make the mistake of thinking you're speaking to my grandmother when you're dealing with me. Her ideals are largely my ideals, her power is my power, but her experiences are not my experiences. I will act how I see fit based on the position I hold and the information I am privy to."

I stared at each of them in turn. "If you can't accept that my opinion of them is different to your own, that's fine. Though I respect each of you, I don't need your approval. I loved my grandmother. I risk my life every day for *her*. I've killed twice to avenge *her* death. Her approval is all I'm after, and don't you fucking dare insinuate that I won't do what needs to be done."

Gathering up the few files and my phone, I strode to the door and glanced back. "Call me child again, Sir Olythieu, and see what happens."

13

Something was buzzing.

I whacked Kyros. "Bumblebee."

"It's *your* bumblebee," he grumbled, rolling over me.

The buzzing stopped, and I relaxed.

"What?" he snapped. "You woke her up."

An irritating whining replied.

"Mosquito." I decided, nuzzling under the blankets.

Kyros snorted. "She thinks you sound like a mosquito."

I cracked an eyelid open. "Whosit?"

"Frannie."

Frannie was too innocent a name for that demon. "Make beeping sounds and hang up."

Kyros was straddling me, chest bare, firm muscles on display. *Holy shit.* Not a bad way to wake up.

"Oh, the fashion show," he murmured, grimacing my way.

I shot up, glancing at the alarm clock.

The vampire pushed me back down. "She'll be there in thirty."

"She better make it twenty."

Kyros disconnected, and I tried to sit again. He gently shoved me back down.

"I've got to shower," I said, batting at his hands.

His mouth covered mine, and I forgot the rest of my argument as I threaded my hands through his toffee strands.

I moaned into his mouth, arching upward and eliciting a hiss from him.

Snarling, Kyros broke away, lowering his head to the neckline of my silk camisole. *Lower.*

He sucked my nipple into his mouth, and I choked, writhing under the blanket between us as my entire body filled with fire.

"Ky—" I gasped, trying to kick the blanket barrier away.

His tongue lapped and he latched onto the other side, making me choke on a scream.

And then he was *gone.*

I sat, shoving away the thick blanket to chase him.

He stood across his lair, the circle sofa between us, grinning.

"Something to think about before tonight," he said, disappearing into the bathroom.

Bastard.

Motherfucking bastard!

The shower turned on, and the sound of his low whistling filled my ears. Even *that* turned me on at this point.

Staggering toward the kitchenette like the R-rated version of *Bambi* my life had become, I filled a glass with water.

The fashion show.

Exchange blood with vampire.

I sipped on my water. "Fuck. What a day."

At least Kyros was happy about it. Then again, what guy wouldn't be happy when guaranteed sex was on the horizon? The thing was, we hadn't had our usual discussion about the terms of this exchange.

And we needed to.

He exited, a towel wrapped around his hips.

Focus, Basi.

"Kyros?"

"Yes, mate."

My stomach fluttered. "We need to talk about the exchange. I have something I want to run by you."

Nerves erupted. None of them mine, and I studied his tense back. What? He thought I'd call it off?

I set my glass down and walked over.

As soon as I reached him, he spun us so my back was to the wall.

"Is everything a power play with you?" I asked, folding my arms.

He shrugged a shoulder. "Being an alpha makes some things necessary, yes. I ease the power in small ways to prevent it exploding in big ways. Does that bother you?"

"I'm getting used to most stuff, I guess," I mumbled, trailing off as I stared at the drop of water rolling down his neck.

He dipped his head down. "You had a suggestion."

I frowned up at him. "Yes."

"What was it, my beauty?"

It was...

Oh, yeah.

I took a breath. "Last time, I didn't like that others saw me during the thrall. It's normal for Vissimo, but it embarrassed me to be seen like that by your sisters."

His face hardened. "You can't be left alone, Basilia. I won't be able to handle that."

"If you listened, you'd realise that's not what I'm saying," I said, glaring at him.

Kyros quirked a brow. "You just stomped on my foot."

Not my problem. I'd given up on getting rid of the petulant stomp. I drove a golf cart around my estate now. Maybe I'd just embrace the hair toss and the hands on hips, too, like the brat I had enough money to be.

"You deserve it for kissing me and ditching."

His voice deepened, and the dreamy haze entered his eyes. "Your nipples are still hard."

And they'd probably stay that way until tonight. "I'm showering."

He latched onto my wrist. "What were you going to say?"

I tugged it free. "I was going to ask if *you* could stay with me during the thrall, but I've changed my mind."

Kyros's shock radiated through me, the searing blast soothed by his overwhelming want.

Slamming the bathroom door on him, I tore off my camisole and sleep shorts, setting the shower to lukewarm. I stepped in and grabbed my body wash left over from the last thrall. I refused to bring any clothing here, electing to bring a bag each time I stayed, so the toiletries were my only possessions in the lair.

Kyros hadn't said anything, but I knew he was bursting to demand I fill up one of the drawers in his dresser.

Lathering the lemon myrtle wash over my skin, I picked up my razor and set to work checking for body hair and ensuring my skin was smooth. Making quick work of my hair, I dried and moisturised my body in record time.

Towel wrapped tight around my frame, I marched back into the room and grabbed my clothes from the night before.

"You can borrow some of my sweats," he said, eyeing the pantsuit.

I had an understanding with Safina, and a deal was a deal. Plus, I didn't want to go down the boyfriend and girlfriend sharing clothes route.

Disappearing back into the bathroom, I dressed, and towel-dried my hair.

"Laurel is waiting to take you to Green," he said.

I looked at him for the first time.

Whoa.

Double whoa.

He wore a burnt-red blazer over a white shirt. Dark blue trousers and a belt that matched the blazer completed the smart-casual look. The sight of him dressed like that made my toes curl.

"Going somewhere?" I said hoarsely.

"To Frannie's fashion show," he said. "Pissing me off by putting my mate on the catwalk is pointless if I don't attend."

True.

"And if other men get to see you walking in a fashion show, I'm sure as fuck making sure they know you're taken."

I bit my lip. "Jealous, are we?"

"With you, always. Jealous of the time you're not with me. Jealous of the conversations you share with others. Jealous of the way you let your butler do everything for you but won't let me serve you a plate of food."

The words were delivered without a trace of bitterness. What was I meant to say to that? I hovered uncertainly.

"Everyone will be there," he said, continuing on as if he hadn't admitted to being jealous of Fred running around after me.

I licked my lips. "When you say *everyone*..."

"My parents too."

I ran my hand through my hair. "Great."

"I'll see you in a couple of hours," Kyros said as I grabbed my phone and walked to the door. Still shaken, I waved overhead in response.

The vampire called after me. "Basilia?"

Wrenching to a halt, I peered back at him. "Yeah?"

He bowed low. "I would be honoured to join you during your thrall."

Heat filled my cheeks as he straightened and fixed me with a smouldering look that I immediately titled Ovary Magnet.

"Okay. Good then," I said breathlessly.

Dammit.

His lips curled.

"Bye," I blurted, turning to run down the stairs as fast as my suddenly feather-light body could carry me.

My butter-blonde hair was dead straight, falling to just below my breasts.

Maybe it would cover whatever garish outfit Francesca put me in. As soon as I'd entered the main tent on the cordoned-off main street in Green, she'd marched me to a director's seat in make-up and disappeared.

I'd done a few catwalks for charity during my final years in high school. And some of those *buy a date* type events where they made everyone parade around before the auction.

"Look up," the make-up artist said.

My look was smoky eyes with a deep-plum lip. Nothing like the diamanté crap I'd expected her to subject me to. The artist didn't bat a false eyelash at the scarring on my neck before covering it with goop.

"*So glad you could make it,*" Francesca said on the other side of the curtain.

A woman sniffed. "*You paid me to be here.*"

No. She. Didn't.

If there was one voice whinier and more nasally than Francesca's, it was the voice of Harriet Gregorian.

"Look down," the artist said.

I gladly obeyed in a bid to hide my glare. I loathed Harriet Gregorian for many reasons. At the very top of that list was what she did to Tommy. The other girls may have held her down and ripped her clothes off with varying degrees of enthusiasm, but Harriet was the instigator. She was stupid and vicious to the core. The most dangerous combination in the world.

"Basilia," Francesca spoke from behind me. "Do you know Miss Gregorian?"

My lips twitched. That little brat. She'd done her homework. "The name does ring a bell. One of my maids, perhaps?"

The artist drew away, and I opened my eyes to witness Harriet's thin-lipped reaction.

"I thought you went to school together?" Francesca said, tapping her lip.

"We did," Harriet said, recovering. "We moved in different circles."

I moved by myself is what she meant.

Tilting my face to each side to check my appearance, I then winked at Harriet, drawling, "Honey, we still do."

Francesca's blue eyes met mine and her lips curled. She directed Harriet into the seat beside me and disappeared again.

Yeah, right.

Like she wouldn't listen to every word.

My phone buzzed.

What's so funny?

I typed a reply to Kyros.

Francesca brought in my high school arch nemesis to mess with me.

I'd fought off a psychotic vampire and it was hard to be anything but amused by Francesca's ploy, but maybe I'd dial up my reaction and make her feel like she'd won. Of all the siblings, Francesca kept me at the greatest distance. This could be a good time to build a bridge.

"I hope you checked into rehab after the appalling scene at your grandmother's funeral," Harriet said as the hairstylist started work on her.

I smiled at her in the mirror. "Not yet, actually. Maybe you could give me the name of the one you last attended."

She narrowed her eyes. "Everyone was talking about what you did. What an embarrassment you made of Agatha."

"You knew her so well."

"Everyone knew her well enough. Most of my childhood was spent at your estate."

That was a stretch of the fucking truth.

Unfortunately, Harriet had latched onto one subject that would get to me. The secret to dealing with rich bitches was to never let them know. "Then you knew what she thought of you, Harry."

The curse of being called Harriet—the nickname, Harry. It had

135

always sent her into a tantrum. Her emerald-green eyes flashed daggers.

"No one knows what anyone really thinks of them," she shot back.

I tossed my hair. "You don't know what I think of you? You sure?" Winking at the man styling her hair, I stage-whispered, "*She knows.*"

He smirked, wiping it away when Harriet lifted her glare to him.

"That Gregorian temper of yours is showing, darling," I said, inspecting my manicured nails. They'd painted them plum to match my lips. The tone was more severe than I tended to wear, but maybe I should give it a go sometime.

"You think you're so fucking above everyone, Basilia. Guess what, you aren't shit without your name. Being a Le Spyre doesn't make you untouchable."

She was spot on. I wasn't shit without my last name. Been there, experienced that.

"You're right, Harry," I said, pursing my lips. "On all counts."

She didn't answer me, watching me warily. No matter how many of these verbal sword fights I won, she always came back for more. Like besting me once would be her crowning glory. That was the way of the world I lived in though.

Pathetic.

"However, I'm a hell of a lot more without my name than you'd ever be without yours." I held up a finger. "And yes, in comparison to a Gregorian, I am fucking untouchable. You should remember that."

Harriet jerked forward in her seat, fists clenching.

"Ladies? How are you getting along?" Francesca popped into existence between us.

I tried to look vaguely pissed off.

Her smirk widened. "Basilia, come with me. I'll show you to your outfits."

Ugh, here we go.

Francesca led me to a rack directly behind the stage curtain, and my heart dropped out my ass.

"Lingerie," I said dully.

Bitch!

She peeked down and grimaced. "I hope you shaved."

Only because the act kept me sane. "Don't you worry about that. I expected to be dressed in monstrosities."

Anger sparked in her gaze. "I don't *design* monstrosities."

No, she didn't. I looked up her label as soon as Gerome dropped me in this thing.

I *had* expected her to make an exception for me.

"Which end do I start at?" There were five outfits—a bustier, negligee, camisole, and frilly panty set, a strappy number I couldn't make head or tail of, and a normal bra set.

"Bustier," she said, pointing to the back. "Change behind that curtain. You'll have three minutes between walks."

No kidding, there were at least twenty women and ten men in here.

I took the hanger and disappeared behind the curtain, joining another five women. Stripping off, I pulled on the G-banger first and forced my boobs into the bustier. *Jesus,* I was going to slip serious nip in this getup. Best not bounce too much.

An assistant came in and arranged my outfit, tugging up the thong, and yanking the garters into place before shoving me into blue-steel heels to match the set.

I pulled a face at the closest woman, who grinned, buck naked.

Francesca placed me at the front of the queue.

"You're such a shit," I told her.

She didn't respond. Smirking Francesca was no longer home. The vampire arranged my hair around my boobs that were nearly pushed up to my chin before pulling my bustier higher.

"My organs didn't need to be where they were anyway," I murmured.

She circled me, nodding. "Walk, pose, come back, grab the next outfit, change, and get in line. Your posture is excellent. Emphasise the bust on this one and the curve of your waist."

She snatched my phone away, shoving it in her pocket.

Even over the deep murmur and bustle back here, my new and improved ears made it impossible to ignore the crowd on the other side of the curtain. Music had started and a sultry beat created the sensuous backboard for a breathy soft-jazz singer.

The assistant who'd dressed or maybe violated me gripped the curtain rope. Francesca stood just behind the woman, determination lining her face.

The assistant counted down softly. "Ten, nine, eight."

The beat picked up, and the crowd hushed.

Fuck.

I was nervous.

What a time to decide that because Kyros was in the crowd. I needed to smash this out of the park. Usually, I didn't give walking in heels a second thought. Now, I couldn't remember how I managed walking on mini stilts. Should I put more swing in my hips? I didn't want to look like I was trying too hard.

"... five, four...."

"Think of Kyros," Francesca snarled.

Ooh, good idea.

Drawing up that morning's activities, I smiled as heat filled me, the current under my skin skyrocketing.

I blinked a few times as the curtain was drawn back and didn't need Francesca's hiss to start my walk.

The stage was straight and had no steps. *Thank fuck.* I kept my chin high while walking, clinging to the current moving just under my skin. What did I usually do with my arms when I walked? They felt so awkward right now.

Reaching the end, Francesca's hissed words echoed in my ears. Cocking a hip, I drew a finger along the top of my breasts, following the top of the bustier. I pushed the same hand down my side accentuating my narrow waist, scanning the front row for Kyros.

Ew. Henry Gregorian was there—Harriet's asshole dad.

His beady eyes drank me in.

Through our bond, I focused on Kyros's rampant appreciation and slight anger as I sauntered back up the runway, passing a brunette woman in a sheer black leotard.

I passed the curtain and hurried to my rack, grabbing the white negligee.

The assistant came in and helped me out of the first outfit and into the next, grabbing handfuls of my boobs to position them.

More than I got this morning.

Not that Kyros had received anything since the fourth exchange except my sleep grope. I had blue nipples, but his balls must be shrivelled and fallen off at this point.

"White negligee," Harriet sneered, changing into a siren-red number beside me. "How cute."

She actually looked pretty good.

"Don't steal that," I said. "I hear you have a theft problem."

Her face paled.

Thank you, Gina.

I rejoined the line, a bolt of adrenaline racing through me now I'd walked once. Harriet slipped in front of me just before I started my second run.

"Watch and learn." Harriet sauntered out, swinging her hips for all she was worth.

If Shakira was right and hips didn't lie, then Harriet Gregorian was a porn star.

"Go," Francesca grunted, ushering me out.

Kyros would be in knots over this number. One, he loved white. Two, anything that made me look vaguely innocent—like my glasses —turned him on big time.

I gasped as his reaction hit me. Working to control my expression, I couldn't help the rise and fall of my chest as my entire being vibrated with the tension between us.

Scanning the crowd, my eyes fell on the box at the very back, where a row of suspiciously large people loomed. I focused on the massive shadow to the right of the middle giant—who I assumed was King Julius.

The shadow shifted, and I smiled. *Yep,* that was Kyros.

Striking a pose, I disappeared behind the curtain soon after, repeating the chaotic process of throwing off one outfit to slip into another. Three minutes was *not* a long time when the worst-case scenario was getting shoved out onto stage half-dressed.

Next was the camisole and frilly panty set. I thought it was cute, but Kyros's reaction during my walk told me he preferred the white negligee. *Surprise, surprise.*

I strutted past Harriet on the stage and beamed at her. Her glare could have curdled milk. Man, she *really* hated me. What a weird grudge to fixate on. I'd done nothing to her except humiliate her a few times before ignoring her—and be born into a richer family. Was there seriously nothing bigger in her life to focus on?

The strappy black number was next and pushed the boundaries of the three-minute change time. The assistant clipped the choker around my neck while I rolled on the second thigh-high. She fastened the hem into the garter belt and gave me a once-over.

"Don't trip," Harriet hissed as I hurried past.

"Shouldn't be a problem. There's no trash on the runway until you step on it," I replied.

Fury twisted her face as I was dragged away.

Francesca adjusted the central strap that connected my choker to the middle of the bra. Strappy was the word for it. The bra was a criss-cross of satin. One band circled my waist. Panties under a garter belt, low denier thigh-highs, and black stilettos finished the look.

This time, the stilettos gave me no choice but to swing my hips.

I ignored the crowd, basking in Kyros's roaring approval as I posed at the end, hooking a thumb under the waist strap and biting my lip.

Total hussy.

Ignoring Henry Gregorian, who was almost drooling, I swung my sexy butt back in for the final outfit.

This was kind of fun. Maybe Francesca was only 99 percent of a brat—I was willing to admit when I was wrong.

The last one was a half-cup royal-blue set with a thong.

"*Um,*" I said, glancing down. "I'm not sure half a cup is enough."

The assistant eyed the precarious balance of my chest. "Don't make any sudden movements."

She checked the fastening—it was one of those bras that did up at the front.

I hurried to join the line when she was done.

Francesca checked Harriet over, shoving her through the curtain, and then glanced at my chest. Her brows shot up. "Careful now. Don't breathe."

Everything else fit perfectly. This was totally planned.

A few catcalls went up during Harriet's walk, the flash of cameras flickering through the crack in the curtain.

"Go time," Francesca said, drawing the drape back.

Carefully placing one white-heeled foot forward after the other, I did my best to glide down the stage without bouncing too much. Were my nipples showing because I was one sharp breath away from losing the battle.

Kyros liked this one too. A lot. Or maybe my nervousness turned him on too. Kind of made me want to buy a few things, but that was a definite line. Him watching me strut in lingerie via the medium of a catwalk, sure. I wasn't doing the show for him. Buying lingerie for him was way too personal. Like I'd be claiming him as a mate in return.

You'll drink his blood, but not wear nice panties.

When I'd come clean about everything, maybe then I'd consider wearing sexy things for him. If he still wanted anything to do with me.

Harriet posed, bending in half and sliding back up. My smile widened, and I felt Kyros's answering amusement.

Clever man, don't appreciate anyone else.

I searched for his shadow at the back again.

Oof!

Long legs tangled around mine and I went down like a sack of shit, Harriet Gregorian on top of me. The audience gasped, those sitting in the front seats shooting to their feet.

Nails clawed at my front, and then Harriet clambered off me.

As a woman with a bigger than usual chest, it was impossible not to feel the sudden freedom where the bra had cut in seconds ago.

Harriet smirked down at me, and I glanced at my chest.

The crowd gasped again, a horrified, *excited* murmur filling the tent.

"Oh my god! Are you okay?" Harriet whined, clutching either side of her face.

She wasn't going to help me up?

I gave her the benefit of the doubt for a second that I'd walked into *her*, but we were nearly over the stage edge on my side.

Bitch.

Sometimes the only way out of the mess was to wade further in. Fixing a smile on my face, I got to my feet. Gripping her shoulders, I air-kissed both her cheeks. Her smile dropped faster than her father's income would in the next hour.

Turning to the crowd, I held the two ends of my bra closed at the front. Until I reached the end, that is.

The crowd's shocked roar as I shimmied out of the bra was quite possibly the pinnacle of my life to date. Giving everyone a good look, I pivoted to walk back...

... Only to witness a petite woman with chestnut hair spear-tackle Harriet off the catwalk.

"Tommy?" I wrenched to a halt as Harriet screamed.

Harriet's shrieks punctuated the chaos I'd created by flashing the crowd. Tommy was laying into her like a fucking cage fighter.

But Harriet Gregorian was larger than her by far.

She shoved Tommy back, and my eyes narrowed to slits. Forcing back the urge to launch into the fight and kick Harriet's ass myself, I instead turned to look at her father.

He was already on his feet, but he tore his eyes from the fight when he felt my cool gaze.

I will ruin you, asshole.

And I absolutely would. The Gregorians really were trash. Maybe it was time to take them out.

He rounded the catwalk.

"*Harriet.*" His voice unfurled like a whip.

She froze, her fist positioned above Tommy's face. She was on her feet in a second. Blood trickled from a cut on her cheek and her nose.

"Daddy?"

Oh, brother.

"Stop disgracing yourself," Mr Gregorian snapped, striding to her. He hunched slightly as though that would make everyone forget this scene.

"But, Daddy, you saw her." She glared down at Tommy. "You better get ready to lose everything you fucking own, bitch."

Tommy laughed, clutching her side as she got to her feet. "I don't own anything. Have fun winning nothing."

Harriet snarled, lunging forward.

"*In the car,*" her father shouted, grabbing her around the waist. "*Now.*"

He shot a nervous look my way, and I didn't allow so much as a twitch to disturb the hard mask I'd put in place. If Tommy was hurt, his family could kiss the estates goodbye.

I walked to Tommy and reached down a hand to pull her onto the stage.

"Basi, your boobs are out," she whispered.

"Do they look good?"

"You betcha, lovely."

Happiness flooded through me. Looping an arm around her neck, I directed her back down the catwalk.

I had no idea why she was here. Or why she'd forgiven me fully enough to attack someone rich enough to bury her. I just knew that I'd never been more grateful for anything in my life.

We couldn't talk about it with Vissimo about, but when we entered the backstage area, I spun her toward me.

Her chestnut eyes shimmered and she hugged me tight, not saying a word.

I rested my head atop hers. "I'm so happy you're here."

She kissed my cheek, squeezing my hand.

How was this possible?

Tommy pulled away first.

"You're bleeding," she said, peering at my knees. "The cow wasn't even subtle about going for you. She pretended to trip, but everyone saw her clawing your chest."

Four vertical nail marks marred the middle of my chest, where she'd ripped through the clasp.

"That's gonna sting," I grunted.

"I'll find a first-aid kit," she said, disappearing into the next room.

The assistant fetched me the shirt I'd worn while in make-up, and I watched as the remaining women navigated the catwalk. Francesca went out to make her bows to the audience, and I escaped the line of models waiting to do the final walk. Kyros's temper was climbing. He needed to see I was okay.

Ignoring the blatant stares of the audience, I walked through their midst, beelining for the box at the back.

I locked eyes with Kyros halfway there.

His eyes were hooded. His fury evident without me needing to see the blazing green of his gaze.

I had one foot on the first step up to the box, when a champagne chute appeared in front of my face.

"Basi dear, I saw what happened," Lady Treena said, rage etched on her face.

"Aunt Treena, I didn't know you were coming." I blinked. How did they hear about this?

She waved a hand. "Hold my champagne, darling."

I obeyed, grabbing the chute, more than familiar with this game.

The older woman jabbed at her phone, tapping her foot as she waited. "Timothy. Answer faster next time. Henry Gregorian. What do we have on him?"

She listened, and I ducked down, tossing back her champagne as quickly as possible.

"I want him out. Entirely. Within the hour," she said. "Don't disappoint me."

Lady Treena hung up and hiccupped, snatching her chute back. "*More champagne.*"

I pursed my lips. "You didn't have to ruin him, Aunt Treena."

"No one draws blood from my goddaughter without being crushed," she said. "Perfect rack though, dear."

Bending, I kissed her cheek. "Thank you." *For talking to me after what I said in the meeting.*

She rested a hand on my shoulder.

"I want Henry Gregorian gone," a thundering voice clapped overhead.

Sir Olythieu snarled into his phone, cane gripped tight. "When do I want him out? *Yesterday*, Hannah. Do I need to spell everything out for you?" He hung up.

"What are you doing?" Lady Treena demanded. "I already ruined the Gregorians."

Sir Olythieu replied calmly. "Not if I get it done first."

He searched my gaze, and I did the same right back.

Exhaling, he took my hands. "Are you okay, Basilia darling?"

I gripped his hands. "Yes, but if you two have already ruined them, I'd like to buy their estate. It's opposite mine. I can build a bridge over the road and see what speed I can reach on my golf cart."

He kissed the back of my hand. "A wonderful idea. Perhaps redecorate the house though, darling. Gaudy new-money opulence. You know the type."

"That little cunt."

"Dame Burke," I greeted, turning.

"Have you two ruined the Gregorians yet?" she boomed. When they nodded, she reached into her purse, pulling out her phone. "Thought so. I'll humiliate them."

We watched her barrel away.

Phew. Harriet just well and truly fucked her family. I was just going to ruin Henry for a few years, not for life.

"Champagne," Lady Treena bellowed. "Bartley, help me find a filler upper. Poor people have no idea."

Sir Olythieu presented his arm. I wasn't fooled for a single second.

They knew the vampires were here today. They probably knew they were in the box right behind us.

My oldies just drew a line in the sand while showing me everything between us was okay. That made me feel so much stronger.

I ran up the steps, straight into Kyros's waiting arms.

His quiet growl slipped between us as he stroked my hair, then held me at arm's length. "I saw."

I shrugged. "Yeah, she's been after me for a while."

He peered after my oldies. "It appears she's been dealt with."

His family was all here, aside from Francesca, but they sat watching our exchange in silence.

"Never fuck with old money," I quipped. "They're about as ruthless as they come."

Kyros's gaze was fixed on my knees.

"Tommy's finding a first-aid kit. I'll go sort this out."

"I can handle it," he said, nostrils flaring.

I shoved him gently. "I know." *He couldn't.* "I'd like to find her."

"*Francesca! What happened today? Was it a design flaw?*" a woman said.

Cameras flashed.

Kyros peered over my head, his mouth tightening.

"*Just an incident,*" she answered, the anger in her voice plain.

I groaned and heard Rory's groan too. That wasn't the way to deal with the media.

Untangling myself, I marched down the stairs to where reporters had holed Francesca up.

"Miss Le Spyre! Flashing the audience. I'm certain they won't forget that any time soon."

Stopping beside Francesca, I wrapped an arm around her slim waist and cocked a brow at the man. "They're real too."

He chuckled.

"Can we take your participation in the show to mean the Le Spyre empire supports this label?" a woman asked.

Francesca tensed.

"*Ornate* produces sustainable and ethically-made clothing that meets and exceeds global standards in the Fairtrade Practices Act," I replied coolly. "The designs demonstrate a left-turn from the fast fashion practices that promote slave labour and negatively impact the environment. While upholding those incredible values, Francesca manages to combine the trends of today with a classic feel that ensures women and men can wear her garments for years to come. Her work is nothing short of genius. Long answer short, I wholeheartedly support her outstanding label." I scanned the reporters, arching a brow. "Now, if you'll excuse us. My knees are bleeding, and I'm sure you can appreciate that Francesca will be in hot demand for the foreseeable future."

They snapped pictures as I directed her back through the crowd.

She allowed me to for a full minute before snapping out of her funk.

"All that stuff you said," she said, grabbing my forearm. "Did you mean it?"

"My family name is synonymous with ethical practices, Francesca. I researched *Ornate* as soon as the show was mentioned. If I'd found your label lacking in any way, I wouldn't have walked, no matter the favour I owed Gerome."

A small smile graced her face.

"You need to practice dealing with the media. Let me know if you want help. Or I suppose Rory is decent at it."

"I may just take you up on that," she said breezily, handing my phone over.

Tommy waved from the stage.

"Gotta get cleaned up." I dialled Daniel as I strode toward Tommy.

"Miss Le Spyre."

"Daniel, if there's not already, half-naked pictures of me will be covering the internet."

He cleared his throat. "Already on it, miss."

"Thanks."

"Harriet Gregorian did it?"

"Yep."

"I'll make sure the picture of her ass is the top search result."

I snorted. "Thanks, Daniel."

"All in a day's work, Miss Le Spyre."

I let Tommy direct me to a seat where she set to work on my knees.

I watched her work, shedding the armour I'd just donned to deal with the crisis outside. My hands shook as the impossibility of her presence hit me anew. I didn't dare feel joy even with her tending my wounds.

"Will I live?" I asked in a trembling voice.

She stuck the final Band-Aid in place and scrubbed at the trails of blood down my shins with an alcohol wipe. "I prescribe you medicinal tequila shots for the next three days. With regular consumption, you should bounce back in no time."

"You spear-tackled Harriet Gregorian off the stage," I informed her gravely.

Tommy's face was grim. "Yeah. I did."

I cracked a grin.

Her chin wobbled.

We reached for each other, rolling on the floor as we hooted our damn heads off.

"What were you *thinking*?" I asked between gasps. "You're the height of her legs."

Tommy sucked in a breath. "I saw red when I realised she ripped your bra off. What kind of low-life trash does that?"

I wiped my eyes. "Daniel's wiping everything, but I need a video of that. We'll add it to our time capsule."

"The one we dig up each year to add stuff to, but end up going through the contents because we can't wait ten years?"

Yep.

A shadow fell over us.

Tommy tensed.

So did I.

"Basilia," Kyros said. He studied my knees. "I see Tommy has taken care of you."

I sat, and he gripped my arms, pulling me to my feet without effort.

"Uh, yeah. I'll be ready to go soon."

"There's an afterparty." He shot a look at Tommy, who was dusting off her hands and butt.

"No, thanks. Let's just head to your place." I hesitated, glancing at my friend. We had a lot to talk about if her change of heart wasn't a moment of insanity.

Kyros smiled. "I can pick you up in a few hours if you prefer."

He was smiling, but inside he was devastated.

Tommy grabbed my arm. "You have a date planned. Don't worry about me. I'll head back to my place and we can catch up another time."

"Tom, please don't go back to wherever you're staying. Go to the estate."

She peered up at me, her eyes filling.

"Your father too."

Her throat worked as she swallowed, and I wrapped her in my arms. "I won't take no for an answer. I'll be away for a few days, but there's an ice-cream musical marathon with our names on it when I get back."

"Love you, Basil." She sniffed hard.

A fierce protectiveness surged within me. I didn't know why she was here, but I was determined to never let her go. "I love you more, Tom."

14

"I know you like my house better, but I thought you might want a soundproof room for this thrall," Kyros said. "I'd prefer guarding a space with only one entrance if truth be told."

I nodded, nerves fluttering in my stomach as he navigated the car through Green. "What will happen?"

We'd been through four thralls but never spent one in the same room.

"Sex, Basilia. Lots of it. I won't hurt you though, if that's what worries you. My urge to protect you is greater than the urge to mate, as you know."

I stared ahead, not really seeing anything. "Okay."

He shot me a look. "You were having fun on the catwalk in the beginning. Before that woman." A menacing growl filled the vehicle.

"I was, actually." Francesca shoved a bag into my hand before I left too. "It wasn't all bad at the end. Tommy came back."

Kyros was quiet.

"You can tell me how that came to happen any time you'd like." I arched my brows. "I saw the weird looks between you two."

He directed us onto the freeway. "Two days ago, I went to the hostel where she and her father were staying. I spoke with her and explained the situation with Theodore."

I stiffened. "That's all you did?"

"I didn't compel her," he growled.

Consider me surprised that hadn't even crossed my mind. "I meant that Tommy was inconsolable two weeks ago. How the hell did you convince her?"

He pressed his lips together. "I showed her the video."

I gasped. "The video of me killing Theodore?"

Kyros clenched his jaw.

"How could you do that?" I demanded, twisting to stare at him. "She *loved* him."

"She loved what he made her love. Your friend didn't love Theodore Tonyi. When she saw what he did to you in the video, Tommy understood the distinction. Just as she understood what you'd done for her and what you went through. I went back to the hostel this morning and asked her to attend the fashion show."

I was *appalled* he'd shown her the video.

I'd shrivel up and die inside if I had to watch Tommy go through that.

"Please delete the video," I murmured, crossing my arms.

"I'd like nothing more," Kyros said. "My father has ordered me to watch your ordeal until I can control my reaction to it."

Shock hit me. "That's *sick*."

"It's working," Kyros disagreed. "At first it took me hours to calm down. Now I can get through the video without breaking too many things."

"How have I not noticed that?" A wrinkle formed between my brows.

"I wait until you're asleep. At the start, I'd return to find you strangling the pillows."

I'd sleep-reacted to his anger? "I wish you wouldn't do that to yourself. I don't want you to see me that way."

"To see a courageous woman fighting off a man who has every advantage to save the person she loves?"

151

I fell silent.

When he pulled into the garage of *Kyros Sky*, my nerves returned full force. Neither of us spoke until we entered the elevator.

"Thank you for letting me handle what happened today," I said, studying my appearance in the mirror. I couldn't wait to wash the make-up off my face. "That meant a lot."

Kyros's gaze landed heavy on me. "I couldn't trust my reaction. My eyes were too bright."

Oh.

"That's something you value, I take? Your ability to handle situations like today?" He pressed.

Today was a craziness of its own. "I value your confidence in me, yes. You can physically handle nearly anything, and you have so much experience. I find it empowering when you trust me to protect myself."

He was quiet on the walk to his lair.

I could feel him mulling over what I'd said, so I entered the bathroom without disturbing his reverie and stripped out of the shirt and royal-blue underwear.

The water hit the long scratches down my chest and stung like shit, but I twisted my hair into a knot and scrubbed the stress of the show away, cleaning the layers of make-up off my face.

Sighing happily, I dried off and wrapped the towel around me.

A quick peek in the bag Francesca gave me revealed the white negligee I wore earlier. With the nail marks, it wouldn't look as cute.

Clad in the towel, I entered the room.

Kyros had removed his red blazer and shoes and sat on the round sofa with his legs outstretched. I perched on the edge, staring around his lair and wondering how many walls would remain in three days.

"Are there a lot of other Vissimo who do multiple exchanges with humans?" I asked.

"The term is mate, Basilia. Not multiple exchanges," Kyros said, tipping his head back against the sofa to meet my gaze. Toffee strands splayed over his face.

He was so fucking handsome.

Reaching over, I brushed them back into place. "I know."

His gaze softened, and he caught my hand, kissing the back before releasing it.

"Yes, a few. One clan in particular, Koani, have a history of relationships with humans—not necessarily with their permission. That's where I discovered information about how long it would take you to adjust after the fourth exchange."

"How long will it take this time?"

"Not as difficult. You'll need to minimise exertion for everything, but these changes aren't as dramatic. You'll have around 10 percent of the speed and strength of the weakest of our kind, whereas the strength of your senses matches theirs."

I loosened the knot in my straightened hair as I remembered the words in the mating ritual book. "Are you ready for how powerful you'll become after this exchange?"

My joke fell flat.

Dang.

"What I mean to say is that I'm sorry you don't get much from mating with a human," I said, clearing my throat.

He cast me a strange look. "I have more power than I can always control, Basilia. The thought of holding more inside terrifies me daily. Our blood sings for a reason, and that's because you are powerful in other ways; ways that won't cause me to—"

"—wreak havoc on the world?" I finished softly.

More than my conversations with them, I'd started to pay more attention to the differences between Kyros and his siblings, and the way the clan minions treated him in comparison. The difference wasn't that Kyros was the crown prince or slightly more powerful—which was the assumption I'd made long ago. It was because he would be *the* most powerful vampire in existence one day.

"You kept your potential destiny awful quiet, fang man," I whispered.

His gaze darkened. "Who have you been talking to?"

Gina. Laurel.

"It doesn't matter. Why didn't you tell me?"

"You were scared enough."

I sighed. "I could share that fate, Kyros. Will you always decide how much you think I should know because you're worried I can't handle it?"

"If you let me."

That deserved a massive eye-roll, and I gave it to him.

Kyros tugged my arm, and I toppled onto his lap with the grace of an ice-skating donkey but managed to keep a hold on my towel.

He *arranged* me so I sat across his lap.

Kyros trailed a finger over the top of the largest scratch, and I hissed at the sting.

A shadow crossed his eyes.

"Kyros?"

"I like it when you call me Ky," he interrupted. "Even if you only called me that because ecstasy robbed you of two-syllable words. *Ky—*"

I couldn't recall saying that, but I had no doubt my mind was otherwise occupied at the time. My lips twitched. "Is that what's happening?"

"Yes."

I'll give you that one.

I hesitated, deciding to voice something that had weighed on my mind since after the attack. "You've said a couple of times that you've compelled people in the past. Who are they?"

His lips curved. "Jealousy."

Something I hoped to never feel. "It seems that way."

Kyros wrapped his arms around me, bringing his lips against my ear. "You're jealous, but not murderously so. If you shared blood with another, I'd kill them without second thought. I'm not sure I could stop myself."

I shivered, knowing he spoke the cold truth.

"I've shared blood with other humans and one vampire in the past," he said. "One exchange with each of them, simply to control them. They're dead now."

Thank fuck for that.

"They were all male."

I blew out a breath. "Okay. Thanks. I guess the thought bothered me."

"It's a weak male who prefers a jealous woman. Though with everything you're doing to push me away, I can't deny your possessiveness soothes my ego."

Not bothering to deny my possessiveness, I straddled him. "Nothing can hurt your ego. Are we going to break the place then?"

A laugh startled out of him. "You want to break my lair?"

Ha! He said lair.

"*Please.* Three days of sex. You can't tell me your mind hasn't drawn up all kinds of fantasies. What surface? What position? How many times?"

His fangs descended.

Fascinated, I stroked one, careful to avoid the sharp tip. He closed his eyes, shuddering.

My voice was dry. "I'll take that as a yes."

"I haven't had three days off in one hundred and thirty-five years."

"You think you're having three days off? Maybe this won't be quite as good as I expected."

His smile was smug. "You know better than that. I've been dreaming of this since the first exchange. I plan to enjoy every millimetre of your skin several times."

Good. Because it was burning up.

I dropped the towel, meeting his gaze. "Don't break the sofa, and that's an order. Everything else is fair game."

Kyros gripped my hips through the pooled towel. His green eyes held a wild edge as he took me in slowly.

"You're so beautiful, mate. I'm not sure what I did to deserve you."

Heat rushed to the surface, chasing the trail his eyes made over my frame. I fidgeted as the current between us inched higher, spreading to my curled toes and trembling fingers. Soon, I wouldn't be able to control myself.

I didn't plan to.

"*My mate,*" he said fervently.

Kyros leaned forward to trail his tongue between my breasts over the long scratches, and air lodged in my throat.

"I've been hard all day," he said against my stomach. "Watching you walk in that lingerie was fucking torture."

A sassy retort died on my lips as he took one of my nipples in his mouth.

Wait.

Not this time.

I was sick of being the receiver. Sensing the shift in my mood, he rested back, watching me with dark curiosity. I smiled and started on the buttons of his shirt.

"What are you doing?"

"Undressing you." I peeked up through my lashes, shoving his shirt off his shoulders.

His body vibrated, and my eyes fluttered closed as I relished the precarious control he had over the urge to touch me—to *claim* me.

Admiring the firm expanse of his chest, I undid his belt and drew the zipper of his trousers down.

His breath hitched as I trailed my nails over his erection through the material.

"Lie down," I instructed.

He shifted us before easing onto his back, fangs fully descended now. I grinned saucily, inching his pants down until he sprang free.

A sound—half growl, half moan—slipped between his teeth.

Sweeping my hair aside, I didn't waste time taking him in my mouth.

Our groan filled my ears. The *feel* of him between my lips. *Jesus*, the taste of him. That had to be the blood bond because no woman could actually like that shit.

Except I did.

Holy fuck, did I ever.

He hissed as I bobbed and retreated, licking his length. Paying attention to every bit of available satin skin. I wrapped my hand around his base, not breaking the steady pace of my lips and tongue.

Kyros tortured me this morning.

I was returning the favour.

The vampire cursed in a blur of words, collecting my hair when it fell in a thick curtain between us.

I circled my tongue around his tip, and his hips jerked as he shouted.

Smirking, I retreated, drawing my nails down his thighs until some of the tension drained from his body.

Then I went back for round two, pushing him closer to the edge.

"Enough," he panted.

Ignoring him, I took as much of him in my mouth as possible. His deep groan was music to my ears for the split second before I was flipped onto my back.

I winked up at him.

"Disobedient," my vampire purred, his eyes burning green. "You give me orders but ignore mine."

"You don't want me to finish what I started?" I asked, tilting my head.

His smile faded and his hot menace made my entire lower half clench.

"I wouldn't say that, vixen." Leaning down, he kissed me, prying my lips apart with his tongue.

I sighed, savouring the warm sensation of his mouth and lips.

He pulled back and knelt on the ground, positioning his head between my legs. *Oh, god.* A low cry fell from my lips, drawn from my very soul, as he applied a hard and slow pressure with the flat of his tongue. My toes curled to cramping point, and I arched upward, hands clutching my face.

"Fucking *goddess*," he said raggedly.

He did the same thing again, and I rode the wave of pleasure, using his face as he set a steady pace. My body rose and fell in crests. My hips jerked and his lips curved against me, unrelenting with the constant pressure and speed.

He knew I wanted more.

It didn't matter though.

The cloud-like awareness took over. White-hot bliss was around the corner, and the finality of how this would end only pushed me higher. My body slackened as languidness took over—my toes unfurled, numbness crept over my mind, my body was rendered powerless against the intensity of his masterful mouth.

"*Fuck*," Kyros hissed, his massive hands tightening on my thighs. "I can feel you coming."

His words hardly reached me. The bomb detonated. I imploded, *everything* within me drawing into a tiny point before pleasure catapulted outward.

Kyros pinned my legs wide open as I came apart with the force of my orgasm. My choked gasp turned to a scream as his fangs entered the inside of my thigh.

"Ky—" I cried out.

His growl was savage. He pulled blood from my femoral artery, and I froze as the ecstasy somehow surged *higher*, transporting me into territory I would never return to.

Or so I thought.

His finger slid inside me, working in and out. I shouted, bucking against the arm pinning me down.

Rapture.

Bliss.

It couldn't end.

I didn't want it to end. A whimper left my lips.

The vampire licked my leg, before pulling me up to my knees, his finger still hooked inside me.

My body shook with the force of aftershocks. Ripping snarls filled his chest and the room, but I felt nothing but an inferno of desire. He slid his finger free of me and rose to stand, so my face was level with his hips. Holding my heavy gaze, the vampire bit his wrist.

My heart thundered as he brought his wrist to the middle of his chest.

Thick blood trickled down his torso, and I didn't give my actions a second thought. My tongue was ready to intercept the stream. I sucked and swallowed, making sure not to miss a single drop as I cleaned his rigid abdomen to the soundtrack of his growls and groans.

I craned to reach higher, pulling myself up using his arms to lap at the trail of red coating his centre line. I wanted it all.

Higher.

A soft whine slipped from my lips as I suckled all the way to his wrist.

I snatched at his arm, greedily latching my mouth around the wound to draw as hard as possible as the insatiable fire of the thrall bore down on me.

I wanted to be consumed.

Kyros spun me in his arms, my mouth still clamped around his wrist.

His blood. The feel of his hardness against my back. It was too much and not enough.

His lust slammed into me, and he hooked one of my legs with his free arm. Reaching down, I rose on tiptoe and positioned him at my entrance before slowly sinking down.

We both sighed, a brief pause in the desperate, pulsing chaos.

Then the fire rose to a desperate inferno.

In a blur, Kyros hooked my other leg, my knees bent over his forearms. Arching, I looped my hands behind his neck as he spread me wide in front of his tower window.

"*Mine,*" his low voice rumbled in my ear.

I twisted my head and claimed his mouth. My eyes surely blazed brighter than his. I tried to move my hips again as he pulled out so only his tip was inside me.

It was useless.

I was at his mercy.

My vampire enjoyed that, but he was waiting for something.

"*Mine,*" I growled back.

Kyros shoved into me.

15

My feet hooked around his ass as I helped his slow thrusts into me.

Our gazes were locked. Nearly nose to nose, sweat slickened our bodies. We existed alone in bliss, and there wasn't any hurry.

My vampire's pulses were almost lazy, and I smiled sleepily up at him.

"Mine," he whispered, trailing his nose from my jaw to temple.

I gripped his forearms as our bodies tightened and we crested a wave that was one of thousands.

This wouldn't end.

Our world would always be shared pleasure, equal pleasure, double the joy for experiencing it myself and through him.

"Ky," I breathed, my blinks slow and heavy.

"Mate."

He stayed inside me, rolling us to the side. My mouth was tender, and so his kiss was whisper soft.

Kyros tilted my chin, and I frowned at him, shivering as the fire surrounding me edged away.

I blinked at the loss of it, exhaling shakily with my sudden terror.

"There's nothing to fear, my beauty. The thrall is ending," he said, kissing my forehead.

The thrall?

I frowned as the last of the mindless fire drained away. Pushing up, I peered around us.

I gasped.

Oh my god. The thrall!

"Is there anything left?" he rasped, not budging his focus from my face.

I glanced down. We were on top of blankets on the floor. "The sofa. Thank you."

Kyros snorted.

My jaw dropped as I glanced around. Because I remembered everything this time.

Every. Single. Thing.

What was I supposed to say after three days of mind-blowing sex with a vampire? "I didn't black out."

He eyed me. "You didn't?"

I shook my head. Sex in the shower, on the dresser, the bed, the walls, the kitchen bench, and the mirror. It was all there. "How am I still standing?"

"You're not," he drawled.

Someone was feeling proud of himself.

Honestly? He should.

He brushed his thumb along my collarbone, eliciting a sigh. "You heal faster now, and I helped you a few times, if you recall."

Blood flooded my cheeks. "I recall."

"Thought you might."

I shifted, and my eyes widened. "You're still inside me!"

Kyros peered down. "So I am."

I choked on a laugh.

He pulled free, and I did my best not to acknowledge the mounting heat in my cheeks as he did. We'd never done this part before—the *immediately after sex* part.

He cradled me in his arms, holding me tight.

"I don't want to stand in case I can't," I admitted after a few minutes.

"I'm not sure I can manage it either."

"Wait, you're saying I wore your ass out?"

"I already knew you were creative, vixen. That quality extends to the bedroom."

Grunting, he got to his feet with me in tow and weaved toward the bathroom.

Kyros *really* couldn't walk. My body shook as he leaned against the tiled wall in the shower and slid to the ground.

"Would you rather walk?" he asked, setting me on the tiles beside him. We'd broken the shower partition and the mirror. *Damn.*

I reached up and turned the shower on in answer.

Tried to.

My jaw dropped as the handle came away in my hand. "Shit. I broke the shower."

Kyros grinned. "Well, we're fucked because I can't walk any farther." He took the black handle from me and fitted it overhead, twisting. Water poured out, and when it warmed, I slithered on my belly under the jet.

"Oh my god, you need to feel this," I said, laying there as the water pounded down on my aching body. This is why I didn't do exercise other than swimming. Exercise came with consequences.

Kyros gripped my ankles and pulled himself beside me.

"That feels incredible," the vampire murmured, his eyes weary.

"Would it be bad to nap here?"

The graphite tiles felt like a cloud. My limbs were so heavy. I needed to sleep for a week. Because of sex.

He mumbled, "Waste of water."

"*Mmm*," I murmured.

Fingertips grazed my cheekbones. The sensation lulled me, and my body relaxed.

I was powerless to open my eyes.

"I love you, Basilia Le Spyre," Kyros whispered.

With the last of my conscious effort, I rested my hand against his chest and smiled.

"Bitch, get up."

"Better have my money," I snapped from sleep's hold.

Tommy snorted. "Bitch better have my money? I actually get that one."

No. Only Kyros got my delirious waking-up talk.

I squinted over my shoulder. "Dayzit?"

"Friday morning. 8:00 a.m. You slept for eighteen hours."

No shit.

My last memory was of stumbling into the house after Queen Titania dropped me off because she was the only other person who knew the code to Kyros's lair. Everything between the end of the thrall and now was a hazy blur. "*Whoa.*"

Tommy's hand rested on my chest. I peered down and only twigged when she clawed her hand.

The scratches were gone.

Tommy threw off the bedspread.

Yep, my knees were healed too.

She held up a hand, wiggling her five fingers. I nodded after a beat, realising what she was asking. And this time, Kyros and I exchange more than blood and sex. What we'd shared was so much more.

Fuck.

My body was begging me to go back to sleep, eighteen-hour slumber notwithstanding. But Tommy was here, and apparently, five days had passed since the fashion show.

"Office," I croaked.

"I was given instructions to make sure you read this."

I took the note from her, squinting.

Remember you may be a little faster and stronger, true mate of my eldest son.

- Queen Titania

I blew out a breath. "You read it?"

Tommy's eyes were wide as she nodded.

That's my girl.

Recalling Kyros's words to exert myself less, I pretended my body was wading through mud as I sat and then stood.

That felt too slow.

I pretended I was moving through water instead of mud as I walked between the bed and door. "How did I go?"

Tommy squeaked, "Jerky."

Crap.

Picking somewhere in the middle, I reached for the door handles.

"Better," she murmured, sounding faint.

Focusing on my arms, I imagined the force needed to move a feather and pulled. The doors opened halfway. *What's heavier than a feather?*

I imagined gripping a stick and pulled again. The doors crashed against the walls either side.

"Oops," I said as Tommy gasped.

I'll work on that.

Clinging to the watery-mud sensation, I walked through the house beside a very quiet Tommy. As soon as we reached the office, she shut the door and ran for the noise-cancelling button.

She turned to me. "Holy fuck. You're a vampire."

I held my hands apart and wriggled the fingers of one. "Human." Then I wriggled the fingers of my other hand before slicing through the middle.

"You're somewhere between?" she said, circling me. "Faster and stronger. Anything else?"

I didn't know how to tell her about the changes after the last thrall, so she had no idea my senses were better now, unless Kyros said something. Thinking of Dumbo, I touched my ears. Then thinking about when I'd next get to the spa for a facial, I touched my eyes, nose, mouth, and skin in turn. "Senses."

"Is this normal?" Tommy asked in a strangled voice.

I dipped my head.

Her breath came fast. Giving her a moment, I walked to the desk at a hopefully normal pace and picked up each of the objects in turn, trying to find the right level for my strength.

Kyros would have some tips.

At the thought of him, my stomach swooped, and fierce longing swept through me. Lust was there, but *this* wasn't the same.

Where was he right now? What was he doing? A quick check told me he was asleep. I wanted to be next to him, hugging his back, breathing him in.

Which wasn't good. *At all.*

What was I thinking? I should have spent the thrall with his sisters.

Shaking my head, I faced Tommy.

"You'll be better able to protect yourself," she whispered, and her face firmed. "Good."

My confusion over her presence here was strong enough to edge between my longing and despair. "Tom, I love that you're here again. And Kyros told me what he showed you. It's just... I need you to explain what's going on in your head because I never expected to see you again after our last conversation."

I perched on the desk as she sprawled on the chaise.

"Okay," she said, taking a deep breath as she rolled onto her back. "Here's the list. I loved Theodore—or the person I thought he was. I've never let myself feel that much for a person. Then once I had, he was gone and you were here. I couldn't blame him, and I couldn't accept he was a Vissimo or that he'd lied. My mind went into overload. I could see that you were having trouble telling me what you needed to, but I couldn't listen to the words coming out of your mouth. I didn't even blame you. I blamed Kyros. Through you, he'd killed Theodore."

She swung up to sitting. "Kyros found me and showed me the video. He made me watch it three times. After that, I chose to watch it a fourth time so the truth sank in." Tommy dropped her head into her hands. "Basi, how can *you* forgive *me* after that? Kyros told me that you walked right into the hands of the triplets, making sure he couldn't follow you. They placed a bomb around your neck. Fuck, you must have been terrified out of your mind."

Lifting her head, she looked at me. "You did that to save my life. Then you came back to tell me my boyfriend was a psychopath so I could move on. And I slapped you around the face for it."

"I deserved it, Tom," I told her. "I failed to protect you when I brought you into this mess. You were depending on me, and I should have insisted on meeting Theodore. Looking back, it was so obvious. It's just that he was in your life before I knew about any of this. Which is zero excuse, really."

Her face slackened. "That's ridiculous. That's... no."

Yes.

"How are you doing?" I asked softly. "He still broke your heart. You nearly died from whatever he gave you."

Tommy peered up at the ceiling, blinking several times. "I've wondered whether it's better or worse that Theodore wasn't who or what I thought. He'd be dead now, but at least I'd be able to mourn the love we shared. I feel like because the person I loved was a lie, my grief is a lie too. Like I have no right to feel the way I do."

I crossed at human pace to join her on the chaise, very carefully wrapping an arm around her shoulders. "Can't you grieve the lies though? Even if you find it hard to mourn the man you loved?"

She wiped her face, sniffing hard. "I'm not sure how I have tears left. I wish they'd stop. I'm so angry at him."

"He paid for what he did to you and my grandmother."

Fresh tears squeezed from her eyes. "Kyros told me about Agatha too. The three of them stressed her heart until it gave out. Fucking sick monsters."

Sadness over my grandmother didn't always weigh heavy, but today her words hit me hard. "Yes, they did. So there are two more to kill."

"They must be pissed about their brother."

"I'd say so. Especially when one of them pressed the remote button that set off the bomb."

A cruel smile unfurled across her face, then her vulnerability snapped back into place. "I'm not sure it was always Theodore I spent time with, Basil."

I stilled.

"I think they took turns," she whispered.

Letting her go in case I accidentally hurt her, I said, "You're sure?"

"He'd act strangely sometimes. I thought he was tired or stressed about work. There were moments when he couldn't recall something we'd discussed the day before."

I brought her into this world, and she'd been used by three guys. *Raped.*

"Tom," I said, my voice breaking. "I am so sorry for bringing you into this. I should have been stronger and kept pushing you away. I'm just so fucking *sorry.*"

She cut off my babbling apology. "You said yourself that Theodore approached me before you knew about vampires. Your position in the tower—the mating thing with Kyros—drove him to hurt me in that specific way, perhaps. But he—*they*—were always going to use and hurt me in some way. You had nothing to do with how they treated me, apart from being my friend. And that's not a burden you're allowed to take on."

Being the poor friend of a rich woman had consequences that Tommy occasionally struggled with, but it never should have led to this. But maybe I shouldn't blame myself entirely for the actions of a supernatural race I hadn't known existed until recently.

I rubbed my nose. "I hate when you're logical. Let me feel like shit."

"Whatever. That's a cop-out. *You* just had three days of sex that turned you into superwoman. *I'm* miserable. Your mission is to pretend the shit out of happiness, so I can continue to wallow."

I snorted. "Pretend the shit out of happiness. What have you been watching?"

"*Truth Ranges.* I wouldn't need to explain that quote to you if you were a real fan."

"Take that back."

"Nope," she declared.

Standing, Tommy held out her hand. "Come on. Let Fred cover estate jobs today. You're mine until midnight."

I slapped my hand into hers, and she reeled away, clutching it.

"Fucker!" she hissed.

Shooting to my feet, my eyes and ears weren't ready for my new speed. I sprawled across the low table, whacking my hands down as I tumbled over it and landed on the carpet.

I groaned, rolling onto my back to glare at Tommy.

Her shoulders shook as she nursed her hand. "Don't glare at me, I didn't make you do that. But I'm so glad you did."

She tipped back her head and laughed, tears streaming over her cheeks.

Scowling, I clambered to my feet, dusting myself off. Apparently I needed to practice using my senses with the new additions to my body.

"Change of plan," Tommy announced, taking my hand. "Let's go to the nut orchard and figure out how to manage your superpowers."

Baby powers, more like it.

I pursed my lips. "Maybe that's a good idea."

16

I stared at the latest *Ingenium* forecast.

Eighteen days.

That's how long Clan Sundulus had until Fyrlia triggered the end cascade. They'd purchased two properties in Black yesterday for astronomical prices.

They sensed the kill. They were hunting their enemy—cornering them.

I had to move without delay. Yes, I'd hoped to do this without Sandra being compelled, but I'd also been stalling for personal reasons.

I couldn't lose these people.

"Basilia? Your thoughts?" Rory broke my reverie.

I jumped and stared around the table. It was Friday and Kyros had returned from King Mikael's side just after one. The others were here. "On what?"

"On investigating their finances," he snarled, fangs descending. "They're throwing ridiculous sums of money into every industry."

I lifted a shoulder. "So would I if I sensed the kill."

No one reacted to the statement.

Kyros was quiet.

Whatever Mikael and the Fyrlia royals were doing to him during the Friday get-togethers, it was taking a toll. I knew for a fact he wouldn't fill me in, but for now, I was just satisfied with his contentedness when we were in close quarters.

And that's why I had to do this. The thought of him never forgiving me was unbearable, where it never had been before. If I let my lie go any further, that was the risk.

I drew in a breath, settling at his earthy scent.

"What's the final plan?" I glanced at my phone. The call with King Julius was in five minutes.

Lalitta's gaze was fixed on the table. Rory looked murderous. Gerome grinned so tightly I thought his lips may snap off. Safina had her arm around Francesca. Neelan was still. Lionel watched everyone else, sadness in his eyes.

Fuck it all.

No amount of research was going to confirm what Sandra's fate would be. I was talking to business owners. A deal could be negotiated. That was my only option.

She'd emailed this morning asking for more funds and an update. The worry in her short message was clear. Dragging this out wasn't fair for anyone.

Time to come clean.

Panic pulsed through me.

Clearing my throat, I said, "I've found something."

Kyros was already watching me.

The others didn't budge.

I took a breath. "Proof of foul play in the Mr Ringly deal."

A hand was over my mouth.

Neelan cautioned me with his hazel eyes.

I pried his fingers away, nodding to show I understood his warning. "Before I tell you what I know, a deal must be negotiated to protect the human witness from being harmed or controlled in any way."

Safina pulled out her phone. "Father will want to handle this."

Kyros held up a hand, and she paused.

He held my gaze. "How long have you known?"

I tilted my chin. "One week."

His jaw clenched, but I didn't offer any excuses. I'd already expressed my concerns by opening the negotiation for Sandra's safety.

Kyros watched me. "King Julius will want to speak to you personally. Are you ready for that?"

Nope.

"Yes." I hesitated. "There's more to say when we get out there though."

The *Sundulus* royals turned to face me, their faces smoothing, gazes sharp.

I imagined that was the nicest expression I'd encounter once they heard the truth.

Standing, I collected my tablet and handed it to Kyros as I passed him at the door. The siblings filed out after me from youngest to eldest, Kyros taking the rear.

"The announcement will be late tonight," he announced to the packed Level 66. "Stand by."

No one made a peep.

I weaved through the monitors, setting my mind on what needed to be done.

Keep Sandra safe. Get rid of your guilt. Protect Kyros and his family.

Just thinking of the pending emotional freedom was a relief. They'd be angry beyond measure—my life would certainly be threatened. This was one situation where I could need Kyros's protection from his father, but I was bringing them a trump card. *The key to putting themselves back in the game.* That had to count for something.

We took the elevator down to the garage in two lots, and I felt the eyes of Francesca, Lalitta, Lionel, and Neelan on me.

I made to follow them into one of the waiting SUVs, but Lionel stopped me, pointing to Kyros's car.

"He'll want to ride with you," he said quietly, avoiding my gaze.

Lionel didn't want to look at me? *Ouch.*

Safina, Gerome, Dierdre, and Rory filed into the second SUV, and Kyros took my hand, leading me to his car.

He was still holding my hand even though he had to feel the guilt, anxiety, and fear coursing through me. I wasn't sure if I'd been more grateful to him than in that moment. I smiled at him, but he didn't return the gesture, dropping my hand to enter the driver's door.

Tuning in to his mood, I found fear to be the predominant emotion. Fear about his father's reaction or what I'd done?

Kyros navigated out of the garage and drove in the direction of his parents' mansion. I listened in on his mood as the minutes ticked by, respecting his desire not to speak.

He broke the tension. "The trip to Frankton Gorge?"

"Yes," I answered.

His hands gripped the wheel. "Is there other information you've withheld?"

Where do I begin? "Yes."

Kyros indicated, pulling over on the freeway shoulder. He breathed hard, eyes closed.

I watched his struggle to regain control, sending soothing vibes his way.

"I am about to take you into the territory of a stronger Vissimo," Kyros said in a guttural voice I could barely understand. "It goes against my instincts to allow that when I'm unsure of the outcome."

"You're afraid things will go wrong," I said.

So am I. But only at the thought of losing you.

Kyros turned to me, and I blinked against the brightness of his eyes.

"Are you certain about the hand you're about to play?" His voice rumbled through me and my heart squeezed.

"As sure as I can possibly be."

He searched my face. "Then I suppose I'm meant to let you proceed."

It would be funny if he wasn't so torn apart inside. "Yes, Kyros. That's how you'll protect me this time."

A wrinkle appeared between his brows.

I paused. "You'll be there to protect me physically too. Even if it's unnecessary." His father couldn't kill me without causing his son to lose control.

It was an insurance I didn't want but could need.

Kyros's eyes dimmed to near-normal wattage as he pulled out onto the freeway again. Silence returned until my thundering heartbeat formed the drumroll for our drive into the property of King Julius.

Fuck.

I could not screw this up. Kyros was important to me. *That* was indisputable after what we'd shared.

Apparently, so were his siblings.

"That doesn't make this easier," he said, glaring at my chest.

Yeah, my heartbeat was an inconvenient sign on my discomfort. "I know."

Kyros took my hand when we exited the car, squeezing it this time.

I stopped him, looking up. "Thank you."

Then I untangled my fingers, heading into the house before him. I marched through the halls and through the interior courtyard, climbing the stairs toward the chamber where I'd first met King Julius.

I listened to the shuffling of the Vissimo within.

Everyone was there.

I inhaled, scenting the saltiness of my perspiration. Gathering myself at the top of the stairs, I strode through the iron and wood doors.

King Julius sat in his throne, dressed in his usual coarse sarong—Queen Titania was seated beside him in a robe.

The royal siblings stood four at the base of the stairs, leaving an opening for Kyros and me.

I stopped in the middle and curtsied. Kyros stopped several steps behind me, obeying my wish to do this alone. I was alone in appearance only, perhaps, but that distance was driving him to the edges of his control.

"Human." King Julius greeted me.

The last few times he'd spoken to me, I'd been Basilia or Miss Le Spyre or *mate of my heir* if he was feeling really nice.

He held up a letter. "King Mikael sent a letter tonight after his time with my heir. It is addressed to you."

The king held it out, and after mentally checking Kyros for confirmation, I climbed the ten steps to take the envelope, dread filling me.

The wax seal wasn't broken.

"Why is my enemy sending you mail?" he asked in a soft voice that shot fear through every fibre of my body.

I inhaled. "For the very reason I plan to reveal tonight. I'd like to discuss information surrounding the Mr Ringly deal and the background to what pushed me to investigate it personally."

When I sealed the fate of you and eight of your children.

The king hummed, leaning forward. "Open the message."

I stared at him, my palms growing slick with sweat. No, I had to start with the information.

"Now."

My chest seized at the icy promise behind the word. I pried my finger under the seal.

It wasn't a message; it was a photo.

I drew it out, and choked on my inhale, covering my mouth as the photo tumbled from my grip.

Sandra.

What remained of her.

The picture was of her severed head, her mouth twisted grotesquely and her eyes wide and glassy.

Bile surged up through my throat and I battled it, listening to Kyros's quiet growl at my back. I retreated two steps toward him as his father swooped down and regarded the picture.

He flipped it over, reading aloud. "*Good try.*"

Oh my god. *Sandra.* "They caught her."

How had they known? I took twenty-five Indebted with me. My team would have noticed anyone following us from Bluff City or within listening distance.

King Julius straightened, his face hard. Queen Titania rested a fleeting hand on his knee.

"Explain," he boomed.

I jumped. "It's a picture of Sandra Hoyt. S-She's dead."

"I can see that, human."

"Father, she's in shock," Kyros murmured from the bottom of the stairs.

And that meant jack shit to the Vissimo king before me. I shook my head, grabbing at the tatters of my ruined plan.

"She was the councilwoman assigned to Mr Ringly's case until June last year. She transferred to Frankton Gorge and his case was then transferred to Julia Dinh. I tracked Miss Hoyt down a week ago and questioned her."

Hands shaking, I drew out my phone, locating the video.

I pushed Play.

"*At first, I started receiving a list of my family's addresses in the mail. It took me a while to realise I only received them after a phone call with Mr Ringly. First the letters turned up in my mailbox, then on my desk when I returned from the printer or the bathroom. Once, the letter was left on my pillow in my bedroom. I went to my supervisor for help...*"

The video was ten minutes long, and I held the phone aloft, wondering if ten minutes had ever seemed so long.

"*Miss Hoyt,*" my voice sounded as she trailed off, "*why do you believe you received the letters? Why do you think your supervisors and the police wouldn't help? And why do you think the man with brown curls and hazel eyes was following you?*"

"*I wouldn't approve Mr Ringly's DA. Agricultural land is of greater need to Bluff City than more residential land. What's the point of building more houses if our ability to feed the population doesn't also increase? The people threatening my family, myself, and my career wanted me to approve the rezoning plan. I'm certain of that.*"

The video ended.

"You found her one week ago," King Julius said, resting back.

"Yes, King Julius." I kept my gaze on the armrest of his throne.

He held the picture out to me.

Hands shaking, I took it, bracing myself before looking again. There was a date on the picture. *Yesterday.*

"The recording of her testimony is useless," he said, blue eyes never colder. "Now she is dead."

The feeling of falling overcame everything else. It swamped my horror over Sandra's fate. Because I could *feel* Kyros's fear and his struggle not to join me on the stairs.

He was trusting me to handle this, and that was so hard for him to give.

His siblings were barely breathing.

The king's hand curled. "Arrogant *human*," he spat.

My gaze dropped further.

"Why was this note addressed to you?" Queen Titania asked in a steady voice.

She wasn't any easier to look at than the king. Not when she was the mother who would survive, minus a husband and with only one of her nine children. Even if she hadn't given birth to all of them herself—which is something I'd never insult her by asking—she would die for any one of them.

My heart thudded pathetically. We all heard it.

And still Kyros hoped... *hoped* this was part of my plan.

I'd betrayed him and the only people he cared about.

Taking a breath, I said, "Because when the Tonyi triplets took me hostage, I made a deal with King Mikael."

Even the king hadn't expected that.

I continued. "I told him about the bluff you played with the Mr Ringly deal so Tommy would live."

Lalitta gasped, and yet I couldn't turn to face her because Kyros's pain froze me to the core.

Disbelief. Anguish.

"Acceptance," I whispered as Kyros's disbelief dissipated to be replaced with bitter betrayal.

My insides *shook* as hardness overcame him. I was left reaching for his emotions, fingernails scratching at a rock wall.

Queen Titania closed her eyes.

"You couldn't be compelled though," Kyros whispered. "You offered the information *freely*."

I swallowed three times before recovering my ability to speak through the emptiness of his absence in me. "Yes. I honoured the deal once Tommy was delivered to a hospital."

The king's blue eyes bored into me, but the pain bursting from the vampire at my back was of greater importance. I had the presence of mind to back down the stairs before facing Kyros.

I flinched at the hatred on his face.

"You sacrificed the lives of my entire family for one human," he spat.

"She's my family."

"I'm your family too." His roar was terrible to behold.

None of the siblings looked at me aside from Safina.

I jerked back at her burning hatred.

"You've killed my daughter," she whispered, voice shaking with loathing.

Kearra.

I sucked in a breath. The entire bloodline would be executed aside from the queen and Kyros. That included her daughter.

Horror suffused every part of me.

Torment filled Kyros's voice. "*Why?*"

I'd already told him.

But he wanted to know why I'd hurt *him* this way. Why I'd gone after the one thing he valued in life—his family.

"There was no other choice," I told him simply.

"The *choice* was seeking my help when the triplets first contacted you," he growled in my face.

I tried to breathe through my reaction, clamping down on the urge to collapse in a heap.

"The choice was telling me what you did as soon as you woke." Kyros's hands clawed. "The *choice* was coming to me when you

177

discovered the possible discrepancy in the council papers. Mr Ringly transferred his bank loan to one of Fyrlia's banks. We thought they were protecting their investment. The debts of his drug dealer were suddenly paid. Every planning breach we'd taken note of was cleared up overnight. We thought Julia Dinh was playing us."

I lifted my gaze to his meadow-green eyes and part of my soul chipped away.

"*You* were stabbing us in the back," he said. "Is this your fucking revenge for what I did then?"

The lump in my throat made my voice hoarse. "No," I whispered.

Kyros strode past me, and I turned to watch as he knelt at the base of the stairs. "Father, please forgive my lack of judgment."

Lack of judgment.

That's what I was now.

I took the hit, telling myself it was just hurt from his words and not my heart shattering.

"Your idiocy will be discussed at length, but not in front of human trash. Get rid of her."

It took Kyros less than a second to accept the order.

"Leave," he said, his back to me. "Do not return."

I'd expected this.

I'd known he'd be angry.

What I hadn't expected was to feel like a speck of dirt on the bottom of his *Freens* and to *deserve* being there.

I'd betrayed him, all of them. I'd stalled while scrambling to figure out a solution.

Maybe I knew, even back then, that I couldn't handle the look on Kyros's face.

I dipped my head and turned to leave.

"Back out," Kyros hissed.

Tears welled in my eyes. I blinked, forcing them down. I couldn't leave things like this. Desperation clawed at my throat.

"The threat to Tommy's life was immediate," I said, my chest tightening as the stinging behind my eyes swelled. "The threat to the life of your siblings and father was not."

His voice dripped with ice. "*I said get the fuck out.*"

Facing him again, I dropped my head.

So I wouldn't need to witness the decay of whatever messed up and beautiful bond we'd shared.

So the sight of his disgust couldn't haunt my every waking moment for the rest of time.

Stooped, I shuffled backward from the chamber.

"I'm out," I told the table surrounded by my grandmother's friends.

They stared back at me.

It took two days to work up the courage to arrange this meeting. Since Kyros washed his hands of me, I'd thrown myself into estate work in a frenzy even Tommy couldn't contain.

I'd failed my grandmother.

I'd failed these people who had fought the Vissimo every day for nearly three decades.

I'd failed Kyros and his family.

I'd failed the Indebted.

In another fifteen days, Kyros's hatred of me would be sealed with the triggering of the end cascade.

"You're out of what exactly?" Lady Treena asked.

"Level 66?" Dame Burke said, eyes sharp on me.

My mind never left my misery these days, so talking was nearly easy. "And their group."

Mr Hothen swore.

"How?" Mrs Syrre whispered.

Sir Olythieu's eyes narrowed. "They know?"

I shook my head. "Not about this group. I went about Sandra. It was past time."

Turning to Mr Hothen, I closed my eyes. "F got to her first. I'm so sorry."

Shock blanketed his features.

Without a word, he left the room.

"Poor woman," Mrs Syrre said, dashing away a few tears.

Sandra Hoyt was just another person I'd failed. I'd *promised* she would be okay. I was so determined to do right by her, but the rug was pulled from beneath me. The remaining triplets would have worked on her.

Her last moments would have been filled with horror and pain.

I'd been sick too many times to count in the last couple of days.

Mr Dithis leaned back. "The state of *Ingenium* is the same?"

That right there was why the world should fear the people around this table. Death and fear surrounded them at every turn, and here they were, fighting with cold calculation.

I nodded. "Fifteen days."

"The *end* is in fifteen days," Dame Burke asked, blinking.

Sir Olythieu chimed. "Just over two weeks to establish equilibrium again then."

Equilibrium.

That was all well and good. My plan had centred on completing *six* exchanges with Kyros so I could free the Indebted and employ them for protection.

"What I don't understand," Lady Treena said, "is if you betrayed them badly enough to get kicked out entirely, why you aren't dead."

Because I was his true mate.

My grandmother's friends had forgiven me for a few sympathising comments toward the Vissimo. If they knew what happened with Kyros. If they knew how I *felt* for a vampire, they'd never look at me again. They might not join forces against me, but they'd damn-well slam the door in my face. If I was in their shoes, I'd do the same. It was too risky to discuss matters with me openly, never knowing when Kyros may take a dip into my mind. Or when I'd confess everything.

Maybe I deserved that door to slam shut.

If my grandmother was here, I wouldn't be able to look her in the face. Guilt and self-loathing were my constant companions since her death. Only Kyros had balanced those feelings, and I hadn't realised until too late.

Decision made, I dug around in my bag. I drew out the *Vissimo* book on mating rituals. Riffling through the contents, I stopped at the fifth exchange and placed it in the middle of the table.

"Me and Kyros," I said.

Chairs scraped back as they craned to look at the book. Dame Burke studied the title and snatched the book up, gaze darting over the first few pages.

Her eyes widened.

She glanced up at me, her mouth ajar. "You're *mated* to him?"

The others gasped and crowded around her, reaching for the book in turn.

I watched as they skimmed through, reading a bit from each exchange. The location thing, the feelings, the changes to my senses, and the increases in my strength and speed. They absorbed all of it.

I watched as their expression turned from confusion to shock to horror and disgust.

My grandmother's six friends focused on me.

I deserved everything they were thinking and feeling. As surely as I'd played Kyros, I'd played these people too. King Julius was right when he titled me arrogant human. Even if my intentions were sound, I'd handled everything like a fool.

No wonder they questioned my loyalty.

I had no idea who I was loyal *to* anymore. Because how could I want to help both sides at the same time?

The risk for this group to trust me was too high. They were businesspeople well and truly, and I'd become the bad investment.

I'm so sorry, Grandmother.

What a train wreck. Twenty-seven years of sacrifice down the drain in a matter of weeks. All because I'd taken over.

Crack.

Dame Burke gasped, and I dropped my gaze to the edge of the table. Chips of wood came away as I removed my hands.

"You're *one of them*," Mr Dithis whispered.

But I wasn't.

And I wasn't human either. Not anymore.

I swallowed hard and dropped my eyes.

Leaving the files, I retrieved the book that had toppled from Dame Burke's hands.

And left.

17

Tommy plonked down in the seat opposite me.

I stared across the desk at her.

"Snap out of it," she said.

Returning my attention to my computer screen, I resumed typing the email. The great thing about owning international companies is emails came through at all hours of the day, so there was always work to do.

I had no idea what the time was. I didn't want to know.

"It's been five days, Basi. You feel like shit, and I get that. But I feel like shit at the moment, so you can't."

I cocked a brow, signing off on the latest email before sending it. "You're miserable, and so I can't be?"

"Correct. I claimed it before whatever fight you clearly had with Kyros."

Fight. "That doesn't quite do it justice," I said sarcastically.

"Talk."

If I was going to talk to anyone, it would be Tommy. That I didn't want to, told me just how much I needed to. "To save you, I made a deal."

Her eyes darted. "A deal with Clan Fyrlia?"

Focusing on Tom Hanks's autobiography, I inclined my head.

"To save me?"

I nodded again.

"Making a deal with Fyrlia when you're sexing Sundulus is a big no-no, I'm assuming," she said, tapping her lip. "Kyros found out about it."

His entire family. "Big time."

Tommy stood, pacing. "Was the deal you made win or lose *Ingenium* stuff?"

I levelled her with a steady look.

She sank back into the seat. "Fark, Basil."

Fark, indeed.

Her mouth set. "They can't end the game before you win though. How do we even things up again?"

I loved my best friend. "That's what I've been trying to do for the last few weeks."

"I see." She tapped her mouth.

She did?

"Then I revert to my original statement," she said, bounding up again. "Snap out of it."

I was trying. I just felt so damn lonely. And angry. And full of regret.

Blood bond aside, Kyros had occupied a space inside of me. When he was butting his nose into my life each day, I hadn't realised just how large that chunk was.

The void now was big.

Really big.

Tommy yanked on my hair.

"Ow!" I shot her a glare.

"Listen good, Basil," she said, hunkering down. "You made that choice to save me, and I'll never be able to repay that, so as a poor substitute, you're about to receive the pep talk to end all pep talks."

Oh, brother.

"How long until Sundulus loses?" she pressed.

Thirteen days if the forecast for the end cascade proved correct.

Focusing on the pay schedule for my Churchill team—who I hadn't contacted all week—I muttered, "Nearly two weeks."

She brought both hands down on my knees, and I jumped.

"Then you still have time. There's time to win him back even if you can't win the game."

I frowned. Win him back? "Do you even like Kyros?"

"No. But I hated him before, so total dislike is a leap in the right direction. I think I could barely tolerate him given ample time."

Okay.

"The point is," she said, sighing, "that you're legit miserable without him, and he cares for you enough to get your best friend back. From what I've read in that mating rituals book, this is a permanent kind of deal."

We could still be apart though—as torturous as that was. The pain in my chest from our separation surged each day. I'd considered standing outside the tower to see if the pain would dissipate, but Kyros would feel me there.

If the sensation continued to heighten, I might not have a choice.

"He *is* the game," I managed to force out. "He'll never speak to me again unless I correct what I did."

Tommy sat back on her heels. "Well, how do you do that?"

"That's just it. I can't."

Fyrlia caught me digging around Sandra somehow. Sundulus had kicked me out. I was fresh out of ideas, and the oldies hadn't been in touch since I upended the *I'm Kyros's mate and have vampire powers* bin over their heads.

"Tom," I said in a low voice, "I let Grandmother down so badly. I can't win for her. I can't even restore balance. And without that, Kyros won't look twice at me."

The list of people I'd failed played over and over in my mind like a horror movie without end. In the couple of hours of sleep my body demanded, their faces haunted me. I'd avoided everyone—Laurel, the Indebted, Tommy, and even Fred.

Tommy gripped my chin, smooshing my cheeks. "Where's the Basilia I know?" she snapped.

I stared at her.

"You don't like something, you change it. You want something, you get it. *That's* the spoiled brat I know."

I pried free of her grip, rubbing my jaw. "That started great."

"It was all great," she said savagely. "Tell me, what do you want?"

We were nose to nose, and I felt my heartbeat thudding in my ears.

"No lies, Basil," Tommy said. "Don't tell me what you think I want to hear. Or what others expect of you. What the fuck do you want?"

I closed my eyes.

"Open them!"

Jolting again, I obeyed. "Kyros."

Kudos to my friend, her nose didn't even wrinkle.

"You want him," she repeated. "Then *get* Kyros."

Words slipped from my mouth. "If I get him, then I betray my grandmother and everything she worked for."

I slumped in defeat as my voice trailed off, avoiding Tommy's intent chestnut gaze.

Tommy blew out a breath and perched on the desk. "That's a moderate problem, I'll admit."

There was nothing moderate about it.

"Your grandmother hated Vissimo. And you're literally banging one."

"This is the worst pep talk I've ever had." I tried to stand and she shoved me back in the chair.

"You leave when I say you leave."

Uh, pep-talk Tommy was scary. "I can't give up everything she worked for, Tom. She *died* because of this bullshit. I tried my best to keep things going, but I failed. I've failed everyone."

Tommy's eyes narrowed. "If you won the game? What was the plan?"

I blinked a few times. "The plan was that I'd make that decision in twenty years when I was smarter. Because winning would take at least that long."

"You're smart now, Basi. And confident too. You're just doubting yourself."

Felt like I'd been doubting myself for twenty-one years and nine months.

Tommy tapped my temple. "The answer is in here. As much as I'd like to advocate three months of ice-cream musical dates to get over the fucker, that's not going to happen. You have a deadline, girl. Best get going."

Two weeks.

Kyros could be out of my reach in *thirteen days*. Was there a chance to win him back? Tommy gave me hope for that possibility. In a weird yet effective way.

"Best get going," she repeated.

I peered at her. "You already said that."

"Yeah, but in motivational things, they always chant a slogan. Haven't you seen *Good Will Hunting*?" She slapped my knee. "Best get going."

"Ouch. Stop hitting me!"

"Best get going."

I stood, trying to fend her off as she herded me around the table.

"*Best get going.*"

Snorting, I dodged her. "Seriously, stop it."

She started whacking my body, chasing me to the door as she continued her chant.

"Oh my god, Tommy! I'm getting going. Or whatever. Stop." Using my extra speed, I caught the book she'd tossed at my head.

The book fell from my hands to the ground, and the heading of the chapter caught my eye.

Rights of Human Mates

I paused, staring at the page as Tommy continued her beatdown.

She panted, stopping the abuse. "Best get... Wait, what happened?"

A stillness came over me. It was the calmest I'd felt in five days. I bent down to pick the book up.

"Tom."

"Yeah?" She craned over my shoulder to read the heading. "Something got your brain juices squeezing?"

"You have a beautiful way with words, my friend." But yes, kind of.

"What do you think I need to do?" I asked slowly.

Tommy snorted. "I ain't the billionaire here."

"No." I agreed seriously, taking her hand. "You're my friend, and the best one I'll ever have. I trust your judgment where I don't always trust my own. What am I doing wrong?"

The smile faded from her lips. "You're catering to everyone else's expectations."

I needed to address those expectations then.

And decide what I could live with. Because she was right. I had less than two weeks left.

"I'm heading out," I told her, striding for the door.

Tommy didn't let go of my hand, and I dragged her along with me. "Just one thing before you do."

She licked her lips when I stopped and glanced back.

"Your grandmother, Basil," Tommy said, smiling. "She was a hell of a woman. She left a hell of a legacy. But she isn't here. If she was, I think you'd be surprised by what she'd have to say. Remember that Agatha Le Spyre had faults just like any other person, and most importantly, remember that you're not her. You can't be satisfied with life if you're chasing after her definition of happiness and success. The woman I knew wouldn't have expected you to. In fact, she'd have some cutting things to say if she caught you doing it."

I closed my eyes, allowing her words to seep into my bones for later. There was truth in them. I just needed to find that conviction for myself. "Thank you."

"Any time. Where are you going?"

Where else did I go when my feelings overwhelmed me?

I opened my eyes. "The theme park. Don't wait up."

I stared at the text and hit send.

I'm sorry

Saying more than that felt like an excuse.

I'm sorry but I did what I felt was right. I'm sorry, but I'm going to fight to make things right now.

I felt Kyros focus as he read the message, then listened in on his bitter response.

It was the response I'd expected, but it still hurt.

Bad.

"Here are the boxes, Miss Le Spyre," Rosie said. "Are you certain you don't require assistance?"

A string of my staff entered my grandmother's suite clasping flattened cardboard boxes. They began to set them up.

I inhaled deeply and glanced around my grandmother's room, the scent of lavender not as strong as it once was.

"No, thank you," I answered. "But please bring up a few vases of lavender."

She curtsied, and I grabbed my phone, plugging it into the speaker I'd carried in.

The slow swing of Nat King Cole's "Unforgettable" filled the room.

As the staff finished making up boxes behind me, Rosie reappeared with the vases of lavender. They retreated from the room, leaving me alone.

I opened Grandmother's closet, a heaviness settling on my shoulders as the soulful lyrics washed over me.

The last tangible signs of my grandmother's personal life were in this room. It was a life that a select few ever saw. Only family, really, and Lady Treena. Even the rest of the oldies never stepped foot in her private suite. That was the kind of woman my grandmother was. Removing her things from this space felt like I was removing her from my life. The jewellery, the clothing, the smell, the décor—the way things were arranged as she'd liked them.

She'd always slept here. Her presence filled every corner. In my memories of her, she'd occupied this space and always would in my heart.

Because she was taken from me so quickly. Before I was ready. The trauma surrounding her death had locked my grief in time.

I couldn't see the suite as anything else.

And maybe I didn't have to yet.

Maybe I never would.

Perhaps packing up her things was the first step. Or a trial. I could see what happened after it. What I felt like doing next.

I picked up a box and approached the bathroom. It seemed like the most impersonal space. Packing up toiletries was stupid, yet I couldn't throw them out. I sniffed her bath salts, a lump rising in my throat as I remembered baths in here with Tommy when we were seven or eight years old.

I placed the lavender salts in the box, and smelled her shampoo, conditioner, and body wash in turn before doing the same with them. Maybe one day I'd have the capacity to donate or throw things out. Today wasn't that day.

All her cosmetics and care products went into the box, but I placed her favourite peach-coloured lipstick on the bed. Maybe I'd use that.

I pivoted in a slow circle, my socked feet sliding easily on the floor. I placed my hands on the waistband of my black hot pants, blowing my hair off my cheek, then smiled as my grandmother's reproach of *don't let your hair cover your face* rang in my ears. I obediently flipped my ponytail over my shoulder, feeling the long strands settled against my back left mostly bare by the black sports bra.

I wish she was here to deliver her tongue-lashing reproaches in person.

I miss you so much.

Traipsing to the dresser, I started splitting the jewellery into pieces I'd keep and pieces I'd put in the safe. I placed her wedding rings onto the *keep* pile, pushing a gold and emerald necklace to the other pile while trying not to think too hard about what I was doing.

I'd spent every night in here for months after my parents' death, and then every other night for two years. Even into my late teens, I'd sneak in to sleep beside my beloved grandmother.

She'd never acknowledged my presence with more than a pat on my hand, but sometimes I'd wake to find her hand on my forehead, with her still fast asleep.

Never again.

Yet I had so many wonderful memories with her.

Watching her shut down spiteful comments from her rivals without batting an eyelash.

Indulging in too much brandy and actually taking off her blazer while out of her room.

Her straight back.

Her steady gaze.

Her blatant love for me.

I placed the right pile of jewellery on the bed next to the lipstick and set the other in a box that I jotted the words *for the safe* on.

Replacing the cap, I knelt on the ground before her wardrobe, lavender filling my senses.

A tear slipped down my cheek, and I dashed it away. "I need help," I whispered.

To *her*.

Closing my eyes, I drew forth the image of my grandmother's face. Her flinty eyes and penetrating topaz gaze.

Yesterday, I spent five hours on the Ferris wheel at the theme park reading through the Vissimo law book and the *Ingenium* rule book.

I'd come to the realisation that the only person I needed to justify my actions to was Agatha Le Spyre. But I couldn't because she was gone. And that was why I'd tried to justify them to everyone else—my oldies, Kyros, his family, Tommy, Fred, Laurel.

If Grandmother was here, we would have spoken, agreed or disagreed, and moved on long ago.

My grief and my desire and need to respect and uphold my grandmother's wishes was crippling me.

I needed to come to terms with what I could bear to do.

Drawing up the memory of her, I murmured, "I can't do exactly what you wanted me to do. Everything has changed."

I'd said something similar to her when I stopped associating with Harriet Gregorian and her horde, and I still remembered her reply.

Have your standards, Basilia. Stick to those standards, but always be ready to flow into a different path. That's why we draw lines in the sand, so we can move them as we grow. Rigid idiots snap in half, and my granddaughter is no idiot.

She'd been right, of course. I outgrew my rich friends the moment they hurt Tommy. After that day, I drew a new line in the sand. I'd drawn new lines at least a dozen times in the last three months.

Nothing was set in stone.

Nothing except my love for her, and what I shared with Kyros. That would never go away.

Would my grandmother like Kyros? If he wasn't Vissimo, that was. Tall, handsome, business-minded, intelligent, and a good dresser.

I grinned.

Yes, she'd approve.

It shouldn't matter that he'd have fangs. Agatha Le Spyre hadn't shied away from other races and cultures. Even with her hatred of the vampires in Bluff City, I believed that she would have become accustomed to Kyros in time. After trying to force him away. Knowing him, he'd probably enjoy the challenge.

She may have disliked him, but she would have respected him.

As I'd always respected her.

I needed retribution for my last family member; for the way she'd died and for her efforts to free the humans here from Vissimo control.

In spirit, I hoped to still achieve that for her and her friends.

It just wouldn't be in the way they liked. Nor in a way they might understand.

I didn't even know if such a thing was possible yet.

I drew in a slow breath, holding onto the memory of my grandmother's face.

Always be ready to flow into a different path.

The end of the path was set. *Ingenium* had to be won, and that couldn't alter. But everything up until that point *could* alter within the rules of the game.

I swallowed hard.

There were many things I did want in life but living as she did... not one bit. In the throes of bitter anger after Kyros's subterfuge, I threw myself into revenge. And I'd really believed that I could live the double life, the two roles remaining cleanly separated on either side of my line in the sand.

The line that was distorted beyond measure at this point.

I had to re-draw it.

With a new plan.

My grandmother smiled in my mind, and I thought back to the moment I left the estate. In a rage, I was certain she couldn't understand how trapped I felt.

Why did I need to follow in the family footsteps?

I hadn't wanted that life.

I'd thought her as furious as me, but in my mind, the vision of her was entirely calm.

Go after the life you want, she'd said, watching as I flung down my electronics in a huff and grabbed my *Elegance* pack.

I will, the memory of myself hurled back.

She arched a brow. *Good. Then I've raised you right.*

I batted open my lashes.

My grandmother's legacy wasn't contained in her efforts in *Ingenium*. I was her legacy. The 10 percent growth of the Le Spyre fortune under her management was her legacy. Quiet grace. Firm truth. Sharp intelligence.

That was my grandmother's legacy, and everyone who knew her well felt the weight of that in their hearts.

How could I ever think she'd want anything more than my happiness and the happiness of her friends?

I couldn't be my grandmother. She'd never wanted me to be. But I could heed her advice.

Go after the life you want.

A tired smile spread across my face as I stood and grabbed the first of her skirt suits, folding it gently into the box at my feet.

"I will, Grandmother," I whispered.

There were twelve days to do so.

18

The phone rang, and I paused in my frantic typing to swipe up the handset.

"Miss Le Spyre, it's Daniel."

"Yes, Daniel?" I said, my knee bouncing with impatience.

"We've had a visitor the last few nights," he said. "At first I thought it was one of your guests, but he doesn't dress in black leather."

I stilled. "What does he dress in?"

"A suit. I got a still of his face last night, and I believe he's your male guest. Kyros, was it?"

I would have cracked a grin over the term *male guest* if my mouth wasn't suddenly so dry. Kyros was visiting the estate at night. "What time?"

"Around 5:00 a.m., miss."

After playing *Ingenium*.

I guessed the only reason I hadn't charged down to his tower was because he'd been sneaking here at night. Which tore all romance from the gesture. He was coming close enough to satisfy the blood bond so we didn't have to actually see each other.

"Should I alert the authorities?" he asked.

I settled back in the cushioned chair. "No. Don't do that. Next time he shows up, send me a message. Don't call, just message."

"Copy that."

As soon as I hung up, the phone rang again.

"Miss Le Spyre, your ten o'clock appointment is here."

"Thank you, Fred. Send him in."

Fernando strode in a moment later, closing the door, and turning on the noise-cancelling. "Miss Le Spyre," he said, bowing low.

He'd lost the fear from our first exchanges, but he kept up the appropriate sheepishness. To my knowledge, his brothers and sisters were still treating him like a piece of shit.

Fernando's information had proven invaluable so far, and I'd decided that if Laurel agreed, he'd be freed alongside the others. If I managed to pull anything off, that was.

I still needed the sixth exchange to occur with Kyros. Not only to free the Indebted, but to have any chance of putting my new plan into effect.

Even then, I'd be relying on Kyros's forgiveness for any of this to work.

"Fernando. Report," I said, giving him my full attention.

He bowed again. "You were right. Sandra Hoyt was under compulsion to report. She's tied to Gina. As soon as you left Sandra's house, she had to phone Gina and tell her everything. But she wasn't compelled to do more, so she still ran and managed to evade them for five days until they caught up."

I should have brought her with me that day. She never would have managed to report with my Indebted around.

That was a grievous mistake I'd live with for the rest of my life. The memory of Sandra and Rhys would forever stain my hands red even if I hadn't personally killed them.

"Fyrlia's status in *Ingenium*?"

He clasped his hands behind his back. "King Mikael speaks of how he'll kill King Julius and the Sundulus royals. He speaks of how he'll treat Queen Titania, and how he'll make his eldest son *see the light*."

My stomach flipped at the thought that Mikael may get what he'd so desperately sought for one-and-a-half centuries. He didn't deserve Kyros.

"What's the feeling between the Fyrlia siblings? Has the divide between the remaining Tonyi triplets widened?"

The vampire dipped his head. "Now that Trenit and Tynan are at each other's throats, the other siblings have regained the upper hand in the power struggle. I believe King Mikael is once more gravitating toward the counsel of Gina and Hector."

That made sense. Breaking the rules could cost Fyrlia dearly at this crucial point in the game. "Anything else?"

He hesitated. "Prince Kyros had his weekly visit with Fyrlia. I thought you may be interested to know that King Mikael goaded him with your recent actions."

It was the fuel I'd given the king to drive a wedge between us. I'd *told* him to use it to save Tommy's life.

I swallowed. "And?"

"Prince Kyros defended you against all his attempts to besmirch you."

Defended how? I wanted to know, and yet it was important to keep Fernando at a distance. "Very well. I'm particularly interested in whatever you can dig up on Fyrlia's plans for the coming week. Please report back in two days with what you find."

He bowed again and left.

I tried to regulate my breathing.

Kyros was defending me to Mikael? What did that mean? Was it just a ploy to undermine his enemy? Or had he reasoned through what I'd done and reassessed?

The churning emotion within him hadn't abated in the slightest. Kyros was as disappointed and furious and shocked as he'd been when the traitorous words left my mouth.

I also knew that the interpretation of his feelings was subjective. How many times had I used that ploy against him? Or focused on a memory to distract him from what I truly felt?

Pulling out my phone, I typed another text. My being needed

Kyros desperately, but my plans required him too. The lives of his family, the freedom of the Indebted, and the livelihood of the humans in Bluff City depended on it. Nothing would happen unless I managed to get him in the same room as me.

I could work with angry Kyros, but I couldn't work with absent Kyros.

I'm sure you have questions

I sent the text and hesitated before adding:

Time is running out to ask them.

Nine days to be exact.

Like a dog waiting for its owner to come home, I listened in on him as he read, uncertainty spread through me at the jolt of sharp yearning that ran through him for a split second before his rage slammed down once more.

Pressing the button under the desk, I grimaced as my ears popped and the sounds outside the room disappeared. I was used to hearing the movements of Fred and the Indebted around me these days; it was uncomfortable to have the sense dampened.

I scrolled through my numbers to Winston and rang my Churchill team.

"Miss Le Spyre," Eva's voice trailed down the line. "How can we help you?"

Holding the phone between my shoulder and ear, I finished the email to her. "I'm sending you an email with *Foremost* and *Live Right* figures. The team will cease all other projects and focus on an audit of all Foremost and Live Right holdings."

"We regularly track their acquisitions," she offered. "How would you like our focus to alter?"

"Go through every single asset Foremost and Live Right has ever purchased, every *cent* of their income. I'm also sending you the names of other companies they own that are unrelated to real estate. I need the team to assess the holdings of these as well. In no more than seven days, I require the net worth of each company. These numbers need to be entirely accurate, Eva. That's very important."

My Churchill team operated with almost zero possession of the facts and reasons for the tasks I set. This was just another day at the office for them.

Through my work at Sundulus, I had an in-depth knowledge of the various public faces of each clan. I had to use that knowledge now to see if what I owned could save Kyros's family.

I needed to know if my Bluff City assets were worth enough to make a difference.

Go after the life you want.

I was going all in.

"Understood, Miss Le Spyre. I'm reading over your email now and will respond with any queries. The team will be pulled from their normal tasks and reassigned to this audit. Would you like the acquisition teams to continue their work?"

I'd already spoken to Tommy. "Yes. They will continue their work."

The more I owned in nine days' time, the better.

I might have enough to bring Sundulus and Fyrlia head to head again. But what I really wanted so very desperately was to trigger the end cascade.

Against Fyrlia.

I wanted to end this for good.

I hadn't slept, so when my phone vibrated, I sat in a movement much too fast for a human.

Blinking against the glare of light, I read the message from Daniel.

He's here, Miss Le Spyre

Phew. Here goes.

I didn't bother creeping to the windows overlooking the south of the estate. If he was here, he was focused on me.

Taking a breath, I slid back the window and leaned out. Putting all my regret and sorrow into the word, I whispered, "Kyros."

He mentally jerked.

I peered into the thick darkness, wondering if he could see me. "Please come inside."

His longing was an echo of mine. Through the other ugly emotions, even now, our want for each other remained.

"Please," I repeated.

Retreating to the bed, I perched on the end, and waited.

I had no idea what to expect from him. That we couldn't be separated endlessly was painfully apparent to both of us, yet he didn't want to be in my company any more than the blood bond dictated.

That hurt a lot.

But I couldn't blame him for it.

My bedroom doors opened, and Kyros entered, not bothering to shut them after.

I didn't look up, fully occupied by the onslaught of emotions exploding from him. *Fury. Betrayal. Yearning. Lust.*

"You came," I said, my voice shaking.

It probably meant he was unable to resist the call to claim me, but my mind clung to the tiny hope his reason for coming had nothing to do with the blood bond.

He stalked around the room, keeping a wide berth from me.

I was grateful for that. My head spun with his presence and scent. The urge to go to him, to *wrap around him*, was almost undeniable.

"I'm not surprised you can't look at me," Kyros said, bitterness unfurling like a whip.

The gloves were off.

Stiffening my spine, I tilted my head back when he stopped before me.

A meadow-green gaze met mine. Impossibly handsome as always, the only clue to how the vampire really felt was in the bone-deep weariness in his gaze as he looked at me.

Hollow.

I did that to him.

Him to me.

His family to mine.

Mine to his.

At this point, I'd lost track of who'd wronged one another. All that was left was his emptiness, my guilt, and the threat against those we cared about.

"You must have questions," I said softly, leaning back to put distance between us so my body recalled it needed air to survive.

I blinked through the vibrations and haze cloying my mind, pushing and whispering to take him. To make him mine.

The vampire loomed over me. "What makes you think I want to hear anything from your mouth when you've spent the last month lying?"

Hmm, probably double that time, actually.

"You wouldn't be here if you didn't," I answered.

"I needed to look upon the human who single-handedly killed my family. Perhaps I wanted to gaze upon her and wonder how I never saw who she really was."

He didn't believe the words, but he wanted to. More than anything. That felt worse.

Kyros's throat worked. "The uncertainty and guilt holding you back from accepting me. It wasn't anything to do with your doubts about me or my family."

I took a shallow breath. "No. I couldn't cross that line while lying to you."

"Maybe there's a shred of decency in you."

The sarcastic words stabbed into my heart. "Kyros, I tried to make things right. You know I did."

He scoffed, turning away. "You tried to pull yourself from the grave you'd made for yourself."

I stood. "That's not what happened."

Kyros whipped back, green eyes flashing. "Then why did you wait until you had proof to bring the matter to our attention? *Why*, if not to save your own hide?"

Because I didn't want to see this look on your face.

Blowing out a breath, I watched him pace around the suite. "The end cascade. When is it?"

The glance he threw my way asked if I was crazy.

I braced myself. "I know it doesn't seem this way, but I care about your family too." The shits had wormed their way into my heart at some point. It even bothered me that Julius would die.

"Do you often secure the death of those you care about?" he asked, cocking his head.

Focused on his emotions, I did my best to brush aside the comment.

His lust was swelling.

Like it had in the past, his urge to rip off my clothes spurred my libido higher. Our bodies were swimming around each other, touching, scenting, listening, and heating. Constantly.

I gulped back air. *Hot* air. The room was stifling. Not big enough for both of us.

While I still had faculty of my brain, I edged around the bed to stand by the open window. The cool air did nothing to soothe the uncomfortable heat building in my body.

"Eight days," Kyros grunted.

Frowning, it took a second to realise he'd answered my question. *Eight days until the end cascade is triggered.* Forecasted to be triggered anyway. It could be several days after. It could also happen any day if Fyrlia scored another big deal or continued to throw obscene amounts of money at properties.

The temptation to tell Kyros my entire plan burned in my throat, if only so he'd stop looking at me like that.

Yes, he'd been forced to interact with me at first. I'd lost count of the times the vampire had lost himself to fury over my actions.

Never, *never* had Kyros looked at me like I was trash. I felt like the worst person in the world, the lowest of the low.

But I had a plan that could change his opinion of me. Like so many of my actions in recent times, my *plan* affected others. Other humans. People I respected who I couldn't forcefully manoeuvre if they didn't choose to work with me.

Ironically, Kyros and I fell down more often than not because we didn't confide in the other. There were so many things I *did* discuss with Kyros. Many times where I'd sought his harmless advice.

And still, the same issue remained between us as it had from day one.

The game.

Perhaps I should bring him on board with this plan. Two heads were better than one, after all, but *Ingenium* was why I couldn't bring him in on this last effort to fix everything.

His motives still weren't my motives.

He played to keep his family alive at nearly any cost.

I played because I wanted our motives to be the same.

I wanted the game gone.

I wanted to live my life without a constant threat over my head. I wanted that for my loved ones too.

I wanted the humans of this city to be free.

I needed Kyros to be done with this game so *we* could be free.

To ensure that happened, I was willing to betray him one more time.

"Nothing to say?" He pressed.

I scrambled for a reply. "You can feel how that knowledge affects me. Has Sundulus figured out an exit point?"

My mouth dried as he straightened, looking as perfect as the first time I saw him.

His jaw clenched. "You lost the right to know our movements when you betrayed us to the Fyrlia scum."

I flinched as though struck.

"Did you take any convincing?" he whispered, stalking forward until he stood before me. "Did you walk in and give up my family without second thought?"

One hundred and fifty years of constant struggle to keep his family alive. That was fuelling his bitterness now—and that his true mate was the person to lose the battle for them.

I didn't answer.

"Tell me," he snarled in my face.

I tilted my chin. "You know me, so I won't answer that question despite the anger you feel."

"I thought I knew you." He whirled away, and I sucked in a large breath as his scent struck me full force.

Fuck.

Pressing my legs together, I bit my lip on a whimper.

His cruel laughter rang out. "It must torture you to feel so torn. Your body wants nothing but to wrap around mine, your mind wants nothing more than to see me dead."

He was venting, but my ire finally rose in response.

"I don't want you dead. And you won't die," I said calmly.

"You believe I'll live happily in Fyrlia territory?" Kyros hissed. "You think that every day in there won't be hell? My family killed before my eyes. My mother raped. Forced each day to hear their insults against those I love." His voice swelled. "The need to get to you, to claim you, will drive me insane. I won't physically die, Basilia."

"I'm sorry," I whispered. "It was a mistake to handle that situation alone. I know that."

"*That* situation." Kyros fixed both eyes on me.

Folding my arms, I returned his regard.

He blurred to me and clamped one arm around my waist, forcing my head upward with a grip under my chin.

Gasping, I clutched his arms so I didn't topple out the window.

"What aren't you telling me?" His voice was thunderous.

Cool air brushed my back as I tried not to choke on his rage.

His eyes blazed into mine and shock filled me as I understood Kyros was about to compel me. Tears stung my eyes, and the full horror of how badly I'd botched things hit me.

The trust was gone.

Kyros told me he wouldn't compel information from me again

after the fourth exchange. If he did, then the void between us really was here to stay.

I let my body go limp and met his blaring gaze in defeat, curling inward on myself.

On my heart.

The energy between us still thrummed and pounded between my legs. Everywhere we touched, even his dominating grip under my chin seared my insides with toe-curling desperation.

Even as tears slipped down my cheeks, I panted with need.

How did I ever believe the blood bond was forcing me to love him? My emotions existed apart from the bond. *Intertwined*, yes, but the distinction between them was so obvious when I was split in half like this.

His erection dug into my hip. His inhales were harsh in my ears.

"The sixth exchange," he snarled.

My eyes flew to his.

Whatever I'd expected, that wasn't it.

I licked my lips. "W-What?"

His hand loosened. "The sixth exchange. We have eight days."

I blinked, trying to fathom the change of gear. He...?

"You *want* the sixth exchange?"

Kyros regarded me coldly, lips pressed together and showing white. "What I want and need are different things. Once Fyrlia wins, I'll never see you again."

But the sixth exchange would make things exponentially worse, wouldn't it? I'd forced myself to stay away from the tower for nine days, and I'd only managed that because Kyros was sneaking to the estate each night. I physically wouldn't be capable of staying away if this thing between us became stronger.

Already, I felt a constant frantic itch that I couldn't scratch.

To hold *more* of that inside until my dying day.

Hell on earth.

I wet my lips a second time, trying to accept I wasn't hearing things. "If that's your logic, then we'd be better to complete the last *two* exchanges."

Ugly anger churned in him at my words. He didn't answer, shifting away from the window before releasing me.

I rubbed my chin, placing distance between us again as I tried to decipher everything the vampire *wasn't* saying. He was holding something back.

"If the sixth exchange is to occur, it must happen in the next few days to allow for the thrall," he said, gazing out the window.

Blood pounded in my ears.

Did he come tonight to bring this up?

I couldn't believe what I was hearing. *Why?* With everything I'd done to him and his family, with all the horrors he'd just laid out for me, *why?*

I opened my mouth. "I'm just surprised—"

"Do you want it or not?"

Did I want to cleave my soul to him more than it already was? Even when he asked in that way? There were so many reasons to say yes—reasons to do with our situation and everyone who could die.

There was only one reason I *wanted* to say yes. "I do, Kyros."

The three words shocked him, but the stalling of his mind disappeared in a flash.

He didn't face me again. "You'll hear from me."

"When?"

I stared at the spot where Kyros had stood, jerking as the window slammed shut with the force of his slipstream.

19

"You heard everything last night?" I said to Laurel as she switched on the noise-cancelling.

I hadn't slept a wink between replaying the conversation over and over with Kyros and scrambling to ensure everything was in place for when he decided to *drop in* for the sixth exchange.

The black-haired vampire was dressed head to toe in leather like usual, but today there was an edge to her I couldn't interpret.

She nodded. "I heard."

Her tone was tense, and I narrowed my eyes.

"Are you okay with what went down?"

She inclined her head again.

"Okay, well if you'd like to explain why you're being weird, leap in at any time."

I shoved a stack of papers across the desk as she took the seat opposite me.

Laurel's nostrils flared. "These are?"

"Two thousand and thirty-two contracts that I've pre-signed." Giving myself tendonitis in the doing. "Each Vissimo who wishes to take my deal needs to print their name, sign, and date."

The contract was there to outline what I expected from those who accepted my deal—though not legally binding by human standards, by Vissimo standards it was.

Laurel's throat worked as she rifled through the sheets of paper.

"I leave it to the discretion of yourself and Vladymir to collect the signatures of those interested. As soon as I enter the sixth thrall, you can begin dispersing them. No sooner." I waited for her murmured agreement.

Leaning across the desk, I tapped a clause in the middle. "This is a non-disclosure clause. It will last until I personally reveal our deal. For the sake of full clarity between us, I need you to ensure that anyone who doesn't take the deal is kept quiet until that time. Can I depend on that?"

Her face firmed as she lifted her gaze from the papers. The freedom of more than two thousand slaves sat before her.

"Yes," she said.

I didn't doubt her for a second. "Good. The sixth exchange will likely be in the next two or three days."

Laurel sat down, drawing the papers closer as if they may be snatched away at any moment. "You keep your own counsel, Basilia. I know that's because of the fine line you walk between the human world and ours, and between loyalty to your mating bond and those you love. I don't know if I can be part of your plans yet, or even if this is going the way you intended. But when you're ready—"

"I fucked up," I blurted.

She stilled and glanced at the contracts again before relaxing. "Tell me."

The vampire sat with her eyes closed as I poured out everything that had happened since my grandmother's death.

Fuck, it felt good. I could almost feel some of the weight on my shoulders lessening as the word tumbled from my lips.

Maybe this should be heard by Tommy, but I couldn't just blab everything out in a rush like this, and Tommy—as much as I loved her—wasn't a vampire. I'd betrayed just about every Vissimo I knew. The royal ones anyway.

I needed reassurance from a vampire I respected.

When I trailed off, Laurel opened her blue eyes.

"Is that all?" she said drily.

I blew out a breath. "Yeah, I know."

She pursed her lips. "Would you like to know what I think based on what you've told me?"

Did I?

Laurel wasn't the kind to spear-tackle Harriet Gregorian because she'd humiliated me. She was the kind to assess the options and decide whether letting me finish the catwalk or stabbing Gregorian on the walk home was the best course of action.

"Yes," I said, meeting her gaze.

"You have a complex about Jessica Alba wearing black leather because you secretly wish you could wear it all the time."

"Oh my god," I exploded. "I just handed you my bleeding heart, and you come back with that." Despite how crappy I felt after a sleepless and emotionally draining night, my lips lifted at the corners.

My friends were terrible at pep talks.

Laurel's eyes brightened. "I knew there was a smile left in you somewhere. We've all been worried about you."

I leaned back in the chair, crossing my arms.

"*Ingenium* has spanned more than one hundred and fifty years, Basilia. You've played the game for a speck of that time, and yet you blame yourself for the outcome."

Because I brought the end cascade about. Kind of.

"You're vocal about your hatred for games, and so I imagine the real reason you're so conflicted is because of your betrayal to Kyros himself."

Ouch. I knew she wouldn't pull punches. "Yeah."

"He has come to the property each night except the first," she told me.

I glared. "Thanks for the heads-up."

She shrugged a shoulder. "Until you exit the sixth thrall, the Indebted have a pretence to keep up. You both needed space after what happened with King Julius."

I sighed. "Maybe. Kyros more than me."

Laurel shook her head. "Do you remember when I asked you what would happen to your loyalties when Kyros claimed you for the sixth time?"

The thought of him biting me nearly elicited a groan.

She quirked a brow. "You assured me that you'd do what needed to be done because you loved your grandmother."

I stilled.

"It can't have been easy to find yourself between that love and a new love. Not when both loves are immortal. When I say you both needed time, I mean it. There has been a change in you since the theme park. Am I to take it that you decided on a side?"

My grandmother.

Or Kyros.

That's what she was asking me.

I tipped my head back, interlacing my fingers. "No sides. Just what's right."

"And what's right, Basi?"

Right was freeing two thousand slaves.

Right was ending a battle over a child that never should have started.

Right was doing what made me and those I loved happy.

"I can't win the game, Laurel," I said softly.

That ship had sailed well and truly.

Her eyes were on me. "Do you need to win? This was never your game to play."

From the moment I met Kyros, it was.

"He will live." Laurel pressed. "You'll have protection of a Vissimo army. *You* could take him back by force."

I had considered that. Part of me would love to take what I wanted.

Except that would hurt the Indebted.

And... "If I don't save Kyros's family, he'll never look at me again."

She pulled a face. "He offered the sixth exchange. Don't you wonder why?"

The thought had kept me up since his visit.

"He's angry at you," Laurel said. "He feels betrayed and hurt. Just as you did not so long ago. But you overcame that. So will he in time."

This vampire was two hundred and eighty years old. I *should* believe her. Except I could feel what Kyros felt, and enough had happened to me that I knew some scars never left. I would always be haunted by imagining how the triplets killed my grandmother. I'd always relive that terrified, desperate moment when I'd dropped the bomb into Theodore's open jacket. I'd never forget the call from Theodore telling me he had Tommy or the way the floor seemed to disappear beneath me.

Kyros was meant to just *get over* the slaughtering of his family? What then? We'd live happily ever after until I died and he went berserk?

No.

Maybe the game had spanned generations before I came along. But this was different for the same reason Trenit and Tynan were at each other's throats after Theodore's death. I'd dropped the bomb, but Trenit clicked the button.

There had been bombs around the necks of the Fyrlia and Sundulus royals for one hundred and fifty years.

But I had clicked the button that would destroy Sundulus.

That was why Kyros would never forgive me.

"I can't win the game, Loz," I said, expression grave. "I can't fulfil my grandmother's legacy in *Ingenium*."

She frowned at me. "Then what are you going to do? Why do you need us?" Laurel glanced at the papers for the billionth time.

I'd free the Indebted regardless of my situation. The only thing stopping me was the uncertainty of when the sixth exchange would occur. Until that happened, I wouldn't rest easy.

Everything in the coming week could blow up in my face.

Ten days ago, I strutted into a situation I felt completely prepared for and it went to shit.

Now, I planned to strut into a situation I couldn't *possibly* prepare for because it was now the only avenue left where Kyros and I might regain a semblance of what we'd once had.

For that, I'd do anything.

I regarded the woman across the desk. "I'm going to give everything I own in Bluff City to Clan Sundulus."

Her mouth rounded.

Couldn't blame her. There were more things that could go wrong with that than right. For one, I could only speak in formal situations if Kyros granted me permission. Then there was the tiny thing where I may not have enough assets to actually change the outcome.

I exhaled slowly. "If Kyros's family goes down, it won't be without me giving everything I have to stop it."

"Mr Tetley has resumed work, but I believe it will take time for him to feel comfortable again," Fred said.

I considered that. "I need to speak to him."

Tommy gave him a modified version of what happened with Theodore, but that didn't erase all of our fights since I first entered *Kyros Sky*. Her father definitely knew about them. He'd known me my entire life, but Tommy was his world.

Which was no doubt why he'd agreed to come back at all.

"That might be best, Miss Le Spyre," Fred said, bowing.

He held a finger to his ear. "Lady Treena is pulling up, miss."

I rose, making sure to keep the speed within human bounds. Fred's reaction to my new additions was one that I was putting off.

I strode past him.

"Miss Le Spyre, is everything okay between you and your grandmother's friends?" Fred asked as I reached the door.

Pausing, I glanced back at him. "They seem to think I'm a younger version of my grandmother, Fred. We've had some disagreements."

Fred smiled.

"They expected you to play the game as your grandmother did?" he asked, shaking his head.

Stepping beside me, he drew the door open.

His brown eyes twinkled. "I predicted that you'd be every inch of the Head of Estate your grandmother was. In your *own* way. If your grandmother's friends believed otherwise, that was their mistake. It sounds like they're now aware of the distinction."

My mouth dry, I walked from the room, his words bouncing around my head.

Fred featured in most of my memories on the estate. Maybe not as a part of the festivities—dinners and the like. The butler always popped in, ensuring things ran smoothly.

I'd spent five hours on the Ferris wheel. I read three books and packed up my grandmother's suite. I endured terrible pep talks from Tommy *and* Laurel.

Yet with an errant compliment, *Fred* had convinced me of my path.

Reaching the lobby, I hastily smoothed my expression in preparation for the next onslaught.

Lady Treena's chauffeur pulled around her gleaming steel-grey car. Before he could stride around to open her door, my grandmother's best friend was out of the vehicle, champagne chute raised in the air.

Was she here as a representative of all the oldies or was this a personal visit?

This was old money I was dealing with. If they were on my side, this could be her digging for information on my loyalties. If they'd turned on me...

... Things were about to get ugly when I couldn't afford—and didn't *want*—them to get ugly.

"Basilia," she said cheerfully.

The tightness around her mouth spoke otherwise.

"Aunt Treena," I replied, gesturing to the house.

"No, no. Just here for a fleeting visit, I'm afraid."

This woman was afraid of one thing and one thing only. *Vissimo.*

She took a fake sip of champagne, observing me.

I was glad to see my grandmother's friend. *Really* glad. No matter what happened next, I had no intention of harming my oldies. Just as I had no intention to back down from what I'd said.

My choice was made.

The old woman hummed and reached into her purse, passing me her chute. As had been the way since I hit sixteen, I chugged the contents behind the curtain of my curls.

When I glanced back up, her expression had softened.

She held out an envelope.

I took it on autopilot, exchanging it for her chute.

Lady Treena held her hand to my cold cheek. "We hope to see you there, dear."

I stared at the envelope as she got into her car and disappeared as swiftly as she'd come.

Hooking my thumb under the wax seal that only served to remind me of the last wax seal I'd pried open, I worked it free.

An invitation. To a soiree. Four days from now.

"And what that means, I have no idea." Could be good. Could be a trap.

If all my oldies were there, however, it worked in perfectly with my plan. *If* Kyros deigned to show up in the next day. Attending their soiree during my thrall seemed like a recipe for disaster.

Hiccupping from the champagne I'd necked, I hustled inside. I had so much shit to do that sleep seriously wasn't an option for me.

Entering the office again, I groaned at the stacks of paper from estate matters piling up while I disregarded everything for *Ingenium*. I had thirty-two emails in my inbox. Scratch that, that was if I just counted the emails requiring thoughtful responses.

All of it would have to wait.

Sliding open the desk drawer, I grabbed my Vissimo law book and the *Ingenium* rule book. Reading them had become a ritual. I'd memorised some parts by chanting them over and over when stressed out of my mind.

Knowing the rules of the game was everything. Of *any* game, whether surviving as part of the human working class or in a life-

and-death vampire battle. Each time I'd lost, it was due to ignorance of the rules or uncertainty about the rules.

And sure, lack of experience too.

I was going up against people who had played *Ingenium* for one hundred and fifty years. They'd had two human lifespans *living* the rules of the game. By now, the complexities of this battle were second nature to them. Meanwhile, thus far, I'd had a crash course that barely skimmed the surface.

The door opened.

I didn't budge my eyes from the chapter on the end cascade. "Fred, I may need you to take over estate tasks again for a few weeks. It's piling up."

Fred didn't answer.

I blinked at the sudden thudding of my heart and jerked my head up.

Kyros entered the office, shutting the door before stalking around the room. His gaze darted to the book in my hands.

Shit.

Recovering from my shock, I set the manual on the low table without a word, face down in case he didn't managed to catch the title.

"A bit of light reading?" he purred.

Yep, totally saw it.

"Kyros," I greeted.

I crossed the room and turned on the noise-cancelling.

He froze, no doubt feeling the pop in his ears and the loss of one of his biggest senses.

"More secrets," he muttered.

I ignored the comment, checking my phone.

11:00 a.m.

He strode behind my desk, scanning the contents there before reading the computer screen.

"You about done?" I said, folding my arms.

The vampire didn't answer, completing his circle around the room. The act was an almost exact replica of King Julius when he

215

entered Kyros's home for the first time. With the king, I'd seen it as a protective thing.

With Kyros, I got the vibe I was on trial.

He stopped by the low table and turned the two books over, reading the titles.

I waited for him to demand answers. When he didn't, I couldn't resist saying, "You know I won't rest until I find a solution to this."

Despite the menacing entrance, a quick check told me much of his bitterness was gone. Instead, the bone-deep weariness was in the driver's seat once more. Then again, would I sleep if nine of my family members could be dead in six days?

Ten, I corrected myself, recalling Kearra.

"You expect to find an answer in a handful of days, three of which you'll spend in a thrall?" His green eyes bore into mine.

He was so angry at me. So disappointed and heartsick.

A perverse part of me didn't care because my vampire was standing before me. My *mate*. Maybe for tonight, he could pretend I hadn't signed his family's death warrants, and I could pretend he'd forgiven me.

I lowered my arms. "You're here for the sixth exchange?"

"Why else would I be here?"

Swallowing hurt, I cleared my throat. "Okay, how's it going to work?"

"My siblings are outside. Once I've bitten you, they'll retrieve me. I've spoken with Laurel. She will confine you in your quarters until the end of the thrall."

I deflated.

I'd expected to spend the thrall with him again. Which was stupid of me, really. He didn't even want to be here, but I'd hoped he might be unable to stay away.

He watched me with cold green eyes, and I stared at his slim black tie, thinking over all the times I'd dreamed of loosening it.

"The date for end cascade negotiations is set for the seventh," he told me in a low voice.

I glanced up. Five days from now.

Fuck.

I'd read through the end cascade chapter of the *Ingenium* rule book enough times to know what he referred to by *negotiations*. Though the end cascade would be triggered, Fyrlia could spend months or years buying up the entirety of Bluff City. The rule book stated that the losing clan could call a meeting when the end cascade —the point of no return—was triggered. In exchange for surrendering on the spot, Sundulus could attempt to barter for some of the lives of the royal family.

Negotiating with King Mikael seemed like a useless pursuit. I'd managed to do so, but only because I gave him what he valued most. He'd all but won *Ingenium now*; there was no need for him to compromise on anything else. He'd waited for this moment for one hundred and fifty years.

"I see," I whispered. For all their sakes, I hope Kearra was allowed to live. Surely even Mikael couldn't be so ruthless.

Kyros stepped closer, and my stomach churned as I held myself back from running at him.

Our separation after the fifth exchange made me feel physically sick.

A whimper slipped between my teeth, and I squeezed my eyes shut.

"After the negotiations, I won't be allowed to contact you," Kyros said, his voice straining. "This is the last time we will see each other."

No.

My chest rose and fell with my shallow breaths. "Maybe in time..."

I trailed off because we both knew that wouldn't happen.

King Julius had been convinced. Or at least, he recognised a losing battle. Mikael would keep Kyros from me no matter the cost.

His gaze darkened. "Mikael may allow me to complete the mating ritual with you if I can't be controlled, but he'll never permit you to become Vissimo. He'll try to break me over the next five or six decades and wait until you die and I lose control. Then I'll be his weapon across the ages."

Bile threatened to make an appearance as his words hit me with the force of a sledgehammer. "That's his plan?"

Kyros nodded. "He practiced on the triplets. He'll do the same for me."

My hands curled into tight fists. "You'll never be like *them*."

A wrinkle appeared between his brows. "I used to fear losing control. It's the greatest fear of most alphas. But in five days, most of my family will be dead. I yearn for the darkness losing control might bring."

He wasn't allowed to speak like that.

I did something I hadn't dared to do since everything blew up in my face.

Resting my hands on his chest, I gripped the front of his shirt. "I know things between us are more messed up than they've ever been, Kyros, but please don't give up. There's a way out of this, I promise you."

Never had the urge to admit everything been stronger.

Kyros glanced into my eyes, and his want, his *fierce* want rolled over me. I moaned, choking on a sob at the same time.

"This is the last time I'll see you, Basilia," he said, cupping my face. "As fucking furious as I am for what you did and what it will mean for my family, I can't spend these last moments in anger. If this is the last memory I have of you, of *us*, then I must leave your betrayal at the door."

I let go of his shirt to cover his hands, tears stinging my eyes. "We'll find a way through this."

He let me choke out the words, gaze rapt on my expression. He seemed to be waiting for my tears because he swept the salty droplets away the second they tumbled from my wet lashes.

Closing the distance, he dropped a whisper-soft kiss on the tops of my cheekbones. "Don't cry, my beauty."

If he wanted me to stop crying, that was the wrong thing to say. He kissed my lips as they trembled, slipping his warm tongue into my mouth in a bitter-sweet kiss that would torture me to the end of my days.

I clung to him, pulling him against my body as tightly as possible.

When we broke apart, we were both breathing hard.

"I may not be able to see you," Kyros said hoarsely, resting his forehead against mine. "But I'll always feel where you are. We'll always know what the other is feeling. And sometimes, if we ever draw close enough, we might catch some of each other's thoughts."

Fresh tears coated my cheeks. The picture he painted was unbearable to contemplate. To be so close, to constantly feel the other and never touch them or look in their eyes. To live and die in that way.

"We need to run," I stuttered. "Us. Your entire family. Everyone."

He pressed kisses along my jaw and up to my temple, licking at my tears as he went. "We'd be hunted by all Vissimo."

My chest seized in time to my soul-shaking sobs. "Ky—"

The vampire caught my chin, and I stared at him through wet lashes.

"My beauty," he said in a voice so soft I had to lean forward. "Know that I'll live for each of those moments. I'll wake each night to feel your presence within me. The longing to hear your innermost thoughts will bring me joy across the decades. *Live for me*, my beauty, so that I may experience life through your heart." He rested a hand between my breasts. "Through your soul."

I couldn't see him through the tears.

My words were barely intelligible. "I can't lose you, Kyros. I'm so sorry for what I did."

He pulled me against his chest. "This is not a time for apologies and regrets, *true mate*. They are meaningless with a bond such as ours." He stroked my back. "Our blood sings. It will sing always, across the ages. Never forget that."

Pulling back, I did my best to regain control of myself. He was right. If tonight was our last night, this wasn't a time for tears and pain.

"Before we start," he said, still stroking my back, "I have a few requests."

Anything. "Tell me."

"On the morning of the negotiations, you need to board a private plane with everyone you care about. I am sending all of my Indebted with you."

That couldn't happen.

"I want to stay here," I countered.

His jaw clenched. "I need you away from Bluff City during negotiations. I need to know you're safe. I can't stop you from coming back—this is your home—but if you know what's good for you and Tommy, you won't ever return."

Tommy.

He studied me intently. "For Tommy, Basilia. For me."

I didn't argue the point further.

"Thank you, mate," he whispered against my ear.

A shiver wracked my body. It was surprisingly easy to shove aside the demands of the blood bond when Kyros could be lost to me after this night. "There's more?"

"Yes," he said, peering at the books on the low table. "You may know this already, but when a human mate reaches the sixth exchange, they have the right to purchase Indebted. I know how you feel about their situation, but I urge you to consider taking on my Indebted after the sixth thrall. You have enough money, and they'll be able to protect you where I cannot."

He... was asking me to buy the Indebted. I'd operated in secret this entire time, and yet he was presenting me with a different version of the same plan.

Kyros pulled a slip of paper from his internal suit pocket and placed it on the table. "There are the details for the transfer. When the sixth thrall ends, I'll make it known to the clan who handles administration for the Indebted. You won't encounter resistance."

I'd planned on using three of the Indebted as witnesses to grant my access per another clause, but Kyros was offering to do it directly. On the slip were bank details I'd already asked Laurel to secure.

I had so grossly underestimated this man.

Rising on tiptoes, I pressed a kiss against his lips, looping my arms around his neck. A growl ripped through his throat. "Thank you so much."

"Basilia," he sighed into my mouth.

I threaded my fingers through his toffee strands, pulling back.

"Mate," I told him, not a flicker of humour in my voice. "*True mate.*"

They were different things. It felt insulting to call him anything less.

His growl ripped from his chest, and my skin flushed in response.

"I want to be inside you one last time," Kyros said, chest heaving.

In reply, I lifted my sweater overhead, tossing my T-shirt after it before sliding my shorts down. Kyros didn't look away, unmoving as I went to work on his shirt and pants.

Slowing to draw the moment out wasn't an option as much as I yearned to do so.

"Inside," I said hoarsely, freeing his erection.

How long we could draw out sex would be a test of both of our control. It wasn't as if Kyros's blood was a turn off for me at this point. With each exchange, the taste became sweeter, the texture like milk, soothing and heady. My mouth watered at the thought of biting into him.

I was more than ready for him and grumbled when he dropped to his knees before me.

"One last taste," he said, before latching on to my clit.

A wordless scream shredded my being as my head fell back.

A haze was spreading, flooding my cheeks with fever. I gripped his hair, moving against his mouth, powerless to remain still.

"Ky," I cried out.

He slipped a finger into me and my knees shook. The haze was growing so hot. A sauna. I scrambled to unhook my bra, my legs buckling.

"Too hot," I complained, my mind clouded with fire.

Kyros lowered us onto the chaise and hovered over me. Our gazes locked as he held my knees wide. We held our breath as he moved to my entrance.

He pressed inside me and our moans tangled as tightly as our emotions.

We rocked into each other, an odd calmness to our movements that we'd never experienced outside of the thrall.

I locked my ankles behind his hips, straining to meet every deep, blissful thrust. His fangs lengthened, and I stroked them in time to our rhythm.

His rapture was mine. The pleasure he felt, I did too.

"Fucking perfect," Kyros hissed, sucking one of my nipples into his mouth, careful not to pierce the surrounding skin with his incisors

I arched, clamping around him. His hiss turned to a savage snarl, and he palmed my breasts, hands roaming as frantically as mine.

Sweat from resisting the sixth exchange coated us, but the pressure in my body was building despite my best efforts. The mindlessness that always accompanied the orgasms Kyros gave me was creeping over my senses. That out-of-body moment when I could only fathom ecstasy and the connection to him.

"I love you, Basilia Le Spyre," Kyros whispered.

Heart at bursting point, I opened my mouth, but my answering words turned to a scream as his fangs sliced into my breasts, catapulting me headfirst into the deepest pleasure I'd ever known.

It shook my mind. Shook my body.

Because the pleasure came from us.

And nothing, *no one*, had ever meant more to me.

My true mate.

A pulling sensation on my chest gently tugged me back to the chaise in my office.

In a legless daze, I stared at Kyros lapping blood from my chest as he continued to move in and out of me. A trickle of red escaped his lips as he tensed.

A roar burst from his mouth as he shoved into me, eliciting a fresh round of aftershocks for me. Half wild, I snatched for his wrist, desperate for his blood. My breath hitched, and a *growl* left my lips as my mate pulled his arm away, slowing the pace of his thrusts.

"Now," I demanded, the order morphing to a breathless moan as he pulled me up to straddle him.

I gasped at the fullness of him inside me with the changed position, but wasted no time rocking against him in firm circles.

His eyes were green fire as he bit into his wrist. Cupping the back of my neck, Kyros hovered his dripping wound over my mouth, waiting as I swallowed each mouthful before feeding me more.

I swallowed more and more of his sweet blood, our gazes locked, bodies connected and moving in perfect, beautiful sync.

"I love you, Kyros Atagio," I said hoarsely. Pressing one hand to his cheek, I rested my other palm over his heart.

Our heart.

Red fell freely from his eyes.

And fire slammed into me.

20

I crawled after the morsel, licking my lips.

Hungry.

"Fuck my life," a woman said.

I liked her. Mostly. Not when she wouldn't give me the food.

I blinked a few times at the sandwich on the floor. Something was funny about it. And *ouch*, my knees hurt.

Sitting back on my haunches, I studied the petite woman with new eyes.

"Tommy?" I asked.

Her eyes widened. "Holy shit, is it over? Am I talking with Basil or Coriander?"

I shivered as fire drained from my veins, leaving me cold. I recognised the feeling this time. *The thrall.*

And yep, I had my memories again.

"It's Basil," I rasped at her.

We were in my suite. It was intact—no painted walls, no moved furniture or décor pinecones.

I frowned at the sandwich, tracing the length of nylon tied around the baguette to the stick in Tommy's hand. "What the hell? Are you leading me around the room with a sandwich on a string?"

She huffed and picked up the baguette. "I was trying to get you into the shower."

My lips twitched.

"It was working," she exploded. "*You* try looking after crazy you for three fucking days. I'm never having kids. Ever!"

Shit.

"That bad, huh?" I didn't need her confirmation. It was. It definitely, definitely was.

Tommy winced. "Laurel said it was tame compared to some of your other thralls. You spent most of the time trying to escape to find Kyros. If I wasn't babysitting you and if you hadn't taken me hostage at one point, I'd almost be impressed. And you refused to take off that outfit, so the stink is real, girl."

I peered down at my clothing.

"Fuck," I ground out.

Fucking black leather! Head to toe in the stuff. *Again.* I groaned, running my hands through my knotted hair.

A small squeak escaped Tommy, and I dared her with my eyes to mention Jessica Alba.

"Jessica Alba," she said immediately, snorting.

Ugh.

Forcing my disintegrated standards from my mind, I grimaced, recalling tying sheets together to rappel out my window. I faked sickness on the second day. Called the police a few times.

Crap. Thrall me was resourceful as hell.

"Sorry about the last three days," I said. "Maybe I'll take that shower." *And apologise to the leather gods.*

Tommy stopped me. "Really, it wasn't that bad. Kind of endearing in a way. And you should congratulate yourself for reaching the sixth exchange."

I blanched, gazing at her. That's right. Now she mentioned it, I was where I'd planned to be from the start.

Go me.

While in the throes of revenge, I'd imagined this moment would feel a hell of a lot better.

Forcing a smile, I strode into the bathroom, stopping short when I felt Kyros's focus. The sensation of him within me was so strong. His feelings, his state, now held equal importance with my own. My mind was half preoccupied by him.

And—whoa, what the hell was that?

There was an inexplicable draw from behind me. I spun in a circle. The draw wasn't to the shower, not to something in this room, or on the estate. The feeling was tugging me toward Grey, and my mouth rounded as I figured it out.

Oh my god.

I could feel where Kyros was.

The book didn't say anything about this! Neither did Kyros. Or anyone. But as sure as I stood here breathing, I was sure that if I followed the tugging, I'd end up right by his side.

Where I belonged.

There was no place I'd rather be right now.

The thought of the distance between us sent waves of misery and longing through me. His company was guaranteed joy. Anything else was a sub-par quality of living.

Kyros? I thought his name, focusing hard toward Grey.

Nothing.

Could he hear my thoughts this far away? There were distance restrictions on the mind-reading thing unlike everything else. I was relieved not to hear anything just yet though. Having someone in my mind would be a whole new adjustment period. For both of us.

Turning on the shower, I settled into one of the longest *wash, shave, hydrate* routines I'd ever had. It rivalled the one I went through after discovering vampires. That seemed like so long ago now, yet in reality only a few months had passed.

Everything was different now.

And everything could be stolen away in the coming days.

That couldn't happen—I wouldn't let it. Or I wasn't Agatha Le Spyre's granddaughter.

Business time.

Moisturising a second time, I strode into the room naked.

Tommy was gone—couldn't blame her. I owed her big time for that. She was the only person barring Kyros who I didn't mind seeing me like that.

I dressed for the day I wanted.

Black jeans, white T-shirt, royal-blue blazer, and a feature necklace. Leaving my hair down, I zipped mocha heeled boots into place.

"Princess Laurel," I bellowed, striding from my suite.

"I'm right here."

Cursing, I whirled to the wall, hand clutching the base of my throat.

"And I'm not a princess any longer," she said.

Semantics. "Where are we at?" Usually this conversation would occur in my office. I was done with that.

She straightened. "Please come with me."

I trailed down the stairs out to the pool area after her. Stopping on the patio, I gazed out at the sea of leather-clad Indebted.

Leather-clad *people.*

Laurel rested a hand on my shoulder. "Not everyone could attend, seeing as we're keeping up the charade for now. But those who could be..." She gestured to the huge crowd of enslaved vampires. For a very few of them, their own crimes had landed them here. Most of them were here to pay for the crimes of others.

Decades and centuries never knowing which day would be their last. At the mercy of the whims of their masters.

Whatever was happening in my life, *this* moment made every struggle worth it.

"How many signed the contract?"

"Everyone but Deana. She doesn't believe she deserves freedom. If you're willing to keep the offer open, then we will continue to convince her that our pasts don't define us." Laurel looked into the crowd, and I followed her gaze to the woman who'd accidentally introduced me to Vissimo.

I preferred concise orders over grand speeches, but the weight of this situation—that I couldn't possibly understand the entire significance of without walking in their shoes—chased away my qualms.

Sometimes grand speeches were necessary.

From the top of the patio stairs, I surveyed their silent masses, a tiny piece of me wondering what my staff thought of this gathering.

"I come from a different world to yours," I said in a soft voice. "But in the last few months, I've felt more at home in your company than anywhere else. You are not Indebted, and what happened to you was wrong. Enslaving any being is a disgusting, deplorable act. *You are Vissimo.*"

A murmur ran through the crowd, but they otherwise stood like soldiers, listening intently to my words.

There was so much I could say. That I *wanted* to say, but to put the pain I felt on their behalf into words was an impossible thing. Better that they found solace amongst each other, as I'd found in those compelled as I was. They needed real understanding.

Scanning them for a full minute, I said, "You will work for me for a time, but you need to know that from this moment, you are no longer slaves, you are free. Throw off your chains and live without fear in honour of those who couldn't be here with us today."

Drawing out my phone, I opened my emails. "Let's make it official."

I'd already drafted an email—*yes*, modern-age correspondence—to Clan Gugi with the registration numbers of all the Indebted. Without removing Deana's name from the list, I clicked Send.

Laurel's gaze was heavy on me.

I scrolled through my contacts to Donald Duck and dialled.

"Miss Le Spyre," the head of my financial team answered.

Four rings.

Unacceptable. But I'd deal with that another time.

"Roger," I said coolly. "I'm making a large transfer. Here's the account number."

I smirked as he scrambled for a paper and pen, rattling off the number and account name. He read it back.

"Correct," I replied.

"The amount, Miss Le Spyre?"

I surveyed the Indebted, smiling at them. "Five hundred and twenty-two million."

"Usual currency?"

"Yes."

He hesitated. "What should I file the transfer under, miss?"

I rolled my eyes. "Whatever you want, Roger. Hamburgers. Send me confirmation when it's done."

Hanging up, I descended the steps and perched on the bottom one. Closing my eyes, I tilted my face to the sun and waited.

There had to be more than five hundred Vissimo here, but I could have been alone with only the slight breeze lifting my hair. No one made a peep.

My phone buzzed.

I read the message and then typed the second number from Kyros into my phone.

I held it to my ear.

"Clan Gugi, Indebted division. You're speaking with Sora."

One ring.

That was service. Roger should take notes.

"Sora. It's Basilia Le Spyre. My true mate, Kyros Atagio, contacted you regarding our recent sixth exchange."

"Hold, please."

Please have called. Please have called.

"Mrs Le Spyre, yes. We received his confirmation."

I pulled a face at the Mrs bomb. He absolutely did that on purpose to mess with me.

She attacked a keyboard in the background. "We've also received your email with the codes of two thousand and thirty-two Indebted."

"Payment was just put through," I told her. "How long does clearance usually take?"

"Twelve hours at the most, Mrs Le Spyre. Confirmation of payment will be sent by email."

I grimaced again. *Damn*, longer than I'd hoped. "Thank you."

"Is there anything else I can help you with today?"

Jesus. How often did this woman process the freedom of more than two thousand slaves? "No. That's all."

I hung up and flipped my phone before sliding it into my back pocket.

"I didn't want to be freed." Deana stood before me, rage etched in the hard lines of her face.

She'd lost every shred of innocence in her features since I first saw her wrapped around her human boyfriend.

Waving Laurel away, I got to my feet. "You're free, regardless."

"I didn't sign the contract," she spat.

My brows rose. "No, you didn't. I guess that means you're totally free to do what you want."

Fear widened her eyes. "No."

"Clearly, being free is the harder path for you. If you really want to torture yourself for what happened, choose to live in painful freedom."

A confused frown graced her face.

"Go or stay. If you stay, you work for the same wage as everyone else with the same time off. If you choose to go, you need to wait one week."

I turned to Laurel, who dipped her head.

She'd watch Deana until I let the cat out of the bag.

I climbed a few stairs so the Vissimo could see me. "I'll send word out when final confirmation comes through. Thank you for being brave enough to accept my offer. Now, please listen closely. My friend Tommy is in charge of housing. A list of available houses and the number each rental sleeps will be handed out tomorrow. A team will arrive early next week to start the process of setting up bank accounts, tax numbers, and applying for identification. For the next four to six weeks, until we have everything necessary, you will be paid in cash. You will receive payment from today. I've arranged for your first month to be paid in advance so you're able to purchase various items you need. These funds will be distributed tomorrow."

I studied the slackening faces. "My butler, Fred, will hand out a template budget sheet that I drew up. This will help you spread funds to cover discounted rent, food, public transportation, and other costs of living. Some may not need this, but some time has passed since you had control of money, so I hope the template doesn't come across as insulting. Of course, aside from housing costs, you're welcome to spend your money how you wish."

I took a breath. "Laurel and Vladymir are in charge of the work and housing roster. I'm sure they've notified you of this, but until further notice, you are to continue your current work for Fyrlia and Sundulus. I apologise for this subterfuge, but it is a necessary one."

They were silent as I finished.

"That's it," I said lamely.

Laurel sank to her knees beside me, her head bowed.

Not this again.

In a wave, the Vissimo mimicked their leader, dropping to their knees.

"Enough of that," I said sharply.

They didn't budge.

Blowing out an irritated breath, I dropped to my knees, too, bowing my head to them. Their response wasn't so much a murmur as a shocked intake of air.

Ha! "I'm not standing until the rest of you do," I murmured, lifting my head. "So get the fuck up because my knees hurt."

"We could outlast you," Laurel replied, her gaze cutting to me.

"No doubt," I replied. "So give me the pity win, please."

Laurel rested a hand over her heart. "You are a friend of ours. Forevermore."

I swallowed hard. Did she have any idea what that word meant to me? *My forevermore love.* Something my grandmother had often said to me.

If she could see me right now, I know she'd be so proud.

"We will not forget this day," Laurel whispered.

Her fervent words robbed me of speech, so I just placed a hand over my heart in return.

She stood and the other leather-clad vampires followed suit. I joined them, scowling at their outfits.

"Maybe now you can leave the black leather to Jessica Alba where it belongs," I muttered.

"You spent two days of your thrall in black leather," Laurel replied in an even tone.

I turned away, entering the house. "Prove it."

She called after me. "Look through your phone."

Dammit. They didn't?

I hurried into my office, scrolling through my gallery, settling on a photo of me hanging off one of the posts on my bed.

In black leather.

If I knew Tommy—and I did—there was more than one copy of these photos.

Fuckers.

Leaving the door to my office open, I threw myself into the upholstered chair. Uncomfortable fucking thing. "Fred," I shouted.

Ten seconds passed and he appeared in the doorway. Magic man.

"Can you order me a comfortable chair, please?" I huffed.

"You want to replace the chair, miss?"

I fluttered a hand. "Yes, yes. A comfortable one that doesn't make my ass numb. That kind."

I caught his smile before he bowed and exited the room.

Logging into my inbox, the top email caught my attention.

Churchill Team

Miss Le Spyre, As requested...

I closed my eyes.

The moment of truth.

Did I have enough assets in Bluff City to swing the tide for Sundulus? I needed to make a 4 percent difference to trigger the end cascade against Fyrlia. If I could do that, everything would work out.

A 2 percent difference would restore equilibrium, and the game would continue.

Tommy entered the room. "You look constipated, lovely."

Funnily enough, that's how I felt.

232

"Just an email that could make or break my life. You know, typical Tuesday."

"It's not Tuesday."

Really?

She rounded the desk and rested a hand on my shoulder. "Go on then. Open the mofo up."

Taking a breath, I obeyed, scanning the short message before opening the two attachments.

I scrolled straight to the bottom of both documents, and my mouth dried.

There was no way to know if the valuation for each clan was completely accurate. Fyrlia could have assets I didn't know about.

I pulled out a valuation of my assets from the top drawer. It detailed everything I owned locally, minus the estate.

Hands shaking, I extracted my grandmother's massive calculator from the same drawer and added Sundulus's total to mine.

I compared that figure to the sum of Clan Fyrlia's assets.

"Well?" Tommy strained.

My heart sank.

21

The thick paper of Lady Treena's invitation sat heavy in my hand. I was entering the lion's den tonight with an agenda so fucking ballsy that Grandmother might have raised a single brow.

The gathering was at our usual meeting place at Sir Olythieu's which led me to assume this wasn't a soiree at all but a normal meeting.

Yet someone had gone to the effort of making an invitation.

Which meant Dame Burke organised this—her flair for the dramatic was about as strong as her sailor's mouth.

I'd dressed for a soiree, regardless, slipping into a black and flittering floor-length gown for the occasion. Strapless, it highlighted the curve of my neck and the graceful slope of my shoulders, accentuating the curves of my body that drove Kyros to distraction. White gloves extended to my elbows.

I wish he could see me now.

I hadn't heard from my mate, and weirdly, that felt right. He was gearing up for his battle, and I was gearing up for mine. Our last moment in each other's arms was the memory we wanted to retain if the worst happened.

Two butlers in tuxes bowed and swung the doors of the ballroom open.

Yep, definitely Dame Burke.

The six elite were waiting for me, already seated around the square table in the middle of the huge dancing area. No one spoke as I took my seat and fixed each of them with a level look.

"Good evening, Basilia," Sir Olythieu said in a mild voice.

"Good evening." I inclined my head regally and saw the hint of amusement in his gaze.

Mrs Syrre cleared her throat. "We thought it best to give tempers time to cool so each of us could regain perspective before meeting again."

Mmm-hmm. I peered around. "A lot of effort for a meeting."

Dame Burke grinned as the others glared at her.

I placed my hands on the armrests. "So what's it going to be?"

Mr Hothen stroked his jaw.

I hadn't spoken to him since delivering the news of Sandra's death. He looked the same as ever, but that meant nothing.

"Some of us have been victims of the beasts for nearly thirty years," he said. "Our view of the creatures is unlikely to ever change. Which, from my reckoning, is going to become a regular obstacle in our meetings even if we're united in our overall goal."

I waited. There was more.

"Our larger concern." Lady Treena took over. "Is that you've been forced into a horrible situation. As such, our new goal with regards to these meetings is to free you from this mating ritual you find yourself trapped in."

My anger swelled at her comment, but I tempered it as Mr Dithis spoke.

"From what you've told us, the end cascade will be triggered in two days. Bitter though it makes us feel, it is time to admit the game is lost. The new focus needs to be protecting you. Your grandmother would have wanted that."

They wanted to keep me safe.

I inhaled to restore my own perspective. In their shoes, I would be thinking the same thing. They'd watched me grow from baby to child to teen and into adulthood. As they shoved away their families and severed ties to keep them safe from Vissimo, I was always here—their substitute child.

"I know what Grandmother would have wanted," I said. "To see me happy. Safety doesn't always equate to happiness. Look at the way she chose to live her life, fighting a more powerful race while living in daily fear. She did that because anything less would have made her unhappy."

Dame Burke frowned. "That's what we want too."

"Your assumption is the belief that freeing me from Kyros will make me happy," I said gently.

She reeled back.

I regarded the occupants of the table. "I love him."

Lady Treena covered her mouth, the horror in her eyes plain.

Their shocked disbelief buzzed heavy around the table.

Shrugging a shoulder, I said, "I love a Vissimo."

Sir Olythieu jolted. "What did you just say?"

"I love Kyros," I repeated, frowning.

"No," he whispered. "You said, I love a—" He cut off, staring pointedly at me.

A gasp fled my lips.

I shot to my feet. "Vissimo. Vampires."

"Sundulus. Fyrlia. Ingenium!" My mouth dried as I met their stares.

I clutched my cheeks with my gloved hands.

"What's happening?" Mr Hothen said. "Why can you suddenly say everything?"

I struggled to control my harsh breaths.

"He freed her," Sir Olythieu said. His brows drew together.

I hadn't felt him doing it—but I *was* kind of distracted at the time. And maybe releasing a compulsion didn't feel the same as putting one in place.

"He must have," I said, my voice faint.

Sitting heavily, I dropped my wide-eyed gaze to the table, my mind working frantically.

"He didn't tell you?" Mrs Syrre asked.

I wet my lips. "He said I needed to get on a plane with everyone I cared about in two days. Then he said I needed to purchase Indebted to protect myself. He gave me the details to do so."

"He... gave you an army?" Lady Treena asked.

Closing my eyes, I gathered all my surprise and gratitude and *love*, pushing it to Kyros. I felt his jolt, followed by a searing warmth tinged with regret.

In some ways, I couldn't wait to read his mind. Because what the fuck did that mean?

"Are you speaking to him?" Mr Dithis said.

Opening my eyes, I glanced at the man my grandmother had called Pie. "We can hear each other's thoughts now we've completed the sixth exchange, but not from this distance. We haven't tested that part yet. But we can feel what the other feels, and I can sense where he is."

Dame Burke leaned forward. "What else?"

"One of your butlers is taking a piss forty metres away," I said to Sir Olythieu, then jerked my chin to the far wall. "There is a bug flying in the next room." Inhaling, I sighed. "One of you uses sandalwood body wash."

Mr Hothen made a small noise.

"I can rip a door off its hinges and run one-hundred metres in seven seconds. A small cut in my skin will heal completely within twelve hours." I finished. "These are changes that occurred in the fourth and fifth exchanges."

"And the sixth?" Lady Treena asked.

I tapped my head. "The telepathy."

As they absorbed that, I collected my thoughts. "Now I know where you all stand, I'd like to make the entirety of my position known. It will be much easier now."

He'd freed me.

He hadn't just protected me by removing the compulsion. He'd given me the tools to protect myself. That meant so much.

I interlocked my fingers. "I'm unsure how much of my grandmother's plan you were privy to. I assume that due to my presence on the estate, she kept some of the finer details to herself as I have. Now things are coming to a head, I'd like to fill in the gaps."

Their faces smoothed to a wrinkled replica of what mine was before I blurted the word Vissimo.

No one made a sound. It wasn't from a sense of devotion like the ex-Indebted. Without knowing they did so—because they'd have stopped if they realised—the six elite studied me like crocodiles about to ambush their prey.

I appreciated that they were looking at me like an equal. "The first thing you need to know is that I freed two thousand and thirty-two enslaved vampires yesterday. They are now in my employ for the duration of one year. They previously belonged to Sundulus and Fyrlia. Currently, they're continuing the appearance of working for the clans until I make my move."

Dame Burke's mouth bobbed.

Opening my document case, I removed six sheets and handed them out. "This was my plan for the next sixty years—for my lifetime. In two years, when the last of the real estate had been purchased, I had plans to expand into other industries. In ten years, I would have doubled the assets my grandmother had attained. In twenty years, I would have been a real player on the board. In thirty years, things would have become ugly as I began pressing in on clan territory to take assets back from them. That battle would have continued until my death. At which point—if I'd dared to have a family—I would no doubt pass the reins onto my children."

I studied them as they skimmed over the ten-page summary of my Bluff City domination plan.

Mr Dithis whistled low.

Steeling myself, I continued. "If Fyrlia wasn't a breath away from winning, that might have been my life. I would have played until they killed me or until my death, *but*," I said, lifting my chin, "the situation has changed. As much as I tried to keep myself distant from Kyros, my emotions became involved. The mating ritual altered me physically. Fyrlia is days from winning. The plan must therefore change." I placed my palms on the table and met each of their gazes. "I am not their creature," I said. "I will never be their creature."

Lady Treena and Sir Olythieu relaxed.

"Neither am I my grandmother's creature." I didn't give Mrs Syrre's gasp time to settle in, ploughing forward. "I am not Agatha Le Spyre. If you aren't aware of that, then you need to be. I'm not a replacement for the woman you lost, however much I respected and idolised her. What I am is someone who infiltrated a clan of vampires to do the right thing by her, by you, and by the people in this city. And, I initially thought, for me." I curled my fingers to a fist. "I won't kill people that I care about—Vissimo or other. I *will* take the path that makes me happy and protects those I love."

Looking at my ten-page plan, I tore it in two. "This is not the life I wish to lead. My grandmother did, but I don't."

"You're going to abandon this city?" Sir Olythieu asked coolly.

I smiled. "No. The game must end. *Ingenium* hurts humans and vampires alike. It must be finished, but that can't be achieved in the way my grandmother envisioned, or how I first intended. There's a way we can end *Ingenium* on our terms. Now, I want to pre-empt the next part by acknowledging I've lived through three months of terror in comparison to the years you've spent under *their* control. But I *have* felt terror."

I pulled back my hair. I always covered the scar with make-up before coming. Things were so messed up after Tommy left, and I wasn't sure that I could even answer their questions about how I got it.

"I got this while murdering one of my grandmother's killers," I told them. "Clan Fyrlia wanted my money and they took Tommy to lure me away from protection. Tommy had no idea she was dating one of the Fyrlia royals. He drugged her, and she barely survived. I walked into their territory to save her—a place Kyros couldn't follow without the deaths of his family—and was tortured and beaten. They strapped a bomb around my neck, put me in a ring with one of the Tonyi triplets, and we fought to the death. When he tore into my neck," I dropped my hair to cover the scar again, "I managed to place the bomb from my neck in his jacket. He was blown to pieces, and I barely survived. I have permanent damage to my ears as a result of their torture."

They listened intently. I couldn't gauge their reaction.

"I *will* kill the other two triplets," I told them, my face hardening. "Because they killed my grandmother. For what they did to Tommy. I'm telling you this because I've met the royals of both clans. I've met both kings. I wouldn't pick either as an ally if I had another choice, but if I must choose a side, then King Julius wins every day of the week. When he discovered my betrayal against his clan, he could have killed me."

Though it would have sent his son into a berserk rage, so maybe that wasn't mercy, but I'd leave that out of this.

"What are you leading to?" Mr Hothen said, ice dripping from his words.

"I can't win this game." I'd dreaded saying the words to them, but they slipped from my mouth, followed by a wave of relief. "But I *can* ensure Fyrlia doesn't win—with your help. My team has run the numbers. If I give Sundulus my local assets, I can restore balance in the game." If the numbers were correct—a big *if*.

That got a reaction.

"You're going to *help* them win?" Lady Treena said, her face twisting.

I took the comment in my stride. Part of me had expected to be evicted by now. "I can restore balance, but I can't trigger the end cascade against Fyrlia alone." My exhale shook. "But you need to know that when I give everything I own in Bluff City to Sundulus, I won't be able to recoup my position on the board ever. This is me telling you that our part in the game is ending whether *Ingenium* continues or not." There was one currency the vampires were richer in, and that was time.

"I want *Ingenium* to end. I don't want to waste my life playing it. So

I'm asking for your help," I told them. "Our part in the game is over, regardless, and we can't win, but we can finish it for good. That power is in your hands. With your combined wealth, the result would be a certainty."

Dame Burke snorted. "You want us to give our wealth and assets to the people who have made us live in daily fear. I pushed my *children* away, Basilia. I made them think I hated them and severed all ties with them. I've lost decades knowing them. You want me to hand the victory to half the monsters on a silver platter?"

I met her fiery gaze. "Yes. That's what I am asking. When the game ends, so does their need to control humans to gain an edge. They'd have no reason to continue harming the citizens of this city."

"Apart from feeding on us," she said sarcastically.

They survived on blood donations, but I wasn't about to tell the elite about that particular weakness.

I felt their unrelenting resistance. The others kept their own counsel, but I felt their animosity. If there was time, I'd leave things here for now.

But we didn't have that luxury.

"You know that I love each of you. Each of you was an integral part of my childhood. I didn't have parents, I didn't have many friends, but because of your presence and my grandmother's, I became what I am. So it's with love that I tell you the following. I don't wish to be apart from Kyros. What I do want is to end the game that took my grandmother's life and has harmed so many others. I want to live a full life with Kyros, and that is not possible if Fyrlia wins. I'm asking the world of each of you. In reality, none of you owe me a thing. But I know you must be deathly worried for me. So believe me when I say that just as I found a home with the six of you and my grandmother, I've found another home in Clan Sundulus."

Rising, I pushed the document case toward them. Inside were details of the assets of both clans and my estate. A list of conditions for the contracts between the oldies, myself, and Sundulus were also outlined.

I wasn't just handing Sundulus the means to win without anything in return.

"In two days, I've chartered a private jet to take each of you out of the country. Fred will arrive to pick you up at ten in the morning. I don't know how the final negotiations will go down, but I want you out of the firing zone." I straightened my back. "If you wish to help me, I'll need as many of your local assets signed to Julius Atagio before that plane leaves. If not, then leave with my understanding and my love. We have all played *Ingenium*. It brought you together— and there's some beauty in that. That bond is immortal and greater than any game."

I blinked rapidly, turning away, and whispered, "Goodbye."

Shoving through the doors, I strode through the main house to where Fred would be waiting. Snapping out my phone, I scrolled down to the contact Pepperoni.

One ring.

"Miss Le Spyre," a man answered. Tony headed my legal team.

"Tony. I'm gifting everything I own in Bluff City to a corporation."

Silence met my comment. For a beat. "Understood."

"One of my teams will send through all pertinent documents. There will not be a settlement, but I will send through a list of conditions to include in the contracts. Please ensure they are editable so I can add further conditions should I wish."

My grandmother hired Tony for a reason, and that's because he was the capable son of the lawyer who worked for her father.

"Who's the beneficiary?" he asked, typing in the background.

"Julius Atagio," I replied, spelling the name for him.

"Do you wish the estate to be included, Miss Le Spyre?"

No. My family home had stood here for one hundred and thirty-five years. It was a symbol of the Le Spyre's presence in Bluff City. Giving it up was akin to selling my soul to Clan Sundulus.

I'd sold that a long time ago though, and it was within the boundaries of the new line I'd drawn in the sand.

"Yes, Tony. The estate as well. Everything. Collaborate with the financial team should you need to. There will likely be a delay of several hours before you receive details of my assets. I'm sending the email with my personal conditions for you to begin on immediately."

Without waiting for his acknowledgement, I hung up and dialled Winston.

Eva answered.

"Good evening," I replied, striding through Sir Olythieu's mansion.

Fred fell into step behind me, hurrying forward to open the door of the car when we exited the main house into the front courtyard.

"I need the team on a new job," I told her. Their last job—though they were so efficient I'd absorb them in my other companies somewhere. "Gather the contracts of sale for everything I own in Bluff City."

"Of course, Miss Le Spyre. What would you like us to do with them?"

I pressed my lips together, settling into the back seat of Grandmother's favourite car. "Listen very closely."

22

I sat in the lavender garden, inhaling the scent as I gazed around the tiers.

"Miss, would you like some tea?"

Blinking, I focused on Rosie. "No, thank you."

She curtsied. "The projector is set up by the pool, miss. They're ready to begin the movie when you are."

It needed to be dark for my outside cinema night. Blinking again, I saw it *was* dark. At some point, the sun had gone down.

Exhaustion used me as its play toy, but I couldn't rest until the battle was over. Tomorrow, one way or another, I would have played my last hand.

"I'll come presently," I told her.

She curtsied again and turned to leave.

"Rosie?"

"Yes, Miss Le Spyre?"

"How do you think this area would look if I ripped out the lavender bushes and replaced them with succulents?"

Horror flittered across her face, and I smirked.

Gotcha.

Her expression smoothed. "It would look terrible, miss."

A snort left me. "That will be all, Rosie."

She was totally a poker player in some underground gambling circuit.

Gathering the stacks of papers spread across the wrought iron table, I trailed after her through the hedgeway toward the pool. The laughter and shouts of the gathered Vissimo stretched to me, drawing a genuine smile to my lips. Their silent and watchful days were over. My heart was happy that they were relaxed enough in my employ to make noise.

No matter what happened, I'd cultivate their trust until they were free on paper *and* in mind.

"Basil." Tommy waved from the middle of what had to be two hundred vampires. I had no idea what their roster with Fyrlia and Sundulus was, but whoever wasn't on duty tended to show up. The other day there were over five hundred here. Tonight, under half of that number. Were Fyrlia and Sundulus expecting trouble before tomorrow?

My staff had erected a huge white screen over the length of the pool. Speakers stood at either side and in the pavilions behind the chattering *crowd*. Every pillow and blanket in the house were on the grass right now, occupied by lounging vampires.

... Who appeared to be grouped in clusters that I strongly suspected were harems.

I really hoped the movie Tommy chose didn't have sex in it.

"Hey, girl," she said, shifting over to make space.

I plonked myself down. "Sorry to keep you all waiting. I lost track of time."

"Did it have something to do with those?" Tommy eyed the stack of papers in my arms.

Yeah. Turned out the worst thing was the wait.

If there was anything else to do, I couldn't think of it. I could only pore over every angle of my strategy again and again.

Laurel was on my other side, men draped over her like blankets.

"Will everyone be ready tomorrow?" I asked her.

She dipped her head, squeezing the thigh of a red-haired hunk on her left. "They will. And they'll enjoy every second of it."

Good.

I sighed.

Tommy took the papers from me and set them on her side, tossing a blanket over my legs.

"I take it you haven't heard from them?" she murmured.

My oldies?

No.

They had until ten o'clock tomorrow morning to show with the documents, but I hadn't heard a peep. At the very minimum, I'd expected them to organise another *soiree* to hammer out the final details.

I was going in alone, and I couldn't blame them for their decision. My oldies had only ever seen the tormentor and the executioner in these beautiful creatures. If I spent three decades in the company of the Tonyi triplets, I'd never help them in a million years.

Even for me, for the memory of my grandmother, I'd asked too much of them. I knew that, but desperation drove me to ask anyway. Regardless of their answer, they'd deserved to understand what was happening and that our part was drawing to a close.

Without their help, I might be able to restore balance to *Ingenium*. But what if Fyrlia had made large purchases in the last twenty-four hours? Tommy had pushed the acquisition team hard over the last few days. They'd acquired four more properties, but there was no way to really *know* I had enough.

The uncertainty of the outcome kept me up each night. My hair was limp. Circles marred the area beneath my eyes. I felt tense to snapping point.

The movie started, and I smiled as the intro music played. *The Boat that Rocked.* One of my favourites.

It had sex in it.

Grimacing, I glanced around, wondering how long these horn-dogs would last. I gave it twenty minutes. Perhaps I shouldn't be so judgmental, considering that if Kyros was here, we'd be halfway through the seventh exchange.

Closing my eyes, I focused on him, and my insides shook at the defeat and misery filling him. There was an undercurrent of determination, too, but he felt *so fucking terrible.* I followed the thrumming beat north. He wasn't at his tower or our Lyall Bay property. Maybe his parents' place? Their family would have gathered together for their last night.

If I'd thought separation was hard after the fifth swap, it was nothing on how I felt now. Fear about tomorrow wasn't the only contribution to my appearance. I was draining away to nothing the longer we stayed apart.

That scared me more than anything.

If I failed tomorrow, both of us would fade to a whisper. For me, I'd survive and live a half life. For Kyros, King Mikael's work would become that much easier.

Three days without him and I knew without a shadow of doubt that if he was taken from me, I'd spend the rest of my life trying to free him. Because I needed to.

Because I wanted to.

That was a game I'd never stop playing.

Tears gathered behind my eyes as his morose mood deepened.

I couldn't take it. Sliding out my phone, I tapped out a message.

I love you, Kyros <3

Hesitating—because part of him must still hate me for what I did —I pushed Send.

I tapped out another.

I'm going to fix this. Your family will be okay.

Staring at the message, I hovered my thumb over *Send.* The thing was… I couldn't promise that. If I gave him false hope now and lost, I'd never forgive myself.

Tommy rested her head on my shoulder, laughing as the new DJ boarded the ship and broadcasted for the first time.

I hunkered back against the cushions, wrapping my arm around her shoulders.

A soft moan rose from behind us.

Yep, there they went.

"Uhm," Tommy said. "Can't help but notice there are clusters of men with a sole woman, and clusters of women with a sole man."

Pretty sure my crew had been aware Tommy knew about them for a while now, but now I'd freed them, I made no secret of it. And with the compulsion removed, I'd told her everything—from the moment I'd dropped off my résumé to now.

As much as I worried about her growing ease with the *Vissimo*, I also wanted to foster it. I wanted her to know that not all vampires were monsters after what she'd been through. My bestie was strong. *Literally* sitting in the middle of hundreds of people with fangs.

"What are you trying to say?" I asked. "That they're into harems or something?"

"No, no," she said quickly. Then paused. "Are they though?"

I flashed her a grin. "Most of them, yes. Vissimo can't reproduce easily, so they have multiple partners." I wasn't sure why some grouped around a man and others around a woman, but I knew everyone had a harem of their own and was part of another harem too.

Maybe they alternated days.

She straightened and peered around. "Interesting concept."

My gaze narrowed at the purring quality in her voice. "Interesting, how?"

My friend eyed a slender male with blond hair to his shoulders.

"Do you think he plays an instrument?" she whispered.

And we were back on the miserable musician kick. "No idea, Tom. Please tell me you're not going to form a harem."

She shrugged a shoulder. "Maybe I've been looking at life wrong. Why choose, you know?"

Belatedly, Tommy shot me a look.

"Yeah," I said drily. "You may be talking to the wrong person about that."

She snorted. "True."

I wondered if we were ruining the movie for everyone. "You're on the rebound then?"

Tommy had kept to herself since learning the truth about Theodore and his brothers. She needed to talk about everything. Except who *could* she talk to about vampires except me and those of them in my employ? I hoped we'd be enough. Her trauma could come out in any number of ways, and I knew from personal experience that grief often lured people into a false sense of security before returning for a smackdown months or years down the track.

"Sure, why not?" she said breezily, glancing around again.

That she was looking at a Vissimo to scratch the itch was kind of surprising.

I tucked my hand in hers. "As long as you're careful. And as long as you talk to me if you're ever not okay."

Tommy squeezed my hand. "You know I will." She peered at my phone. "You gonna send that or what?"

I'm going to fix this. Your family will be okay.

Kyros hadn't replied to my first text.

Laurel tapped my knee and showed me her phone.

I scanned the flight details from Kyros.

"Tomorrow at eleven," I murmured.

"We have orders from Kyros to ensure you get on the plane with your staff and Tommy."

Well, that isn't happening.

I met her blue gaze. "When do the negotiations start?"

"Eleven thirty."

"Good." If there was too much time between my flight and the gathering of the two clans, I had no doubt Kyros would personally come to ensure I left. He could feel my location, so I had to keep up the guise until it was too late for him to interfere.

Laurel returned her attention to the movie, and I peered down at the message I'd typed out. If Kyros suspected anything was amiss, he'd ensure I couldn't attend the negotiations.

As much as tomorrow was about saving his family, it was also about representing my grandmother.

"I'm sick of keeping secrets from him, Tommy," I said, moving to push the damn button.

She snatched the phone away. "Before you do though."

"I don't get to choose?"

"This time, I'll let you. But listen first. From what you've told me, you seriously fucked up with Kyros and his family. Like really, *really* bad. Like—"

I arched a brow. "I understand how epically I messed up, Tom."

"Good," she said. "Which leads me to my point. Kyros is a crown prince. Which means that when all goes to plan, you'll be a princess and maybe a queen one day."

That was a terrifying fucking thought. Did we have to go there now? I reached for the phone. "I'm sending it."

Tommy blurted, "If you're going to be queen one day, you need to show everyone you are a queen."

Hand in the air, I stilled.

My bestie leaned in, expression dead serious. "Erase your mistake from their minds. Kick Fyrlia's ass into the ground and your screw up will look like a mastermind puzzle piece in an elaborate plan. Do it by *yourself*, Basil, for those you love, for those who need your protection, and show the immortal world you're Kyros's equal."

I inhaled. "Wow. That's heavy stuff. I just didn't want to get his hopes up if I couldn't make good on my promises."

Tommy slapped the phone into my palm. "Become the queen or always be the princess, Basilia Le Spyre."

Laurel and the others around us stopped talking.

Maybe Tommy had a point. I had something to prove to so many people that I'd forgotten my *future* people—Kyros's family. Their clan. How could these people ever respect me if they saw me as the consolation prize to the man who'd be the most powerful vampire in existence.

I didn't want Kyros to be ashamed of me. Never again.

And I wanted to be proud of myself.

I deleted the text and slid my phone away.

"Queen Basilia," I murmured, testing it out.

Tommy rolled her eyes. "Y S I S."

"What can I say? That rich shit sticks."

Facing the movie, I tuned into Kyros's emotions, settling in for what would be a long night.

23

"Do you have everything, Miss Le Spyre?" Fred asked.

I held up a heavy overnight bag. It was one of ten. The rest were loaded in the boot. "I think so. You'll pick up my oldies soon?"

He bowed. "Yes, miss."

"Once you've dropped them off, stand by to pick me up," I told him. "I'm attending an important meeting today and I'd like to leave it in my grandmother's car. If you'll drive me."

Fred was as much a part of this as anyone else.

His sharp eyes glinted and he glanced at my overnight bag with new understanding.

"This is it then?" he asked in a low voice.

I'd told him the truth about Laurel and the others—and that they worked for me now—but his distrust would take a while to fade. If ever. He was too loyal to forgive anyone with fangs.

"In my way, yes, this is it," I replied, gripping his shoulder. "Thank you, Fred."

"Miss Le Spyre, if you prefer, I can see Don to escort your grandmother's friends while I accompany you."

Tempting. Vissimo recognised that my butler wasn't like other humans. But if two thousand vampires couldn't protect me, he certainly couldn't.

I smiled at him. "That means a lot, thank you. But not this time. I'll text you the address."

"As you say, Miss Le Spyre." He bowed again.

I clambered into the SUV next to Tommy, and Kelsea slid in after me.

"To the airport, please, Laurel," I instructed.

Surprisingly, exhaustion finally claimed me last night. I didn't feel refreshed, but some energy had returned to me. Tommy's work on my hair and make-up covered the other signs of my drained body.

I was dressed in black heels, a tight pencil skirt that highlighted my figure from waist to half-calf. I wore a white scoop-neck top with tight sleeves to my elbows. Demure, sophisticated. There for business.

My hair was back in a chignon, my make-up flawless from sooty lashes to ruby lips.

I looked the part.

I didn't feel the part.

Only people with nothing to lose could be that cocky. Being a Le Spyre, I didn't feel vulnerable very often, but at least my time off the estate gave me a crash course I'd never forget.

Everyone was quiet on the drive.

A distant part of me still hoped to hear from my oldies, their Bluff City assets outstretched. They wouldn't have drawn it out needlessly to torture me—that I did believe in.

They weren't coming.

"All set?" Tommy asked.

The contents of my stomach were sloshing and could appear at any moment. "As much as I can be."

"We'll have to wait at the airport as long as possible," Laurel said. "He wants me to send confirmation when the plane takes off."

He'd be focused on my location until he received that confirmation. Probably because he could feel me preparing to battle.

We arrived at Bluff City's private airport, and I barely registered the clearance checks. She pulled into a hangar housing a large plane. Larger than the ones I'd always travelled in with Grandmother.

Cars began to arrive and my human staff filed out. Mrs Gaughton hopped out of the car, hustling to my side.

"Basilia, I can't believe you're doing this for everyone." She cackled. "My first overseas trip."

Yep. My staff thought I'd sprung a surprise vacation on them.

She dug her bony elbow in my side. "You're sure you won't tell us where we're going?"

Pretty sure, considering I had no idea where Kyros believed he was sending me. Knowing him, somewhere nice.

I stood back as my staff went through the procedure of boarding.

Tommy joined me. "So this is the part where I tell you that I'm not going with everyone else."

"Yes, you are."

"Nope," she replied, leaning against the car. "I'm going into that room with you, Basil. And that special clause you added? I want to read it aloud as I look at their faces."

She'd done such a good job of hiding how she felt, but the bitterness and anger were there in spades.

My friend wanted revenge.

I was familiar with the feeling.

"Tom," I told her. "When I told you about Vissimo, I swore to never let harm befall you. I already broke that oath once, so please don't make me do it again."

She scoffed. "What? You're rich and so you get to decide my life? My actions don't belong to anyone but myself. I wanted to be with Theodore—who I thought he was anyway. Now, I want to spit in the faces of the other two. Most of all, I'm going to be there by your side because I'm your fucking best friend."

I cut her a look. "Your body will betray you in there. The royals are strong. Their power will flare. You'll want to fall in a heap and piss yourself."

"I've been practicing with the vampires on the estate."

My voice dropped to dangerous levels. "Practicing how?"

She didn't answer. "I'm going into that room, Basil. The easy way or the hard way. *Give me this moment*, and I accept full responsibility for my actions. If I'm hurt, it's on my head and my head alone."

But it wouldn't be.

Tommy whipped out a hand to clutch my forearm. "You think you'll blame yourself if I'm hurt. Why do you feel like it's different for me? You think I want you walking into that shitshow without me? If anything happens, I'll never forgive myself."

"It'll be—"

"Dangerous. Got that, Sherlock."

I let out a frustrated hiss. "I'll be fucking pissed if you die."

Understatement of the century.

She grinned at me, opening the car door. "Love you, Basil."

Leaving her to bask in her triumph, I paced around the hangar, certain Kyros was watching me like a hawk—I couldn't sit still in the car for an hour when I should be moving into the plane like everyone else.

Did I have everything? I spent three hours that morning cross-checking the piles of documents for the third time.

Everything was in the bags.

Everything except the document in my back pocket.

"The plane is ready to depart, Basi," Laurel reported a while later, moving to my side.

I blinked at the grey wall. I'd been staring at it while running over what I wanted to say at the negotiations. The kings would try to unsettle me—just like Julius did last time.

I had to stick to my script.

There was too much to lose.

"Thank you. Please get someone to make excuses for Tommy and me. Tell them, something urgent has come up."

Fifteen of my Vissimo would go with my staff. The rest of them were called back by Sundulus for the negotiations, so I'd walk into the lion's den with my crew of seven.

Somehow, that felt right.

I waved at my staff as the plane left the hangar. They were safe for now. My oldies wouldn't be far behind, though I doubted the destinations were the same.

I breathed a little easier as the plane took off.

Eleven thirty came and went, and I kept an internal eye on Kyros's emotions, feeling the exact moment his fear began to climb.

"Text him," I instructed Laurel. "There's a delay due to air traffic from the public airport. Expected wait is fifteen minutes."

There was every risk he'd call my bluff, but Kyros was in Grey and the private airport was on the far side of Orange. It would take him twenty minutes to get here at least, and then he wouldn't have enough time to return for the meeting.

Laurel sent the text and her brows shot up at the reply.

"Making threats, is he?" I smirked.

"*Get that fucking plane off the ground now,*" she recited. "*Now* is in capital letters."

Shouty. Couldn't blame him.

But Kyros was on the move too.

"Shit, he's changing locations," I whispered, focusing on the drawing sensation pulling me north. "He can't be coming here."

Ten tense minutes proved he wasn't. He'd relocated to a place in Black.

11:50 a.m.

"Time to get in the car and act like we're moving down the runway." Kyros's anger was mounting, along with his desperation.

Laurel messaged him again as we slid into the car with my crew. Jillian sat on Evie's lap due to Tommy's presence. His relief upon reading the text was immediate, though it dispersed in a flooding rush, replaced by determination and dread.

Increasingly, I found myself yearning to hear his thoughts. Feeling his emotions was like not quite sneezing. That determination could mean anything. Did Kyros have his own plan? A point to negotiate?

Emotions were so subjective out of context.

Laurel looped the car down to the end of the runway and then circled back toward the entrance gates.

11:56 a.m.

My palms began to sweat. Kyros didn't have enough time to stop me now. I'd trapped him in the meeting and thwarted his attempts to keep me safe *again*. This time, I actually felt bad about it because after everything I'd done, I was walking into this battle by myself *again*. And there was every chance Kyros would hate me for it *again*.

We could come back from some things. Not from others.

Doing it this way felt like it gave most respect to everyone hurt along the way.

As soon as Laurel left the airport gates, Kyros's rage slammed into me. I gasped at the force of it, clutching my chest.

"He knows, huh?" Tommy asked drily.

Shit! Did he ever.

"Yep," I choked. "Not happy."

Tommy patted my knee. "Save his family. He'll get over himself."

Betrayal. Fury. Fear. The emotions rolled through me in pulsing waves.

Laurel's eyes met mine in the rear-view mirror. "Directions."

I waded through Kyros's reaction and focused on his location. "Head in the direction of Black. What's there, do you know?"

"That's where the kings roll the dice each night," she said. "Kyros didn't tell me the address of the negotiations. He didn't trust that you'd board the plane quietly, or that I wouldn't tell you."

"Gotta give it to the punk, he knows you," Tommy said, wrinkling her nose.

I smiled. He'd never mentioned me gaining the power to feel his location either, so I assumed he had no idea that was a two-way street.

The drive through Bluff City to Black was one hundred times worse than the wait in the hangar. I clasped my trembling hands together and closed my eyes, trying to regain my calm.

"Do you remember how straight Agatha's back was?" Tommy asked.

Pretty sure I'd never seen it bend.

I straightened in my seat, her stern reprimand ringing in my ears.

Tommy continued. "She always kept her chin tilted, too. And her eyes. She had that *you're a piece of peasant vermin* look down to a fine art."

Taking a breath, I lifted my chin as though my grandmother had tapped her finger underneath it. I remembered the vermin look well. When people pissed me off, my topaz eyes held the same fire.

Tommy squeezed my knee, winking. "There you are."

I tossed her as much of a smile as I was capable of.

"Don't forget why you're doing this, Basil," she murmured.

For me.

For Tommy.

For my grandmother.

My oldies.

For Kyros.

And not to sound like a superhero, but I was doing this for Bluff City too.

My shallow breaths deepened, and the clamminess left my palms. This could go one of two ways, but regardless, I'd conduct myself with dignity.

Dignity my grandmother gave me.

Laurel pulled up outside a large building I couldn't recall glancing at twice in my life. It looked like a conference centre.

Before I forgot, I sent the address to Fred.

Kyros's fury had largely melted away to panic at this point. I sent him as many soothing and calm thoughts as possible, knowing his powers would be bursting to take over.

Get. Away.

I jolted in my seat.

"Basil?" Tommy asked in alarm.

An awed gasp left my lips. "I just heard Kyros in my head for the first time."

"Freaky shit," she replied.

Kyros?

Leave, he shouted in my mind.

Whoa, that was really loud. He followed the order with a barrage of words I couldn't make sense of. I winced, pain stabbing over my brow.

"He wants me to leave," I said, sliding out of the car after Josie.

My crew surrounded Tommy and me, and as I approached the building doors, the steady stream of Kyros's thoughts hammered my forehead.

What is she fucking doing here?

I told her to leave.

She can't be hurt again.

Never.

Protect my true mate.

Kill.

"I need a second," I announced, leaning against the wall.

"What's wrong?" Tommy asked.

If the vampires inside were paying attention, they'd be listening to her. I tapped my head. Aside from the obvious problem of having another person in my head when I needed total focus, complete joy filled me as I heard Kyros's *voice* for the first time.

The mental sound—if that's what it could be called—rumbled through my body just as his voice rumbled through me in real life.

Kyros, I'm okay, I thought, testing it out. *I'm coming inside—*

His thought cut me off. *Over my dead body.*

I'm going to do my best to save your family, I said.

Using every inch of the focus I'd cultivated since my senses came in, I gathered the rapid stream of his shouting voice and did my best to box it up. I only managed to hush him to a whispering volume that had a bead of sweat trekking down my back.

It would have to do.

Straightening, I strode to the doors, nodding at two of my Vissimo who opened them. I winked at them—because bravado—and headed directly to where I could feel the thrum of Kyros.

He was debating whether he could leave the room.

Kyros, the last time you left things to me, the plan exploded in my face. I understand your hesitation, but I'm asking you to trust me again. I'm doing this for you. For us. But I need to have this moment for my grandmother.

His confusion over the last part took over everything else. The way he turned over problems was incredible. As I walked to the second set of doors, he'd come up with ten different reasons for me mentioning my grandmother and prioritised them from most likely to least likely.

None of your theories are right, I told him. *But it's time you know the truth.*

I drew forth everything I'd kept from him—the underground office, the Churchill team, the acquisition team, the stacks of properties I owned in Bluff City.

The tumult of information shocked him to silence, but it wasn't awed. The silence was confused. Shoot, did he even get any of that? I wasn't sure if I'd sent the information in a logical way or if I'd thrown it at him in a pile.

But I hoped he understood enough.

I *wanted* him to know at last. I never wanted to keep anything from him again.

Standing outside the double doors, I braced for the sweaty state two entire clans of vampires would put me in.

Tommy planted herself at my back, and I threw her a searching glance.

Her jaw was set. Her eyes hard.

Laurel shadowed my right. Kelsea, my left. The rest of my crew surrounded me and Tommy from behind. They carried eleven bags, and I held out my hand to take the bag from Laurel.

I took a steadying breath, tilting my chin and straightening my back.

This one's for you, Agatha.

Laurel and Kelsea pushed the doors open.

And I strode into a sea of vampires.

24

Holy shit. Entering a stadium packed with what had to be over six thousand vampires was eerie. Really, less than half of the fifteen thousand vampires that lived in the city had managed to cram in here. It was comforting *and* interesting to note that both sides had prioritised space so most of their Indebted could attend. Guess if a fight broke out, they didn't want their *actual* clan members to die.

Assholes.

The clans were seated in tiers rising on opposite sides. In the middle was the space I usually saw during the dice roll. Instead of the thrones facing off against each other, a long table had been placed in the middle. The kings and queens sat in thrones in the middle of the longest sides, facing off. Their children sat either side of them, also facing off. As I listened to Tommy's erratic breathing at my back, my gaze honed on Kyros to the right of his father.

His thoughts were still spilling over from everything I'd just unleashed on him, but I'd managed to keep his mental frenzy to a whisper. Kyros was painfully aware of my presence, devastated by it.

I strode between the two towering tiers toward the table. In short duration the clans became aware of the mostly human and *actual* human in their midst.

I listened to the conversation ahead of me. I'd expected shouting and blazing eyes and barred fangs, but the calm poise of both sides—the steady pitch of their voices—was the stuff of nightmares.

Almost in unison, the royals stiffened, their conversation trailing away as they turned to me.

Tommy's breathing stopped altogether as I led the way to the table. My own heartbeat thundered as I became the sole object of attention for two kings, two queens, and sixteen princes and princesses.

I stopped at the end of the table between Hector and Neelan. Their faces were cold.

King Mikael waved a hand my way. "Get rid of the human trash, Julius. She has no place here."

Play your own game.

I smiled sweetly at him. "Human mate rights, clause fourteen, section seven. *Unless the transition ritual is invoked at the seventh exchange, the human or elevated-human mate will not speak in formal gatherings unless permitted by their Vissimo counterpart.*"

The king's brows slammed together. He wasn't alone.

I turned to my mate.

Prepared for everything else, I was grossly unprepared to see him now. Toffee strands were slicked back, but I longed to run my fingers through them. Green eyes so piercing, so familiar. I traced the sweeping lines of his lips and the cutting edge of his jaw.

He was wearing my favourite suit.

We studied each other.

Kyros wanted me gone in the biggest way.

What have you got to lose from giving me this last chance? I asked.

Your life, he replied, tapering his other thoughts to project the single answer at me. *Why didn't you get on the plane?*

Would you have done it?

King Mikael's cruel laughter rang out through the amphitheatre. "My son doesn't wish you here, human. Begone."

It was the wrong move.

Outwardly calm, Kyros went from panicked to furious in a beat. I blinked as his rage entered me, forcing blood to my cheeks. *Shit, that's stronger.* Our emotions had influenced each other before, but not to this degree.

Taking a firm handle on my response, I sent through all the calm I could muster. I'd soothe my true mate because he hated losing control. His sadness was my own.

He stilled and rose from his huge chair. My eyes flickered to his mother and father. Both were impassive. I doubted anyone from Sundulus wanted me here, but they also wouldn't make Kyros lose face in this setting.

He rounded the table and stopped a metre from me.

I didn't dare touch him, both of us were battling to control the urge to close the gap and get our seventh exchange on.

King Mikael laughed again.

Fucking tosser.

Kyros's lips twitched.

Fists balling, I met his green gaze, my heart squeezing within me. *So beautiful.*

You've got to let me try, I begged, prepared to leave my dignity on the floor if that's what it took.

Searching my face, he turned away. "Let it be noted that I, Kyros Nicholai Atagio, Crown Prince of Clan Sundulus, give permission for my true mate, Basilia Le Spyre, to speak here."

He was addressing a row of people I hadn't noticed. Dressed in robes, they sat like a panel of judges on the opposite end of the large room.

The woman in the middle nodded, her eyes settling on me. "Clan Leith notes that mate permission has been granted."

Kyros left my side and returned to his seat, each step costing him dearly.

I was on my own.

"I object to her presence," Mikael said, standing. Fury twisted his features.

He didn't believe I had anything useful, though he had to be wondering what was in the bags. Mikael didn't want me here because it would be harder to cleave Kyros from me after.

Good luck.

I don't know if the thought was mine or Kyros's, but I'd been waiting to say something for a long time.

Kyros, I need you to stay seated. This is part of the plan. The Indebted are in my employ now.

"King Mikael," I met his gaze. "Shut the fuck up."

The clans had looked on with nothing more than a murmur, but a shocked gasp hit me from both sides.

I didn't even see him move.

By the time my eyes caught up, the king stood before me, his chest covered with red dots.

Snarls ripped from Kyros's chest, but he hadn't moved, which almost brought tears to my eyes.

Red dots covered my chest also.

"Which of us do you think has a better chance of dodging bullets?" the king asked, regaining his semblance of calm though I could tell he was taken aback.

Laurel held her gun casually as she slid from behind me to stand by my side. "Would you like me to shoot his kneecap off, Miss Le Spyre?"

I pretended to consider that. "Would it grow back?"

"If I blew the whole thing off, it would take a month or so," she answered coolly.

Mikael's hooded eyes slid to her, the promise of murder in every line of his face.

I folded my arms. "He'd still have another leg to get around on though."

Vladymir's deep voice washed over me. "I could get the other kneecap, if you like, Miss Le Spyre."

He took up the position on my other side as Mikael's eyes widened.

The red dots covering my body switched to the king's.

I smirked.

Mikael studied his body before staring at the row of leather-clad vampires at his back. His mouth snapped shut. "Filthy slaves, stand down or each and every one of you will be executed."

Holding up a finger, I tutted. "That's incorrect, King Mikael." I set my bag on the table, turning my face from him as I unzipped it.

"In fact," I continued. "You'll find that the Vissimo in Clan Sundulus and Clan Fyrlia that you mistakenly referred to as Indebted were freed of their debt three days ago. They have graciously agreed to remain in my employ."

I didn't need to look at the two vampires to my right to feel how much this moment meant to them.

"I suggest you take your seat, Mikael," I murmured. "For some reason, my friends don't like you."

One snarl left his curled lips.

"Father," Gina said from her seat opposite Kyros, "the faster we hear out the human trash, the faster we can destroy Sundulus."

I ignored her.

As did Mikael.

"Do I need to remind you of Clause 15?" I asked, tilting my head.

If he touched me right now, Kyros had a right to kill him.

"Father," Gina said again.

I turned and caught the king's wide smile before he resumed his seat.

Phew.

"Stand down," I said to my guards.

A loud boom echoed as the better part of two thousand vampires snapped their heels together, standing erect, guns at their sides.

Pride filled my chest.

Mate, Kyros said, his tone strained to the point of snapping. He needed me closer. Picking up my bag, I walked around the table and edged in between Kyros and Rory.

Setting the bag down, I pulled out the first chunk of documents pertaining to over nine thousand properties.

"I won't beat around the bush. I'm gifting the entirety of my Bluff

City assets to Clan Sundulus," I declared, setting the stack before Kyros.

"Quaint," King Mikael said.

"That amounts to nine thousand and thirty-six properties." I continued. "Thirty-two businesses. And a range of shares in local corporations."

Kyros had frozen, *in and out*. As had his siblings.

Clearly, he didn't receive that part in my mental heads-up earlier. *Oops.*

Everyone here knew the significance of that number. It was nearly all of the properties belonging to overseas owners—or so they'd thought.

Tommy's ragged breathing was the only sound.

Kyros thumbed through the stack, scanning the addresses. He traced my signature at the bottom of each page. Sucking in a breath, he pushed the stack toward his father and reached into the bag for the next chunk.

"Ladies," I said to my crew.

"One moment," Trenit purred. "Correct me if I'm wrong. Perhaps the rules of *Ingenium* suddenly changed overnight. You are compelled by a member of Sundulus. Close though my eldest brother keeps you for now, it does not make you exempt from obeying the order of the game. You cannot sign anything over to them." He leaned forward. "Only *us*."

Kyros answered smoothly. "My true mate is not compelled. I removed all compulsions four days ago."

"We, of course, are unable to verify that, however, given that she cannot be compelled and cleared by an impartial party," Tynan answered him.

Oh. Fuck.

There was one massive fucking hole in my take-down plan. *Shit!*

I took the only path I could think of. "My previous compulsion stopped me talking to humans. Bring in a human in your power. I'll tell them everything I know about Vissimo. There's proof."

"Do a temporary compulsion on me," Tommy said over me.

266

My eyes widened, and I shot her a frantic look.

She ignored me. "Basilia couldn't speak about vampires until Kyros freed her four days ago. You can compel the truth from me."

"And then compel you to keep your mouth shut," Trenit snapped. "Which should have been done by Sundulus already if they suspected you knew of our existence."

His threat was weightless and everyone knew it.

Tommy didn't spare him a glance, peering instead at the impartial clan. "If that needs to happen, so be it."

Over my dead body.

"If Clan Sundulus wishes to accept these properties from the mate of Crown Prince Kyros, my clan must confer on the validity of this solution. If Miss Basilia Le Spyre is compelled in any way, the deal is illegal within the rules of *Ingenium*," a woman from the impartial clan said mildly, looking up from a stack of papers before her as if our dispute was a garden bowl's match.

Please tell me you took everything out, I whispered his way.

Kyros glanced at his father and nodded.

Are you kidding me? What does that mean? I silently hissed.

My mate fixed his gaze on me. *It means that I freed you absolutely, Basilia.*

Thank fuck.

"Confer and give us your ruling," King Julius told the woman from the impartial clan.

Yeah. His wording didn't fool anyone. He hadn't decided to accept shit from me yet.

She bowed slightly and returned to the row of her clan members. "Will the human witness please come forward?"

I clenched my hands to fists, tense as Tommy shot me a veiled look and made her way around the table to approach the woman.

"Each of us will search your mind and vote upon the verdict of allowing your testimony regarding the removal of Miss Le Spyre's compulsion," she told my friend.

My mouth bobbed open. *All of them!* I quickly counted. There were ten.

Surely that—

Tread cautiously, Kyros's thoughts invaded mine.

Tommy didn't hesitate, leaving her bag next to Evie before striding to one end of the line. The male Vissimo locked eyes with her and my friend gasped. But within a minute, he'd released her.

"Next," the woman called.

Blinking several times, Tommy shifted down the row. I swallowed, my hands slickening as she worked her way through the ten vampires.

If this failed, I had to think of something else, but I could only think of my oldies—who were long gone by now. There was Fred, but I just couldn't do that to him.

I was cursing the weakness that made me agree to Tommy being here.

When the last Vissimo finished searching her mind, I met her halfway, steadying her as she wobbled back to where I stood.

"We are specifically interested in the witness's memories pertaining to the difference of what Miss Le Spyre was able to divulge when first compelled in comparison to the last four days," the female said.

Gina cut in. "That doesn't prove there's *no* compulsion on her. If there is any compulsion on their behalf, she is not allowed to deal with Sundulus. If they cannot prove she isn't—"

Gerome cleared his throat. "Clan Sundulus keeps clear records of the compulsion parameters we place upon each human liaison. With my father's permission, I would like to direct Clan Leith's attention to page two thousand and fourteen of the document titled *Human Liaisons.*"

Original. They should have titled it *Enslavement of the Innocent Because Two People Couldn't Agree.*

A towering male next to the woman, who I assumed was the leader or nominated spokesperson, scrambled to find the document.

"Page one thousand, nine hundred and ninety-eight," Kyros said quietly.

There was a page detailing the exact limitations Kyros placed on my mind. Yeah, if I lived through today, I was reading that fucker.

I have nothing to hide, he answered me, a slight nip entering his mental voice.

Consider me still weirded out that mental voices existed.

I lifted a shoulder. *Just for interest's sake.* It was kind of like me wanting to read my medical history at this point. Plus, I could tell he was telling the absolute truth. The whole emotion radar and telepathy combo didn't leave room for ambiguity.

The document was being passed from end to end.

When the last Vissimo in Clan Leith closed the pages, the woman spoke again. "With the parameters in mind, we will now vote."

What? Like an *everyone raise your hand* type of situation? Surely not.

"Everyone raise your hand if you are assured of the validity of Miss Le Spyre and Crown Prince Kyros Atagio's claim that all compulsions were removed four days hence."

I closed my eyes.

After everything, a fucking vote was the straw on the camel's back that made me want to bury my head in the group and pretend none of this existed.

Open your eyes, Basilia.

Obeying, I stared at the six hands in the air.

My knees wobbled and I locked my legs, counting the hands again. Six out of ten.

Sixty percent. Was that in our favour or against us?

A savage snarl ripped from King Mikael's lips. "Preposterous. Clan Fyrlia demands an appeal."

Queen Titania laughed lightly. "The rulings of the impartial clan at the end cascade negotiations is absolute. Do not seek to waste our time, Mikael."

Oh, snap! The cruel king stared across the table at Kyros's mother, undisguised lust in his muscular body.

King Julian shifted.

I shared a look with Tommy, and she dipped her head.

Time to get things back on track. This was our show, not theirs. And I could strangle her later for risking herself like that.

"Please come forward with the remaining deeds," I called over my shoulder.

One by one, my vampire crew of seven set a bag on the table, some of them carrying two. Tommy collected hers and passed it into my hands.

The kings broke off their stares, and I released a pent-up breath.

This is my show.

I opened the bag and removed the top sheet, setting the page before my mate. It showed the tallies of Fyrlia's assets against my own in combination with Sundulus's assets.

Are those numbers correct? I asked him.

He studied the sheet intently.

I left Kyros's side as he perused the document. Facing the royals at the head of the table, I said, "If Clan Sundulus accepts these gifts, they also accept my terms."

King Julius lifted his head at that.

Picking up the closest contract, I flicked to the second page. "Regarding the execution of Fyrlia royals. If Clan Sundulus should win, all royal children will be allowed to live." I squinted at the page. "Oh, hold on. Tommy, could you help me with this part?"

My friend licked her lips, joining me at the head of the table. I held the document so she could see.

Her voice didn't tremble. "All royal children of Clan Fyrlia will live, barring Trenit Tonyi and Tynan Tonyi." She said the words and raised her head to look at them on the far side of the king.

"Fucking a human was a bore, but we did enjoy taking turns," Trenit said, a death metal T-shirt visible beneath his blazer.

Tommy's gaze dropped to his T-shirt before flicking back up to his face. "Your cock is smaller than your brother's."

I snorted, sliding out my phone. Three messages from Fred. What did he want?

That doesn't bode well.

Passing the phone to Tommy, I shot her a pointed look. She studied the screen for a second and took the phone.

Jillian and Evie peeled out of the amphitheatre after her.

I returned to my conditions. "Special condition one, section two. My true mate, Kyros Atagio, will be allowed to kill Trenit and Tynan Tonyi in any way he deems fit."

My mate's mental roar of approval drew a smile to my lips. "King Mikael will, of course, be executed."

I stared at the queen by his side. "You, I am not so sure of."

In comparison to Queen Titania, she was nothing. By *human* standards, she was one of the most beautiful women I'd ever seen. She'd stood in the sidelines as her lover fought for the child of another queen. Though she appeared timid at first glance, her eyes cast down demurely, I was of the opinion that no one could survive Mikael that long without a backbone of steel.

"I killed two of your children," I said, watching her closely. "Two more will die."

Her head snapped up, fire dancing in her almond-shaped hazel eyes.

My gaze sharpened. "That's why I'm unsure if you should live or die. What mother could ever forgive the person who killed her babies —no matter how fucking psychotic three of them are?"

She tried to veil the hatred in her eyes, but it was too late.

"Vladymir," I called to where he stood as a hulking giant beside Laurel. "How did Queen Zofia treat you and your comrades while you were in her power?"

He bowed low to me. "She was kind to us when she could be, Miss Le Spyre. She treated us like we were people."

"When her asshole husband wasn't around, I take that to mean," I said, pretending to deliberate though I'd already made my choice.

I focused on her again. "You will live, Queen Zofia, because you treated people you considered slaves with respect. Look at me with that hatred in your eyes again, come against me or my loved ones in any way, shape, or form, and I will slaughter *all* of your children. And you better believe that's already in the contract and legally binding."

She wet her lips, eyes rounding slightly.

I pressed my lips together. "I leave it to King Julius's discretion on how to deal with living Fyrlia royals, but they're to stay alive."

Hopefully I don't live to regret that.

"Special condition two," I said, reading the contract in my hand. "There will be no further compulsions of Bluff City humans by Clan Sundulus. Section two, the compulsions on the listed names will be removed."

Lady Treena would be free when Mikael was executed. The compulsion on everyone else would need to be removed willingly.

The clans were growing louder and louder from where they watched on.

"Silence," the woman from the impartial clan snapped.

They resumed their quiet, not managing to achieve total silence.

"Special condition three," I continued. "My *Vissimo* employees will be allowed to live in nine hundred of the gifted properties for the space of two years at the specified discount rent rates, should they wish." One year while they worked for me, and another because I'd fucking felt like it.

"Four," I said, noticing the Sundulus royals were already skimming through the conditions on their own.

"You want Kyros in exchange for the gifted houses," Safina said, levelling me with a look. It wasn't filled with loathing like last time, but she regarded me coolly. Hopefully there'd be time to regain the ease we once had.

Kyros pinned me with his gaze as I nodded.

"He will be *mine*," I answered her. "King Julius will relinquish control over his son in entirety." I stared around the table of vampires. "All of you will relinquish whatever fucking claim you think you have on him."

Possessiveness burst through me. "A one-hundred-and-fifty-year battle over a child." My face screwed up as I looked at the two kings. "What the fuck were you both thinking dragging your lovers and family into that bullshit? You think you can *own* a man like Kyros or get him to do your bidding? Pathetic."

King Julius spoke for the first time. "Pathetic to protect what is mine?"

Basilia. The warning in Kyros's voice was edged in fear.

Guessed I should be nice to my future father-in-law. "If you take my gifted properties, Kyros is no longer yours to command."

Julius tilted his head back. "He will be yours to command instead?"

My brows shot up. "No, King Julius. Kyros will command himself."

A glimmer of something shone in his father's eyes.

"For the record," I snapped at the Fyrlia clan in the tiers, jabbing a finger in Mikael's direction, "anyone with fucking eyes can see whose son Kyros is. Jesus, how did you people follow that sack of shit for so long?"

His eyes flared, and the power made my knees shake.

Kyros's gratitude washed through me, warming me. I straightened my back, locking my knees so I didn't collapse.

"In line with that," I said, taking a breath, "I'd like both kings to make formal apologies to their families and their clans."

Gina regarded me. "What incentive does my father have to agree to that, Miss Le Spyre?"

Tynan and Trenit soured—no doubt because she didn't call me human.

"If he wants six of his children and his wife to survive, he will," I replied coolly. "You'll survive anyway, Gina, seeing as we have a standing deal from when you sold out the triplets."

Her family turned to her, and Gina glared at me.

"You could have given Sandra Hoyt a clean death," I told her. "But you didn't." Or failed to put an end to her brother's sadistic torture of the woman.

Gina dropped her gaze to the table.

King Julius rifled through the property deed and attached contract. "The conditions are the same on each contract?"

"They are." All except one. The contract in my back pocket had a special condition attached.

Do the numbers check out? I silently asked Kyros.

I can't say. We haven't presented our final figures yet. You underestimated our figures by one hundred and thirty thousand.

Fuck. Which meant I may not be entirely accurate with Fyrlia's numbers either. *Will it be close?*

He nodded.

King Julius stood. "True mate of my eldest son, I accept your conditions."

No surprise there.

He had to know the numbers would cut it close, but he had nothing to lose and everything to gain. Kyros was a businessman and he'd learned it from someone.

Julius rounded to my side and promptly dropped to his knees, facing his family. "For one hundred and fifty years, I have forced each of you into a battle that stole your freedom. For that, I'm sorrier than words can adequately describe. My only defence is that I love each of you more than my own life. I could not give up a single one of you to another. Thank you for fighting with me for your eldest brother's freedom," he said hoarsely, head bowed. "The only life you have known is this one, and that guilt will reside with me always."

As apologies went, that was fucking incredible.

I blinked several times as he regained his feet and towered over me.

Dipping my head, I gestured to the bags. "Sign and they're yours."

"Each property will need to be processed," the woman from Clan Leith said.

"Neelan, Dierdre," the king said, still holding my gaze, "take the bags to them."

"Yes, Father," they murmured.

He still held one of the deeds in his hand. Flicking to the first page of the attached contract, he pointed at a date under the property details. "This property was purchased nearly thirty years ago. Before your birth. These are the properties we believe to be owned by offshore investors or used as holiday homes. Why do you have such a magnitude of Bluff City properties?"

I tilted my chin. "King Julius, thirty years ago, you angered the wrong woman." I glanced around the table of royals. "All of you did."

My grandmother should be here to crow her own victory, but I'd do my best to make up for her absence.

I narrowed my eyes on Kyros's father. "The clans fucked off my grandmother by compelling her friends. From that day on, she entered your little game as a third player. She moved her assets internationally to remove herself as a target and began to purchase properties under offshore aliases. When she died, that responsibility was passed to me."

The king's cold scrutiny barely touched me because I was so furious on my grandmother's behalf.

"You would give that up for us?" he said quietly.

I stepped closer. "You're lucky I'm not my grandmother, King Julius—your children and my Vissimo friends showed me another side to your race, one my grandmother never witnessed." I glanced at his eldest son. "And you're lucky I love your son."

I fell into Kyros's green eyes, only snapping out of it when the papers smacked down in front of the impartial clan.

There were ten members from the impartial clan. The papers were stacked in tall columns next to the vampire on the far left.

Each had a calculator.

As the first vampire whacked numbers into his calculator, he passed each deed onward to the next vampire to cross-check.

Ten cross-checks seemed like overkill, but I was glad for it. And never more nervous in my life.

I closed my eyes, turning away from the Fyrlia royals. Over nine thousand deeds had to be processed. Even at Vissimo speed, that would take time.

"Lucky," Julius murmured to himself.

I peered up at him.

The regard of the ancient predator crashed over me.

"We'll see," he said, returning to his throne.

25

The last thirty minutes of my life were some of the worst I could remember.

For me. For Kyros, his family, and his clan.

Tommy had returned to my side, and my Vissimo crew flanked us.

Nothing but the whisper of paper and the frantic tapping of calculators sounded in the amphitheatre. I held tight to the paper with the asset figures for each clan, knowing my estimates were pretty much useless.

The woman in the middle stood without warning.

My mouth dried, bile surging in my throat.

"We've processed Miss Le Spyre's figures," she stated, casting me a curious look. "And found them accurate. Clan figures were submitted this morning and have been processed." Rounding the table, she passed both kings a sheet of paper. On the way back, she paused and passed me a third.

I couldn't hide my fear.

But my heart dropped at the bottom figures. Seven million dollars in assets separated the clans.

So fucking close.

Kyros's devastation was like a battering ram to the gut.

Mikael laughed with Trenit and Tynan.

I reached into my back pocket, dragging out the final deed that I really hadn't wanted to pass over.

Their laughter trailed off.

"There's one more," I told the woman from Clan Leith.

In a flash, my wrist was gripped with iron strength.

Kyros pried the papers from my finger, unfolding it. He stared at the title and glanced back up at me.

Your estate, he said.

He didn't like it.

My estate was worth eighteen and a half million dollars—ironically not the most expensive property I owned in the world. Certainly the most sentimental.

What use are walls if you're not in them with me? I replied.

Kyros held the paper out of my reach. *It's your home.*

Scowling, I crossed my arms. *The conditions on it are different, if that makes you feel better.*

He flicked to the second page, skimming the special conditions. There was a buy-back clause.

When Clan Sundulus wins, my estate will be gifted back to me, my heir, or my children, I said to him.

I could bring Sundulus back into the game with a tiny edge, but I couldn't win *Ingenium* for them. The battle could reign for a hundred years more, by which time I'd be dead.

Kyros had front row seats to my reasoning, and a growl rose in the back of his throat.

Placing a hand on his chest, I stretched up on tiptoes and pulled the contract from him. Then I scuttled back because *fuck*, my libido was sick of talking.

On wobbling pins, I placed the contract in front of the woman. "This one too."

King Julius would accept the special condition.

The ten vampires still cross-checked the new total. Kyros came up behind me as she stood.

"If King Julius of Clan Sundulus accepts the conditions of the final contract, then that puts Clan Fyrlia at a 0.15 percent deficit. The end cascade is not triggered."

It took everything I had not to collapse in a heap.

The end cascade wasn't triggered. Kyros wouldn't be taken from me today. His family wouldn't die.

Today.

Ingenium would continue, but that life was preferable to the grim alternative. *By far.* How could I be disappointed when this could have ended in so much death and heartbreak?

Not only had I undone the damage I caused, Sundulus now had an advantage. A small one, but an advantage nevertheless.

I hadn't dared to dream things would work out this way.

"I accept Miss Le Spyre's conditions," King Julius said. "And I consider myself lucky indeed."

I turned to him, and he inclined his head. The action was echoed by his queen and children. Behind him, Clan Sundulus went a step further, bowing at the waist.

A phone buzzed.

Glancing back, I watched Tommy rattle off a text on my phone.

Lifting her head, she winked at me.

The doors boomed open.

Fred walked in, escorting Lady Treena.

I jerked, sucking in a breath. My legs remembered how to work, and I hurried to intercept them.

"Aunt Treena," I said in a low voice. "What are you doing here?"

Glaring at Fred, I returned my focus to her familiar face.

She held her champagne chute aloft. "The thing about forcing people onto planes is you must ensure they actually leave."

Kyros's grim amusement rocketed through our bond, and I shoved back with a mental pout that only made him want to pin me down and bite me.

I peeked past her to see the rest of my oldies trailing into the amphitheatre.

Dammit. Each of them had dealt with vampires for at least fifteen years, but that didn't stop me from worrying about their hearts. I never intended for them to be in the room with both clans.

Lady Treena rested her free hand on my cheek. "You don't think *we* would miss this, do you, darling goddaughter?"

... Maybe not.

I rested my hand over hers. "No, Aunt. Of course not."

Taking her arm, I led her to the royal table. She clicked her fingers at Fred, who placed a case on the table and opened it.

"All of my Bluff City assets were going to my goddaughter upon my death anyway. I never had children because I couldn't bear to bring them into contact with your race. Basilia has been my only joy over the years. If I trusted her with my money after my death, then I don't see the point mistrusting her with everything when I'm *nearly* dead," she said, sniffing as she studied the vampires with disdain.

She extracted the top document, sliding it into the middle of the table. "These are my conditions. Most echo those in her own contracts. Mine has the addition that my assets will revert to Basilia after the game is won."

She'd managed to strike twenty royal vampires speechless.

I bit back my smile.

Lady Treena faced King Mikael—her tormentor—and held her chute aloft. "Fuck you, Mikael. I hope you rot in hell."

She brought the chute to her lips, tipped her head back, and my jaw dropped as she skulled the contents as only a lady could.

Aunt Treena just drank her champers. The proceedings should shock me more, but *that* took the cake.

Shit!

"I hope he's worth it, Basilia," she said to me.

A lump rose in my throat. "I hope you'll see that for yourself. *Thank you*, Aunt Treena."

"So like Agatha," she whispered back, a tear sliding down her cheek.

Leaning down, I kissed her cheek.

Neelan took the conditions to his father while Dierdre took the suitcase to Clan Leith.

The tap of Sir Olythieu's cane announced his arrival.

He set his case on the table, taking both my hands. Bending, he dropped a kiss on the back of each.

"Sir Olythieu," I said in a trembling voice. He was the one I least expected to be here. Not because he didn't love me, *because* he did love me—and was just like my grandmother. Totally unpredictable and unrelenting.

"That's uncle to you," he scolded.

"Sir Uncle," I replied impishly.

He pursed his lips against a smile. "A sound compromise." His face hardened as he faced the royals. "I am compelled and cannot directly transfer to Clan Sundulus."

I arched a brow. *Of course* my oldies thought of that.

"My Bluff City assets have been gifted to Basilia. She may do what she wishes with them. If she chooses to *lend* them to you, the assets will afterwards revert to her again. My international assets will be kept for my children—with whom I never had a relationship. I pushed them away because of you. Their survival has been my one triumph in life, but it has been a cold one."

Queen Titania dropped her gaze.

"The locks on my mind will be removed tomorrow at 9:00 a.m.," he said in a voice that brooked no defiance. "You can be assured that if anyone but this young woman came to us and asked us to save you, they'd be six feet under and rotting in their grave by now."

King Julius wasn't cowed by the man beside me.

... If Sir Olythieu was a vampire, I wonder who would win between them.

I kissed his cheek, and he cupped my face between his wrinkled hands.

"You were right," he said. "Agatha only wanted you to be happy. Forgive an old fool?"

I gripped his hands. "You're many things, but a fool isn't often one of them."

"I give you a portion of my wealth and you give me a backhanded compliment."

Choking on a laugh, I pulled away.

He untangled himself, and Mrs Syrre took his place.

She copied Sir Olythieu's approach, signing over her assets to me to lend to Clan Sundulus as I chose, but the sadness in her huge emerald eyes was almost worse. Neelan fidgeted in his seat, and I was glad she'd managed to get under his skin.

Mr Dithis's suitcase was huge.

It was a feat that he managed to collect the documents in only three days.

"My assets will revert back to me," he said, cocking his head my way. "Most of my wealth is in this city, so unless you want to care for me when I'm old, I need my money back."

He was compelled to Fyrlia and could deal with Sundulus directly. A relief, really. I didn't want to be responsible for all their wealth too.

I smiled. "I'd care for you."

His brown eyes softened. "I might hold you to that, sweetheart."

Kill.

Frowning, I searched for Kyros. Oh my god. Was he jealous?

He's my uncle, Kyros.

How can you care for him when you'll be caring for me? It was immediately followed by, *He'll be dead within ten years.*

I gasped.

She wasn't meant to hear that.

"It's true then," Mr Dithis murmured, pressing a kiss to my forehead and shooting a look at Kyros. "About the telepathy?"

"Sure is," I replied.

He pulled a face. "Good luck with that."

Yeah. I had a feeling there'd be a whole heap of acceptance ahead of both of us. Communication was kind of not our strong suit *at all.*

It will be, mate.

Mr Hothen slammed his case on the table.

My brows shot up.

"Which one of you killed Sandra Hoyt?" He stared murderously at Clan Fyrlia.

There was a beat of silence.

Hector spoke. "My two brothers." He jerked his thumb at them.

Mr Hothen spun to me. "Are they dying?"

I sighed happily. "They are, Uncle Hothen. Painfully, I hope. Kyros is handling that."

The silver fox glanced back at my mate. "My condition is that they die in the same way Sandra did. If you can assure that, my assets will reach you through Basilia and revert back to me."

Kyros's arms were crossed, highlighting the expanse of his muscular chest.

"It will be my pleasure," he answered, a ghost of a smile quirking his lips.

Trenit and Tynan paled.

Mr Hothen looked Francesca up and down, sneering. "And of course, the limitations placed on me will be removed tomorrow at 9:00 a.m."

Dame Burke squeezed in when he left, setting down her case. "You pathetic cunts."

Safina jolted, exchanging a glance with Gerome.

I tucked away my grin.

Lalitta didn't show a flicker of surprise.

"All my local assets are Basilia's now. For some reason she wants you to have it," she said, shoving the case to King Julius. "Give it to Basilia after. I'm out of this fucking shithole."

Her fury melted as she looked at me. "Basilia, my love. I'll be on a tropical island somewhere."

Every piece of this woman was abrupt, but she had the biggest, most dramatic heart of any of my oldies. I pulled her into my arms and squeezed her tight. "I know better than to change your mind, but please tell me you'll visit."

Tears burned my eyes.

She turned her head to Kyros as I released her.

"I think you'll find that all six of us will be dropping in *regularly*," she said with a scowl. "And if that oversized bastard treats you wrong, we will use the entirety of our wealth—not just the Bluff City portion —to cripple him permanently."

I didn't doubt her for a second.

Kyros was inclined to find her threat funny, but the humour was tinged with gratitude. He liked that someone would cripple him if he hurt me.

Weird.

She kissed my cheeks, pinching them slightly—Dame Burke was *that* aunt—before marching off.

My oldies had come in like a tidal wave. They disappeared in the same way. Not acknowledging the vampires further, they left.

I held Vladymir's gaze. He nodded and signalled. Thirty leather-clad Vissimo peeled away from the masses and followed my grandmother's friends.

Fred lingered.

I shot him a look and he visibly wilted. The action gave me pause.

We'd all fought our battles. My oldies had to put aside a generation of injustice to be the bigger people. Kyros had to trust me. I had to trust myself.

And Fred?

He'd had to disobey a Le Spyre.

Striding to my butler, I wrapped my arms around his middle. "Thank you, Fred."

He was as stiff as a board, and I listened to his thumping heart until he relaxed and placed his arms around me. "Please forgive me for the breach in your trust, Miss Le Spyre."

I squeezed his arm and looked up at him. "There's nothing to forgive."

He bowed. "Then unless you require something else, I'll be waiting in the car, miss."

The butler strode out to the symphony of processing papers and the renewed surge of tapping on calculators.

I'd already run the numbers on the Bluff City assets belonging to my oldies.

For my grandmother, I'd restored the game.

For my grandmother, they'd just won it.

Maybe I should have catalogued Mikael, Trenit, and Tynan's defeat, and watched the moment they realised their lives were forfeit.

But I'd done this for revenge *and* love. Right now, love had taken over everything else.

Kyros was focused on me from where he loomed in front of the vampires from Clan Leith, witness to the thoughts running through my mind. The same sense of wonder filling my mind was rampant in his.

Well, kind of. The wonder was mixed in between thoughts of me in bed and how beautiful and strong I looked.

Not that *my* thoughts were innocent.

Walking to him, I dared to place my hand on the centre of his chest again. Gathering my determination, I thought. *I want you, Kyros. You know I do.*

Good. Because my father technically just sold me to you.

My lips twitched, but I let my seriousness take hold again. *The win is yours. Ingenium will end.*

If Fyrlia decided to battle to the bitter end, it could take months to years depending on how steeply the odds were stacked against them after the input from my oldies.

I stared at my hand on his chest, wanting to relent to the temptation of the seventh exchange with nearly everything I had.

Except one thing.

The same thing that had always stood between us.

Kyros, if you want me after everything that has happened between us, then come to me without games. Ingenium will always be a memory and a lesson to hold close. But only you and I will continue on.

His green eyes were solemn.

I lowered my hand, unable to bear another second of being so close to him with the burning under my skin.

... And with *Ingenium* still in the way.

On this issue, I would be unrelenting.

Taking a breath, I pushed my thoughts toward him again. *If you can't come to me without games, don't come at all. I won't have you any other way.*

Breaking away from his gaze, I strode for the exit, my army of vampires falling in behind me with booming steps.

26

Four months.

King Mikael decided to take things to the bitter end—or so I assumed.

The day after I gatecrashed the end cascade negotiations, I'd received a letter that cordially invited me to remain at the estate for the remainder of my life.

Signed, King Julius.

How nice of him.

"Drink this, babe." Tommy shoved another monstrosity under my nose. This one was orange.

I cast her a baleful look. "That crap won't make me feel better."

Only Kyros could do that, but Tommy was determined to keep me chugging along. Each day she forced one of these health juices down my throat before shoving me into the pool to swim laps for an hour.

Not to mention the meditation and massages.

If I could be happy through her efforts, I'd be a fucking joy.

For the last four months, I'd existed as a shadow. The first few days were better—when I kept expecting Kyros to turn up at all hours of the day and night.

Food tasted like sawdust.

Laughter was hard to come by.

Music pissed me off.

If Tommy, Mrs Gaughton, my oldies, and my Vissimo friends weren't here, I'd be halfway to death's door.

Cruelly. *Ironically*. Along with my enjoyment in life, the negatives had disappeared too. Every trace of fear and uncertainty and mistrust that ever sat between Kyros and me was eradicated by misery.

The doubts I'd carried seemed so small now.

The blood bond was unrelenting with its desperation to force me off the estate and onto his lap. Unfortunately, I had the presence of mind to instruct Laurel and the others not to listen to my orders on the matter four months ago.

They'd prevented me from leaving the estate twenty-five times.

Turned out, I'd used all my luck sneaking off the property to save Tommy. They'd confiscated all the frequency generators in the house after I tried using them to get away. With the damage to my ears, I didn't have much of an advantage. They heard me coming far before I heard them.

The blood bond was shoving my body to exhaustion, wearing me down physically and mentally so I'd cave and crawl to my mate. It was helped by my very real misery.

I missed Kyros so damn much.

Sighing, I sipped the orange slop through my bamboo straw.

Tastes like horseshit.

Then why are you drinking it?

I frowned. *Tommy makes me.*

Then I assume it's for your own good.

I slowly straightened, my mouth full of the carrot juice. As though she had a radar, Tommy whipped around.

"What is it?" she demanded. "Don't spit that out."

Kyros?

Yes, my beauty.

I spat the juice out over the bench, startling everyone in the kitchen. My guards tensed, immediately on high alert.

Falling off the stool, I barely had the presence of mind to keep my speed regulated for my human staff as I raced toward the thrumming of Kyros.

He was by the pool.

It wasn't the first time he'd come closer. I'd feel him in Orange or Black sometimes—occasionally right on the border of Black and the Estates.

Never this close.

Never on my property.

This had to mean something. I couldn't bear it if he left again.

It means something.

His voice rumbled through me, eliciting a sob. I tore out of the patio and rested my eyes upon him for the first time in four months.

My feet stilled as I looked upon him. The icy winter wind whipped my hair around my face, and I lifted a hand to push back the obstacle to my vision.

He was here, but I didn't know how to go to him.

It meant too much.

Like I could shatter into a million pieces by taking a single step closer.

My eyes drank him in—because if that was all I got of him, I'd take whatever scraps possible.

He wore a green shirt, sleeves rolled to expose his muscular forearms. He'd partnered it with khakis. If there was one thing I loved more than my vampire in a suit, it was seeing him dress smart casual.

Because that look belonged to me.

Come to me, my beauty.

I startled at sounds behind me.

Tommy was out of breath, even though she'd been joining me in the pool each morning. My guards hadn't overtaken me, so I could assume they'd figured out Kyros was here.

Tommy gave me a not-so-gentle shove. "What the fuck are you waiting for? Go get him, tiger."

Kyros strode toward me, done with waiting.

I ran.

His growl filled the air as I traversed the last few steps and launched myself against his body, seventh exchange be damned.

That was the last thing on my mind.

Crying so hard I felt my ribs may crack, I wrapped my arms around his neck, latching my ankles behind his back. His arms wrapped around me, and Kyros held me close.

"Shh, Basilia. I'm here now," he said in a low voice, turning his back to those watching us from the patio.

My voice couldn't form words through my tears.

His thoughts were whipping through mine too fast to comprehend. *That's right.* I didn't need a physical voice.

What took you so long?

Kyros inhaled me, squeezing me tighter. *Never let her go. Smells right.* "You were clear about how you wanted me. You always have been."

Four months, I thought brokenly. *I thought you weren't coming.*

He set me on my feet, hands running down my arms. "You're so fucking beautiful."

I can't breathe around her. Mine.

Fresh tears spilled over my cheeks at the uncontrolled torrent of his thoughts. I hope he never learned to control them because his mind was the most wondrous thing I'd ever beheld.

My queen. In a rabbit onesie.

Peering down, I frowned at the outfit.

Shit. Where's the short dress when I need it?

"You don't need anything," he murmured in my ear, sending a violent shiver through me.

I wrapped my arms around my waist. "I've been cold. Tommy dressed me..."

He reached back and flipped the rabbit ears hood up. "Perfect."

If he thought so, I wouldn't correct him.

Kyros tilted my chin. "Laurel, Vladymir, stop me if this goes too far."

He kissed me then. Tears, wet lashes, red face, and all, *he kissed me* and the world righted. We sank into each other, and determining where he started and I ended was an impossible task. One shared feeling and one shared thought existed in the warm space we could remain lost in for eternity.

The sensation transcended the physical.

I was inside Kyros and he was inside me.

With the steady pressure he exerted, I knew he'd protect me to his dying breath. Nowhere was safer than in his arms. He pressed his tongue between my lips, and I sighed, opening for him as I reciprocated. Panting, Kyros cut off the kiss, turning his head aside.

I'd climbed back up his body. In a haze, I threaded my fingers through his toffee strands and used the other to draw his face back to mine.

"We don't turn from each other," I told him in a dreamy voice.

This close, I could see the deep bruising circling beneath his eyes. His usual golden hue had waned. He didn't appear to have lost weight or muscle, but a weight hung around his neck.

I brushed a thumb over his bottom lip. "You're tired."

"As are you," he said. "But it will be better now."

Is Ingenium over? I asked.

Kyros's mouth curved. "My father executed Mikael yesterday morning. The surviving Fyrlia royals formally admitted defeat. As expected, the decision to draw out the game until the bitter end came from Mikael. My father still honoured your terms despite Mikael never apologising to his family as you requested."

Saw that coming from a mile away. Actually, I had to step up my hyperboles with my vampire senses. Saw that coming from *one hundred* miles away.

Kyros's mouth bobbed as he listened in on my thoughts. He blinked a few times before continuing. "I spent the day with Trenit and Tynan and executed them late last night once they were broken."

Whoa. I knew what my mate was capable of, but his enjoyment of the task demonstrated a bloodthirstiness I'd have to acclimatise to. The two times I'd killed made me feel sick.

He'd spoken loudly, but I turned to check Tommy had heard.

Her eyes were shining—whether from our *Notebook* moment or the news of Kyros's torture session, I had no idea.

"Thank you," she said to Kyros. "I still dislike you, but a little less."

I nearly grinned at that. Until I saw Fernando wrap an arm around her waist.

When the fuck did that happen?

Marcus approached on the other side, taking her hand, and my jaw dropped open.

Holy shit. Tommy has a fucking harem!

Kyros's shoulders were shaking. "What are you going to do about that?"

Marcus would be put on best-friend trial to see if he was worthy. Fernando could get the hell off my friend. He wasn't anywhere good enough—fucking traitor.

My mate stilled, lifting his head to peruse Fernando. *He was the spy?*

Oops. Guess that's out of the bag. I wondered if you already knew about him, actually.

Your relationship with the Indebted was growing. I decided to leave the matter to you, he surprised me by responding.

"Well, don't beat him up now, please," I murmured against his mouth.

A growl rumbled in Kyros's chest, the snarl about to whip out in challenge.

Later, mate. Another day. Next week or next year. Once you've satisfied me. I nipped at his bottom lip.

He tore his glare from Fernando. "We don't have time anyway."

I tensed. "What does that mean?"

"It means that my father and family are expecting us." He glanced at me uncertainly after.

The idea wasn't abhorrent to me. I'd missed all of them too.

Well, most of them.

I nuzzled into his chest. "As long as we have contact at all times, I can put up with that."

I'll never let you go, my beauty. Never again.

My mood lightened when I realised Kyros was driving us to his Lyall Bay property. Pulling into the garage, he proceeded to drag me onto his lap.

I gasped as fire scorched everywhere he touched. Pain and pleasure.

"Your rules," he teased. "You said I had to maintain contact at all times."

It was a gasp, not a complaint.

His lips curved and he kissed my nose.

Once out of the car, I wriggled until he put me down. I was already in the fucking rabbit onesie. Only using my legs to walk could redeem me.

Grabbing his hand, I tugged Kyros down the hall, listening to his silent laughter. Why this was funny, I had no idea.

The voices ahead of us trailed off.

I drew back, eyeing him.

Are you laughing because of the rabbit onesie? I asked.

He grinned. *Just feeling grateful that we're here in this moment, true mate.*

The truth. And a thought I could appreciate the weight of.

We entered the open-plan living space hand in hand.

There wasn't a single second of awkwardness before Gerome swept me into his arms. My hand was torn from Kyros's as his brother spun me in a blurring circle.

I was too tired for spinning.

Tapping his shoulder, I groaned. "Enough."

The tall, dark, and handsome vampire set me down immediately.

Kyros's growl swelled, telling me he *might* have caught my mental description of his brother.

Oops.

I was passed into the arms of my first crush next.

Rory beamed down at me for a split second before Kyros ripped me away.

Crap, those thoughts were going to get me in trouble.

"Damn right they will," he said, brows drawing together.

Kyros clamped me against his body, and I waved lamely at the other siblings. I'd wondered if the betrayal would still be held against me, but I couldn't see a shred of bitterness or blame on their perfect faces.

Still, *Ingenium* ended yesterday. Who knew what feelings could arise in time? I really hoped there were no hard feelings.

Kyros pressed his forehead to the back of my head. *They don't. They wouldn't dare after what you did for us.*

I just undid the damage I'd caused.

You gave up everything you owned in Bluff City to help us, including your family's home. You entered the lion's den with no idea whether what you had would be enough. You did it for the love of your grandmother and love of me.

I'm glad you see it that way.

We all do, he replied. *Including my mother and father.*

The king and queen sat on the window seat, holding hands. It weirded me out when they did normal human stuff. Be a tyrannical ruler or not, but pick a damn side.

Kyros snorted. *Why would he when he knows the uncertainty unsettles you?*

The king pulled that shit on purpose?

My eyes narrowed. *A worthy foe.*

Deep, rumbling laughter burst from Kyros's lips.

"Thank fuck you're back," Neelan said. "He's been a pain in the ass. Bitching and moaning and moping."

"Glad to be back," I answered him solemnly. Kyros allowed just enough freedom for me to squeeze his brother's hand.

"You look haggard but happy. Once you sleep, you'll look much better," Dierdre remarked, devouring a slice of cheese pizza.

I erupted in mental hoots. *God,* I'd missed her. "Thanks, Dierdre."

Kyros was watching me closely. What? He hadn't realised I found her hilarious?

He shook his head, and I grinned.

293

That pizza smells so good. I'd had no appetite in months. With a tendency toward the skinny of my optimal weight, I was now a size too small to be healthy. If Tommy hadn't force-fed me, who knew what state I'd be in.

I should have worked harder.

I missed something the king said, glancing up at Kyros, a wrinkle between my brows. He avoided my gaze and Dierdre's low growl when he stole her pizza box.

Ugh, nope. I wasn't coming between a vampire and her food. One, she was female and that was a general no-no. Two, she had fangs.

"I'll grab something else soon," I said.

King Julius stood in front of me.

Heart thumping, I stared at the ancient Vissimo.

"I can't recall the last time a human ignored me," he said in bafflement.

The queen called. "It's their mind-speak, lover. It distracts my son and my daughter-in-law."

Whoa, whoa, whoa.

The king held out his arm, studying my face closely. Checking how haggy I was?

"What's going on?" I took his arm.

"You would know if you had listened," he replied.

I inhaled and my stomach gurgled.

Exhaling loudly, Kyros's father swiped the pizza box from his son before marching us out the front door.

"I'm glad to see you, true mate of my eldest son."

He wasn't calling me human, so things could be worse. The king led us to the fire pit where Kyros once tried to set up a romantic date. If he did it again, I'd be all for it.

A small smile escaped me before I sobered.

I could only smile right now because things happened to work out. Four months later and I still felt as though everything could disappear.

The king sat on the swinging chair, gesturing to the quarter of bench space left next to his huge frame. He handed me the pizza box, closing his eyes.

Well, okay then. I took out a slice and munched on it, nearly pooling into a puddle on the ground at the cheesy goodness.

Kyros mentally snorted before receding.

Dierdre wasn't getting any of this back.

"The first time we met," Julius broke the silence, "I asked you why you returned to my son's tower. You said *to win the game.*"

... Yeah.

"My arrogance allowed you to get so far. That was a good lesson for me." He regarded me through those predator's blue eyes, but there was a glimmer I wasn't used to seeing. "You played your hand well."

I wasn't even sure I liked this guy and the praise still felt good. Guess not growing up with parents would do that to a gal.

"I have two questions," he said.

... Were they rhetorical?

The king crossed an ankle over his knee, glancing at his pants in annoyance. I'd only seen him wear a sarong in the confines of his own home. Guess he liked the freedom.

Which was a pretty gross thought, really.

He watched me closely. "When you gave up my family to Mikael in exchange for your friend's life, did you intend to give us all your Bluff City assets?"

Nope. "At that point, I still intended to win the game."

The answer drew a smile to his lips out of all things. "What changed your mind?"

A lot. "I didn't wish to spend my life that way." I wanted to spend it with Kyros, pursuing the things I found important before the crazy explosion of my life.

The king studied my face as I took another mouthful of cheese pizza. *Holy shitballs*, this was so fucking amazing. Though maybe I shouldn't eat too much. I'd have to put in some serious training to regain my ability to eat a full pizza.

"If you were older than twenty-five, I'd call that wisdom," he said.

King Julius could call it whatever he wanted. I wasn't a normal twenty-two-year-old because I wasn't a normal nine-year-old. I wasn't raised in an everyday world.

"Then again," he said, voice softening. "Grief does that to us."

It was eerie how well he could read people—it couldn't just be me.

"Another question," he declared, making me jump.

My stomach churned. *Ugh,* too much pizza.

Dammit.

"You bought my son from me," the king said, his eyes narrowing. "Why?"

"To be clear, I don't see what I did as owning him," I answered. "I see it as ensuring his freedom."

"You own my son." He lifted a shoulder. "In my day, we sold people all the time."

That... really hadn't changed in Vissimo culture from what I could tell.

But crap.

His question required an answer that could offend him. This was the obstacle that prevented any real relationship forming between us.

"I don't like the way you treat Kyros like dirt," I said, opting for the truth.

He grinned, and I ground my teeth.

"Put your claws away," the king said. "Your past actions warrant that I offer you an explanation."

What's happening?

He settled back. "Kyros will struggle with his powers always, Miss Le Spyre. Like humans, his mind is most flexible until a certain age. For humans, that's twenty-five. For Vissimo, around two hundred and twenty. The biggest battle my son will face in his immortality will be a constant one, a siege. His power is unlike anything I have seen. His strength rivals the stories of the greatest of our kind—mere myths to us now. Since his birth—game aside—that has been a constant concern for his mother and me. Due to that concern, I have pushed him relentlessly from birth—knowing my ability to contain his loss of control had an expiry date. I humiliate him. I hurt him. I dangle the things he wants most just out of his reach. I demand more than perfection from my heir because the world could be left in ruins if he ever loses control."

My jaw dropped open as I thought back over the interactions with King Julius.

Refusing his permission for the exchanges.

Choking me in front of Kyros.

Flaring his eyes to push my body to the limits, *in front of Kyros*.

Forcing his son to watch the video of the fight with Theodore over and over again.

He did it out of love and devotion.

Absolute love. He feared having to kill Kyros.

I *understood*.

"What about when you found out about Sandra Hoyt?" I asked him.

He tipped his head back. "No. Then, I was going to kill you. I'm an alpha, too, so it was good practice. It's not often my control gets tested anymore."

Phew.

"Six hundred years and even I am not infallible. But two things stopped me." His endless blue eyes settled upon me as he straightened. "My son would have lost control if I killed you."

There was something else? Because that was the only thing I'd considered.

"Secondly, I had an inkling you would still prove worthy."

I didn't say anything, unsure how to respond, but my curiosity couldn't be denied. Who knew when King Julius would want a deep and meaningful again? This was probably a once every decade occurrence. "Why?"

"Your blood and Kyros's sings, Miss Le Spyre," the king replied. "I do not know you well. I doubt you know yourself well. I *do* know my son. A partner worthy of him must be extraordinary indeed."

I tried not to fidget.

"Kyros could have told you this if you'd asked him, by the way,"

Julius said, his lips twitching. "As much as he enjoyed your feistiness each time I humiliated him."

He did?

I'd felt terrible for him, and he'd *liked* my response. My eyes narrowed.

"As much as he enjoyed being purchased by you, I'd wager," the king added. "This is what happens to strong men when a strong woman knows her worth."

Kyros and I would be having words about the owning thing. I'd freed over two thousand vampires in direct opposition of that concept. "So you'll need to continue being mean to him," I said, wrinkling my nose.

"No," the ancient vampire said, lips quirking again. "I don't believe so."

He stood, towering over me.

I clutched the pizza box to hide the sudden shaking of my hands.

"In one-hundred-and-fifty years, I managed to make my son lose control four times in his first three decades of living. Most of those in his very first years. Since knowing you, he has lost control at least three times by my count. I have high hopes that trend will continue, *especially*," he tapped my temple, "as you can calm him down also."

I stared. *What?* I wasn't taking over that role! Not happening.

"I couldn't have planned your trip to Gingers to see Gina better myself," the king said. "Well done."

That was one time!

...And then when Gerome compelled me. That wasn't my fault.

Betraying his family.

Shit. I totally drove Kyros mad.

The thought only made me smile. He was so screwed.

The ruler turned to leave but paused when he reached the path. "True mate of my eldest son."

"Yeah?" I'd nearly congratulated myself on getting through the conversation alive.

That'd learn me.

"Kyros seems to believe you don't wish to become Vissimo. With a reminder of what will happen to Kyros at your death, I suggest you reconsider."

Four months apart had removed a lot of my last doubts. The time was spent processing everything I hadn't had *time* to process since entering *Live Right*.

The concept of fearing what Kyros and I shared was ludicrous to me now. The obstacles between us, insignificant.

I wasn't human as it was.

Leaving Kyros alone in this life made me feel sick. "I have to be invited."

The mating ritual book still sat in my underground office, the chapter on the seventh exchange unread. Fernando and Lauren only detailed the first six exchanges as I never expected more would happen.

The king studied me. "Welcoming my son's mate, a formidable power in her own right, to join him in immortality and one day rule by his side is my honour. I invite you to join my clan, Basilia Le Spyre, and my family as a Vissimo." The ruler rested a hand against his heart and inclined his head to me.

My mouth dried.

He did? He was seriously asking me to join his family? For real?

What was I meant to say to that? There was probably a formal response.

"Be sure it is what you want," King Julius said, not waiting for my fumbling reply. "There's no going back."

27

Kyros had demanded a two-day *settlement period* to my decision in case I got cold feet.

Glad to see winning *Ingenium* hadn't robbed him of his business sense.

I'd dragged every detail of the process from him and his siblings after consulting my various books back at the estate. All without losing contact with Kyros for longer than it took to shower—that took skill.

"Basilia? Can I have a word?" the queen asked.

We'd gathered at the king and queen's mansion for the transition ceremony, and she was dressed in a sheer sarong and nipple pasties with tassels.

"Uh, sure," I said, squeezing from between Lalitta and Francesca.

Lalitta gave me a little push. Francesca didn't budge an inch to help. So things were pretty much the same now *Ingenium* was over.

I followed the queen to a small lounge I'd never been inside. Kyros tended toward practical space. His parents did not. This place was a sprawling maze that made no sense—unless it was a representation of King Julius's mind.

She tugged me to sit beside her. "I wanted to talk about the transition."

The queen was the perfect counterpart to the king, really—in terms of her perfect nipples and how she balanced him. She popped up sporadically to smooth situations and keep the peace in the family. I'd gained acceptance from her and Angelica right at the start, simply for being the force that reminded Kyros he needed to live, but I hadn't spent much one-on-one time with her.

"We haven't had much time getting to know each other," she said in her sultry voice.

"I was thinking the same. There hasn't really been time."

She leaned back. "We'll have nothing but time after the transition."

If I survived it. Because that wasn't assured.

You will, Kyros's furious thoughts burst into my thoughts.

His fury wasn't directed at me but the situation. He was tied in more knots over the transition than me.

An alpha's blood was necessary to trigger the change, but survival depended on the strength of the other six vampires involved. There was surely a connection between the seven blood exchanges in the mating ritual and the seven Vissimo needed to change a human, but no one knew what that connection was. Of course, there was a clan dedicated to solving the mystery.

It would have sucked to be the guinea pig for figuring out the answer, was my opinion on the matter.

The queen took my hand. "I wanted to speak with you about my grandchildren."

My brain slammed on the brakes. I choked on my own spit. "What grandchildren?"

Oh my god, does Kyros have kids?

None, my beauty. Mother's scaring her off. Intercept.

Kyros started moving through the house toward us.

"Any children you may have with my eldest son," she clarified.

I blew out a breath and then realised I shouldn't relax yet. "I'm twenty-one, Queen Titania. I can't say that's on the radar for me yet."

"Which is why I must talk to you." Her eyes were so beautiful, like the meadow inside a teardrop. It was no wonder her children were the most perfect creations I'd ever seen.

She blinked, glancing down. "Vissimo don't reproduce easily. It has taken me three hundred years of copious sex with many men to birth two children."

Kyros turned on his heel at the mention of *copious sex with many men*.

I withheld my grin. Just.

The queen sighed. "My point is that you'll only have one sexual partner because mates are unable to share each other," the beautiful vampire continued. "I couldn't rest easy without telling you how unlikely conceiving will be for you. False hope in motherhood is the greatest challenge Vissimo females face. You will have an eternity with my son, yes, but you need to be aware that eternity may not include children."

My ideal future had always included children. Two or three.

I was twenty-one, but I'd seen the veiled heartache within Vissimo women *and* men. Angelica was nearly two hundred years old and had never mentioned children. And she had a harem.

Yes, I wanted children with Kyros one day. If they didn't come, I liked to think I could find joy in my nieces and nephews. Or maybe by helping human children in need. Kyros was enough, and that would always hold true, no matter the heartache I may feel in the future.

"I don't understand eternity, Queen Titania, so I appreciate that what you're saying is probably above my comprehension," I answered. "Children aren't on my radar yet. If I remain human, Kyros and I are incompatible. There may not be a high chance of conceiving once I'm Vissimo, but that's more than zero chance."

"There's still time to have a child with a human male," she said quietly.

She was telling me to sleep with another man.

"I wanted to present it as an option," she added, spotting my shock.

Kyros's guilt was heavy.

Why do you feel bad? I asked him.

Because a human male could give you children.

Not all the time. What makes you think I'd want children with anyone else?

He thought about that. *You wouldn't.* The reply was accompanied by an arrogance that shoved aside every trace of guilt.

I mentally rolled my eyes.

"Any children I'm lucky enough to have will be fathered by Kyros," I told the queen.

My mate's purr vibrated down our connection sending a bolt of lust through me that coated my vision in white for several breaths.

The queen dipped her head. "Go into your next life knowing the odds."

"Thank you, Queen Titania. I hope to." I smiled.

She turned her head. "Someone has arrived."

"Probably Gina," I said. "That means everyone's here."

My request for Gina to be one of the seven vampires went down harder than a sack of wet shit.

I won the battle on the basis that Gina was as powerful as Safina, and my survival was therefore better assured.

I liked the Sundulus siblings, but none of them had reached maturity, so most weren't strong enough to suit Kyros's standards for my transition. I respected the path Gina chose to walk despite how and *who* she was raised by. And well... I wanted to bridge the divide between Fyrlia and Sundulus. The Fyrlia clan had merged with Sundulus and that process would go smoother if the opposing royals were seen to be getting along—or making an effort to get along.

I asked Gina two days ago. To my surprise, she gave me an instant yes.

"One last thing, daughter," the queen said, twisting to grab something behind her.

I sucked in a breath at the endearment.

Daughter.

The word made me tremble inside.

You have parents again, my beauty, Kyros said.

One of his parents was fucking terrifying, but now I'd jumped through Julian's hoops, I truly believed he'd protect me as ferociously as any of his children.

Like a father should.

And the queen just gave me a sex talk. Or encouraged me to have sex with a stranger and get pregnant... which I guessed was the opposite of a sex talk. Still, she'd talked with me to protect my heart.

I swallowed back the lump in my throat. I *did* have parents again.

Kyros started walking toward us again, drawn by my urge to cry.

A gift bag was deposited on my lap.

"What's this?" I asked the queen.

The queen touched my knee, standing. "A welcome to the family present. Join us when you are ready."

She left the lounge room, and I opened the bag.

Oh my god.

I drew out white lingerie—a bralette with a maze of silk ties, a tiny G-banger, garters, and stockings. I hadn't had a mother-in-law before, but this seemed like an unusual gift to receive from one.

Kyros entered. He stilled when he saw what I held.

"Put it on," he growled.

Laughter threatened to burst from my lips. I dropped the garments, resting my head back on the armrest. He placed his hands either side of my head and kissed me upside down.

"You want to see me in that tiny thong?" I asked breathlessly.

I wanted to drink my mate's blood.

I wanted to claim him for eternity.

To wake beside him always.

Kyros choked, his green gaze blazing down into mine. "Stop thinking about blood or I'll take you right now. We only have one chance to make you Vissimo."

"Your mother gave me that lingerie."

Horror blanketed his face and he reeled away.

I didn't want to hurt Titania's feelings by laughing, so I confined my thigh-slapping roar to my head, clutching my stomach when Kyros eyed the white scraps in disgust.

He was effectively turned off.

Placing the gift back in the bag, I stood and wrapped my arms around his neck.

"It's time?" I nipped his bottom lip, swaying into him and groaning at the contact.

White edged my vision.

His erection dug into my stomach.

Soon, we'd be able to touch without needing to make arrangements for a three-day thrall. Freedom to be naked with Kyros at every hour of the day.

Yes, please.

His mother had said my chances of conceiving were low.

I had a feeling Kyros and I would enjoy the practice.

He captured my mouth, splaying his hands across my bare upper back and ass. "I can't think straight when you think like that, Basilia."

His hands shook against me. I tucked my head under his chin, panting hard.

Are you ready, true mate? he asked, wrapping his arms around me.

I took a full breath, my heart never lighter or happier. *I'm ready.*

I'd dressed in a simple white silk gown with spaghetti straps. The material covered me from breasts to just below my knees.

I was spread out like Da Vinci's *Vitruvian Man* on a slab of cold graphite. The seven most powerful vampires I knew loomed over me. Their fangs were out.

The casual observer could mistake this for a virgin sacrifice.

They'd be wrong on two counts.

I frowned at Kyros. *I don't even get a chuckle for that one?*

If he could think about anything other than the tiny risk I may not pull through the transition, he would have laughed.

Tough crowd.

Though I only had the urge to because I was borderline hysterical about what happened next. Turned out the decision was the easiest part of this.

Rory stood in line with my right arm. Vladymir was in line with my left. King Julius stood at my head beside Kyros. Gina was stationed at my left leg and Safina at my right one. Laurel was positioned by my stomach after Kyros decreed the males were only allowed to bite my top half.

My mate was torn between glaring at his father, Rory, and Vladymir, but seemed mostly focused on the Viking.

I can always kill him after.

I didn't laugh at his thought because, truthfully, this would be one of the hardest things my mate would ever do. Now that I had a mate and we'd completed more than four exchanges, it was impossible for me to forge connections to any of the gathered vampires, but Kyros had to allow six other Vissimo to drink my blood and feed me *their* blood.

He'd once told me that would make him jealous to a murderous degree.

Closing my eyes, I thought of a gentle tide on a summer day and nudged soothing thoughts toward my mate. *True mate*, I thought at him, knowing the endearment would help.

Don't worry, my beauty. The prize is having you by my side forever. I'm not capable of jeopardising that.

There's no doubt in my mind about that, I answered.

Not one shred of it.

I cleared my throat. "On a scale of one to ten, how much will this hurt?" I only had movies to go off, and if they were to be believed, the coming moments would be excruciating.

Kyros towered over my prone form, and I was torn between checking out his junk or his face.

"I'd be happy with either," he answered, lips twitching.

"I hate when they do that," Gerome complained from where he and the other siblings—barring Rory and Safina—waited as spectators. Tommy wanted to come, but I wasn't at the point where I felt comfortable with her around the royals.

Kyros held my gaze, and I felt my mind cloud, a heavy languidness filling my body.

"You will not feel pain through the transition," he ordered, leaning down to brush my cheek.

He straightened and blinked, but the heaviness filling my limbs didn't dissipate.

"You compelled me," I slurred, my eyelids heavy.

He smirked. "Last time I'll be able to."

Yeah, right. You're a freakin' powerful Vissimo.

My mate studied the gathered vampires, his mouth twisting into a wry smile. *You're about to be a powerful Vissimo, too, Basilia. Believe me.*

I wouldn't be a weakling one?

Cool.

"Eldest son," King Julius said, gripping his shoulder. "Are you ready?"

That was my cue to ramp up the soothing vibes for my mate— easy with the warmth weighing down my body.

"I am, Father," Kyros answered, his meadow-green eyes on mine.

King Julius crouched on the ground by my head. He had a sarong on, and I wasn't cool with the position change. The queen's nipples deserved a Twitter page, yes, but that's where I drew the line when it came to the swinging bits of Kyros's parents.

My mate blanched.

"Daughter," the king said loudly, reminding me this was a big deal. "Are you certain you wish to join our family forever?"

I needed Kyros in the same way I needed shelter, food, and air. *Family*, I *wanted* with every fibre of my being.

My eyes stung at his daughter bomb, and I really hoped his question wasn't rhetorical.

I nodded. "I'm sure."

The king stood again. I wrinkled my nose, my eyes flicking to Laurel. She was smirking.

Bitch.

I smiled at her though, and then the others.

"Thank you all for helping me," I said softly.

Gina cocked her hip. Safina didn't outwardly react. Vladymir winked, and Laurel's smirk faded. King Julius arched a brow. And my mate...

He flooded my system with every ounce of love he carried for me.

"We drain and then fill," King Julius growled, crouching again. I barely managed to avert my eyes in time.

Jesus! Give a girl some fucking warning.

Kyros smoothed my hair away from my neck, and my heartbeat thundered for all to hear. The other vampires bent over my limbs while Laurel curled over my stomach.

Fuck, fuck, fuck.

Focus on me, mate, Kyros whispered in my mind.

His eyes captured mine before he brushed his lips against my forehead.

Soothe Kyros.

Inhaling, I focused on the gentle tide and the sunshine again, blanketing him with it as he kissed the pulse in my neck.

"We'll see each other soon, vixen," Kyros murmured against my skin.

"*I'll be the one in a blood-splattered white nightgown,*" I replied mildly.

Fangs sliced into my flesh.

EPILOGUE

"Open your eyes, my beauty."

Through thick lashes, I gazed up at the other half of me.

"Such beautiful eyes," Kyros whispered.

The transition left my skin flawless and glowing, my hair lighter and silky smooth, and my body was effortlessly toned and lithe. My topaz eye colour also remained, which made my mate ecstatic.

His prediction wasn't wrong. At twenty-two years of age—or a six-month-old Vissimo—my power was strong. Stronger than Gina and Safina's powers combined. Because I was made and not born a vampire, my powers wouldn't ever mature and grow like theirs, but that was fine by me.

After six months, lapses in dialling down my strength and speed to human norms were still a regular occurrence—particularly when my mate's body distracted me. He'd made it into a game that I had no objections playing.

I stretched, basking in his avid attention to my body. "I'm glad you think so."

"I have a goddess for a mate," he said, leaning to kiss the swell of my breast.

Because being a multi-billionaire wasn't enough in life, my ties to

Kyros technically made me a princess. Tommy said she'd make it her life's work to prevent it going to my head, so I wasn't too worried.

I moaned as his hands swept up my torso. He inhaled from my neck to my temple, and settled on top of me, lowering his mouth to mine.

I shifted to give him better access and let my knees fall apart so our bodies were aligned.

He was hard.

If I had a dick, it'd be in the same state.

Kyros laughed into my mouth.

"Don't like that visual?" I asked innocently.

He responded by kissing me until I was breathless.

A knock sounded.

"Enter, Laurel," Kyros said.

My friend obeyed, her stomach entering before the rest of her. Turned out Vladymir was in possession of powerful seed—Queen Titania's words, not mine. Laurel was five months along, and *definitely* showing.

I pursed my lips, eyeing the stretch of her leather top. Someday soon, she'd have to stop wearing leather.

And when she did, I'd never let her hear the end of it. Because Jessica Alba.

Which is why she hadn't taken the stuff off yet.

Laurel's eyes narrowed on me. "Queen Titania called to remind you of the clan gathering."

Oh, man. That was today?

Kyros groaned into my chest.

"We need to go," I said, trying to convince myself. "It's kind of a big deal."

King Julius had declared an official event to celebrate the merging of the two clans. He was also introducing me for the first time as his heir's mate, so we were kind of the guests of honour.

Our two thousand and thirty-two guards didn't belong to Sundulus, but they were invited after I stomped my foot and tossed my hair a few times.

"I had other plans," he grumbled, inching his mouth closer to my nipple.

"What's the time, Laurel?"

"Ten o'clock," she answered, leaving the room.

Our routine had settled halfway between human and Vissimo hours. We went to sleep at one or two and woke late morning.

Though Julius no longer had power over his son's decisions, we decided to enter into business with the clan across every industry. Kyros had made it his personal mission to regain every cent of the money I spent saving Sundulus from *Ingenium*.

This game didn't hurt anyone. Business was a game I was okay with.

That I *loved*.

We managed the Le Spyre estate together. We lived under the same roof—going between the estate and his Lyall Bay property. We'd fallen into a rhythm that felt free and safe—and that allowed for ample play.

I'd worried that Kyros would find life boring after *Ingenium*, but the international scale of estate business genuinely excited him. As did the notion of having time off and enjoying other important things.

Like every episode of *Truth Ranges* in existence.

That's how I knew we were true mates.

But some things had been harder for him. We were still part of Clan Sundulus, but he no longer directed thousands of Vissimo each night.

I knew the presence of my guards was soothing to him on an intrinsic level. He made it his business to enquire about their finances and ambitions to guide them where possible. If they'd been hesitant to accept his help at the start, six months of continued interest had rid them of lingering animosity.

Meanwhile, for the foreseeable future, it was my goal to lobby the clans and abolish the act of enslaving the family members of criminals.

That was between our efforts to expand the Le Spyre accounts to fund my life's work. The world contained too much corruption—particularly within large corporations, in many industries, and in government. Immortality made changing that less of an impossibility and more of an ultimate challenge. The work had to be done under an alias—with the whole *I'll never die* thing—but now I had eternity to take the evil fuckers in this world down.

They had no chance.

Kyros's phone blared. He stared at the screen.

"It's the finance guy. What's his name again?"

"I don't know. Did you sack Roger or not?" I asked.

A menacing smirk widened his lips. "No. I simply reminded him why this job was so important to him."

I snorted. He made the poor guy shit his pants in other words. "Go and answer then. I have a meeting with Clan Gugi soon."

He hummed, kissing me soft and deep. We pulled apart long after the phone had stopped.

He gave me a hot look that warmed every inch of my skin before striding out of the suite. We'd moved down the hall to Grandmother's old room when I became Vissimo. Moving into a new space made the room feel like *ours* instead of just mine.

I didn't want Kyros to feel this house wasn't as much his as mine.

"Kyros Le Spyre," he snapped, moving away down the hall. "This better be good."

His amusement rose in answer to mine.

Pretty sure our human staff thought we were crazy for swapping last names seemingly at a whim. But no, we just had two different races to juggle and it was easiest to use the mortal last name for the mortal world and our immortal last name for the *immortal* world.

Not that we were married or anything. Marriage seemed like a quaint joke after merging my blood, mind, and soul with another, and my mate agreed.

The call with Clan Gugi came and went without incident. I had a feeling their professionalism and help would disappear the second they learned I was researching how best to shut down their clan's cause for good. If there weren't any slaves, there was no need for a clan to handle the registration of slaves either.

Tommy was in our room when I returned from the call.

Her jaw dropped.

"What's up?" I said, hugging her from behind.

"Uhm, nothing really. Just that there are two fucking crowns here. That kind of thing."

No way.

I peeked over her shoulder. "Shit. There are. Who do you think they belong to? Bet they're bastards."

"Probably some rich bitch. And a balding middle-age man. Total buttholes."

"Most likely."

Seriously though. The thought of a naked Kyros in a crown was doing things to me.

"Lover," a man called from the hall.

Males never entered this suite because they wanted to survive.

"Hey, yourself," my friend purred, untangling from my embrace.

Dang.

I didn't even know this one's name, but I could assume that my friend's harem was now at five vampires.

She kissed my cheek. "Send me a photo of you in the ballgown and crown, lovely."

I checked my phone. "I don't leave for an hour."

Tommy glanced at the man. "Yeah, I know." She grinned at me and then leaped for lover number five.

Should I be happy or worried? Six months and I constantly bounced between the two.

I hid the two crowns as Rosie entered to help me into my dress. I listened to her frantic heartbeat now that I was a predator. Her poker face had been severely tested in the last six months, but she hadn't left. None of my human staff had left, actually. They got on with their jobs in the same brisk manner as always.

My grandmother had only hired the best.

Kyros entered as Rosie was twitching the royal-blue velvet gown into place.

He swallowed audibly.

The head maid smiled at me and made scarce.

"Mate," he said thickly, like the words were stuck in his throat. "There aren't words for your radiance."

My cheeks flushed. "You're great for my ego."

My breasts were pushed up and displayed atop the sweetheart neckline of the floor-length gown. The corset cinched my waist—and the pockets would hold my phone. It was a more severe cut and colour than I usually wore, but it seemed to suit the person I was now.

He bowed over my hand, kissing the back. "You take my breath away daily. Dressed like this, I won't be able to breathe all night."

Guess I'd better keep my mouth glued to his then.

For safety reasons.

"Two crowns arrived," I said as he stared at me.

He didn't blink. "Where?"

I crouched, sending my dress billowing up around me. Drawing out the box, I set it on the bed.

Both crowns were gold, but one was noticeably larger—both for a bigger head and in the thickness and number of sapphires inlaid in the ornate settings.

It was beautiful.

Taking hold of it, I turned to Kyros.

Rising on tiptoes even in heels, I watched my mate, holding the crown aloft.

"Crown Prince Kyros Nicholai Atagio," I said grandly, lowering the heavy gold circlet onto his head.

Meadow-green eyes held me captive. They were impossible to resist and I hadn't done anything that silly in six months. I leaned in to kiss him, but Kyros sidestepped me.

I stumbled forward, whirling with a frown.

He picked up the smaller crown. A large sapphire occupied the front peak, diamonds and sapphires formed flowers around each side.

The smile faded from his lips as he returned.

He held the crown over my head. "You bring my life meaning, mate."

I rested a hand on his heart, waiting for the once-a-minute beat.

Thud.

I smiled.

"Princess Basilia Atagio," he said, arching a brow. "You belong to me for the rest of eternity. Best get comfortable."

My true mate lowered the crown onto my head.

The End

COMING IN 2020

Supernatural Battle: Werewolf Dens

ACKNOWLEDGMENTS

The lifestyle of an author requires a very specific type of support from our loved ones.

To my husband, for understanding my whims

To my family, for understanding my whims

To my friends, for understanding my whims

Mostly, I'd just like to thank those close to me for understanding my whims.

My beta readers for this series were so enthusiastic, and they deserve an extra big thank you for their dedication to this series in the early draft stages and throughout.

A large thank you to the *Vampire Towers* launch team for your time, excitement, laughter, tears, and slight book aggression. I enjoyed it all.

To the readers of this series, I greatly appreciate your effort leaving reviews to help me smash some long-held personal goals. It's truly motivating to hear of you talking about Basi and Kyros in the community and beyond.

As Basi would say: <3 <3 <3

This series is dedicated to one of the most important people of my life. My nan passed away during the first draft of *Blood Trial*, and Basi's grief throughout the series is certainly my own.

Many parts of Agatha Le Spyre were inspired by my lovely nan - not the billionaire part (lol) - but certainly her wisdom, capability, loyalty, kindness, iron will, sharp wit, and love of Tom Hanks. I wish you could have known her.

We shared a great love for books, travel, and the craft of writing, and immortalising parts of her in *Vampire Towers* is something I'll cherish forever.

Happy reading,

Kelly St. Clare
Escape Into Fantasy

BOOKS BY KELLY ST. CLARE

Supernatural Battle

Vampire Towers (Paranormal urban romance)

Blood Trial

Vampire Debt

Death Game

The Darkest Drae (Dragon shifter romance)

with Raye Wagner

Blood Oath

Shadow Wings

Black Crown

The Tainted Accords (Royal fantasy romance):

Fantasy of Frost

Fantasy of Flight

Fantasy of Fire

Fantasy of Freedom

Novellas:

Sin

Olandon

Rhone

Shard

Pirates of Felicity (Pirate fantasy romance):

Immortal Plunder

Stolen Princess

Pillars of Six

Dynami's Wrath

Veritas

Eternal Gambit

Mortal Trinity

The After Trilogy (Dystopian romance):

The Retreat

The Return

The Reprisal